HATRED
AND
RETRIBUTION

HATRED
AND
RETRIBUTION

Fraud of the Ages

By
JEREMIAH STONE

HATRED
AND
RETRIBUTION

Copyright © 2017 by Jeremiah Stone

World Ahead Press is a division of WND Books. The views and opinions expressed in this book are those of the author and do not necessarily reflect the official policy or position or WND Books.

Paperback ISBN: 978-1-944212-66-7
eBook ISBN: 978-1-944212-67-4

Printed in the United States of America
16 17 18 19 20 21 XXX 9 8 7 6 5 4 3 2 1

CONTENTS

CHAPTER 1

THE 11:11 PHENOMENON
AND QURAN 9:111

Perpetually, I live in the eye of the spiritual hurricane. While I am not into numerology or into the occult and I reject outright the numerics of 11:11, these numbers do follow me periodically. They have impacted me in life threatening ways to the point where I ask myself if there is a world beyond the visible and the natural? Is there an unseen world of the supernatural, other than Adonai and Yeshua?

There is a global phenomenon in which people who have been selected, are experiencing 11:11 sightings. The spirit world is trying to communicate with us and to warn us of coming awesome events. It has been said that these sightings are an inducement to walk through a mystical portal into another reality, and into another paradigm. The 11, 11:11 and 1111 worldwide visualizations are premonitions of fatalistic future events. In Illuminati numerology, the number 11 is the number of judgment, destruction, and the death of humans. Consider that the World War I cease-fire was signed at the eleventh hour, on the eleventh day, of the eleventh month as in 11:11:11. On June 4, 1963, through President Kennedy's Executive Order No. 11110, control and power was transferred from the privately owned Rothschild Federal Reserve Bank to the United States Department of the Treasury. This demonic connection was President Kennedy's death warrant. These types of connections make the number 11, with its multiples, a favorite number of satanists. On the other hand, 1111 is also considered to be an angelic number and the sightings to be angelic promptings to encourage people to wake up to the murderous verses in Muhammad's Quran 9:111: "they fight in the cause of Allah, so they kill and are killed."

"They fight in the cause of Allah, so they kill and are killed."

—Quran 9.111

In contrast, **Revelation 9:11** reads, "They have as king over them the angel of the bottomless pit; the name in Hebrew is Abaddon, and in Greek he is called Apollyon." The God of Heaven is calling out His earthly armies across the globe to herald the imminent return of Yeshua the King of Heaven.

In my personal experiences, the 11:11 numeric has been an ominous omen. Millions of selected people from across the world are experiencing similar 11 or 11:11 or 1111 experiences. Most 1111 experiences are visual manifestations. However, my 11:11 encounter was a physical and a tangible event involving demonic entities and angelic intervention.

On November 11, 2009 (9:11:11), I was caught up in the middle of a battle between two opposing forces from other dimensions. I had lived in Fort McMurray, Alberta, Canada. Today, the rapidly expanding Islamic population in Fort McMurray has outgrown its existing Markaz-Ul-Islam mosque. Work is in progress on a $60-million project that will be the home to a second mosque for their Insha'Allah Friday Prayer. Why is Fort McMurray such a magnet to attract this rapidly growing Muslim community? Is it because Fort McMurray is at the vital nerve center and at the heart of Canada's energy infrastructures? Why are there so many Muslim transport truck drivers passing through Fort McMurray to the oil sands?

November 11th, 2009 was my 9/11/11/11 supernatural awakening that changed my life forever. Because I had been analyzing the Quran and because I had been researching Islam for the previous eight years, I became a target of radical Islam's physical and spiritual attacks. Because I had been probing Muhammad's Islam on the Internet since September 11, 2001 (9/11), I had a 9/11/11/11 encounter with death from worldly physical forces and from otherworldly demonic forces behind

Quran 9.111. My privacy had been compromised severely at Keyano College in Fort McMurray. I was monitored online. Even the cleaning staff knew what I was researching online. They knew where I slept. On November 11, 2009, at 11 minutes past midnight, I experienced an unavoidable brush with death. Crossing the overpass onto Highway #63, I had just turned left down the long narrow merge lane going south, when I was met with a fast-moving car coming toward me up the down ramp against traffic. Because concrete barriers blocked sight of the approaching headlights, suddenly at bumper-to-bumper kissing range, there was no time and no room to move out of the way. Since two physical objects cannot occupy the same space at the same time, a crash was unavoidable. Yet miraculously, our vehicles passed by each other or through each other. This otherwordly passage of vehicles can not be explained through the laws of physics. There was not a shadow of a doubt that there was Divine intervention which saved me from severe crippling injury or death. In revelation given to me, the 9/11/11/11 attack upon me was an Islamist suicide vehicle. As in Nice, France, so it was in Fort McMurray, Alberta, Canada, only seven years earlier. Ever since that otherworldly encounter with death at the overpass, the tyranny of fear has been removed from my life. Personally, that event was the Lord's Passover at the Overpass. I often consider that since God is for me, then who could be against me? His intervention for me at the Fort McMurray overpass was Divine endorsement of my exposure of Islam to the world within this book. However, after my book is in print, I do expect a fatwa against me.

For thirty years, I have prayed **Psalm 91. Psalm 91:9-11** promises:

> Because you have made the Lord your refuge, the Most High your habitation, no evil shall befall you. . . . *For He will give His angels charge of you to guard you in all your ways.* On their hands they will bear you up, lest you dash your foot against a stone."
> (**Psalm 91:9–11**, emphasis mine)

Daily, He splits the Red Sea for me. I am alive because of many angelic interventions. Archangel Gabriel continues to be on guard for me. He has spared my life repeatedly. Gabriel is my protector and my continuing enlightenment.

In **Matthew 4:1–11**, Satan quotes **Psalm 91:11** and Psalm 91:12 to Jesus. **Psalm 91:9–11**, which is about being guarded from death, is the very antithesis of September 11, 2001 as 9/11 and Quran 9.111. Because verse 9 and verse 11 are the key verses, **Psalm 91:9-11** can be written as **Psalm 91:9/11**. Adonai, the God of Heaven, the Sovereign of the Universe, foreknew Muhammad's future Quran 9.111 and the Islamic 9/11 take down of the World Trade Center Towers. Adonai sent His messenger Archangel Gabriel to King David with the words of **Psalm 91**. The cosmic control and foreknowledge of Adonai cannot be discounted.

It is no accident that this angelic dialogue is a discourse involving four Archangels. I was chosen by Hashem, also known by the name Adonai, as the transcendent God of Heaven, to dive deep into infinite waters to uncover and to expose this Islamic Fraud of the Ages which is attacking His Son Yeshua Messiah with its stated goal to break the Cross of Christ.

At a distance, the four Archangels evaluate the words of the author. "I hate to splash some cold water and buckets of scalding water here." True to form, and as a great source of sowing both seeds of doubt and revelation, Archangel Uriel declares, "First and foremost, Islam is a political ideology destined for worldwide conquest. Islam is a virulent political ideology masquerading as a religion. It is more than likely that the Augustinian monks and their Vatican stooges, who wrote the Quran for Muhammad, performed their usual 'spiritual' revisionist quackery by distorting **Psalm 91:9-11** into Quran 9:111. Be aware that the Islamic Antichrist is coming soon to kill the Christians and the Jews."

CHAPTER 2

"CAREFUL, I OUTNUMBER YOU.
WE ARE LEGION."

On February 12, 2016, *FOX News* announced that the cell phone encryptions of the two jihadist terrorists who massacred fourteen people in San Bernardino were so sophisticated that the best technology minds in the U.S. could not crack the code. On February 16, 2016, the FBI requested the assistance of Apple to crack the code. The next day, Apple CEO, Tim Cook, refused to hack into the shooter's phone. A federal judge demanded Apple comply. Again, Tim Cook refused. He stated that building a "backdoor" into the iPhone would compromise and undermine Apple's cell phone security system across the globe and that it would undermine decades of security advancements. Apple's Tim Cook stated that the issue was about privacy and that hacking the phone would set a precedent for further government encroachment upon privacy. To surrender to the government's demand would be to allow our government to violate our freedom the same way Muhammad's radical Islamic leaders do.

It is interesting that the radical Islamic State (ISIS) uses advanced technology to try to force humanity back to Muhammad's primitive and barbaric world of the seventh century. This is just more of the dualism of Muhammad's radical Islam. They may not be as highly advanced as others, but they do know how to use technology to their advantage and for their cause. In my extensive research, I have searched through Islamic websites to uncover their history. Many of the religious and secular Islamic sites attacked my computer with tracking cookies, viruses, spy-ware, mal-ware, and Trojan horses. They have even caused physical damages to my computer hard drives, which I have had to replace repeatedly. In the last three years, I have been attacked twenty to thirty-five times per search. The attacks upon my computer are escalating in frequency. Even my research editor experienced attacks. One night she heard a booming voice from a website warn, "Careful, I outnumber you." Clearly, she had been trespassing in forbidden territory. The words *"Careful, I outnumber you,"* are part of the dialogue from the movie trailer for the film *Gods of Egypt*, which hit the big screen around that time. The words *"Careful, I outnumber you."* are found in many other contexts, including in the Bible. Similar words in the New Testament are found in the Gospel of **Mark** in verses **5:6-13** which read that the demon-possessed victim had said, *"My name is Legion, for we are many"* (5:9). In *Gods of Egypt* the powerful god Horus was the Egyptian solar deity who was the son of Osiris and the Egyptian goddess ISIS. The ancient Egyptian god Thoth, the alleged "inventor" of writing and the supporter of Horus, was considered to have been the scribe of the underworld and the one who said in the movie, "Careful, I outnumber you." It is ironic that ISIS used the god of writing of the underworld to intimidate and to threaten an author who is writing to expose Muhammad's radical Islam.

The loud outburst inside the presumed safety of my editor's own home, traumatized her and drove her into a state of panic and fear, for herself and for her child. The assault took far greater technical sophistication by radical Islam than simply using a sophisticated Apple iPhone, and the timing means that Islamists are monitoring our Internet probes. Are other Islamic researchers facing similar aggressive intrusions?

By using the words of Thoth, an Egyptian god associated with the underworld, and by enlisting Horus, to attack my editor on the Internet, associates ISIS with the Egyptian trinity of Osiris-ISIS-Horus. Injecting **Horus** the Egyptian sun god also associates the trinity of **Osiris-ISIS-Horus** with Roman solar worship and validates the reason for the switch to Sunday worship by the Vatican. Because the Vatican was the driving force behind the authorship of the Quran, this linkage makes for another unholy divinity. In another high-profile unholy trinity, and one which is visible in the eyes of the entire world, the Egyptian phallic obelisk in St. Peter's Square in Rome, the phallic symbol of Cleopatra's Needle in the City-State of London, and the George Washington Monument in the City-State of the District of Columbia representing an Egyptian phallic symbol, associate the ancient Egyptian gods with today's ruling elites. Why are these ancient pagan Egyptian gods and goddesses central in our Western societies today?

This book exposes the gods of Egypt, the gods of Babylon, and Muhammad's association with Allah the moon god. Radical ISIS is desperate to shut down any *factual* exposure of Muhammad's Allah and his unholy and ludicrous, sex-crazed apocalyptic paradise.

This quasi-novel is based upon easily-verifiable historical events. All players and participants are real. The Spirit World is recognizable. Many characters date back to ancient times and much, much earlier. However, some conversations cannot be verified.

Humanity always has been surrounded by angels and demons; angels of light and angels of darkness. But in these scary, violent and malevolent times, as the world hurls itself feverishly towards its rendezvous with the Unknown, the age of angels and devils is heavy upon us. We are living in the dimming twilight of the approaching darkness which will be of an intensity never before known to mankind. In this fractured world of evil, humanity is separating, fragmenting, and alienating. Mankind is living on the knife's edge of eternity. We are heading toward the imminent Apocalypse. The Four Horsemen are visible on the horizon.

Archangel Michael addresses the God Squad saying, "From its very beginnings in the Garden of Eden, humanity has majored in hatred, in killing, and in defiance of the God of Heaven. In His response, Elohim/Adonai has reciprocated with judgment and with His Divine retribution. Today the world faces Muhammad's Islam as the greatest Fraud of the Ages that is at apocalyptic war with Adonai and Yeshua Messiah."

CHAPTER 3

TWILIGHT GATHERING
OF THE EAGLES AND THE RAVENS

In the gloom and doom of an approaching storm, the God Squad of four Archangels is gathered in a tight circle as they summarize historical events from antiquity.

Archangel Michael announces, "before the creation of mankind, the war in Heaven was driven by a power struggle for supremacy which was linked with Luciferian hatred of Adonai, the God of Heaven. From the creation story until today, the dark history of humanity has been dominated by Satan's hatred of the Creator of the universe, propelled by man's hatred of his fellow man, and animated by Muhammad's radical Islamic hatred of Adonai as the God of Abraham, the God of Isaac, and the God of Jacob.

"The senseless road rages on today's streets and highways are the metaphor for Muhammad's irrational, hate-obsessed murderous rages against the kafirs, the non-Muslims, in the Arabian deserts of the seventh century. Muhammad's hatred is being extended worldwide in the second decade of the twenty-first century." It is obvious that Archangel Gabriel is deeply distressed with his archenemy of fourteen centuries. "Muhammad's terror has evolved and metastasized across the world and into America. Muhammad's Islam is determined to destroy Western Civilization. The jackals of war are past the door. Islamic State first chose the title ISIS. Was this title an accidental or a deliberate attempt to flaunt the Egyptian Queen of Heaven with the same name? The jackals already are inside the house. Radical Islamic imperialism is upon our heads."

"ISIS is a sophisticated terrorist group which is Internet-savvy and shockingly proficient in social media high-level encryption. ISIS is determined to force the world back to the Arabic seventh century."

"In His Ten Commandments, Elohim, the God of Heaven and the God of Abraham, says, 'Thou shalt not kill.' However, Allah commands to Kill! Kill! Kill! as in 'Strike off their heads,' 'Slay the idolaters,' 'Make war on the infidels,' 'Seize them and put them to death,' 'Strike terror into the enemy of Allah,' 'Slay them wherever you find them,' 'Put them to the sword.'" Michael continues his historical exposure, "the Quran and Sharia Law exhort to kill the kafir; kill the gays; kill your daughter if you catch her in adultery; kill your daughter if she disobeys you; kill your apostate son. It's kill, kill, kill by Muhammad's ISIS in Paris, in Brussels, in San Bernardino, in Orlando, in Istanbul, in Dhaka, in Baghdad, in Medina, and in Nice where Allah mowed down children and toddlers with a transport truck. In this Age of Hatred, the spirit of hate is running rampant."

With a quizzical look, Uriel asks, "Sharia Law? What is this Sharia Law?"

"As written by Muslim historians Sahih Muslim and Sahih Bukhari, the writings in the Hadiths are the basis of Sharia Law across the Muslim world," explains Michael.

"What are these Hadiths?" Uriel inquires.

"The Hadiths are about what Muhammad said," Gabriel replies. "They are mostly about Muhammad's words. The Hadiths are influential. However, the Hadiths are not as authoritative as the Quran, which carries the major weight. In terms of sacredness, the Hadiths are second to the Quran."

Archangel Raphael waves his arms as he expounds, "Islam denies that Jesus Messiah is the Son of God, denies that He died on the cross, denies that His blood atones for the sins of mankind, denies that He rose from the dead, and denies that He sits at the right hand of God his Father. In Muhammad's Quran, Allah states that if you say that Jesus is the Son of God, you will burn in hell. As

> "When you meet the unbelievers in the battlefield strike off their heads."
>
> - Quran 47:4

part of its formal doctrine, because Islam is the only religion that denies the divinity of Jesus Christ, Islam is the religion of the Antichrist. In **1 John 2:22**, the Apostle John wrote, "This is the antichrist, he who denies the Father and the Son."

"Hear this!" Archangel Michael continues, "Pope Francis has declared that the God of Abraham is the same Supreme Being as the god of Islam. In the Quran, Muhammad's Allah declares that Jesus is not the Son of the God of Abraham. The murderous killings of children and infants in the name Allah make it clear that the God of Abraham is not the Allah of Muhammad. The God of Abraham is as far removed from the Allah of Islam as Heaven is removed from Hell. This is the new *Chrislam* or the new *ChrIslam* of Pope Francis."

"This is head-shaking stuff!" exclaims Archangel Uriel. "Pope Francis has stated that, 'Authentic Islam and the proper reading of the Koran are opposed to every form of violence.' What is proper reading? Quran 47:4 reads, 'When you meet the unbelievers in the battlefield strike off their heads.' This was not a Quranic suggestion. It was Allah's unconditional demand— Striking off heads is undeniable Quranic violence."

"There are other verses," says Gabriel. Reading from his tablet he continues, "In Quran 2:191–192, Allah admonishes Muslims to, 'Slay them wherever you find them.'. . . 'put them to the sword.' In Quran 2:194, Allah commands, 'If anyone attacks you, attack him as he attacked you.' Quran 2:216 reads, 'Fighting is obligatory for you.' Quran 4:89 leaves no doubt about Allah's intentions: 'Seize them and put them to death wherever you find them.'"

> Allah admonishes Muslims to, 'Slay them wherever you find them.'. . . 'put them to the sword.'
>
> - Quran 2:191-192

Scrolling down his tablet, Raphael joins in. "Quran 5:33 speaks the shocking truth about Allah's Islam, saying that kafirs 'shall be slain or crucified or have their hands and feet cut off on alternate sides.' Ouch!"

Uriel throws up both arms asking, "Kafir! Kafir! Kafir! What's a Kafir?

"The Arabic Muslim polite name for a non-Muslim is *infidel*," replies Michael. "That's the gentle label used to the face of a nonbeliever. But behind their backs, a kafir is anyone who is not a Muslim whom they denigrate with choice low-level descriptors."

"It's much worse than that. A kafir is the lowest form of life, an outright scum, a most disgusting, wicked, and evil human." Gabriel expands upon this portrayal. "It's Islam's ugliest form of contempt possible to describe nonbelievers. Muslims can cheat them, deceive them, lie to kafirs, and with Allah's permission, it is proper to enslave, to torture, and to kill a kafir."

"The greater part of the Quran is about the kafirs."

"Repeatedly, the Quran states that Muslims constantly should be putting pressure on kafirs," continues Gabriel. "This condition of war against the Kafirs is universal and is required for all Muslims to perform."

"War against the kafirs is the number-one rule of Islam for all Muslims to follow," exclaims Michael, who ought to know.

"Remember," interjects Gabriel. "We were listening when the Quran was being created fourteen hundred years ago. Here's another Quranic blast. In Quran 9:5, Allah exhorts Muslims to 'Slay the idolaters wherever you find them.' In Quran 9:36 Allah commanded, 'fight against the idolaters.' Quran 9:39 threatens, 'If you do not go to war, [Allah] will punish you sternly, and will replace you by other men.'"

"Allah's Quran 9:73," adds Michael, "terrorizes with these words: 'Prophet, make war on the unbelievers and the hypocrites and deal rigorously with them. Hell shall be their home.' Quran 9:123 is more and more of Allah's commands to slaughter as, 'Believers make war on the infidels that dwell around you.' These are shocking and undeniable commands straight out of Allah's Quran," grieves Michael.

Uriel throws out another chilling zinger in which Allah commands his followers to, '"Strike terror into the enemy of Allah and your enemy,' says Quran 8:60. There is nothing peaceful about Quran 33:60–61 which curses the hypocrites who want to sit on the sidelines, threatening them with

> Allah exhorts Muslims to "Slay the idolaters wherever you find them."
>
> - Quran 9:5

death: 'If the hypocrites and those who have tainted hearts …do not desist, we will rouse you against them. Cursed wherever they are found, they shall be seized and put to death without mercy.'"

On a roll and gathering speed, Michael reads from his copy of the Quran, "Here is more of the same. In Quran 48:13, Allah told Muhammad, 'As for those that disbelieve in Allah and His apostle, We have prepared a blazing Fire for the unbelievers.' It's all about the threat of hellfire!"

"Here is proof from other sources." Uriel addresses the God Squad. "Islamic scholar Sahih Muslim wrote that Muhammad had said, 'Certainly, the gates of Paradise lie in the shade of swords.' And Islamic scholar Sahih Bukhari wrote almost identical words claiming Muhammad had said, 'Be aware that Paradise lies under the shadow of swords.' Allah is about cutting off heads, just as ISIS is doing today."

"Strike terror into the enemy of Allah and your enemy,"

- Quran 8:60

Gabriel interrupts, "Muslim renowned historian Sahih Bukhari wrote that Muhammad punished the men of the Uraina tribe by cutting off their hands and feet and letting them bleed to death. Muhammad ordered that their hands and feet be cut off and their eyes gouged out with hot pokers. They were thrown on jagged rocks, their pleas for water ignored and they died of thirst, who abandoned Islam. Death is the sentence for leaving Islam." Gabriel laments the agony. "This was Muhammad's bloodlust and hatred. This was radical Islamic terrorism. This was Muhammad's barbarous killing which ISIS is duplicating today. This was and is Allah's fundamental authentic Islam."

"Here is another clincher of Allah's hate-driven, murderous rampages," retorts Raphael. "Both Muslim authorities Sahih al-Bukhari and Sahih Muslim wrote in their hadiths and quoted Muhammad's threats as he lay dying: 'May Allah curse the Christians and Jews.' Muhammad died while cursing the Christians and the Jews: 'The last hour will not come before the Muslims fight the Jews and the Muslims kill them. In that day Allah will give voice to the rocks and the trees and they will cry out, 'O Muslim, there is a Jew hiding behind me. Come and kill him!'"

"Sad but true, there are over one hundred verses just in the Quran that call upon Muslims to make war upon nonbelievers. It is clear that Allah is the god of hatred and indiscriminate, mass slaughter. I wonder what Pope Francis had been drinking or smoking when he proclaimed that Islam is peaceful?"

Drawing back the curtain more, Michael exposes more of Allah's hatred. "In Quran 2:63–65," he said, "Allah wrote of the children of Israel: 'You will be changed into detested apes.' Muslim authority Ishaq wrote: 'Allah totally approves of the killing of the Jews, enslaving the women and children.' What can Pope Francis say in response to this obvious hatred and violence?"

As the medical expert in the God Squad, Raphael summarizes, "The Quran is a book of virulent hatred demanding the killing of non-Muslims but especially the slaughter of Christians and Jews as the children of Sarah and Rebeccah. To protect the gullible, because the Quran is hate literature, the Quran should be banned from bookstores."

"We know that Muhammad smoked hashish and marijuana and was probably hallucinating much of his life. That is why he heard strange voices. That is why Muhammad had demonic dreams and saw demonic visions which he had attributed to Gabriel." Michael continues to strip away the veil masking the Quran. "Muhammad was morally bankrupt. He was driven by generational hatred which he had inherited from Ishmael and Esau. The four of us were witnesses to this monstrous Muhammad Fraud of the Ages."

Raphael interjects, "In 2016, ISIS proclaimed that Ramadan is the time to kill for Allah, and kill they did. The ongoing Yazidi genocide is the ISIS version of Muhammad's seventh-century slaughters."

Michael reinforces. "Allah has no limits to his hatred. On August 21, 2016, ISIS used a child to kill fifty-four at a Turkish wedding. Many

> "As for those that disbelieve in Allah and His apostle, We have prepared a blazing Fire for the unbelievers"
>
> – *Quran 48:13*

who were killed were children. Yes, Allah's Hamas teaches children to commit jihadist suicide."

Gabriel summarizes the extent of the virulence in the Quran. "We all know Saudi Arabia, Iran and Pakistan stone adulterous females and throw gays out of high buildings. This is invading France too. Mowing down adults, children and infants with an eighteen-ton truck is a throwback to Muhammad's medieval Islamic barbarity. Now the mosques in America are clamouring for Sharia Law and promoting hatred against America. Sharia Law is supremacist ideology, which is incompatible with Western civilization and incompatible with the American Constitution. ISIS celebrates brutality and flaunts it on social media."

"The United States is approaching the point of no return," adds Archangel Michael. "The belligerent Black Lives Matter movement, which originated under a black president, screams outrage at the same president's failed and bankrupt actions toward the black communities. Reckless Democrat administrations continue to polarize Americans by sex, class, and race. Their ploy is to Balkanize the American States into warring factions that fight against each other."

"At the other extreme," adds Raphael, "the Republican Establishment has been party to the greedy banksters who crippled America with the collapse of the housing bubble in 2008, and somehow avoided jail for their outrageous frauds and thieveries. In 2016, the resentment, the intense anger, and the hostilities in America ran deeply and unpredictably against the establishment powers. But at least they didn't give us the Arab Spring."

"Allah wrote of the children of Israel: 'You will be changed into detested apes.'"

- Quran 2:63-65

"Arab Spring!" exclaims Gabriel. "After five years, the Arab Spring has given way to a hopeless Arab Fall and a disastrous Arab Winter. In reality and in effect, the Arab Spring was an ISIS Spring."

Uriel, the physical sciences expert, launches a mind-bender. "The enigma of these American and Middle East political unrealities is matched by a far deeper enigma as the cosmic hologram."

"Cosmic hologram?" Gabriel echoes. "I can't understand a hologram that I can see. So what's a cosmic hologram?"

"A hologram is an image created by bending light from a physical object. The two-dimensional image appears as if it is three-dimensional," explains Uriel. "Evidence suggests that this world and everything in it are just three-dimensional projections originating from a real universe somewhere beyond time and space. The cosmos and everything in it might be just a super-hologram. Such a reality is beyond human comprehension, but humans know very little about space. As an example, tape recordings of the 1969 Apollo 10 mission, which circled the dark side of the Moon, contain strange "music" signals which could not reach earth. Documented UFO movements defy all the known laws of physics. These objects appear and disappear as if traveling through different dimensions. Even some scientists believe in an infinite number of parallel universes. As the Creator of a multi-universe, what manner of GOD is He? **Exodus 33:20–23** warns that beyond a measure, He is not knowable, 'You cannot see my face; for man shall not see Me and live.... my face shall not be seen.' But WE have seen His face and He talks to us," blinks Uriel.

"The most significant and deadly Fraud of the Ages, is the shroud of radical Islam," Michael declares. "Allah's Quran is an ideology driven by hatred while hiding behind the pretence of being a religion. Allah is the god of hatred, mass killing, and murder. Those at the top of this Pyramid of Fraud know the truth, while the unwashed masses are the useful idiots. While promising eternal sex with seventy-two recycled virgins to young males in Allah's paradise, Islam's goal is to conquer the world and to make everyone submit to Allah. From AD 610, the fanatical spread of Islam began at the point of the sword. Although Islam was stopped over the centuries at Tours, France, at Kosovo, at the Great Siege of Malta, at the Battle of Vienna, and at the Battle of Zenta, today Islam continues with the AK 47, the suicide bomber, the roadside bomb, and the 20-tonne truck. Today, Muhammad's radical Islam strives to obtain and to push the button on the nuclear bomb. Islamic Pakistan already has the bomb. Iran's stated goal is to obtain the nuclear bomb and to wipe Israel off the map. Today, Islam is the black swan that is flying through the Middle East and across the globe as ISIS.

"Over fourteen centuries of ruthless bloodshed, some 300,000,000 lives have been slaughtered in the name of Islam and the Quran. Of that number massacred, 80 million were Hindus, 60 million were Christians, and 10 million were Buddhists. Muhammad's Quran is hate ideology which should be banned."

"We have endured these ruthless, barbaric massacres for fourteen centuries." Tears fall from Gabriel's eyes.

"There is more, so much more," Michael continues. "Egypt's Christian Copts have resisted conversion to Islam for fourteen centuries, during which time they have suffered cycles of persecution. On Orthodox Christmas in 2010, the Nagaa Hamadi Church Massacre was a continuum in the forty-years-long series of violence that has killed thousands of Egyptian Copts. Just prior to the Nagaa Hamadi Massacre, an imam had incited a mob of several tens of thousands of Muslims to cleanse the city of infidel Christians. Since the 1970s, the Islamization of Egypt has marginalized Christians by removing them from all senior government, army, police, and public sector positions. The expropriation of their lands has been promoted. The burning of Christian churches has been encouraged. Imams have goaded Muslim mobs to assault and to kill non-Muslims.

"Remember New Year's Day 2011," chimes in Gabriel. "A car bomb outside a Christian church in Alexandria, Egypt, killed twenty-one and injured ninety-seven as they were leaving Mass. Islamic global terrorist organizations have targeted Egyptian Christians." Archangel Gabriel continues, "In Iraq, the never-ending story of assassinations of Christians continues. Firebombing of homes, kidnapping of relatives, and shooting of Sunday worshippers continue by the old renewed strain of Muhammad's orthodox Islam.

"And in Southern Sudan," Michael exclaims as though they are competing for time to talk, "Christians have been enslaved and tortured by their Arab neighbors in the north. Islamization of Southern Sudan has been a process of assassination and brutal liquidation. Islamic bombings of churches and the killing of Christians in Nigeria and in the Philippines continued on Christmas 2010. Indonesia has a long history of hostility towards Christians. In Turkey, nuns and priests had been murdered. Less than six hundred years ago, Turkey was the home to millions of Christians. Today, Turkey is almost exclusively a Muslim nation. In Pakistan, blaspheming Muhammad or Islam is punishable by hanging. In Islamabad, on January 4, 2011, the governor of Punjab province was assassinated because he criticized Pakistan's blasphemy laws by coming to the assistance of a Christian woman."

"These mass murders are ethnic and religious cleansing in a declared holy war intended to eliminate all Christians and Jews from the Middle East. There exists a deliberate intent to destroy Christian communities. As the example of national intolerance in action, Saudi Arabia, the very heart of Islamic darkness, permits no Jews, no synagogues, and no churches on its soil. Even harmless cartoons of Muhammad are declared to be blasphemy and are punishable by death.

"Tens of thousands of Egyptian Copts have escaped persecution by moving to Canada. During Christmas 2010, many Canadian Copts received anonymous threats claiming that they are dogs defaming Islam. In Egyptian-style, Islamic Jihad of old is coming soon to a Christian church near you. Today, ISIS is slaughtering thousands in Iraq and Syria. Christians are their primary targets. On November 13, 2015, radical Islamists butchered 130 young people in Paris. On December 2, 2015, in San Bernardino, California, a husband-wife team of radical Islamic terrorists murdered 14 disabled Christian adults celebrating a Christmas party. In 2017, radical Islam is on their March of Murder.

"We are living in the age of anxiety. Many Americans are scared to death. Their anxiety is shaking the political landscape. Grassroots movements on both the left and on the right feel that those running America have a secret agenda that is working against them. Paranoia about the roles of big money and big corporations is palpable across the nation.

"Compelled by Ishmael's and by Esau's hatred of women and hatred of Jews, compelled by the Quran's hellfire fear of Allah who demands to kill the Kafir, and compelled by sexual rewards in Allah's paradise, the picture of a peaceful Muslim is the ultimate oxymoron," Gabriel is frustrated that this message is being suppressed and drowned out by Islamic shouts of "Islamophobia."

People choose to ignore the truth. People choose to ignore the hideous ancient past. The books of Genesis, Enoch, Baruch, and Jeremiah, all speak of the Nephilim, the wicked offspring of the watcher angels and the daughters of Cain. The Nephilim were the demonic offspring of these fallen angels with Earth's women. Moses wrote about them in **Genesis 6:4** saying, 'The Nephilim were on the earth those days, and also afterward, when the sons of God came in to the daughters of men, and they bore children to them. Those were the mighty men who were of old, the men of renown." They sought to pervert and to destroy Adam's bloodline. Even before the Garden of Eden, Satan's plan was to degrade Adam's DNA. The Great Flood was intended to drown the Nephilim so as to retain the Adamic DNA. Unfortunately, several Nephilim had survived Noah's deluge and were able to continue their evil bloodline. Following the Great Flood, these drowned giants of old had been chained in the depths of Hell until their release at the end of time. We see them back in the world today. Nimrod may be walking among us.

From Genesis to Revelation, all manner of wickedness has been associated with the metaphor of the woman in scarlet. The crimson strand of forbidden and perverted sex runs from the Garden of Eden to the Battle of Armageddon. In its beginnings with the historical Nephilim, the story of man has been directed and stained by this bloody thread woven into the fabric of world history. Front and center, Allah's promise of eternal paradise with seventy-two virgins has been the key driving force behind Muhammad's radical Islamic sexual perversion.

It is known in Christian circles that deep-seated hatred can open a physical and spiritual star-gate and unleash demonic forces. Ishmael was consumed by a virulent hatred inflicted upon him by two women: Sarah and Hagar. Over many generations, this demonic hatred festered and grew to become a murderous hatred of Sarah that reached its pinnacle of depravity and fanaticism in the person of Muhammad which was woven into the shroud of Islam. Muhammad's hatred of women and his hatred of Elohim had opened other star-gate portals to satanic possession of this maniac monster.

Always the historian, Archangel Michael dredges up Muhammad's early beginnings. "Many generations after Ishmael, the locals of Medina had considered that Muhammad was demon-possessed. Muhammad himself had verbalized that he had felt possessed by Satan. He was the perfect breeding ground for rebellion against Elohim a.k.a. Adonai. Satan came to Muhammad in the guise of our friend Gabriel. But we all know that the Quran was dictated to Muhammad, not by Gabriel, but by Augustinians and by Satan herself."

In spite of the dark days and the gloomy future, four Archangels are on a mission to save a portion of mankind. In the gathering darkness under a chaotic sky, four angelic beings are gathered into a tight circle. Archangel Gabriel points toward the eastern sky and exclaims, "Look at that thin white horizontal thread just above the horizon."

As the galactic observer of the skies, Uriel shrugs it off casually. "No big concern. It's just the beginning of an insignificant twister which likely won't even touch down. It's little more than a dust devil. Not to worry." The four Archangels ignore the twisting white thread. With a devilish mind of its own, and like a python dropping from a tree onto its prey, the white strand snakes and like a cobra, it strikes abruptly downward. It touches down and ravages the ground below it. Instantly, the whirlwind turns the eastern sky black. Within minutes, the funnel spinning spiral morphs into a swirling category 3 tornado, which shreds the rooves off several farm buildings.

As the roaring twister grows louder and more menacing, it spins its way towards the four angelic beings who are huddled in a serious conference. The air is crackling with electricity. Seemingly oblivious to nature's fury, Michael launches into a lesson on changing world demographics. "Within a few short years, the global cultures as we know them today will be vastly different. Sharia Law will stalk the land. Male oppression of women will plummet to depths of darkness yet unknown. Wearing high heels will be a crime punishable with a lash. Clitoral mutilation will be the mandated Islamic standard. For a female, the price of an illicit relationship will be one hundred lashes followed with execution by stoning. As demonstrated by recent Iranian rulers, many of the charges against women will be a sham. Ishmael's revenge upon all women will show no mercy and no limits. Every female will experience a preview of Hell itself. High-profile women who protest the stonings will be arrested and subjected to the most inhumane sexual tortures that only Allah could devise."

Shocked, Gabriel tries to make sense of what Michael has said. "From what you say, the future for young girls in the U.S. and in Canada looks as threatening as that category 3 tornado that is swirling towards us. But how can such a dramatic change happen so quickly?"

"Islamic totalitarian governments need absolute control of their people, but especially control of their women." Michael presents the flip side of unfolding physical disasters on Earth. "As that swirling tornado, humanity is spinning out of control. Islamic females must be kept under the heels of men. Islamic males cannot allow another Sarah or another Hagar or another Rebecca into their midst. Orthodox Islam is unable to clamp down if it cannot censor all communications and Internet traffic. The United Arab Emerites, Saudi Arabia, and China are trying to shut down the free flow of information. By coercion, they will succeed sooner than can be imagined."

Agreeing with Uriel, Gabriel points out, "With chaos in Cairo, Hosni Mubarak showed us how it could be done. He shut down the Internet and the social networking sites in Egypt. Facebook, Twitter, YouTube, and text message services were shut down, thereby crippling initial efforts to coordinate the rioters. Through YouTube and Facebook, the Arab Spring had removed Mubarak. In its place, the Muslim Brotherhood ruled Egypt for a while until the army threw Morsi into jail. With Gadhafi removed from power in Libya, radical Islamic chaos reigns. The U.S. ambassador was murdered in Benghazi by Al Qaeda terrorists. There is civil war in Syria. Assad is using sarin and chlorine gas. With ISIS in Iraq and Syria, we are at a pivotal point in history. At the beginning of the second Iraq war, Saddam Hussein moved his chemical weapons of mass destruction to Damascus, Syria. Today, Damascus is sitting on the largest mass of chemical weapons. That is why scriptural prophecies state that Damascus will go up in flames. The use of chemical weapons by ISIS is a game-changer. The radical Islamic genie is out of the bottle in the Middle East. The crescent moon on the Al-Aqsa Mosque is closed. The closed crescent of the moon indicates world conquest is in process.

"Egyptian Mubarak didn't succeed in squelching all communications but he did set the future pattern. Succeeding U.S. presidents have been given the power to shut down the Internet. With the hand of the U.S. President on the Internet kill-switch, what will be the event to silence Americans and Canadians?" Gabriel queries his inner circle of Archangels.

Archangel Raphael asks, "Since Hosni Mubarak had failed, why is controlling the Internet so very important for the Muslim mullahs?"

With the flick of his right hand, Gabriel replies casually, "Easy answer. Hosni Mubarak was but one person. The mullahs of Iran are many. The mullahs and the imams interpret the Quran and control all of Shiite Islam. However, the mullahs and the imams know that orthodox Islam is on very shaky ground and that it can't withstand scrutiny. Portions of the Quran are simply laughable. All historical records that predate Islam contradict the Quran left, right, and center. The mullahs and the imams do not believe a single word in the Quran. They know that the Quran is political garbage meant to control the ignorant and the fearful. The Internet allows for the free flow of information. That information should expose the Quran as being total domination and as a culture of hatred. But that's not happening. Instead, Muhammad's orthodox Islam has subverted the Internet by spreading disinformation. Nevertheless, the imams and the mullahs are terrified of any threats to their power, especially the truth spread over social media on the Internet. That's why Muslim countries have forced the UN to outlaw and to punish criticism of Muhammad, criticism of Islam, or criticism of the Quran. Labelled as 'Islamophobia,' it is blasphemy to question the Quran."

"Good insight, Gabby!" praises Michael. "Blaspheming Allah the moon god brings the death sentence. Yasser Arafat once claimed that Jesus was the first Palestinian martyr. How's that for twisting the facts? And the Quran is just more of the same revisionist history."

Gabriel provides more insight, "Shutting down freedom of expression and access to information is where Muhammad's radical Islam and all other dictatorships excel. Islam and freedom of expression cannot coexist. It's all about mindless, unquestioning submission to Allah. The imams are the only authorities who are allowed to interpret the Quran and Islam. A democratic Islam is just another Muslim oxymoron. Consider the war in Iraq which was supposed to bring democratic reforms and safety. It didn't happen. As they've been doing for fourteen centuries, the Shiites and the Sunnis continue to kill each other with suicide bombs. Both brag that Allah is fighting on their side. However, it appears that Allah wants nothing to do with justice or freedom of any kind. Allah is about killing unbelievers and apostates."

All four Archangels burst out laughing.

After a brief moment of joy, Michael's face suddenly turns sombre. "Today, from Morocco to Yemen, revolution and anarchy are spreading across Arab lands. The Middle East is in turmoil. The people in Tunisia and Yemen are rioting to remove their dictators. They want democratic freedom."

With a note of sarcasm in his voice, Gabriel casts doubts on that possibility saying, "Muslim democratic freedom? Get serious! The Muslim Brotherhood has been waiting for just this opportunity to take control. They want to enshrine Sharia Law in the Middle East and break the peace treaty with Israel. Hamas and al-Qaeda are offshoots of the Muslim Brotherhood's hidden agenda, which also comes out of the barrel of a gun. The roots of the jihadist Muslim Brotherhood go back many centuries to the Ishmaelite slaughters in Christian Spain and in Christian Constantinople. Just look at Iraq. The Iraq War, as the most intrusive experiment in democratization, has failed. Instead, it has greatly extended Islam's terrorist influence in the world."

"Did I hear you say something about democratic freedom in Iran?!" booms Raphael as he rocks with laughter. "How about freedom in music?"

"Not even in music!" responds Uriel. "Iran's supreme leader, Ayatollah Ali Khamenei has issued an administrative order for the whole country, making it a law that music is not compatible with the values of Muhammad's Islamic republic."

"Once all Internet traffic can be intercepted, censored, or blocked," Michael explains, "then autocratic governments and Islamic theocracies will be one step closer to total control of their subjects.

"But there is more and it gets worse. It's frightening! On April 8, 2010, government hackers in China pulled off a daring coup. They succeeded in high-jacking Internet traffic from U.S. government and from the American Department of Defense websites. China now is in the position of being able to execute a worldwide digital Pearl Harbour upon the United States."

Gabriel asks, "What role will Islam play in this take-down of the U.S.?"

Michael projects his political perspective. "The fifth column disguised within respectable Muslim America looms large! Muslims have been building and grooming their Trojan horse for decades. Through the Internet, radical Muslims encourage martyrs by promising beautiful virgins awaiting them in the afterlife. Continually, Americans and Canadians have experienced homegrown Islamic terrorists who are being encouraged and sponsored by Pakistan, Yemen, and al-Qaeda. Radicalized young Muslims within Canada and the United States will shake North America to its core. Like Major Hassan of Fort Hood infamy, the suicide bomber could be the military Muslim psychiatrist or the Muslim doctor living next door."

"There is much fear of an al-Qaeda or an ISIS nuclear weapon being brought onto American soil." Archangel Raphael reveals. "However, the greater danger is the stealth insertion of Sharia Law and the loss of freedom that will follow such a constitutional assault."

Gabriel interrupts, "As recorded by Moses in **Genesis 16:12**, do remember that I had brought Elohim's message to Hagar four thousand years ago, proclaiming that Ishmael would be 'a wild ass of a man, his hand against every man.' Well, Ishmael certainly turned out to be that brutal beast. However, Ishmael's great-great-great-great-great grandson Muhammad turned out to be far, far worse. He was a plundering, salacious, murdering rapist, a drug addict and a sex addict. His bloodthirsty ideology continued after he was poisoned by his wives. If Muhammad's followers aren't killing Christians and Jews, then Shiites and Sunnis are killing each other. And the killing continues today. In fourteen hundred years, nothing has changed. The imams continue to brainwash and to incite their young studs into a state of mindless, testosterone-driven frenzy. Saudi Arabia continues to build and to fund their madrassa schools for young boys who are taught only the Quran and jihad. It is nearly impossible for humans to defend against unhinged crazies who want to die for Allah so that they can have unlimited eternal sex in Allah's paradise. Whether it was by the sword and by the dagger, or by today's AK-47 and improvised explosive devices, the radical Islamic mind-set has not changed in over fourteen hundred years. Islam is the culture of death."

Michael interjects, "If Muhammad were alive today, and if he were living in the United States or Canada, he would be arrested, jailed, and committed to an insane asylum as an extremely dangerous pedophile, a sexual deviant, and a murderer."

"Not only that," Raphael chimes in with more details. "Less than a hundred years ago, Muslim Turks slaughtered more than a million Armenian Christians. Pure and simple, it was genocide. Today, Muslim holy warriors are murdering Christians across North Africa, across the Middle East and across the Far East. Today, there are no official churches left in Saudi Arabia. The only Christians allowed are foreign workers from the Philippines and India, but then only on temporary permits. Muslims oppress and murder Christians in Egypt, Sudan, Iraq, Nigeria, Southern Sudan, Syria, Iraq, Turkey, Indonesia, the Philippines, and Pakistan. Within hours of the 2011 assassination of the Punjab governor, Pakistani sympathizers put up a fan page on Facebook honoring the killer. They showered him with rose petals. Many thousands of his supporters gushed words of congratulations for killing the blasphemer of the Prophet Muhammad. Half of the responses to newspaper websites cheered the governor's death. The instigators were the clerics. Many supporters were educated middle-class fanatics. This is Muhammad's radical Islam for the entire world to see!"

"We know that radicalization of locals is very much of a problem in North America." Raphael tries to tone down the emotion. "But what about the mind-set of Pakistani immigrants who have come to Canada and to America? Surely they must think differently."

Shaking his head, Archangel Gabriel adamantly replies, "Come on Raphael. After fourteen hundred years of mass slaughter, the mind-set of killing Christians and killing Jews has been seared into Muslim psyches. Allah demands slaughter. As the most dangerous nuclear country in the world, Pakistan is split down the middle and separating further. By allowing Syrian Muslim immigration, Americans and Canadians potentially are importing death to their way of life. Just look at what happened in San Bernardino, California. They need to give their immigration departments a good shake out. Just consider this peace-loving Raufie Imam. He was absolutely unwavering in building the Cordoba House Mosque at Ground Zero, no matter how many Americans are offended. By bending democratic freedoms, Muslims mean to get their way. Otherwise they scream, 'Islamophobia.'"

Michael adds, "Consider this. In order for a culture to survive, it needs a minimum birth rate of 2.11 children per family. History shows that no culture has ever reversed a birth rate of 1.9 per family. As the population declines, so do the culture and the economics."

"That 1.9 number is ominous for Europe," interjects Raphael. "In 2007 the birth rate in France was 1.8 children per family, in England 1.6, in Greece 1.3, in Germany 1.3, in Italy 1.2 and in Spain it was 1.1 children per family. Across the entire European Union, the average birth rate was a frightening 1.38 children per family. European cultural and democratic lights are dimming quickly."

Mathematician Uriel joins the grim statistical fray. "The arithmetic is frightening."

A very concerned and anxious Gabriel pipes up, "However, because of Muslim immigration, the population of Europe is not declining. Recall many ages ago when the four of us had watched the finger of God writing on King Belshazzar's Palace wall in Babylon. Today, the Islamic finger is spelling out the impending doom of European freedoms and cultures."

Archangel Raphael continues the probing and the pushing, "The birthrate of European Muslims is double to triple that of native Europeans. Every imam in every mosque is preaching and encouraging large families. This is how they gain control of a country through immigration and through copulation. From 1990 to 2010, the global Muslim population had increased at an average yearly rate of 2.2 percent. Islam and Sharia Law give absolute license to Muslim males to demand sex whenever they have the urge. Muslim or not, when Sharia Law becomes universal, every male will have total dominion over his four wives and demand unlimited sex."

"In Pakistan, the imams debate about wife-beating." Legal beagle Michael expounds, "One Pakistani imam said that wife-beating is a Quranic provision which must not be questioned. The systematic misogyny embedded in Sharia Law—honour killings, forced marriages, multiple wives, genital mutilation, and treating females as chattel—continues to oppress women in much of the Muslim world."

Gabriel delivers another stinger: "Islam puts women's rights on ice. Women's rights in America and in Canada will become a distant memory as women become sex slaves and baby factories. Honor killings and the threat of honor killings by husbands, fathers and brothers will continue to instil fear and terror into women, which will reduce them to emotional wrecks. Honor killings are outright murder. For shock value and as a deterrent, in families with multiple Muslim wives, when one of them is being stoned to death, the remaining three wives are forced to become spectators ."

A visibly distressed and dejected-looking Gabriel adds, "And you know what twists the knife even deeper? Large European Muslim families are living in mushrooming and crime-ridden ghettos. To add insult to injury, these ravens' nests are full of Muslims on the welfare rolls, adding to the distressed economies and to the perpetual financial crises. In reality, Europeans are turning their future wealth into welfare payments for impoverished Muslims in their midst."

Archangel Michael, who keeps his finger on the global economic pulse, paints a much bleaker picture. "Europe cannot stop its population decline. But it isn't Greece or Ireland or Portugal or Spain, which is of concern. It is Germany that worries me the most. As Europe's biggest and most successful economic engine, Germany's birthrate is at an alarming historic low. Three and one-half million Muslim Turks are giving birth to half of the babies born in Germany. This is Germany's demographic roadside bomb. No other 'religion' is as much dependent upon social welfare and as much connected with crime as Islam. Germany is the sick man of Europe heading for the abyss. Yes, Germany is the dead man walking and does not know it! In spite of this ominous horizon, Germany continues to bring in more Muslim immigrants. It continues to bail out the failing economies of the eurozone. Chancellor Angela Merkel has invited a million Syrian Muslims into Germany. Male Muslim refugees are raping young European girls and women at will, and with little repercussions. Does Germany have a death wish yet again? How long will it be before ethnic Germans scream 'Enough!'?"

Raphael presents a sobering perspective, "Is this the beginning of another German backlash? How long will Germans continue to tolerate this assault upon their sovereignty? We saw how the swift retaliation to the economic downturn in the 1930s brought the world to its knees in 1939. The ethnic cleansing of that era will pale in comparison to what is looming on the German horizon today. The signs are obvious. Will Germany shake the world for a third time with a Fourth Reich?"

Archangel Uriel inserts a frightening scenario. "Recall that Assyria of old was the most brutal and barbaric killing machine of all time. The destination of the scattered Assyrians has been traced to present-day Germany." A stony cold chill silences the God Squad for a full ten minutes.

"The demographics in France are just as explosive and much more sinister," Archangel Michael breaks the silence but continues in the same dark mood. "In France, on pain of rioting and death, Muslim leaders have warned the French police to stay away from Islamic communities. The Muslim ghettos there are no longer sovereign French soil. These French territories are no longer some la-la-land. Now they are Allah-land. Civil disobedience under the guise of worship is the new harassment tactic of Islamic unrest in France. Well-planned provocative, large Muslim prayer meetings spill out of the mosques onto the streets, blocking traffic. Muslim security thugs prevent French police from breaking up the Allah worshippers when they block traffic as they bow to their god in the streets. This Muslim strategy is deliberate intimidation and confrontation. And the Muslims call themselve peaceful. French police have not dared to intervene in these acts of civil disobedience. How long will France tolerate this abuse? Will discontent with the Muslims spread beyond French borders? Sara Ahmed reveals in the book *The Cultural Politics of Emotion* that Europe has been degraded into a culture of fear. Europe is on the threshold of a bloody war." In the May 7, 2017 French presidential election, Marine Le Pen vowed to stop Islamic immigration. Although she increased her vote count from the last election, Marine Le Pen won only one-third of the votes which were cast.

A dejected-looking Raphael adds, "through welfare payments, European governments are funding their own destruction."

"Muslims will use their sheer numbers and the democratic processes to vote Sharia Law into existence," Michael reminds them. "When that happens the democratic age will come to an abrupt and irreversible closure! Fourteen centuries of violent political ideology have shown that radical Islam always will be at war with democracy. It all fits for the coming one world government."

Archangel Gabriel supplies the dismal clincher, "In other words, democratic laws will be used to shut down democratic freedoms in Europe, and eventually in America and in Canada. Americans and Canadians should face the reality that Islam is Muhammad's totalitarian ideology for global conquest. Islam is a murderous political ideology masked by the pretence of religion."

In an abrupt change in the direction of the conversation, Archangel Raphael asks, "Where do the Nephilim fit into this end-time game?"

After many moments of silence, Michael's oblique answer stretches the imagination: "In the book of **Jeremiah**, verse 32:20 speaks of 'signs and wonders in the land of Egypt.' What signs and wonders? Consider how the huge blocks of rock found their way to the tops of the pyramids. It's an engineering marvel, which cannot be duplicated or accomplished even with today's monster cranes. Construction of the pyramids defies human explanation and ability. However, WE know how it was done. We all saw the Nephilim assemble those monstrosities, not just in Egypt, but in many parts of South America. Even today, there are no machines that can cut one-hundred ton rocks and fit them with such precision that even a sheet of paper cannot be slipped between them. We are not affected by gravity, and neither are the Nephilim man-spirits. What role will the Nephilim play before man's final chapter closes? I don't know all the details, and I won't try to guess."

By now the twister has grown into a one-kilometer-wide black funnel cloud, raking the ground, destroying and devouring everything in its path. Within a span of five minutes, the wind velocity and shear exceed those of a Level 5 mega-monster tornado. Like a mammoth vacuum cleaner, it sucks up cars, tractors, bicycles, house rooves, dogs, horses, and cattle, which are seen flying through the air.

However, nothing appears to faze the four Angelic Beings who are engrossed in serious dialogue in their own little world. Although they are inside the shearing winds of the black funnel cloud, they are unmoved and oblivious to its destructive forces. Even the hair on their heads is unruffled. They are untouched by any earthly forces.

Within the funnel cloud, an eerie darkness now surrounds the angelic God Squad. From within this pitched blackness of swirling debris, Michael adds another layer of gloom, "Except through the intervention of Adonai, both France and Germany will be Islamic states by 2050 or sooner."

Above the hissing sounds of this writhing environmental locomotive, Gabriel reveals other nails in the European coffin. "Just listen to the chilling words made by the late Colonel Muammar Khadaffi of Libya who once had said, "There are signs that Allah will grant victory to Islam in Europe without swords, without guns, without conquest. We don't need terrorists; we don't need homicide bombers. The 50-plus million Muslims [in Europe] will turn it into a Muslim continent within a few decades." Muammar Khadaffi is dead but his stated reality lives on and grows year, by year, by year." In the midst of the spinning debris and the choking dust, four Archangels stand speechless while rocking back and forth on their heels.

Uriel delivers a crushing statistic. "Within the next twenty years, the Muslim population of Europe will exceed 100 million. The lights of European democratic liberties are being extinguished as their cultural curtain falls."

"So Europe is burnt toast! But what's happening in the United States and in Canada?" Gabriel asks anxiously.

Uriel answers, "Much the same depressing statistics. The birth rate in both countries is 1.6 per family. There is no possibility of recovery here either. Immigration from Muslim nations is tipping the scales rapidly. Within the next thirty years, there will be 50 million Muslims living in the United States. Within five years, Islam will be the dominant 'religion' in the world."

"Now hear this." Gabriel wades in with other heavy and distressing information. "In 2010, Iran's Ayatollah Ali Khamenei had likened his own leadership to that of the Prophet Muhammad. This is very scary stuff!"

"Scary stuff?" Michael asks before dropping another heavy bit of information. "How about an Islamic Antichrist? How's that for scary stuff? Shia Muslims believe that the soon-coming Mahdi is the Twelfth Imam. However, I do *know* that there is a connection between the Islamic Mahdi and the Biblical Antichrist."

"Mahdi? Who is this Mahdi? Please give us a quick review," requests Raphael.

"According to Shia traditions, this Twelfth Imam, or Mahdi, is the Shiite messiah, and he will be joined by Jesus Christ in their coming bloody battle against Christians."

"Do you mean that young kid who hid himself down a deep well way back in AD 873?" Raphael mocks.

"That's the guy. He is the Mahdi, and he's bringing Jesus Christ with him." This is serious stuff and not a joking matter, "Gabriel speaks grimly. "This Islamic Jesus Christ is coming back as a Muslim, to force Christians to accept Allah, or else this Islamic Jesus will kill them if they don't bow down before Allah."

"Wow! That's quite the story line and quite the stretch of the imagination." In disbelief Raphael states the obvious, "In Islam, Muhammad's Allah demands that free expression and free will must be utterly suppressed and crushed out of existence."

"It's called Muhammad's radical Islamic totalitarianism," Michael joins in to expose the darkness of this age.

That revelation hits like a thunderbolt. With those words, there is a long silence in the heavenly realms before Michael changes the track of the conversation. "Well Gabriel, you escorted the original Muhammad to the nether regions of darkness. Soon you will get the opportunity to escort this dreaming ayatollah to the same pit."

Gabriel whistles in despair. The sparkle in his eyes is gone. There is not a glimmer of hope coming out of any of the Archangels. The pessimism is palpable. Despair is carved into all their faces.

From the depths of his being, Gabriel delivers a prophecy, "The times of anguish and hysteria are waiting in the wings. The judgment of America and the judgment of the Christian Church are unavoidable. Within twenty-four hours of Barack Obama's re-election, he authorized the UN to proceed with banning guns worldwide."

Uriel quizzes, "Well, isn't that a good thing?"

Gabriel shoots back, "It's good for a one world government and it's good if Barack Obama wants to impose military rule."

Uriel replies very slowly and hesitantly, "You don't think that Obama would . . ."

Gabriel finishes Uriel's sentence, "impose martial law? Give your head a shake, Uriel. You've been spending too much time at the Milky Way." Unequivocally, in May of 2017, President Donald Trump had endorsed the second amendment of the U.S. Constitution.

In his despair and with eyes focused upon the ground, Michael dangles a wispy thread of hope to grasp: "As Gabriel just said a few seconds ago, Europe is burnt toast. However, Canada and the U.S. have a bit more time. If dramatic measures in America are undertaken immediately, the conquest can be pushed back.

Gabriel announces, "Shock! Supreme Court Justice Antonin Scalia was found dead on a hunting trip in Texas. He did not join up with his hunting team. Justice Scalia was found dead in bed with a pillow over his head. No autopsy was performed, and his body has just been cremated. Is this conspiracy *theory*, or is it outright conspiracy?"

"This is highly suspicious," exclaims Raphael looking for motives. "Pillow over the head and no autopsy upon a key political person? Now there are major upheavals in re-election headquarters of Democrats and Republicans over the replacement of Judge Scalia." After much opposition from Senate Democrats, on April 7, 2017, Neil Gorsuch was confirmed by the Senate as Supreme Court Justice.

Michael chimes in, "These major political fires will continue to burn in America. What about the Project? Will patriotic Americans choose to walk through this fire?"

"Fire?" queries Gabriel. "You know what happens when Muslims don't get their way. They say that they are offended. When they get offended, they blow things up and then there is fire."

"Two minutes ago," interrupts Michael, "I mentioned the Project. And no one asked me about the Project. Stop sleep-walking all of you."

Saucily and provocatively, Gabriel taunts, "Project, what Project?"

"Project? No. I didn't say Project." Michael stretches out the suspense, "I said, *the* Project. It's *the* Project. Actually, its complete name is the Muslim Brotherhood Project." Now Michael has their undivided attention.

Heading west, the eye of the tornado passes through the God Squad. In its wake, the landscape left behind it is one of utter and scarred desolation. Raphael surveys the scene only to discover that there is no creature left alive and nothing can be salvaged. Only death and destruction are visible through the thick clouds of dust which hang in the air. The only thing to do is bury the dead and clear the rubble by fire.

Raphael muses to his three companions, "It was pure white, and it appeared angelic. This viper started off so innocently, so gently, and so deceptively. I'm shocked to see how quickly a simple white thread transformed itself into this devouring and rapacious terrorist."

"The message is clear," states Michael. "Coming soon, worldwide events of this nature will be unexpected, sudden, and cataclysmic. Many black swans are set to fly." Michael leaves his final statement hanging in the air.

High above, crows and ravens circle the dark scene of the tornado kill zone.

CHAPTER 4

FIVE WOMEN WHO TURNED
THE ANCIENT WORLD UPSIDE DOWN

I n six cosmic days, the Lord God created the heavens and the earth and all plants and all creatures in the waters and upon the land. After each day, He saw what He had created, and He said that it was good. Then the Lord God created man. And God said that it was good. However, when God formed Adam, the pinnacle of His creation, He did not make any affirmative comment. Why not? Is it because He knew that free will was going to be the major downfall of His creation?

Then from Adam's rib, the Lord God fashioned the woman Eve, for Adam.

Not far away stood four Archangels watching Elohim at work. Gabriel comments first. "Did you notice that Elohim formed Eve from Adam's rib instead of using dust as he did for Adam? Is that significant?"

Michael nods, "Very significant! Had Elohim used dust, Eve would have been Adam's equal. However, because women are wired psychologically different, Eve would have been superior to Adam. Similarly, had Elohim taken a bone from Adam's head, then Eve would be his ruler. Had He taken a bone from his feet, Eve would have been Adam's slave. Therefore, Elohim took a bone from Adam's side to show that Eve would be his equal and his helpmate."

In **Genesis 2:24**, Elohim proclaimed, "A man leaves his father and his mother and cleaves to his wife and the two become one flesh."

"Hey, take note," observes Michael, "One husband, one wife. That will be the standard for the ages."

Gabriel exclaims, "Isn't Eve stunningly beautiful? There is no angel in all of Heaven who even comes close to this gorgeous creature."

Supportively, Michael adds, "She's perfect in every way. I'm optimistic. I see only happiness and joy."

But it doesn't take long for Elohim to see His plan derailed again. Eve sees to it very quickly. Because she is wired differently, Eve is open to deception. Unnoticed by Adam, Eve strays away from his side and walks toward the forbidden apple tree.

With snaky Satan whispering in her ear, Eve quizzes to herself, "What's with this tree that it's so special? Eve further thinks to herself, "Now, don't be silly, Eve. It's just an ordinary looking tree and that's just an ordinary looking apple on it. And it does appear to be delicious. Surely, there can be no harm in just one teensy weensy little bite, and the Lord God will never know when I sneak a taste."

At a distance, Adam sees Eve and fully understands the implications of what she is doing. He runs toward Eve and shouts to discourage her, but Eve can't hear or doesn't want to hear. Adam runs as fast as he can, but he does not reach Eve in time to stop her from biting into the apple.

After Eve bites into the apple from the Tree of Knowledge, in a flash, she sees the angel of death. In a panic, she thinks to herself, "Now I shall surely die, and Elohim will create another wife for Adam."

Immediately, Adam realizes that Eve will be banned from God's sight. Adam is determined that he will not lose Eve whatever the cost. Eve was Elohim's work of art and a model never to be repeated in all of human history. Eve was far and beyond any future Bathsheba or any Delilah, or any Marilyn Monroe or any Farrah Fawcett. She was the perfect woman of all the ages.

Michael comments sadly, "Adam is determined *not* to be separated from Eve so much so that he defies the Lord God and bites into the same apple. Knowingly, Adam chooses to disobey God and to follow Eve into exile. Before his Creator, Adam blames the serpent and he blames Eve.

"Furthermore," Michael continues, "Adam has the greater sin. Eve acted impulsively without giving the matter serious consideration. On the other hand, Adam acted deliberately in a cold and calculated manner when he rejected Elohim. His punishment should be greater."

In **Genesis 3:15**, God says to Satan the serpent, "I will put enmity between the woman, and between your seed and her seed; he shall bruise your head, and you shall bruise his heel."

And so, from that point, Satan, also known as Lucifer and as Allah, has hated the woman because she would give birth to the Messiah who would bruise his head. Satan's hatred of the woman continues until the days of Ishmael when it possesses Ishmael. The whole Middle East is aware of Ishmael's inflamed revenge directed against Sarah and against Elohim. For the next twenty-six hundred years, this hatred festers inside the Ishmaelites when it suddenly ignites explosively in Muhammad.

Out of frustration Gabriel replies, "Well if the animal kingdom is any indication of what's to come, then sex will prove to be man's undoing. Just observe that pair of praying mantises which are getting ready to mate. The male knows his fate is sealed even before the mating dance begins. He is driven to enjoy that one fleeting moment of sexual gratification even if it means dying in the jaws of his female. And look at that! She bites his head right off!"

Raphael has been watching silently. "Everything has changed. Now, Eve will know imperfections, sorrows, and pain. Because she will be bearing, breast-feeding, and nurturing children, Eve now has acquired a different genetic wiring. Eve will not think, nor act, nor feel like Adam. Not being able to communicate at the same level will confuse and frustrate Adam. Premenstrual tension, menstrual cycles tied to the cycles of the moon, churning hormone levels, mood swings, child-birth, postpartum depression, menopause, hot flushes, and sagging breasts in old age will add to her distresses and emotional upheavals. Contrary to her husband, in older years, the skin on her face will wrinkle like a dried up prune. The beauty and the glory will be gone. Poor woman! However, that is the punishment for disobedience and for rebellion against Elohim."

Gabriel is quick to interject, "Well, what about Adam's punishment?"

Raphael is just as quick to point out, "Adam will eat bread from a ground that sprouts thistles, thorns, brambles, and nettles. By the sweat of his brow, his body will be weakened and bowed down. At the end of the day, he will be too tired for sex, but sex will always be on his mind. Adam is hard-wired for sex. His imagination will torment him by replaying that last fateful scene under the apple tree in the Garden of Eden."

Gabriel blurts out, "I can see it now. This is going to be a world that's out of control with sexual energy. That's what happens when these humans have free will, but it could not be any other way."

From his stern facial expression, it is obvious that Michael is not pleased with what he has just seen and heard. Without any emotion, Michael comments on this debacle of the ages. He offers a future warning as he speaks solemnly in low tones to his three angelic companions saying, "Did you notice that Satan came disguised as a snake. Yesterday, Elohim told me that this is just the beginning of Satan's mischief with mankind. Elohim warned me that the symbol of the snake will always represent Satan. The snake will be the sign of evil throughout the generations and into the end times. Be ever vigilant when men model goodness and health after the icon of the snake. Leading to the Apocalypse, medical deceivers will come in the name and the likeness of the snake."

Raphael, the medical expert projects, "Future healing of the human body will come through chemicals, potions and drugs which will distort the body and the mind. And these will come under the symbol of the snake." Raphael knew of what he spoke. How fitting it is that the world of medicine and pharmacology uses as their emblem not one but two snakes intertwined upon a pole.

Quite unmoved, Michael shocks his three angelic companions, "Finally, Adonai gave me a special assignment for the remainder of this age. Gabriel, Raphael, and Uriel, the three of you will be working closely with me to intervene where we can to limit the havoc, the suffering, the killing, and the warfare that Satan will unleash in the following millennia. The four of us will be working as a team, and we will need each other's support. All three of you will need special preparation and training." There is a long moment of silence.

For Adam, lust, sex, and hard labor rule his day. Not unexpectedly, Elohim's plan for mankind is turned on its head. Sex really is the rope and the cable that anchors the destiny of man. In its final phases, though, sex will be one of the major instruments of man's destruction."

The God Squad sees two hundred fallen angels coming down upon Mount Hermon. Uriel is puzzled and he quizzes, "Why is this evil bunch here? What are they up to?"

Gabriel shouts angrily, "Look, the "sons of God" are having sex with the daughters of Cain. How can that happen?"

Health specialist Raphael explains, "We all know that angels can change appearance to suit any situation. We do it all the time. But these fallen angels have adapted their bodies so that they can procreate with the women on earth. Read **Genesis 6:4**. It's all in there. The offspring of these demonic unions are the Nephilim, the giant hybrid beings that are twenty to thirty feet tall. This is satanic. This is *not* how Elohim intended it to be."

Gabriel blurts out, "Shocking stuff this is! Don't these young girls and women know that they are in bed with fallen angels, and that these wicked beings mean harm to every living creature? So what is the plan of these angelic scoundrels?"

Raphael shrugs his shoulders, "The plan? The plan!? It's all about mischief-making and subverting Elohim's grand plan. The story of Adam and Eve is in their DNA. Satan's plan is to genetically engineer man's DNA into bizarre creatures under her demonic control and to reprogram humanity to her purposes. And look around us. Satan is succeeding."

Gabriel's adds, "It's that sexual dominance thing again! Satan's hatred of the woman goes right back to the Garden of Eden."

With the passing years, the Lord saw that the wickedness of man and the wickedness of the Nephilim was great upon the earth and that every thought and intention of the heart was only evil continually. It was always sex, lust, perversion, greed, violence, killing, and war. And the Lord God was grieved in His heart and sorry that He had created man on earth. The Nephilim hordes grow in number as the daughters of Cain bed down with the angelic sons of God. The genetic purity of the Adamic race rapidly degrades. Enoch, the great-grandfather of Noah, sees the wickedness of the hybrid Nephilim and understands the implications. Enoch coaches and admonishes his relatives to remain genetically pure. Finally, only Noah and his family remain with their Adamic DNA unspoiled. Only Noah's immediate family is left with pure genetics.

There is silence in heaven. Michael, as the minister of justice, presents the only two options: "This is a very difficult decision for Elohim. Either Adam's race fades into oblivion and evil runs rampant, or Elohim will have to drown the Nephilim in a great flood."

And so it happened, Elohim flooded the world. But not all the Nephilim were drowned. Being of strong spirit hybrid stock, a few survived to shake the earth yet again. However, throughout the ages, Elohim always has found those who would obey Him. Enoch and Noah were two such men. Abraham was yet another.

In **Genesis 15:13** Adonai said to Abram: "Know for a surety that your decendants will be sojourners in a land that is not theirs, and will be slaves there, and they will be oppressed for four hundred years."

In **Genesis 15** and in **Genesis 17:19**, Elohim made a covenant with Abraham saying to him, "Sarah your wife shall bear you a son, and you shall call his name Isaac. I will establish my covenant with him as an everlasting covenant for his descendents after him." But Sarah his wife has other ideas. As she is barren, Sarah has no child. Because she is barren, Sarah becomes resentful and sometimes bitter. Sarah knows of Elohim's plans for a child from her own body, but she chooses not to believe His promise.

Looking upon Sarah, Satan and her understudy Sonneillon assess their prospects for mischief and chaos. "We have a tremendous opportunity to spoil Elohim's plans on a grand scale. We need to find a way to subvert Elohim's covenant with Abraham."

"And just how are we going to be able to accomplish such a feat?" inquires the junior devil.

"Be patient. Just watch and wait. Sarah will create a diversion. In her own mind, Sarah is a goddess. She has no patience to wait for Adonai's promise. This is a woman who will shake the very foundations of Heaven and Earth. And when she's finished, there will be hell to pay for everyone. And we'll be waiting for the payoff."

All four Archangels agree that Sarah is very beautiful. "She doesn't quite measure up to Eve, but Sarah is provocatively attractive," Gabriel says. "She's a queen. Sarah knows it and unfortunately it has gone to her head."

Sarah is beautiful enough that even Egypt's Pharaoh wants to sleep with her, and so he does. That is, until the Lord God sends great plagues upon the House of Pharaoh to wake him up and to make him desist. However, secretly, Sarah enjoys her luxurious palace living and her time with the king of the known world.

Gifted by Elohim with insight, Gabriel understands Sarah very well. He is quick to analyze the emotions at work and quick to comment. "Abraham knows that Pharaoh is ignoring the rest of his harem and spending all of his time ravaging his wife. This does not make for a happy husband."

Raphael ventures, "Abraham never dreamed that Pharaoh would want Sarah as a wife. It came as an absolute shock to Abraham. But he was in no position to refuse Pharaoh. Well, I will tell you that Abraham is really churned up. This sexcapade certainly will put a major strain on Abraham's and Sarah's relationship. No marriage can withstand this manner of fracture and betrayal."

Gabriel interjects, "Abraham lied. He told Pharaoh that Sarah was his sister. Therefore, Sarah was fair game for Pharaoh. So, wasn't Pharaoh's punishment intended to be a wake-up call for Abraham?"

"Of course, it was a wake-up call for Abraham," answers Raphael. "But does Abraham learn anything from this bedroom fiasco which he had created? We will have to wait and see."

Much later, Abraham lies again to protect himself. Once again, Abraham tells King Abimelech that Sarah is his sister. Abimelech takes Sarah to be his wife. But in **Genesis 20:3–7**, God comes to Abimelech in a dream of the night and tells him, "I know that you have done this in the integrity of your heart, and it was I who kept you from sinning against Me; therefore I did not let you touch her. Now then restore the man's wife."

Gabriel adds, "By bringing down plagues upon the House of Pharaoh, and now threatening to kill another king, Elohim has raised warning flags and has rung alarm bells for Abraham and for humanity. Elohim has just thundered out the significance and the importance of the marriage relationship of Abraham and Sarah. Obviously, He has big plans for the two of them, and His design for the ages will not be subverted by any human, by any angel, or by any devil."

Michael frowns with disappointment, "Yes, Abraham is a slow learner and maybe he is a coward also. And once again, Elohim has to intervene to correct him and to rescue him."

"Did you notice in this marital transaction, that once again Sarah is silent?" questions Gabriel. "She doesn't protest to Abimelech that she's a married woman. It just seems that Sarah loves the company and the luxury of kings. Her silence suggests that she doesn't mind being passed around the royal banquet tables and around the royal beds. I do understand women, but I just don't understand Sarah at all."

Always the keen observer, Michael is quick to point out, "As with many beautiful women, with all her feminine wiles, Sarah rules over her husband Abraham. Although he has great faith in God, yet in many ways Abraham is weak-willed. Did Sarah plant doubts in Abraham's head? All four of us had witnessed and heard Elohim promise a son to Abraham. So why was Abraham afraid that he was at risk of being killed that he had to lie to Pharaoh and to King Abimelech? What happened to his faith in Elohim to protect him?"

But Sarah is impatient and she doubts God's promise of a son. Sarah has her own plans for Abraham. Sarah looks upon her Egyptian maid whose name is Hagar.

Recklessly, Sarah proceeds to venture marital misconduct that staggers the imagination. And the entire world has been reeling from it ever since. Sarah says to Abraham, "The Lord has prevented me from bearing children. Go into my maid [and have sex with her] so that I can have children by her." But Sarah thinks to herself, "I know that you will enjoy this young virgin. That should allay your anger at me for all the times that Pharaoh had bedded me. If you hadn't been such a blithering coward, you would have told Pharaoh that I was your wife and not your sister."

In this offer of a virgin, Abraham forgets Adonai's promise of a son. Poor old Abraham is confused as he complains to Sarah. "You must be joking! You want *me* to have sex with your young slave girl!? She's young enough to be my granddaughter.

But Sarah is adamant.

Always the lawyer, Michael analyzes this intriguing interaction between Sarah and Abraham. Solemnly, he raises the question, "Did any of you hear Abraham say anything to Sarah about Elohim's promise of a son? I didn't hear it. Was Abraham just too afraid to stand up to Sarah? Did he disbelieve Elohim or did he choose to ignore Elohim's promise? Or did Abraham have sex on his brain?"

Raphael directs a reprimand, "There he goes again! Three times running, Abraham willingly violates his marriage covenant with Sarah. Man of faith, yes, but this?"

Gabriel adds, "Tsk! Tsk! Tsk! There's that sexual trap at work again. Nothing good for Abraham or for Sarah, and certainly nothing good for all upcoming generations, and most certainly nothing good for the four of us. Mankind and all of us will be reaping the thistles and thorns of Sarah's bedroom madness!"

Abraham's wedding tent shakes for a number of weeks until Abraham is convinced that Hagar is pregnant or when he is just plain physically exhausted. For an eighty-five-year-old man the ordeal is draining for poor old Abraham. He certainly is the envy of all his man servants during those several weeks of sexual marriage misconduct.

What was Sarah doing while this sex escapade was in progress? Was she an observer inside the wedding tent to make sure that Abraham kept within her guidelines? And what were her guidelines? Did Sarah direct the sexual proceedings from inside the stud tent? Did Sarah humiliate Hagar during these bedtime maneuvers? Did she coach and restrict Abraham with suggestions during the performances? Sarah was a very powerful and manipulating personality. One can only guess what she really did. When Hagar realizes that she is pregnant, she looks down her nose upon Sarah with contempt and despises her. With a superior air, Hagar sneers at Sarah with biting and profane words and innuendos. Hagar knows all the gutter language and she uses it liberally with humiliating and stinging taunts. "Hey Sarah, you dried-up old prune, I gave your husband a really good time, not once but many times in the last three weeks. But he's not as spry as some of the younger studs whom I had serviced back in Egypt. Poor old Abraham will need several weeks to recover from too much of a good time. Maybe now he can teach you a thing or two in bed. But I really doubt that because I do know much about you from my mother who was close to Pharaoh's "girls" at the palace. And you should know that palaces have big ears, and lots of them. Pharaoh's "girls" didn't like your arrogant and bossy attitude when you were his favorite lay. They took turns spying on you two in Pharaoh's bedroom. They heard your heavy breathing and your moaning. There isn't much that Abraham can teach you that you already haven't done. We all know that those hundreds of head of cattle and sheep near this tent are Pharaoh's appreciation gift for your wild bedroom performances with him."

Hagar continues, "You can't have children? What happened to Elohim's promise of a son for you? Back in Egypt, all barren cows are slaughtered because they're useless. Now, I'm the real woman in this household, and you should be my maidservant. It's your turn to clean the tent and wash the clothes today. I'm going for a stroll with your husband."

Sarah wheels around and lands a back-handed slap against Hagar's cheek. "Hold that ugly tongue of yours. Don't you look down your nose at me, you Egyptian slut. This was all my idea. I extended a great privilege to you. I certainly regret it bitterly. Remember that you were just a slave whore. I picked you out of gutter, you wicked viper! Is this how you repay my kindness and generosity, you vicious bitch? Just remember, that I still own you. If we were in Egypt now, I would have you whipped for your insolence. I won't take much more of this crap from you! You just may find yourself wandering in the desert with scorpions and cobras for company!"

The war of the wives begins. However, instead of admitting her own folly, Sarah begins the spiteful blame game. Without blushing and with considerable hostility, Sarah berates Abraham and screams at him, "It's all your fault that I am being humiliated. May the wrong done to me be upon your head. I let you have serial sex with my maid. But when Hagar saw that she was pregnant, she now hates me, despises me, and berates me. And Sarah continues to rail mightily against Abraham saying, "May the Lord judge between you and me."

There just was no winning for poor Abraham. Just like Adam before him, Abraham had chosen to follow his wife's wrong-headed leading.

Being the wimp that he is, Abraham abdicates his responsibility. He withdraws, saying to Sarah, "Hagar is in your power. Do to her whatever feels good to you."

Michael waves his plasma sword saying, "And so begins the war of civilizations. The seeds for the end time conflict are planted. We're off to a very rocky start. In years to come, there's going to be a great world battle."

Gabriel comes to Sarah's defence. "I have a serious issue with Hagar. I would spare Sarah's reputation. Sarah did not betray Abraham. It was Abraham who betrayed Sarah. The bride does not have the authority and Sarah did not have a choice. It's the law of the land and it's the law of the times. Abraham did not try to prevent the sexual union with Pharaoh when Pharaoh commanded Sarah to bed. Sure she did submit to Pharaoh and give him pleasure but she was just obeying her husband."

Michael is quick to challenge that position. "None of us were permitted to see it. I don't believe it. How can you say with certainty that Sarah had sex with Pharaoh?"

On the defensive, Gabriel knows that he stands on somewhat shaky ground. "I know, I know, I know! It's all circumstantial evidence. But it's just so easy to read between the lines. Sarah fulfilled Pharaoh's wildest dreams of making love with the world's most beautiful woman. Pharaoh was well pleased with his new harem beauty. Sarah wasn't just a passive lump under the sheets. She was aggressive in everything she did. How do I know? Well, look at the indirect proof. Look at the sequence of events. Because Pharaoh viewed Abraham as Sarah's brother, he gifted Abraham with a very handsome dowry. Pharaoh gave Abraham the wealth of his land. He gave him herds of livestock with male and female slaves. To be as overly-generous as he was, Pharaoh demonstrated that he was very, very satisfied with Sarah. To make matters more compromising for Abraham, some of the Egyptian slave girls were entertainers and belly dancers. It would have been very difficult for a weak-willed Abraham to resist that kind of sexual temptation. We'll never know how Abraham reacted to all those hip-swinging Egyptian beauties that Pharaoh had gifted to him."

Rather timidly, Raphael comes to Gabriel's defence. "We do know that Sarah was barren. Maybe one reason why Sarah was barren was to make sure that Pharaoh did not impregnate her? But we'll never know that either."

Silence prevails amongst the four Archangels.

Hagar runs away from Sarah, but the angel of the Lord (Gabriel) finds Hagar in the wilderness. In **Genesis 16:9** "The angel of the Lord said to her, 'Return to your mistress, and submit to her.'"

"Now that was a tall order for me to deliver to Hagar. No two wives under the same tent could ever have peace between them. The Lord warned as much when He established the one man, one wife policy. There can be no exceptions to this common sense rule.

Upon Adonai's instructions in **Genesis 16:12**, Gabriel again appears to Hagar and says to her, "Behold, you are with child, and shall bear a son; you shall call his name Ishmael; because the Lord has given heed to your affliction. He shall be a wild ass of a man, his hand against every man and every man's hand against him, and he shall dwell over against all his kinsmen."

After delivering this message from Elohim, Gabriel immediately withdraws to the safe company of Michael, Raphael, and Uriel saying, "I heard Hagar call upon Adonai as Elohim whom she recognized as the Lord God."

Michael echoes, "'Wild ass of a man?' This bodes evil for future mankind. Unfortunately, it will be Sarah's unflattering and deadly legacy until the end of time."

When Abraham is ninety-nine years old, again the Lord appears to him and tells him that he will have a son by Sarah. In **Genesis 17:19**, The Lord tells Abraham, "Sarah your wife will shall bear you a son, and you shall call his name Isaac. I will establish my covenant with him as an everlasting covenant for his descendants after him."

In **Genesis 18:10–15**, The LORD says, "I will surely return to you in the spring, and Sarah your wife shall have a son.' Secretly, Sarah was listening outside the tent door. Sarah laughs to herself saying, 'After I have grown old, and my husband is old, shall I have pleasure?' The LORD says to Abraham, 'Why did Sarah laugh?'. . . But Sarah denies saying, 'I did not laugh'; for she is afraid. The Lord God says, "No, but you did laugh."

"Wow! Michael! Raphael! Uriel! Did you hear what Sarah just said?" Gabriel exclaims, "Did I hear correctly? This woman just lied to Elohim. Just like Eve, Sarah just tried to fool Elohim. What manner of person is this woman?"

Michael, Raphael, and Uriel just stand there speechless and dumbfounded, repeatedly shaking their heads."

At the appointed time, Sarah bears a son to Abraham who names him Isaac. Abraham is one hundred years old when his son Isaac is born.

The year is 2020 BCE. The place is the land of Canaan. This is a special day in the tents of Abraham. Everybody's attention and praise are being directed at the three-year-old boy who was born to Sarah. Even the camels are more cooperative as they are caught up in this spirit of celebration. Everyone knows of Elohim's covenant promise to Isaac. All work stops. Everyone is joyous as the feast is in progress. Well, not quite everyone is celebrating. Two glum angry figures stand apart.

Hagar whispers to her son Ishmael, "You are the firstborn. This feast should be for you. Instead, it's for Isaac. That little brat has stolen your inheritance. I'd like to strangle that little turd together with his mother Sarah. Here's a plan. When you have an opening, castrate that little jerk with this knife. Then there will be no other offspring from Abraham and you will regain your inheritance." Ishmael nods his head in approval as he hides the knife inside his cloak.

After the festivities, Sarah sees seventeen-year-old Ishmael mocking and bullying Isaac. Intrigue and murder are afoot.

The God Squad was away from their battle stations and missed this traumatic event between Ishmael and Issac. They return to see Sarah's face darkened with anger and in a sudden state of extreme hostility. Sarah rages at Abraham, "I saw Ishmael with a knife. I saw Ishmael molest Isaac." Sarah's anger is hot and explosive. "Drive out this maid and her wicked son. The son of this maid shall not be an heir with my son Isaac. Get Hagar out of my tents together with that depraved son of hers."

Abraham is greatly distressed. In **Genesis 21:12** we see that the LORD God tells Abraham, "whatever Sarah says to you, do as she tells you, for through Isaac shall your descendants be named."

Statesman Michael states the obvious, "Sarah's command to Abraham is also Elohim's will. Elohim is in agreement with Sarah. There must have been a very, very serious, threatening, transgression by Ishmael for Elohim to give this command to Abraham. At this very moment, Sarah is acting as an agent of the Lord. In all of scriptural history there is no other woman with such influence with Elohim. Ishmael must have transgressed in some most grievous and egregious manner."

So Abraham rises early in the morning. He takes bread and a skin of water and gives them to Hagar, putting them on her shoulder. Abraham gives Ishmael to Hagar and sends both of them into exile into the hot desert. In a single day, Ishmael is dispossessed of home, family, and father. This hard decision carries the Divine approval of Elohim also known as Hashem and as the transcendent Adonai.

Gabriel observes this transaction and gets emotional. With tears running down his face, he sobs to his three companions, "Think about it! Abraham just sent this woman and his firstborn son into the desert with only one skin of water between them, and without male guides to protect them in the harsh desert environment! Without Adonai's intervention, Hagar and Ishmael surely will die within days. Does Abraham know that Adonai will intervene to save them?"

"I didn't hear Adonai the God of Heaven make any such promise," says Raphael, repeatedly shaking his head.

"I heard nothing like that either, but Adonai did say that He would make a nation out of the son of the slave woman," adds Michael.

Gabriel encapsulates, "It's difficult to imagine the callousness of this act by a husband and a father. And what about Sarah? What's she thinking? Sarah has no reason to believe that Hagar and Ishmael will not perish in the desert. Is Sarah hoping that both of them will die in the heat? This appears to be a high measure of revenge and hatred that is destined to impact all of history to come."

Raphael reviews the recent past history of Abraham's household saying, "Seventeen years of animosity, jealousy, conniving, and feminine intrigue have come to a final crisis point."

Michael asks, "What triggered Sarah's high anger and outrage? Was it that she could not stand the competition of another woman? Of course that's true! But why should there have been competition in the first place? Sarah forced the marriage of Abraham to Hagar. Sarah disbelieved Adonai. Also Abraham disbelieved Adonai for a son. Both Abraham and Sarah brought this trouble upon their own heads and upon all of mankind."

Quick to see the psychology at work in this dysfunctional marriage triangle, Gabriel expands on this problem without a solution. "Sure it is true that Hagar was defiant, cold, and mean-spirited. It's true that Hagar refused to obey Sarah. It's true that Hagar gave her lip. These two women had lived in the same household and had hated each other with a passion. This aura of poison and hatred had a devastating influence upon Ishmael. Ishmael needed his father's wisdom and guidance. Ishmael idolized his father who was recognized as a great man in the land. For seventeen years, young Ishmael had lived in this state of animosity, cold war, and emotional tension between two warring women. He had inherited his mother's fears and her hatred of Sarah. For almost four years, Ishmael the firstborn had been taught that Isaac was his competitor who would steal his inheritance. Ishmael would not have had any tender feelings towards Isaac. Likely, Ishmael and his mother were plotting Isaac's demise frequently. For that reason, Sarah always watched very closely over Isaac whenever Ishmael or Hagar were present."

Michael outlines the legal ramifications of Hagar's and Ishmael's scheming. "They both understood Adonai's covenant with Abraham. Ishmael knew that Isaac would inherit the covenant promises that Adonai had made to Abraham. Ishmael hated the covenant, and he envied and hated Isaac. Ishmael was the oldest son, and he should have been the heir of God's covenant. Ishmael saw this as being unfair, unjust, and wrong. Driven by Hagar's hatred, Ishmael despised and rejected Adonai's covenant with Abraham. Ishmael hated Adonai for being unfair and unjust."

Gabriel adds, "Jewish literature charges Ishmael with idolatry and wickedness and characterizes him as being involved in strange worship and as doing evil works. The apostle Paul explains Ishmael's "mocking" of Isaac as persecution. However, in the book of Genesis, the word "*Mocking*" means "to fondle" sexually. Sarah may have witnessed some kind of sexual assault directed at Isaac by Ishmael. Was Ishmael trying to castrate Isaac or was he trying to sodomize Isaac?"

This same word translated as "mocking" was used in a later event in which a much older Isaac caressed or sported with his wife Rebekah. The usage of *mocking* is definitely sexual in nature. It is the same word used by the wife of the powerful Egyptian ruler Potiphar, who accused Joseph of attempting to rape his wife. With Potiphar's wife, it was an accusation of an aggressive sexual act. In both events, the word *mocking* most definitely is of a sexual deed or of an aggressive sexual event.

Gabriel continues to speculate, "Whatever it was that Ishmael did, I now have some measure of understanding as to why Sarah was so agitated and so angry at him. It is apparent that Ishmael tried to rob Isaac of his innocence and perhaps of his manhood."

The disappearance of four key words in an early version of the Bible raises some most troubling issues for biblical scholars. These missing four words record an incident so shocking that these words had been excluded from the Bible by rabbinical scholars. When some versions of the Bible dropped an entire phrase from the passage, the mystery only deepened. Informed sources indicate that these four words record an event of incestuous child molestation. Did Ishmael molest his three-year-old half-brother Isaac? Scriptural usage indicates that some horrific sexual event did occur. Exactly what Sarah saw remains a mystery.

Although the heavenly quad of Archangels was not there to see all of the activities, Gabriel encapsulates the events succinctly, "Sarah's lack of faith and her disobedience have borne bad fruit, thistles and thorns. In the end, Sarah had no choice but to protect Isaac from further harm. Hagar and Ishmael had to be removed and Adonai the God of Heaven endorsed that eviction."

After their banishment, Hagar and Ishmael are crossing the desert wilderness. The noonday sun has made the very stones in the desert too hot upon which to sit. All of the water is gone. Soon, with blistered lips and swollen tongues, even speech is difficult. In anguish, Ishmael blurts out to Hagar, "I love you because you are my mother, but I hate you for what you have done to me. You started as a concubine, a prostitute, and a slave girl. You were permitted to marry Abraham, a rich man. You were given almost everything you could ever want, and you threw it all away for no good reason. Why could you not have been content with that windfall? What else could you have wanted? Why did you have to provoke Sarah unnecessarily? Your hatred has turned me into an ugly monster. And I hate myself for it. You have hurt me, and I hate you for hurting me! And my father Abraham, how could he send me into the desert to die? My father? Some father. I hate him! I hate him! But it was that bitch Sarah who twisted my father's arm and forced me into this desert. I hate her with a passion. I hate her. I hate her. I hate her! I hate women, and I will take revenge on all women for the wrongs that have been done to me. I hate everybody! I will make Sarah pay. I shall punish Sarah's seed, and I shall punish Isaac's seed forever. And my children shall harass and destroy Sarah's children and Isaac's children. There will always be warfare between us. There will never be peace with Sarah's generations. I will see to it. Now leave me to die!"

Ishmael is greatly distressed. He cries bitterly. The Lord God hears the lad crying. He sends Gabriel who calls out to Hagar from Heaven and says to her, "Fear not; for God has heard the voice of the lad where he is . . . I will make him a great nation" (**Genesis 21:18**).

Ishmael lived in the wilderness and became an archer, a man of war. In his imagination and in his driving anger, every arrow which Ishmael shoots is aimed at his fellow man, but especially it is aimed and driven through the heart of woman.

Ten years after Hagar and Ishmael were cast out by Sarah, the quad of Archangels observes Ishmael's life unfold. Michael comments, "Observe Ishmael, the warrior. While tending his goats, he practices his archery hour after hour after hour. He is quite skilled at it. Archery has become his obsession."

"Look at his target," Raphael points out. "Is that not a human form?"

Gabriel swoops in to make closer observations. He darts back in a panic. With a terrified look on his face, Gabriel sputters, "Yes, the target is a human figure made out of wood and desert weeds, and it is certainly in the form of a woman. After I spied out his archery target, I had a close-up look into Ishmael's eyes. I made myself invisible to him.

He did not sense my presence. I was shocked by what I saw and heard. There is much more than just hatred in those eyes. I saw evil, the same evil which radiates from Satan. I fear that Ishmael's hatred has opened the door to demonic possession."

"But it was his words which convulsed me and sent a cold chill through my being. Ishmael kept muttering to himself, 'I hate Adonai! I hate Adonai! I hate Adonai! I will never speak His name to my children.' I shudder to realize that the roots of Ishmael's hatred run so deep. What's worse is that Satan is monitoring Ishmael's every move. Look to our left. Just how does Ishmael fit into Satan's designs?"

As it was their assignment, Michael, Gabriel, Raphael, and Uriel monitor all of these events as they keep their fingers on the pulse of history. But so too does Satan who sees a future opportunity to destroy Adonai's grand design for Adam's race.

And Satan cackles fiendishly as she converses with her junior devil Sonneillon, "Ishmael and his descendants will be one of my weapons of choice to destroy humanity."

The God Squad is always on hand to observe the beginnings of their future travails and the beginnings of the upheavals to come. Leaning on his laser sword, Michael reviews the first twenty-seven years of Ishmael's life, "There's no doubt that the toxic relationship between Sarah and Hagar has transformed a boy into an angry and psychologically twisted man full of hatred, revenge, and murder. Ishmael has become a virulent woman hater. But now Ishmael is warring even against Adonai. Pathological obsessions have permeated his entire life. They have warped him beyond redemption. Ishmael is being propelled by satanic forces of intense hatred."

In stark contrast, and at this very same moment in history when Isaac is thirteen years of age, Adonai tests Abraham. As documented in **Genesis 22:2**, Adonai says to Abraham, "Take your son, your only son Isaac, whom you love, and go to the land of Moriah, and offer him as a burnt offering upon one of the mountains of which I shall tell you."

Mount Moriah is a three-day journey or six days in total. Gabriel notices that Abraham and Isaac leave for Mount Moriah, but Abraham does not tell Sarah about Adonai's command to sacrifice Isaac.

"Abraham is afraid to tell Sarah of Adonai's command. If he tells the truth to Sarah, Abraham is afraid that this trip may launch a major marital war with her."

Gabriel is chagrined, "Did you see that Abraham and Isaac left without telling Sarah that Isaac will be the sacrificial lamb? Sarah is not given a chance to say a final good-bye to Isaac. Events will not be pleasant when Sarah finds out six days from now."

After a three-day journey to Mount Moriah, Abraham obeys Adonai, builds an altar, binds Isaac, and lays him upon the altar. Abraham raises the knife to slay his son.

As he zips in to block the knife, Gabriel motors, "That's my cue."

After Gabriel positions himself to shield Isaac, as detailed in **Genesis 22:11–12**, the Lord calls to Abraham saying, "Abraham, Abraham! Do not lay your hand on the lad or do anything to him; for now I know that you fear God, seeing you have not withheld your son, your only son, from me."

As recorded in **Genesis 22:16–18**, the Lord continues saying to Abraham, "Because you have done this, and have not withheld your son, your only son, I will indeed bless you, and I will multiply your descendants as the stars of heaven and as the sand which is on the seashore. And your descendants shall possess the gates of their enemies, and by your descendants shall all the nations of the earth bless themselves, because you have obeyed my voice."

There to witness this monumental interaction of all the ages and standing in absolute awe is the elite God Squad. In this flurry of events, it takes more than a few minutes for them to understand the significance of this transaction as they discuss it among themselves.

Michael is the first to comment. "Now that was a mighty huge request to ask of Abraham. As they traveled to Mount Moriah, Abraham had three days to consider, to reconsider, and to sweat about Adonai's command to sacrifice Isaac. Yet Abraham did not question nor did he hesitate. He was not about to betray Adonai yet a fourth time."

And legal-minded Michael chimes in, "Did you hear that both times Adonai called Isaac as 'the only son' of Abraham? The only son?! But Adonai does not mention Ishmael. It is obvious that Ishmael is not part of Adonai's covenant with Abraham."

Raphael confirms Michael's observations, "Yes, both times I heard Him say, 'your only son.'"

"I heard the same," Gabriel echoes. "Why does Adonai refer to Isaac as Abraham's only son when clearly that is not the case?"

After several moments of silence, Michael replies slowly and deliberately. "In Adonai's economy, it is true. Only Isaac is the son of promise. Sarah's machinations were completely outside of Adonai's eternal goals. Hagar and Ishmael never were part of Adonai's plan. Adonai could not and would not allow His original intentions and His original design to be violated and derailed by the disobedience of a woman and a man. At Sarah's age of ninety years, Isaac's birth was a miracle recognized by the local populations and far beyond. What is born of flesh is flesh, but what is born of spirit is spirit. Ishmael was born of marital misconduct and folly, intrigue and of the lust of the flesh. Isaac was born of the Spirit and of promise."

Uriel raises a troubling question. "Why was it necessary for Abraham to be tested so severely to the point of human sacrifice?"

Michael has a ready answer. "Three times Abraham had disbelieved and had disobeyed Adonai's covenant promise; once with Pharaoh, once with King Abimelech, and once with Hagar. Abraham's marriage to Hagar was a decision of the flesh that never should have happened. Because of Abraham's disbelief and disobedience, a much higher level of testing was necessary. But there were other compelling reasons."

When Abraham and Isaac return to their tent, Isaac is ecstatic and in a state of euphoria because he too had heard the voice of Adonai. Isaac blurts out the events to Sarah his mother.

Sarah's face and ears turn beet red as her eyes narrow. With her voice quivering with anger and cracking with emotion, Sarah is barely able to get her words out. Choked up, Sarah calmly requests, "Isaac, please go out and water the camels."

When Isaac is safely away from the tent, the pottery starts to fly. Gabriel does the count down, "A plate... a water pitcher... a cup... another cup... a saucer... a third cup... and another saucer... That's a lot of Pharaoh's expensive pottery gone to waste. For an old man of 114 years of age, Abraham is skilled at ducking and dodging the flying glass. It's good for him that Sarah's aim is not accurate."

Now Sarah's words come flying too, "You lying and deceiving jerk! You left with Isaac and didn't tell me that you were going to kill him on the altar? If you had told me that you were taking Isaac to sacrifice him, I would have beaten your head in with this camel brush, you coward. All of the heathen tribes around us sacrifice their children to their gods. And is your Adonai any different? For ninety years, I had been waiting for this child, and you were going to kill my Isaac on the sacrificial altar? Over my dead body, you would have!"

With perfect calm and assurance, Abraham calmly replies, "It was you who disbelieved Adonai. He sent us away from Ur to a safe place. At a distance, you and I witnessed the strange and bizarre heavenly holocaust of Sodom and Gomorrah. Since then, we have heard horrible reports about the effects of that mushroom fireball from Heaven. For the last fifteen years, no one has been able to live in or near the devastation of Sodom and Gomorrah without falling sick and dying. Adonai spared our families from that poisonous cloud by sending us far from that region. Before that cataclysm from Heaven, you heard Adonai tell me that you would conceive a son. Yet it was you who insisted that I have sex with Hagar. And it all has backfired upon you and upon me. And my Ishmael is wandering the desert somewhere because of your wiles. Is he alive, or is he dead? I do think of Ishmael every day, and it hurts me deeply."

"Well, well, well, just listen to you. You were ready to kill my Isaac, but you were so afraid to die that you stretched the truth and made me out to be your sister with Pharaoh and with King Abimelech. You were prepared to let those two studs have their way with me until they got bored. Nice guy, you man of great faith. But a great husband you never were and even now you are not!" With all the force which she is able to muster, Sarah flings a water jug that narrowly misses Abraham's head.

"Tsk! Tsk! Tsk! Just another dysfunctional family!" Archangel Gabriel clucks.

But Raphael has a different version of events. "Before Adonai renamed them, we know that Abram and Sarai were of upper class society. Abram was a Sumerian nobleman and Sarai was a Sumerian princess. As Abraham's wife, Sarah had expectations of being treated as royalty for the rest of her life." On that note, Angelic silence prevails across the heavens.

Shortly after Sarah's emotional upheavals, which followed the near-sacrifice of Isaac, Sarah dies. God does not speak to Abraham again. As the cosmic spiritual authority, Gabriel analyzes the events of Sarah's life and death: "As the queen of the family, Sarah ruled without true faith in Adonai, and she died in a state of rebellion and disbelief in Adonai the transcendent God of Heaven, leaving behind a legacy of hatred and global end-time upheavals."

Many years later, as disclosed in **Genesis 27:28–29**, and in another cosmic deception of the ages, the God Squad is present to hear an aged, blind, and dying Isaac mistakenly blessing his son Jacob saying, "May God give you of the dew of heaven, and of the fatness of the earth, and plenty of grain and wine. Let the peoples serve you, and nations bow down to you."

"Take note that Isaac did *not* say to 'Jacob' that Adonai the transcendent God of Heaven should give to him the blessing of Abraham, so that he and his descendants would possess the land which God had given to Abraham." Michael is concerned saying, "It was a bit of a hollow blessing."

"Why is that?" asks Gabriel.

"Even though Isaac was blind and dying, he did hear and smell a rat, the rat of deception. Instinctively, Isaac knew that the son who had bent down before him and whom he was blessing was not Esau." Michael expands his declaration, "Isaac suspected that he was being deceived."

Many years later, the God Squad is present to hear an aged and a dying Jacob (now renamed as Israel) summoning his twelve sons. As recorded in **Genesis 49:10**, in their hearing, Jacob/Israel says to Judah, "The sceptre shall not depart from Judah, nor the ruler's staff from between his feet, until he comes to whom it belongs; and to him shall be the obedience of the peoples."

With considerable satisfaction in his voice, Michael summarizes, "It is legally clear that Adonai's covenant with Abraham has been passed from Isaac to Jacob/Israel and then to Judah."

Seven generations after the death of Ishmael, while in the heavenly records library, Archangel Gabriel reviews the stacks of hard drives of future events. He is overcome with emotion and sobs, "Ishmael was the first born of the misogynist ideology that is sweeping through his descendants throughout Arabia. The children of Ishmael are virulent woman haters. None of them mention the name of Adonai, the God of Heaven.

"As the Lord through me had foretold to Hagar, Ishmael became a wild ass of a man who fought against everyone including his own family." Gabriel continues, "Ishmael made sure that he passed his hatred on to his children and to their children. Throughout the generations, Ishmael's descendants have been in perpetual warfare with each other, against their neighbors, and against Adonai."

As the overseer of the earth, of the sun and of the galaxies, Uriel is curious about this turn of events. "I deal with physical matter. Its behavior is predictable. But these humans are something else. Why are Ishmael's generations filled with such hatred? Why the hatred toward women? Why are there widespread sexual abuses of children among the Ishmaelites?"

All three of Uriel's companions want to jump into this conversation at the same time. But Gabriel is quicker off the start. "In the eighteen-year Battle of the Wives, Hagar intentionally humiliated Sarah. When Isaac was born, Hagar and Ishmael both knew of Adonai's covenant with Abraham, that Isaac would inherit his father's birthright. Hagar and Ishmael despised Isaac even before Isaac was born. But when Ishmael was caught in an act of forbidden sexual misconduct with Isaac, Hagar lost the War of the Women. Then it was Sarah's right to protect Isaac and to punish and to humiliate Hagar."

Michael expands upon Gabriel's explanation. "Being driven out of Abraham's camp into the wilderness was a disgrace that became the topic of gossip far and wide throughout the surrounding lands. It was a humiliating and shameful event for Ishmael. Losing his father figure as a role model turned his humiliation and shame into virulent hatred. Yes, hatred of Abraham his father, hatred of Sarah, hatred of Isaac who stole his birthright, hatred of his mother Hagar whose bad behaviour fed this ugliness, and hatred of Adonai who had made the covenant with Abraham and Isaac!"

"Bitterness, resentment, and hatred continue to eat away at Ishmael and at his descendants." Raphael picks up on this toxic theme, "Ishmaelite hatred of women runs deep. Men will kill their sisters, kill their daughters, and kill their wives if they show any signs of independence. Ishmaelite men will not tolerate a Sarah or a Hagar in their families. Their societies have developed a culture of shame. Ishmaelites receive any negative external event as humiliation.

"Ishmael's descendants are obsessed with regaining the honor which was lost in the desert sands of old." Raphael continues his analysis, "Even now, it explodes in acts of terrorism. Ishmael's seed is in a continual feud with itself, with its neighbors, but especially with the descendants of Sarah, of Isaac and of Jacob."

After he sits down upon a nearby rock, Michael continues with expressionless calm, "Across many cultures, it has been long-standing tradition that the first-born inherits the birthright. Ishmael, as the firstborn, feels that Adonai had robbed him of his birthright. Ishmael sees Adonai as his enemy. Even now, Ishmael is seeking desperately to find a replacement for Adonai. Any god except Adonai will do for the descendents of Ishmael! For the Ishmaelites, the name of Adonai is anathema. Over time, the Ishmaelites adopt Allah, the moon god, as their deity. They revise history and they revise the Bible to read that Abraham had placed Ishmael and not Isaac upon the sacrificial altar. The Ishmaelites claim that it was Allah who had made the covenant promise which was passed down to Ishmael. The Muslims of today have determined that the name of Adonai will not pass their lips."

Finally, with a deeply pained and troubled look, Michael encapsulates the future historical path, "Unfortunately, Ishmael's obsession to even up the score will continue to be directed against Sarah's seed until the end of the age. All of history is in preparation for the final showdown between the legions of Allah and the forces of Adonai."

Approximately twenty-six hundred years after Ishmael's death, his direct descendant with the name of Muhammad rises to become the prophet of Islam. Ishmael's generational bitterness and hatreds are channelled through Muhammad's radical Islamic Quran as the most virulent anti-Jewish and anti-Christian religious creed that the world has ever known. Islam's exclusive mantra of "There is no god but Allah and Muhammad is his final messenger," continues to be the slogan of civilizational warfare today. As foretold by Gabriel in

Genesis 16:12, some four thousand years ago, "You shall call his name Ishmael; He shall be a wild ass of a man, his hand against every man and every man's hand against him; and he shall dwell over against all his kinsmen.'"

"Have you ever seen a donkey kicking in all directions? Its behavior is genetically programmed." Gabriel continues his metaphor, "As the donkey, Ishmael was genetically programmed for vile conduct toward Isaac, hatred of women, and hatred of Adonai. This verse meant that there would be perpetual warfare around Ishmael. Without a doubt, this prophecy is the most disturbing and tragic verse in the entire Bible. Because of the warfare between the women in his childhood, because Adonai had 'deprived' him of his firstborn status, because he had lost his inheritance to Isaac, because his father had abandoned him into the desert, and because of his hatred towards the two women who had wrecked his life, Ishmael's destiny was sealed forever for the worse. At some point in the future, Sarah will be required to give an account for engineering mankind's greatest tragedy and its greatest crisis which is unfolding and which is yet to come."

Archangel Michael summarizes, "Eve, Sarah, Hagar, and Rebeccah messed up big time. By their bad conducts, they determined the direction of mankind forever. Including Adam's Lilith, five dysfunctional women turned the ancient world upside down and set it onto a downward spiral from which it would never recover."

While living in the land of Canaan, Abraham had sent his trusted servant and messenger to far away Haran to look for a wife for his son Isaac. As a complete stranger in Haran, Abraham's messenger meets a young maiden named Rebeccah at a public well and asks her to draw water for him. Rebeccah does so willingly, and then voluntarily, Rebeccah draws water for all eleven of his camels, thereby showing her genuine good heart. For Abraham's messenger, this is the sign that Rebeccah is God's chosen wife for Isaac.

Like no other, the story of Rebeccah and Isaac is a compelling love story. As one of the most romantic sequences in the Bible, **Genesis 24** reads, "And they (her parents) called her and said to her, 'Will you go with this man?' She said, 'I will go.'" Rebeccah travels with Abraham's messenger to meet her future husband Isaac in Canaan. "Then

Isaac . . . took Rebeccah, and she became his wife; and he loved her."
While she lived, Rebeccah remained Isaac's only love. For the first
twenty years, when Rebeccah was childless, this picture-book marriage
of Rebeccah and Isaac appeared to have been made in Heaven. Because
of Adonai's intervention, Isaac was born when his mother Sarah was
ninety-years-old. Isaac's name means "to laugh." In his joyous disposition
of being born miraculously to a ninety-year-old mother, Isaac frolicked
joyfully with his wife Rebeccah, whom in playful endearment, he had
lovingly named Rivka as being his heart partner in marriage. Rebeccah
is the only woman in the Bible who was given a loving pet name by her
husband. In the evil world of deceit, and until she derailed, Rivka was a
beacon of light. Although **Genesis 24** reads that Isaac loved Rebeccah,
it does not indicate that Rebeccah loved Isaac.

But when Rebeccah became the mother of twins, this seemingly
perfect marriage disintegrated with disastrous ramifications that affect
billions of lives today. Suddenly and dramatically, Rebeccah changed
and became a markedly different woman from the young, optimistic
bride-to-be who had left her family and rode out from Haran to marry
her dream lover in far-away Canaan.

During Rebeccah's pregnancy, the twins fought each other within
her womb and caused Rebecca so much physical distress and anguish
that she despaired of living. **Genesis 25:22** reads, "The children
struggled together within her." Because God foreknew that Esau would
despise his birthright, He made it known to Rebecca that He would
bless Jacob, who was the younger twin. Adonai's decision was made
before Esau and Jacob were born. **Genesis 25:23** reads, "And the Lord
said to her, 'Two nations are in your womb, and two peoples, born of
you, shall be divided; the one shall be stronger than the other, the elder
shall serve the younger.'"

The date is twentieth century BC. The place is Canaan, inside the
tents of Isaac and Rebecca. On special assignment from Adonai, the four
Archangels are monitoring the family proceedings with great concern.

"Twins fighting each other inside the womb?" asks Uriel.

Health and wellness specialist Raphael explains, "This is a rare
condition, but in some cases, it does happen. In order to create more
space for itself, one fetus will kick, knee, or punch its sibling. However,

within Rebeccah's body, the fighting was painful and extreme, a sign of the troubling events to come."

Gabriel presents the spiritual perspective, "Satan is well aware of God's promise to Abraham and to his future children, so she launches her attacks upon the unborn children inside Rebecca's womb to prevent fulfillment of Adonai's covenant."

"Did Rebeccah favor Jacob because God had told her that Jacob would rule over Esau?" Archangel Raphael treads upon speculative ground, "What if Rebeccah had not been forewarned by God? Would she have behaved differently toward Jacob?"

"We may never know the answer." Michael states the facts, "However, after being enlightened by Adonai, Rebeccah is doing everything that she can to make sure that God's prophecy will come true. Just as her mother-in-law, Sarah, who had disbelieved God's promise and gave her maid Hagar in marriage to Abraham, Rebeccah also has stooped low with her lying and her clandestine scheming to secure Jacob's destiny.

"As the queen upon the family throne, Rebeccah aspires to be the king-maker as well."

"In this dark, twisted, and sinister chapter of Rebeccah's deception, a secret estrangement now is separating Rebeccah from Isaac." Gabriel adds, "For unknown reasons, the Rebeccah-Isaac love story has degraded into a tale of marital discord and sibling rivalry. Isaac is favoring and elevating Esau while Rebeccah is pampering Jacob. Every day, Jacob and Esau are being brought up in the wickedness of favoritism and injustice in a broken home. What turned the beautiful lovers' dream of yesterday into today's marital nightmare?" Silence follows.

Twelve years pass. Jacob and Esau have become radically diverse personalities in character, in disposition, in livelihood, and in religious inclination.

"Just as Ishmael before him, Esau has become a rough, daring, crude, wild ass of a man living in the wilderness, while Jacob has become a refined young man who prefers to live in the tent with his mother." Raphael ventures further into the realms of genetics. "Why are these twins so markedly distinct from each other?"

"It has everything to do with their different upbringings by Rebeccah and by Isaac," Gabriel explains. "Obvious parental preferential treatment of the children has bred jealousy and strife between Esau and Jacob, jealousy which will end in sorrow, separation, and generational hatred."

"Isaac was faithful to Rebeccah,' Raphael expounds, "but Rebeccah becomes unfaithful to Isaac in two major ways. Rebeccah has cheated her oldest son Esau out of his birthright. Then Rebeccah cheats Esau out of his father's blessing so that Esau loses all respect for his mother. In his anger toward his mother, Esau leaves home and marries heathen, idolatrous women. To escape from his brother Esau who is determined to kill him, Jacob is forced to run away from home. This is total family disintegration."

"Birthright is the sacred inheritance of the eldest son." Gabriel goes deeper, "The significance of birthright cannot be minimized and cannot be overemphasized."

"By impersonating Esau and by stealing his blessing from Isaac, Jacob partook of his mother's sins against Esau and Isaac." Raphael pushes deeper, "With Rebeccah's preplanning and coaching, Jacob the younger twin uses deceit and outright fraud to steal Esau's birthright from him. This was a treacherous plan hatched out by a treacherous mother. It's not how you start, it's how you finish."

"In his blindness, Isaac believes that he is blessing Esau and tells Jacob the Deceiver to "Be lord over your brothers" in direct defiance against God whose word was that the older sibling would serve the younger." Michael is shocked by Isaac's outright rebellion against Adonai the God of Heaven, "In his wilful disobedience of the Word of God, Isaac tries to give away the Promised Land to Esau whom God hated. The hatred between Esau and Jacob parallels the hatred between Ishmael and Isaac. In both cases, the mothers were the subversive forces driving these hatreds."

The great nation which sprang from the roots of Esau was known as Edom. Over the millennia, the Ishmaelites (who have hated Sarah and Isaac) together with the Edomites (who have hated Rebeccah and Jacob) have teamed up with the enemies of Israel. Today Edom is Saudi Arabia, which suppresses women's rights. Today the legacy of

Sarah and the legacy of Rebeccah are Sunni Islam, Shiite Islam, and Muhammad's radical Islamic terrorism. Today the legacy of Sarah and the legacy of Rebeccah are Sharia Law and the patriarchal domination and subjugation of females across the world of Islam. Today adherence to Sharia Law or compliance with Sharia Law is espoused by the Islamic world. Sharia adherence or Sharia compliance leads to jihad. Worst by far is Ishmael's and Esau's legacy of hatred of Adonai, the God of Heaven. Both Ishmael and Esau rebelled and turned to Allah, the god of Muhammad as the god of Hell. Today, Muhammad's ISIS is butchering its way across the globe.

Truly, Isaac's Rebeccah was one of five women who turned the ancient world upside down and who turned the world of today onto its head. This vicious and hateful family feuding of four-thousand years ago, opened the doors to the closure of this age with the return of Yeshua Messiah as the Son of God, as the King of kings, as the Lord of lords, and as the God of the universe.

CHAPTER 5

THE BOOK OF DANIEL

The central theme in the book of Daniel is apocalyptic judgment. Daniel chapter 2 is called the foundation of Bible prophecy. The metaphorical animals in the book of Daniel are the lion, the bear, the leopard, the goat, and the ram. The lion represents Babylon, the bear represents the Medo-Persians, and the leopard represents Greece. The lion, the bear, and the leopard are unclean carnivorous animals. The fourth beast is a composite of these three carnivores.

As often as they are not on a mission, Archangels Michael, Gabriel, Raphael, and Uriel are stationed around the throne of God. Gabriel is a key figure in the book of Daniel. In the angelic realm, Gabriel's role has been the most varied. He has served as warrior, avenger, protector, revealer, interpreter, messenger, and as guardian. Gabriel was the messenger angel, the interpreter, and the angel who had revealed Daniel's dreams. His range of authority covers the whole spectrum from the fierce avenging angel who smote the Assyrians, to the gentle Archangel who foretold the birth of Jesus (Yeshua) to Mary. Gabriel is one of the strongest and most powerful of all the angels. Yet Gabriel could not overcome the demonic prince of Persia. Unseen to the eyes of the world, underneath the supernatural veil, spiritual combat goes on behind every major world empire. That Satanic standoff with Gabriel speaks to the power of the demonic realm and what humanity will face in the final spiritual shakedown that is to come.

The date is the latter half of the second decade of the twenty-first century. The time is *now*. The place is inside the ancient Babylonian palace of King Nebuchadnezzar and upon the exact site of its ancient ruins that have been in restoration since Saddam Hussein began its rebuilding in 1983.

The four Archangels continue their gathering in the rebuilt throne room of King Nebuchadnezzar. Michael breaks the silence, "Across the pages of recorded history, Earth has been in crisis since the days in the Garden of Eden. Prevailing and continuing cosmic planetary catastrophes have overlain humanity's battles against satanic powers. Adonai and Yeshua (Christ the Messiah) have determined that man's destiny has been interwoven and will continue to be interwoven with the forces of nature which He had set in motion at the creation of the Universe some fourteen billion years ago. Through the Great Flood, the Red Sea exodus from Egypt, and the global calendar change of 701 BC, it is clear that mankind is not in control of its destiny. But as a senseless donkey kicking in all directions, mankind continues to ignore and to deny Adonai's messages throughout the ages."

"It is very clear that even under intense pain and disaster, mankind refuses to recognize the Author of the cosmic and earthly cataclysms and to bow before his Creator." Gabriel is distressed with mankind's wilful blindness. "This very day, His church as His bride continues to stray into the apostasy of denial. His church mouths the right words but contradicts them by the reality of its actions and its inactions. Time and again, Israel and Judah were punished for their renegade behavior, even to the point of being driven out of their lands and taken captive by their enemies. As the crown prince of Babylon, Nebuchadnezzar defeated the Egyptians at Carchemish. He defeated the Assyrians in 605 BC. Then on his way back to Babylon, Nebuchadnezzar took hostages of Judean nobility. Daniel, Shadrach, Meshach, and Abednego were among the Jewish captives taken to Babylon. Following the death of his father King Nabopolasser, Nebuchadnezzar ruled Babylon as king from 605 BC to 562 BC. The Babylonian Empire lasted from 609 BC to 539 BC, a span of seventy years."

Michael picks up the narrative, "Every chapter in Daniel deals with some aspect of the final battle at the end of this age. Daniel pointed out that the Antichrist would emerge from the geographic areas of the Roman Empire. Daniel's accounts all began in the year 603 BC. In chapter 2:1 Daniel wrote, 'In the second year of the reign of Nebuchadnezzar, Nebuchadnezzar had dreams, and his spirit was troubled, and his sleep left him.'"

Daniel not only described the giant metal statue of a man in King Nebuchadnezzar's dreams, but he also interpreted the meaning behind this metaphorical statue. In **Daniel 2:32**, Daniel told King Nebuchadnezzar, "The head of this image was fine gold, its breast and arms of silver, its belly and thighs of bronze, its legs of iron, its feet partly of iron and partly of clay."

"Michael, here are Yeshua's directives to me which I had relayed to Daniel. It was Daniel who then wrote about you and about me in **Daniel 10:13**: 'The prince of the kingdom of Persia withstood me twenty-one days; but Michael, one of the chief princes, came to help me, so I left him there with the prince of the kingdom of Persia.' Then in **Daniel 10:21**, Daniel had written, 'there is none who contends by my side against these except Michael, your prince.'"

With tears overflowing his eyes, Gabriel chokes back his words, "This very determined angelic prince of Satan, who stands behind the king of Persia, did not want me to reach Daniel. However, I left out a verse. I did not write that I was being beaten up quite badly for twenty-one days by this prince of Persia, and if you hadn't arrived, I just might not be here today."

Across a distance of several meters, the expressions of camaraderie exchanged between Michael and Gabriel bring a warm glow to Nebuchadnezzar's throne room. The energy waves flowing between them were both visible and palpable.

In the emotions of those moments, Gabriel inquires of Michael, "Why did it take twenty-one days for you to come to my rescue?"

"Why? Here's why. The stargate portal to Babylon was sealed and guarded by the powerful demonic prince of Persia. Recall that Daniel was fasting. He had written in 10:2–3 that he 'was mourning for three weeks' and that he 'ate no delicacies, no meat or wine . . . for the full three weeks.' It was Daniel's fasting and praying that enabled Yeshua Messiah to unseal that stargate portal so I could cross into the Persian domain to assist you."

"Thanks for that explanation, Michael. When I next see Daniel, I will thank him for intervening."

Uriel inquires of Gabriel, "Why is the book of Daniel of such strategic significance for understanding Adonai's timeline of events?"

"Why?" asks Gabriel. "Because it foretold and detailed events that would occur hundreds and even thousands of years into the future, right down to the final conclusion of history. Progressively, many predictions in Daniel have been fulfilled. And every fulfilled prophecy had been accurate to the year and even accurate to the very day. The precision timing of these multiple fulfillments is the stamp of truth, authority, and credibility, not only for the book of Daniel, but also for all prophetic utterances in Isaiah, Jeremiah, Ezekiel, Joel, Micah, Zechariah and Malachi. At the very least, the exactness of fulfillment in Daniel is shockingly compelling. There is absolutely no wiggle room to challenge or to deny its accuracy and its authenticity. Daniel's prophecies are a prelude to the book of Revelation and they confirm the prophecies of Revelation and vice-versa. Daniel summarizes all of prophetic history into a few short pages. There is not a single sentence nor a single phrase nor a single word of fulfilled prophecy which wavers in its absolute precision. Daniel is the most commanding, prophetic book in the Old Testament and **Daniel 9:25** is the most powerful single verse in that book."

"What do you mean by *commanding*?" inquires Raphael.

"Many prophecies in the Books of Isaiah, Jeremiah, Ezekiel, Joel, Micah, Zechariah, and Malachi are yet to be fulfilled," explains Gabriel. "For skeptics, these books are just not sufficiently compelling. However, the book of Daniel is persuasive in that much of it has been fulfilled. Daniel is undeniable proof that Adonai is Who He had said that He is. Daniel is undeniable proof that Yeshua as Christ the Messiah is Who He had said that He is. In the book of Daniel, Adonai accurately predicted occurrences which took place 476 years later. Only the God of the universe can predict and fulfill prophecy accurately and to the day.

"I have read in **Daniel 2:32–35** about the metal statue in Nebuchadnezzar's dream," Uriel interjects. "The interpretation which you gave to Daniel in his dream said, 'The head of this image was fine gold, its breast and arms of silver, its belly and thighs of bronze, its legs of iron, its feet partly of iron and partly of clay . . . a stone was cut out by no human hand, and it smote the image on its feet of iron and clay, and broke them in pieces; then the iron, the clay, the bronze, the silver, and the gold, all together were broken in pieces, and became like the chaff . . . and the wind carried them away, so that not a trace of them could be found. But the stone that struck the image became a great mountain and filled the whole earth.' So, you gave this dream to Nebuchadnezzar and then you gave the same dream and its interpretation to Daniel. And you say that this very short prophecy goes right to the close of this age? But why would Adonai and Yeshua Messiah choose to entrust such an important prophecy to a cruel heathen king and to an enemy of Israel, but especially to someone who had just demolished Jerusalem and destroyed the temple? I just don't get it."

"Yes, this prophecy goes right to the final bell when Yeshua Ha-Mashiach better known as Jesus Christ returns to do final battle. King Nebuchadnezzar was the perfect choice for Christ the Messiah's prophecy. Christ chose to manifest His power to the whole world through the most powerful, the best-known, and most-feared king on earth. And King Nebuchadnezzar posted and advertised Yeshua's revelations all over his kingdom. King Nebuchadnezzar's postings and admissions are indisputable. Seven years after he had recovered from his psychosis, Nebuchadnezzar even wrote the fourth chapter of Daniel and then he sent it all over his kingdom. In his records, Nebuchadnezzar included the story of the fiery furnace with Shadrach, Meshach, and Abednego. King Nebuchadnezzar provided prime time advertising for Yeshua Messiah. He was like a reporter working for *CNN* or for *FOX* News, but of a much higher profile. Then this heathen king became a convert to the God of Daniel. It just doesn't get any better or more compelling."

Uriel chimes in, "Retired mathematician and quantum physicist of guided missile fame, Dr. Charles Missler figures that he will see Nebuchadnezzar in Heaven.

"I was present in the palace and I do recall the arrogance of King Nebuchadnezzar's grandson Belshazzar, who threw a large drunken party for his ruling elite. In his daring defiance of the God of Heaven, King Belshazzar and his guests drank from golden temple vessels that King Nebuchadnezzar had stolen from the temple in Jerusalem.

In his drunken mockery of Adonai, King Belshazzar got an instant response from the King of Heaven who allowed the armies of Cyrus the Persian general to ride under the city gates, into his palace, and under Belshazzar's nose.

"And here is what Daniel had witnessed and had written in **Daniel 5:5–6**: 'Immediately, the fingers of a man's hand appeared and wrote on the plaster of the wall of the king's palace. . . . Then the king's color changed, and his thoughts alarmed him; his limbs gave way, and his knees knocked together. Another way of saying it is that 'the joints of his loins were loosed, and his knees smote one against another.' That's a polite way of saying that King Belshazzar of Babylon had crapped his royal pants loosely." As the four Archangels react to that hilarious statement, Uriel continues. "Well now listen to what the prophet had written in **Isaiah 45:1** about this very day some 150 years *before* Cyrus was born. One hundred fifty years before Cyrus was born, Isaiah had called Cyrus by name: 'Thus says the LORD to his anointed, to Cyrus, whose right hand I have grasped, to subdue nations before him and ungird the loins of kings.'"

Gabriel expounds, "Again, there are those words, *ungird the loins.* They have the same meaning. So, even Isaiah talked about kings crapping their drawers in fear of Adonai."

"It is no wonder that Satan's prince of Persia did not want you to reach Daniel." Raphael is intrigued, "Please explain **Daniel 9:25** to us. This is a tough verse to understand. Just what makes this single verse of cosmic significance, Gabriel?"

"First and foremost," answers Gabriel. "There is no room to dispute the hard facts of mathematics. **Daniel 9:25** was designed to be a purely mathematical prophecy of precision, so that it could not be challenged. Before I detail my explanations, let me quote to you **Daniel 9:25–26** which I dictated to Daniel some twenty-six hundred years ago. It reads, 'Know therefore and understand that from the going forth of the word to restore and build Jerusalem to the coming of the anointed one, a prince, there shall be seven weeks. Then for sixty-two weeks it shall be built again with squares and moat, but in a troubled time. And after the sixty-two weeks, an anointed one shall be cut off.'

"Bible prophecies are interpreted to be in weeks of years. A day is a year. The total time in **Daniel 9:25** was 7 + 62 or 69 weeks. The 69 weeks of years was 69 × 7 or 483 years. Across the entire world and across all cultures, the length of a solar year prior to 701 BC, was documented to be 360 days. Therefore, the time in **Daniel 9:25** was 69 × 7 × 360 which equals 173,880 days. But, that is only half the story."

"That's easy to understand," replies Raphael. "It's the second calculation that is causing me great mathematical difficulties."

"Okay, now I will get to this harder part," explains Gabriel. "The decree by the Persian King Artaxerxes to permit the rebuilding of the walls of Jerusalem was made into law on March 14, 445 BC. Yeshua's triumphal entry into Jerusalem, when He allowed Himself to be called King, was on April 6, 32 AD, just four days before his crucifixion. The time between 445 BC and 32 AD was exactly 476 years."

Archangel Raphael interrupts Gabriel, "But I count 477 years."

"Don't forget," explains Gabriel, "that there was no zero year. The calendar went from 1 BC to 1 AD. So you have to subtract 1 year from 477 to get 476 years. But there's another way to confirm that number. Simply divide 173,880 days by the length of our solar year of 365.24219879 days, and we get 476.06767 years, or rounded down to 476 solar years."

"So far, so good, but today our calendar is 365 days, with no decimals after it," challenges Raphael.

"I will adjust for that," says Gabriel. "There are three separate calculations which are needed here. The first calculation is to convert 476 years to days, by multiplying it by 365 as in 476 × 365 or 173,740 days. In the second calculation, I will make an adjustment for the omitted quarter of a day with its missing eight decimal places as in 0.24219879."

"This 365¼ days to eight decimal places is 365.24219879 days." Uriel the mathematician interrupts, "But that's one strange and awkward-looking number. Why did Christ the Messiah make it look so unwieldy and problematic?"

"Why?" challenges Gabriel. "Here's why. Yeshua Messiah wanted to send the message to the whole world that **Daniel 9:25** was no mere coincidence and that even with eight decimal places, His timing was designed to be precise. And precise it was, right to the very day."

"Shocking precision. But now every year we have this awkward looking quarter of a day or to be precise 0.24219879 part of a day left over, which forces us to adjust our calendar with a leap-year day every four years."

"Okay, okay, I get it." Raphael continues the math, "Over 476.06767 years, when we do the simple arithmetic of 476.06767 × 0.24219879, we get 115.30297 days to adjust for the leap years."

"Right on!" Uriel appreciates the mathematical precision of this prophecy. "But even as a scientist, I need a calculator to multiply a five-decimal place number by an eight-decimal place number to get a number with thirteen decimal places. Wow! And way back in Daniel's time and in the time of Jesus, this calculation would have been impossible to perform easily or to fake it."

"Agreed and agreed," Gabriel interjects. "And 115.30297 days to account for leap-years means that the time for the leap-year adjustment was 115 days, and into the 116th day. To repeat, we are setting aside 116 days for the 116 leap years."

"It's great for me to understand because I'm good at math," squeaks Uriel.

Gabriel proceeds to develop the final arithmetical step, "In the third calculation, we determine that the time from March 14 to April 6 is twenty-four days. Finally, we add these three sets of numbers: 173,740 days plus 116 days plus 24 days to get 173,880 days."

Gabriel rotates his computer pad so that the trio of Archangels is able to see his calculations on its screen. "Seeing is believing. Here's the final summary and the mathematical picture on my computer screen:

445 BC to 32 AD = 476 years *or* 476 × 365 =	173,740 days
116 days for 116 Leap Years =	116 days
March 14, 32 AD to April 6, 32 AD =	24 days
Total =	**173,880** days
And Daniel's 69 weeks of years was 69 × 7 × 360 *or*	**173,880** days"

With expressions of shock and awe, Uriel abruptly stands upright from his throne room chair. He spins around to face his three companions saying, "Daniel's sixty-nine weeks of years were exactly 173,880 days. Both numbers are in perfect sync and they overlap to the very day. There is no room for denial. No one can challenge this math."

"Amazingly, in my prophecy which I gave to Daniel in verses 9:25 and 9:26," explains Gabriel, "the prince's rendezvous with death was projected towards a distant horizon 476 years into the future. The numbers in both calendars add up to the very day. By both calendars, the 360-day calendar and the 365¼-day calendar, the two numbers are identical. Beyond the level of the mathematics necessary only in astronomy and in long-range rocket science, this was precision prophecy and incredibly accurate synchronization across two different calendars, across two different solar orbital alignments, and down to thirteen decimal places of exactitude. A distant metaphor or allegory of this ultimate precision would be like sending a rocket probe to the tiny dwarf planet Pluto at the outer rim of the solar system and executing a soft landing on its surface which is more than 7,000,000,000 kilometers away."

"This is mind-boggling stuff," exclaims Uriel. "As we understand it, **Daniel 9:25–26** is based on the 360-day calendar. But the actual day-count from Artaxerxes' decree of March 14, 445 BC to Jesus' triumphal entry into Jerusalem on April 6, 32 AD, was based upon our 365¼-day calendar. Over 476 years, both calendars were synchronized with such incredible accuracy. Even more astounding, Daniel through Gabriel made his prophecies in 594 BC, which was 626 years before Yeshua's entry into Jerusalem on a donkey in 32 AD. King Artaxerxes' edict of 445 BC, which allowed the rebuilding of the walls of Jerusalem, came 149 years *after* Daniel's prophecy (594 BC–445 BC). This long-range revelation makes **Daniel 9:25–26** all the more unimaginable and compelling. The scientific communities must stand in awe of this undeniable predictive disclosure."

During the minutes of shocked, stony silence, the four Archangels shake their skulls in stunned speechlessness.

Michael breaks the silence, "**Daniel 9:25–27** are prophecies in a capsule from alpha to omega, from Genesis to Revelation. **Daniel 9:25** is the pivot point around which all Bible prophecies revolve. **Daniel 9:25** is the standard by which all individuals and all nations will be judged. There are only two choices offered in this verse. Based upon this prophetic mathematical precision, either accept that this Messiah Prince is the King of kings, or reject Him at your eternal peril. In just two verses, and in a nutshell, **Daniel 9:26** and **Daniel 9:27** give a glimpse of the horrors that will unfold at the end of this age."

"Many dissenters accuse that Daniel had been written after the facts," states Uriel.

"But the facts on the ground say otherwise," Michael comes to the defence. "The stamp of authenticity on the book of Daniel and on **Daniel 9:25** comes through the Septuagint. The Greek translation of the Hebrew Bible, known as the Septuagint, was written between 285 BC and 270 BC. That was 301 years before the crucifixion of the Prince. So the *lie* is a given because Daniel, the Torah, the Tanach (Tanakh), and the Septuagint had been widely distributed after they were created. At the very least, even after 301 years, fulfillment of prophecy to the very day is still compelling enough precision. And let's not forget the confirmations from the Dead Sea Scrolls."

"Hey! Hey!! Hey!!! Keep foremost in mind that it was I who gave the *first* dreams and prophecies to Daniel in 603 AD, and Daniel recorded them." Once more, Gabriel comes to the defence of his prophecies and their date, "more dreams followed in later years. Through Yeshua Messiah, I was the source and I am the authority on these precise events."

"Well, let me qualify that boast just a little bit," decrees Michael, "It was Yeshua (Jesus Messiah) who was the ultimate, final source and the final and highest authority. This is what Jesus had said in **Matthew 24:15**, 'So when you see the desolating sacrilege spoken of by the prophet Daniel, standing in the holy place.' Jesus was referring to **Daniel 9:26-27** and to **Daniel 12:11** which say, 'desolations are decreed. And he shall make a strong covenant with many for one week; and for half a week he shall cause sacrifice and offering to cease; and upon the wing of abominations shall come one who makes desolate, until the decreed end is poured out on the desolator. . . . And from the time that the continual burnt offering is taken away, and the abomination that makes desolate is set up.'"

"Here in these verses, you read that Christ the Messiah uses the derivatives of the word *desolating* four times, thereby endorsing the book of Daniel." Michael concludes, "That's absolute confirmation."

"Well that settles it firmly and conclusively." Then in a quick change of direction, Uriel inquires, "But why would King Artaxerxes sign into law a decree to rebuild the walls of Jerusalem? It makes little sense or logic to allow the re-emergence of an independent state within his kingdom, and especially an independent state which could refuse to pay taxes to Persia. Israel and her God had a known history of causing major problems for surrounding powers who wanted to control it."

"Some history of those times will provide clues for Artaxerxes' decision." Once again, Michael the historian rides to the rescue, "It's mostly about the Greeks. The beginning of troubles for Persia began with the Athenian triumph over the Persians at the Battle of Marathon in 490 BC. This victory fired up and inspired the Greeks with regard to their potential. Ten years later, in 480 BC, King Xerxes of Persia had won the Battle of Thermopylae, but later in that same year, he was soundly and decisively defeated in the major naval Battle of Salamis. Xerxes watched from shore as he lost two hundred ships and fifty thousand men to the Greek navies. In his humiliation, and on the advice of Queen Artemisia, Xerxes retreated to Persia. But before he left, and in his fury, Xerxes watched his army set fire to Athens. A year later, in 479 BC, Xerxes tried again. In this last land engagement during his second invasion of Greece, the Persian army was absolutely slaughtered at the Battle of Plataea. In the annals of warfare, it was massacre and annihilation like no other. Out of an army of 300,000 men, only 3,000 survived. Consider the magnitude of this carnage. It was a 99 percent wipeout. According to historian Herodotus, this resounding Greek victory marked the launch of Greece toward its golden age. But it also marked the beginning of the decline of the Persian Empire. The Greek star was in steep ascendancy, while the Persian sun was setting just as rapidly.

"The Persian military triumph over the Greeks in Thermopylae was designed to give Xerxes a false sense of confidence. Historian Herodotus records Xerxes' recklessness in committing all of his naval resources to the Battle of Salamis. Xerxes' ally, Queen Artemisia of the Persian province of Caria, was a commander in the Persian navy. Against the advice of the other commanders, Artemisia discouraged Xerxes from venturing into this battle. She knew that the Greeks were far better skilled in naval warfare, and she knew that the waters around Salamis were too dangerous for Persia's large ships."

Gabriel boasts again, "However, I encouraged Xerxes to ignore Artemisia's advice. In the days before his crushing defeat at Salamis, as *the* messenger of Yeshua Messiah, I gave Xerxes nightly dreams and visions of grandeur, supremacy, and triumph in the coming 'Battle of the Seas.'"

"Well done, Gabriel" congratulates Michael. "But why was Xerxes so determined to crush Greece? He even watched from his throne at the foot of Mount Egaleo as his navy was obliterated. Why did Xerxes put himself at high risk as an observer but especially onto the front lines at the Battle of Salamis?"

"It was pure desperation," explains Gabriel, "because of Daniel's predictions and prophecies that Persia would be smashed by Greece. Xerxes was given daily reminders. Xerxes was being hammered by nightmares, which I sent to him with increasing frequency. It always was the same finger of fate. I continued to send to Xerxes dreams, nightmares, and flashbacks of a disembodied hand, writing *his* name in flames on *his* palace wall. Greece always was the looming nemesis on his horizon. The dreams of the writing finger were burned into his very sub-consciousness. Xerxes was so terrified by the prophecies in the book of Daniel that he felt compelled to conquer Greece and to remove the threat of this kingdom so that Greece would never be a menace to Persia. Xerxes was determined to deny fulfillment of **Daniel 8:7** and to spit into the face of God."

"Xerxes was petrified by that verse," states Michael. "In that prophecy, Daniel wrote about the flying he-goat, claiming to be 'enraged against him and struck the ram and broke his two horns . . . cast him down to the ground and trampled upon him.' Thanks to your dreams, Gabriel, **Daniel 8:7** terrified Xerxes 24/7. But Xerxes was quite unlike Nebuchadnezzar who, after a bout of insanity, finally did acknowledge Daniel's God. In contrast, daily, Xerxes was unyielding while crapping his drawers in fear and trepidation. King Xerxes refused to bow before the God of Daniel, the God of Heaven.

Gabriel details another series of deadly events. "After the destruction of his army by Greece in 479 BC, another war erupted out of Xerxes' bedroom. Xerxes ended his marital crisis by disposing of his wife and deposing her as his queen. Xerxes then married Esther, the Jewess, who became his replacement wife and queen."

"Xerxes' wars against Greece were about defiance—defiance of the word of God and defiance of the God of Daniel. For his rebelliousness, Xerxes was met with staggering defeats at Marathon, at Salamis, and at Plataea. Militarily, Xerxes' spirit of defiance was crushed, and his life was ended with his palace assassination."

Michael brings more ancient Middle East history before his angelic colleagues. "King Artaxerxes remembered that Queen Esther's cousin Mordecai, the Jew, had uncovered the plot to assassinate his father Xerxes. Because of Mordecai's alertness and loyalty, his father Xerxes' life was spared. For that reason, Artaxerxes had warm feelings towards the Jews and a debt of gratitude to repay. His father had married a Jewess. He knew that Esther was very supportive of his father and very considerate to Artaxerxes."

Gabriel brings more history of intrigue and murder to his three friends. "Artaxerxes also remembered that Esther had managed to convince his father Xerxes to have Haman, who was the second in command, to be hanged. Not only did Artaxerxes respect the Jews, but he also feared them. Artaxerxes really couldn't trust them either. In the end, Xerxes was murdered in yet another intriguing palace coup. His son Artaxerxes grabbed the throne after the messy murder of his brother. However, in the midst of all the continual palace plotting and conspiracy swirling about him, Artaxerxes remembered the Jews in his midst."

"Yes," Michael interjects. "Artaxerxes remembered the Jews for reasons other than gratitude." Michael provides the background for the swirl of intrigues, mayhem, and palace coups. "Artaxerxes placated the Jews for reasons of practicality, but especially for reasons of security and self-preservation. With his life constantly under threat, Artaxerxes didn't need a possible fifth column threatening his throne. What better way to promote good will *and* to neutralize a possible risk than by granting to the Jews the freedom to return to their homes in Judah."

"But," explains Gabriel, "King Artaxerxes was most anxious and distressed for other reasons. He was losing sleep over the rise of Greece and its future threat to Persia." Gabriel was only too pleased to review the prophetic revelations that he had brought to King Nebuchadnezzar and to Daniel. "Artaxerxes was running scared. He was painfully and personally aware of his father's three defeats in Greece. He knew about Nebuchannezzar's dream in **Daniel 2:1** and Daniel's interpretation in **Daniel 2:32** that the bronze belly and thighs of the metal statue represented Greece. Artaxerxes also knew about the four-headed leopard with the four wings of a bird in **Daniel 7:6.** Artaxerxes was aware that the leopard with four heads and four wings was another symbol of Greece, a flashback and a reminder that disturbed his every dream. But what really worried and churned Artaxerxes immensely were the two verses in **Daniel 8:5–7**. It was that rapidly flying male goat with the large horn between its eyes, which 'struck the [Persian] ram and broke his two horns . . . cast him down to the ground and trampled upon him.'"

Once again, Michael joins Gabriel in reviewing the prophetic history of Babylon, Persia and Greece. "Artaxerxes realized that the forward pointing horn between the eyes of the goat meant sure death for the ram. Artaxerxes knew that the bronze belly and thighs in the statue, the speedy four-winged leopard, and the flying goat with the 'conspicuous horn between his eyes' were three different warnings about the same looming disaster. These three different metaphors were about Greece destroying Persia at some date in the near future. What Artaxerxes didn't know was *when* Greece was going to invade Persia and come after him. He knew that the Greeks were hell-bent on revenge for his father Xerxes' invasions of their country, and for burning Athens. Over and over again, Artaxerxes read the prophecy in **Daniel 9:25** concerning the rebuilding of the walls of Jerusalem. Artaxerxes knew about the fiery furnace, the lions' den, and the fiery writing on the palace wall by the disembodied hand. His mental turmoil was destroying his sleep and driving him deep into drink and despair."

Gabriel brings to memory more traumas and tyrannies of the ancient past. "Then there was another recurring nightmare, which was the massive lightning bolt from the God of Israel which fried to death 185,000 Assyrians as they surrounded Jerusalem in 701 BC. That lightning bolt, which I had directed at the Assyrian army, melted and fused their armor, swords, and spears. In 701 BC, with the massive lightning bolt from Mars, the thunderclap and the shock wave were heard and felt thousands of miles away. Every time Artaxerxes saw the lightning bolt and heard the thunderclap in his nightmares, he was convulsed into a whip-like snap, right out of his bed. As the time of the prophecy drew near, I watched him every evening. In his private chambers, he would drink a lot of wine and cry a lot. Night after night after night, the fright of that nightmare thunderclap caused him to catapult upright in bed in a cold sweat. Artaxerxes hated to go to bed. Minute by minute, he lived with the Sword of Damocles hanging over his head. By March 14, 445 BC, Artaxerxes was a terrified emotional wreck on the verge of a complete physical and mental breakdown. He would agree to anything that would bring him peace of mind."

Raphael offers his medical assessment. "After each thunderous lightning bolt, his heart raced and his blood pressure spiked. His bed sheets would be soaked in sweat and his sleep was over for the night. Bouts of heavy drinking only made his physical condition worse. Artaxerxes was suffering from clinical depression and another more severe mental disorder called Post Traumatic Stress Disorder (PTSD). After returning from battle, some soldiers are traumatized in a similar manner when they experience being shot at in their nightmares. They relive their traumas over and over and over again. Artaxerxes was living with yet another fear: the perpetual threat of a palace coup. His father Xerxes had been murdered inside the palace and he too had loads of enemies. Artaxerxes even questioned if he should trust his cupbearer, Nehemiah. The threat of being poisoned always had hung over his head."

"The starting date of **Daniel 9:25** had to be March 14, 445 BC," declares Gabriel. "One does not deny the will of the God of Heaven and sleep well. Artaxerxes was an emotional wreck, waiting for the other shoe to drop.

"Without royal permission from Artaxerxes, Ezra the prophet had started to rebuild the walls of Jerusalem. But when the Samaritans complained and petitioned him, King Artaxerxes had the walls of Jerusalem torn down and the gates burned down again. In his anguish, Artaxerexes realized that he had violated **Daniel 9:25**. Now he was waiting for a different shoe to drop. In addition to suffering from PTSD, Artaxerxes was suffering from irritable bowel syndrome. Even before Nehemiah his cupbearer had made his request, Artaxerxes already was crapping his drawers daily. When Nehemiah approached him with the request to rebuild the walls of Jerusalem, Artaxerxes had an immediate vision of a disembodied handwriting on *his* palace wall, but this time with Artaxerxes' name being carved in stone. He also remembered Daniel's prophecies about the Greeks, and he knew that the Greeks were strengthening and stirring in the north. Artaxerxes did not want another Daniel-type visionary to emerge with more bad prophecies for him. In his distressed emotional and physical states, Artaxerxes melted and capitulated without a whimper of objection. On March 14, 445 BC, Artaxerxes signed into law the decree to rebuild the walls of Jerusalem."

"This was the decree of the ages," Michael declares. "This decree was *the* cosmic accomplishment and the turning point of global history that continues to echo from the ancient past and right up the corridors of time. Today, we stand and celebrate that epic moment almost two and a half millennia ago."

After several moments of solemn silence, Uriel returns the conversation to ancient Babylon, "Let's go back to the times of Nebuchadnezzar. What caused him to unravel so badly?

"Nebuchadnezzar was a cruel and arrogant tyrant," explains Gabriel. "In 597 BC, six years after I had given Yeshua Messiah's dream interpretation to Daniel, it was King Nebuchadnezzar who went out of his way to capture Jerusalem. With the revelations I had given to him through Daniel, Nebuchadnezzar further infuriated Yeshua Messiah in 586 BC when he destroyed Jerusalem and the temple. Divine Judgment was inevitable. However, we also need to balance this out with Yeshua Messiah using Nebuchadnezzar as His instrument to judge apostate Judah for flaunting His sovereignty."

There is a long pause before Raphael ventures, "Nebuchadnezzar made matters even worse for himself by rebelling against Adonai's plan when in his pride he erected a huge golden statue of himself. King Nebuchadnezzar pushed matters past the point of no return when he forced all of his subjects to bow down and worship his statue. Ever since Daniel had prophesied that Nebuchadnezzar's empire would be ripped away from Babylon and given to another kingdom, Nebuchadnezzar was running scared. The shadow of the Medo-Persians already had fallen across Babylon. Nebuchadnezzar knew that they were the adversarial kingdom, and that his days were numbered on the short side. His sleep became badly fractured. He began to act erratically. His intense fear of future invasion took a devastating toll upon his health. Nebuchadnezzar too developed uncontrollable irritable bowel syndrome. Living with intense fear of the future, Nebuchadnezzar, the King of Babylon, also was crapping his pants every day."

Gabriel adds, "Nebuchadnezzar was given much from Adonai, including the revelation of the statue in his dream and its interpretation through Daniel. But he ignored Adonai. In his pride, he threw it all away. Nebuchadnezzar had to be punished for his misconduct and for his rebellion. Raphael and I teamed up to teach him a lesson. Then I gave the king another disturbing dream from the Most High. In his dream, he saw a giant tree that grew to heaven. The tree was cut down, but its stump and its roots were left to re-grow. I revealed the dream to Daniel that the giant tree was King Nebuchadnezzar and that the Most High would drive him out from among men and that he would eat grass like an ox for seven years until he dropped his pride and acknowledged that it was Adonai who ruled his kingdom. In **Daniel 4:13–16**, King Nebuchadnezzar wrote, 'I had a dream . . . a holy one came down from heaven and cried aloud and said thus, 'Hew down the tree and cut off its branches . . . but leave the stump of its roots in the earth. . . . Let a beast's mind be given him; and let seven times pass over him.' Now, Nebuchadnezzar had many more reasons to worry about his safety and his future."

Raphael gives his medical perspective. "Under extreme stress and sleep deprivation, Nebuchadnezzar went mad, stark raving insane. In his hallucinations, he believed that he was an ox, and he ate grass like an ox for seven years before his kingship was restored. Today, this kind of mental derangement is a form of mania and delusion known as zoanthropy."

"Belshazzar succeeds the Babylonian throne after the death of Nebuchadnezzar," explains Gabriel. "With no uncertainty, in **Daniel 8:20** and **Daniel 8:21**, King Belshazzar was told bluntly by Daniel of his vision of the ram and the goat, 'As for the ram which you saw with the two horns, these are the kings of Media and Persia. And the he-goat is the king of Greece; and the great horn between his eyes is the first king.'"

"Was King Belshazzar worried about Daniel's vision?" inquires Uriel.

"Like his grandfather Nebuchadnezzar before him," continues Gabriel, "Belshazzar was a very worried man. To dull his worries and his emotional pains, Belshazzar partied hard and drank wine with his nobles from the Jerusalem Temple vessels of the Lord of Heaven. Belshazzar continued to disregard and to defy the Lord of Heaven until that fateful night when I had revealed to Daniel who wrote in his book at **Daniel 5:25–28**. In front of a thousand of his guests, a disembodied hand and finger wrote on Belshazzar's palace wall, "*MENE, MENE, TEKEL, PARSIN.*" Daniel translated those words, '*MENE*, God has numbered the days of your kingdom and brought it to an end; *TEKEL*, you have been weighed in the balances and found wanting; *PERES (PARSIN)*, your kingdom is divided and given to the Medes and Persians.' 'That very night, Belshazzar the Chaldean king was slain. And Darius the Mede received the kingdom.'"

"Babylonian King Nebuchadnezzar and Babylonian King Belshazzar were particularly stressed out by the book of Daniel. I should know because I was present to observe both of them." Gabriel tells his buddies, "Nebuchadnezzar and Belshazzar knew about Isaiah's prophecy concerning Cyrus and emerging Greece. Cyrus was a leader of high morals and of high ethics. More than one hundred years before Jerusalem was destroyed, Yeshua Messiah declared through His prophet Isaiah, that Cyrus would be the anointed shepherd of His people who would perform the rebuilding of Jerusalem. In **Isaiah 44: 27, 28**, Isaiah wrote of Yeshua Messiah as the One 'who says to the deep, "Be dry, I will dry up your rivers"; who says of Cyrus, "He is my shepherd, and he shall fulfil all my purpose"; saying of Jerusalem, "She shall be built," and of the temple, "Your foundation shall be laid.""'"

"In **Isaiah 45:1** and **Isaiah 45:2**, the prophet foretold the birth of Cyrus and his exact name nearly 150 years before Cyrus was born." Michael adds detail to the prophecies concerning Cyrus. "Isaiah foretold the jobs for which the Creator had anointed Cyrus as His servant and had predestined him to perform in his global plan for humanity. Through King Cyrus, Yeshua Messiah had set into motion His seventy-week prophecy that carved in stone the exact year of Yeshua's death and His resurrection eventually leading to His rule over the entire Earth. Isaiah wrote, 'Thus says the Lord to his anointed, to Cyrus, whose right hand I have grasped, to subdue nations before him and open the loins of kings, to open doors before him that gates may not be closed. I will go before you and level the mountains.'"

Raphael is amazed at the language used in the Bible, "There it is again. Yeshua says that He 'will open the loins of kings.' I find it humorous that kings will be crapping their drawers in front of Cyrus. I am more amazed that these words were a threat which came from Yeshua Messiah Himself. I can just imagine his shock when Cyrus read that Yeshua Messiah had named him and designed his destiny almost 150 years before he was born. And this came from the God whom he did not know or worship. **Isaiah 45:4** reads, 'For the sake of my servant Jacob, and Israel my chosen, I call you by your name, I surname you, though you do not know me.'"

"**Isaiah 45:9** appears to be a warning to King Cyrus to honor the fearsome power of Yeshua Messiah as, 'Woe to him who strives with his maker.'... **Isaiah 45:13** extended more encouragement and very specific instructions to Cyrus to put pressure upon him to comply, saying to him and about him, 'I have aroused him in righteousness, and I will make straight all his ways; he shall build my city and set my exiles free, not for price or reward, says the Lord of hosts.'"

Uriel picks up on Raphael's dirty laundry line, "Cyrus was told in no uncertain terms what Yeshua's expectations of him were. Under those expectations, Cyrus would make sure that he followed Isaiah directions to the very letter and beyond, likely erring on the side of extreme caution and generosity. I would guess that after Cyrus had read these verses in Isaiah, he too was crapping his drawers in absolute fear of Yeshua."

"The Creator God of Israel foreordained the birth of Cyrus," explains Michael, "for the express purpose of returning the people of Judah to the land of Israel and to decree the rebuilding of the Temple and the walls of Jerusalem. Here are the words about Cyrus as recorded in the book of **Ezra 1:1–3**:

'Now in the first year of Cyrus king of Persia, that the word of the Lord by the mouth of Jeremiah might be accomplished, the Lord stirred up the spirit of Cyrus king of Persia, that he made a proclamation throughout all his kingdom and put it also in writing: 'Thus says Cyrus king of Persia: the Lord, the God of heaven, has given me all the kingdoms of the earth, and he has charged me to build him an house at Jerusalem, which is in Judah. Whoever is among you of all his people, may his God be with him, and let him go up to Jerusalem, which is in Judah, and rebuild the house of the Lord, the God of Israel—he is the God who is in Jerusalem.'

"And just how had King Cyrus been made aware of Isaiah's prophecy directing his life? Maybe Daniel had told him or maybe Ezra the priest had told him or maybe Nehemiah had told him, or maybe he had read **Isaiah 44:27, 28** or **Isaiah 45:1–9**, or maybe he had read **2 Chronicles 36:22–23**. No one really knows."

"It is clear that Daniel's prophecy, as revealed to him by Gabriel, had to begin and end exactly to the day and on schedule. The timing of the seventy-week prophecy was absolutely critical."

"Cyrus was not a believer and neither did he acknowledge the God of Israel." Gabriel asks, "So why would Yeshua use pagan King Cyrus to achieve such a monumental work that would take humanity to its very end time conclusion?"

"For the same reason that He had chosen Nebuchadnezzar," answers Michael. "Both kings were high profile rulers and both began as heathens. Yeshua was telling the world that He would accomplish

His will even through unbelieving dictators. It was Cyrus who set the wheels in motion for all future prophets and all their prophecies that followed. Cyrus was one of *the* key men of all the ages and the timing of his decree had to be precise. Yeshua is seldom if ever early, but He is never late. And it's always precision timing."

In 331 BC, according to **Daniel 8:5–7**, metaphorically and with lightning speed, Alexander the Great, the flying goat of Greece, broke both horns of the Persian ram and trampled the Persian ram to death."

As the key Archangel in the revelations to Daniel, it is Gabriel who has special insights. "The book of Daniel is a warning, an omen and a harbinger. The intent of a harbinger is to give a forewarning and to awaken God's people so that they will avoid impending destruction. But the harbinger of Daniel is different. The warnings in Daniel are not direct. They are unspoken. They are subtle. They are unconditional and they are irrevocable. As with the unconditional necessity to destroy the Nephilim, the worldwide Flood was unavoidable. In the same manner, the book of Daniel is intended to give preparation time. There is no escape from the prophecies of Daniel. The prophetic book of Daniel contains all the codes to the harbingers leading to the cataclysmic judgments to follow, and to the final judgment yet to come."

"The book of Daniel was and continues to be the harbinger of destiny." Michael summarizes the awesomeness of Daniel saying, "This little book of twelve chapters had been making waves across the eastern Mediterranean and across the sands of the Middle East since it was written onto scroll. From within the prophecies of the book of Daniel, there is preparing massive tidal wave upheavals about to erupt that will shake the heavens and the earth at the closure of the curtain upon this age."

"Just as Nebuchadnezzar, Belshazzar, Cyrus, Darius, Xerxes, and Artaxerxes knew about Daniel from their historical records, so too did the three Persian Magi who visited baby Yeshua Messiah in the stable some six hundred years later." Michael jumps across multiple pages of history. "And just as vividly today, the Iranians, the Iraqis, and the Palestinians know of Daniel's prophecies. But it's all about defiance and about their overwhelming hatred of the Jews, hatred of Christians, and their hatred of Adonai and hatred of His Son Yeshua Messiah."

As it was recorded across the Babylonian and Persian Empires, the Magi astrologers of Persia knew of **Daniel 9:25**. They had studied Daniel's book diligently, and they believed what Daniel had written. Daniel's prophecies projected the forces of fulfillment, credibility, respect, and fear. These highly educated and influential Magi, who determined the destiny of Persian kings, knew of the decree of Artaxerxes on March 14, 445 BC. For 445 years, the Persian Magi priests counted down Daniel's sixty-nine weeks of years. From this date of March 14, 445 BC, they knew and anticipated that death of the Prince had to be in 32 AD. Except for the guiding star, they had an approximate idea of His birthdate but not the place. But the Magi were prepared. They came to worship this Messiah King of Eternity, and they came bearing gifts of gold, frankincense, and myrrh. Gold was the gift fitting for a king. The gold sustained Jesus, Mary, and Joseph after their flight to Egypt.

"Then there were Jesus' silent years, from thiteen to thirty." Michael exposes unknown history never before revealed. "There were seventeen years of silence. Where did Yeshua go? He was a thirteen-year-old with all the power of the universe at his finger tips. We were His God Squad and His wall of protection potentially against all the demons and all the angels of Hell. King Yeshua Messiah went to find the three Magi who were the magistrate priests and the astrologers of Persia to thank them for their gifts thirteen years earlier. Yeshua carried with him the gifts of incense and of myrrh unopened with the seals of the Magi still in place and intact as the sign of authenticity. This was the reunion of all reunions. There were tears of joy. Yeshua Messiah came to the Persian Magi to teach them about His birth, about His reasons for coming to earth, and about His coming crucifixion. We know that secretly these three Persian Magi were present anonymously in Jerusalem to witness His crucifixion."

"It's those two last kingdoms of the metal statue of Nebuchadnezzar's dream in Daniel 2 that puzzle me," announces Raphael. "It's clear that the head of gold was the kingdom of Babylon, the breast and arms of silver were the Medo-Persian kingdom, the belly and thighs of bronze was the kingdom of Greece and the legs of iron was the kingdom of the Roman Empire. But it's this fourth kingdom that really troubles me.

Daniel 2:40 says that this fourth kingdom is, 'strong as iron, because iron breaks to pieces and shatters all things; and like iron which crushes, it shall break and crush all these.'"

Gabriel responds, "This fourth kingdom was the conquering Roman Empire, which ruled with iron fisted control, but the Roman Empire was culturally laissez-faire. It allowed the nations it absorbed to retain their customs and their gods. In reality, it was *not* the Roman Empire that would 'break and crush.' Until Judea rose up in rebellion and until Judea was destroyed in 70 AD, the Romans didn't mess with temple worship or with the Jewish religion. As much as Rome hated Christianity, it allowed a high level of cultural and religious permissiveness. Even under heavy persecution, Rome allowed Christianity to spread throughout its empire until it became the state religion under Emperor Constantine. Quite contrary to Rome, it was and is Muhammad's Islam of Allah which breaks and crushes."

Michael adds his perspective analysis. "The answer lies in the two legs of Daniel's metal statue. One leg was the Western Roman Empire while the other leg was the Eastern Roman Empire. The Western leg of the Roman Empire collapsed in 476 AD while the Eastern leg survived almost a thousand years before the Muslim Ottoman Turks crushed Constantinople in 1453 AD. Christians and Jews were driven out or slaughtered by the sword. The Ottomans continued their genocides into the twentieth century when during 1915 - 1917, they slaughtered up to four million Armenian Christians. The Ottoman Empire was dismantled in 1923 and the beast of Revelation suffered its near-fatal head wound."

"Then the fifth kingdom was represented by the statue's feet and toes, which were partly of iron and partly of clay." Gabriel reaches back in time to his revelations to Daniel in chapter 2:41–43: 'as you saw the feet and toes partly of potter's clay and partly of iron, it shall be a divided kingdom; but some of the firmness of iron shall be in it, just as you saw iron mixed with miry clay… and as the toes of the feet were partly iron and partly clay, so the kingdom shall be partly strong and partly brittle… As you saw the iron mixed with miry clay, so they will mix with one another in marriage, but they will not hold together, just as iron does not mix with clay.' Toes of iron mixed with clay speak of civil war."

"But what's the *meaning* of the feet and toes of iron mixed with clay?" asks Raphael. "I understand the iron, but what is the clay and what is its significance?"

Gabriel, the universally recognized authority on Muhammad, provides the answer. "Even before Muhammad was poisoned by his wives, there already existed two factions of Muslims warring against each other for the leadership of this marauding band of thieves and murderers. After Muhammad's death, the followers of his widow Aisha were in a battle to the death against the followers of Muhammad's daughter Fatima and her husband, Ali. Fatima was murdered. Because Fatima was the closest child to Muhammad and because she supported Muhammad in his difficulties, Fatima is the object of respect and veneration by the Iranian Shiite Muslims and hated by Sunni Muslims."

"The Shiites believe that Muhammad's wife Aisha did not conduct herself in an appropriate manner. They have no respect for Aisha and believe that when their Mahdi, the twelfth imam returns, he will resurrect Aisha and have her whipped in public. In contrast, because Aisha was the wife of Muhammad, the Sunnis of today assert that to criticize Aisha is to criticize Muhammad. Today, after fourteen centuries, the battle between Muhammad's daughter Fatima and Muhammad's wife Aisha continues to rage. This vicious, internal and mutually destructive tearing of the flesh was foretold by me way back in **Genesis 16:12** when I brought Adonai's word to Hagar the mother of Ishmael by prophesying that her son Ishmael, 'shall be a wild ass of a man, his hand against every man, his hand against every man and every man's hand against him; and he shall dwell over against all his kinsmen.'"

"We see the fever pitch of the Middle East cauldron in the Arab Spring which birthed ISIS and produced a highly unstable and unpredictable warring environment," interjects Michael. "The fallout is political chaos and barbaric killings. It's Sunnis against Shiites. The emergence of ISIS has raised Middle East heat past the broiling point."

"There are other reasons," explains Gabriel, "why the feet and toes of clay mixed with iron are not holding together, and why they never will hold together. There are huge racial and ideological divides in the

Muslim world. Arab Sunni Saddam Hussein fought an eight-year war against Shiite Iran. Aryan Shiite Iran is propping up Alawite (Shiite) Bashar al-Assad of Syria with military equipment and Iranian fighters. Sunni Saudi Arabia is desperately afraid of Shiite Iran, which is building a nuclear bomb in order to bomb the Saudi oil fields and Israel. Sunni Saudi Arabia is aiding the Sunni rebels in Syria to stop Iran. Israel has a plentiful supply of nuclear weapons and so does Pakistan.

"To the north Turkish leader Recep Tayyip Erdogan has alienated most of the Muslim Middle East as he strives to resurrect the Ottoman Caliphate and to rule over the Muslim Arab world as the Caliph. The Russian military presence in Syria and in Iran to support Alawite al-Assad has raised major existential threats for nuclear-armed Israel. This lethal mix of distrust and hatreds is waiting to explode into Armageddon."

"The Alawites are a Syrian Islamic sect which follows the Twelver School of Shiite Islam," expounds Michael who brings more depth of understanding to the Islamic cesspool of killings.

"If we didn't read it for ourselves in **Genesis 16:12**, who would have thought that Ishmael's legacy would turn out to be this toxic?" queries Gabriel who is anxious to share his involvement. "But let's move on with the prophecies. I came to Daniel in a dream, and I gave to him a vision, which distressed him greatly and which he recorded in **Daniel 7:7–8**: 'After this I saw in the night visions, and behold a fourth beast, terrible and dreadful and exceedingly strong. It had great iron teeth; it devoured and broke in pieces, and stamped the residue with its feet. It was different from all the beasts before it; and it had ten horns. . . . and behold, there came up among them another horn, a little one . . . speaking great things.'"

Gabriel continues, "In **Daniel 7:15**, he expresses his anxiety and his alarm about this frightening beast with eleven horns. Daniel had written, 'As for me, Daniel, my spirit within me was anxious and the visions of my head alarmed me.' Daniel was so greatly distressed by this exceedingly terrible beast that he inquired to know more about it and its eleven horns, but especially about that little horn. As if for emphasis, Daniel recorded his concerns again in his writings at **Daniel 7:19**, 'Then I desired to know the truth concerning the fourth beast, which was different from all the rest, exceedingly terrible, with its teeth of iron and claws of bronze; and which devoured and broke in pieces, and stamped the residue with its feet; and concerning the ten horns that were on its head, and the other horn which came up . . . which spoke great things.'"

"Iron is the metaphor for the legs, for the feet and for the toes of the statue, while bronze is the metaphor for the belly and for the thighs of the statue." Archangel Michael contributes his insights. "So these kingdoms are the last three kingdoms of the statue. Today, geographically, these lands are controlled by Muslim nations. **Revelation 13:2** throws more light onto the statue: 'the beast that I saw was like a leopard, its feet were like a bear's and its mouth was like a lion's mouth.' The lion, the bear, and the leopard are the same three animals of Daniel's revelations."

"This fourth terrible beast of Revelation is a combination of the first three beasts of Daniel 7, which represented the Greek kingdom, the Medo-Persian kingdom, and the Babylonian kingdom all combined." Raphael is intrigued by the image duplication. "Strangely though, **Revelation 13:2** presents them in *reverse order* to **Daniel 7:3–6** which reads, 'And four great beasts came up out of the sea, different from one another. The first was like a lion and had eagles' wings. . . . A second one, like a bear . . . another, like a leopard, with four wings of a bird.' This was no accident. I believe that the order of the beasts is indicative of the origin of the Antichrist. The pre-eminence of the leopard speaks of swiftness and firmly puts this beast as coming from the lands controlled by the Greek Empire of Alexander. Today, the lands occupied by these first three beasts and their former kingdoms of old, are controlled by Muslim nations that surround Israel."

"I stood back and watched in shock as the Ancient of Days came to Daniel and spoke to him and to me," exclaims Gabriel. "Daniel recorded this revelation from the Ancient of Days in **Daniel 7:23–25**: 'As for the fourth beast, there shall be a fourth kingdom on earth, which shall be different from all the kingdoms, and it shall devour the whole earth, and trample it down, and break it to pieces. As for the ten horns, out of this kingdom ten kings shall arise, and another shall arise after them. . . . He shall speak words against the Most High, and shall wear out the saints of the Most High, and shall think to change the times and the law; and they shall be given into his hand.'"

Gabriel continues, "Daniel was very much preoccupied with this terrible beast, with its eleven horns, and with this eleventh king. I told Daniel that the eleventh little horn was the Antichrist and the desolator, but he did not understand it. Although I gave to him the verses 'And the king shall do according to his will; he shall exalt himself and magnify himself above every god, and shall speak astonishing things against the God of gods. . . . He shall honour the god of fortresses,' which he recorded in **Daniel 11:36–38**, these words did not bring to him the inner peace which he had sought.'"

Michael delves deeper into end-time disclosures. "We know that Allah-inspired Islam was brewed in Hell's kitchen. The Antichrist will be *the* spiritual beast of Daniel and of Revelation who will force his satanic religion worldwide. **Revelation 13:4**, which reads, 'Men worshiped the dragon, for he had given his authority to the beast, and they worshipped the beast, saying, 'Who is like the beast, and who can fight against it?' reinforces **Daniel 11:36–38**. Remember in the Bible, the name 'dragon' refers to Satan."

"And now we'll analyze **Daniel 9:26–27**, which I had revealed to Daniel," announces Gabriel. "It reads, 'And after the sixty-two weeks, an anointed one shall be cut off and have nothing; and the people of the prince who is to come shall destroy the city and the sanctuary. . . to the end there shall be war; desolations are decreed. And he shall make a strong covenant with many for one week; and for half the week he shall cause sacrifice and offering to cease; and upon the wing of abominations shall come one who makes desolate, until the decreed end is poured out on the desolator.'"

"This reads much like the satanic performance of Antiochus Epiphanies of the Seleucid dynasty," says Raphael with astonishment. He volunteers an alternate perspective, "From 171 BC to 165 BC, for more than six years or 2300 days, Antiochus Epiphanies butchered the people of Judah and desecrated their temple. Epiphanies was a type of the Antichrist to come. It is most revealing that he came from the Seleucid wing of the Greek Empire, and that he came from

Syria. **Daniel 9:26** reads: 'the people of the prince who is to come shall destroy the city and the sanctuary.' We should expect to see the emergence of a northern leader from the general region of Turkey, Syria, and Iraq, that is, from the ancient Seleucid Empire. Islam rejects Adonai and rejects His Son Christ the Messiah of the Bible in exchange for Allah of the Quran. In the same manner, the Antichrist rejects the God of his father Abraham. 'The king shall do according to his will; he shall exalt himself and magnify himself above every god, and shall speak astonishing things against the God of gods. He shall give no heed to the gods of his father, or to the one beloved by women,' wrote **Daniel** in **11:36–37**. Muhammad's followers do not worship the God of Abraham, or the God of Isaac, or the God of Jacob."

Gabriel continues, "The Antichrist will 'give no heed' and show no regard for the Lord God of the patriarchs. The Antichrist rejects Adonai, the God of the Bible and rejects His Son Jesus as Yeshua Messiah. Yes, in this one single breath-taking verse of **Daniel 11:37**, the Antichrist of hatred is contrasted against the God of love Who is beloved of women. In contrast, Allah hates women with satanic passion. Allah the god of Islam is the god of war and the god of jihad. Soon after his eviction from Heaven, Satan the Dragon has been masquerading as Allah. Hiding behind the name of Allah, Satan has been craving worship and exaltation ever since.

Yeshua's judgment *cannot* be turned aside. The only hope is in the coming Prince named Yeshua Messiah. Islam is pushing hard for a confrontation with Christ the Messiah. Because the Quran is irreversible, the final judgment also is irreversible. The apocalyptic curtain is coming down and the control switch is locked out in the hands of Yeshua Messiah."

CHAPTER 6

THE VATICAN AND ISLAM: THE POWER BEHIND THE POWER

AUTHOR'S NOTE: Most of the Quranic references quoted in this chapter come from the Koran, translated by N. J. Dawood (Penguin Book, 2003). By clever design, to fool the gullible and the uninformed, the Koran uses the name "God" in place of "Allah." For accuracy, I have substituted the name "Allah" for the name "God" because the god of the Koran (Quran) is *not* the God of the Old Testament and Allah is *not* the God of the New Testament.

Khadijah and Waraquah are historical figures who were instrumental in the rise of Muhammad, the prophet of Islam. Waraquah was a theologian priest well versed in the Bible. Waraquah was Khadijah's cousin. Both were unwavering Roman Catholics under close Vatican authority. Khadijah was born in AD 555. She was Muhammad's first wife from AD 595 until her death in AD 619 in Mecca, Saudi Arabia. Khadijah's and Muhammad's daughter Fatima was and continues to be the significant and strategic figure bridging Shiite Islam and Roman Catholicism today. In the eighth century, during the Islamic invasions of Spain and Portugal, the city of Fatima was named after Muhammad's daughter. In 1917, Fatima, Portugal, gained worldwide recognition when the city became associated with the Apparitions of Mary, known as the Queen of Heaven. Muslims continue to make yearly pilgrimages to Fatima in Portugal. Appearances of Queen of Heaven phantoms are increasing across the entire world today. Under Vatican directive, Muhammad's "revelations" in his Quran were contrived, constructed, and documented by Augustinians during Muhammad's lifetime.

The year is AD 593. The place is outside of a Roman Catholic Cathedral near the outskirts of Mecca. The four Archangels Michael, Gabriel, Raphael, and Uriel are huddled in a conference behind a sand dune.

Michael reveals that Adonai has given them another major assignment. "There is an important event happening tonight in the Catholic Cathedral. All I know is that the four of us need to be present. We will be informed then about plans afoot that will shake this globe in the future."

Black, massive, billowing storm clouds are seen full circle on every horizon. Multiple lightning strikes illuminate the evening skies as strong winds whip up the sands, reducing visibility. In this clear standoff between angelic and demonic powers, the air is electric with expectation. In the gathering gloom of the deepening twilight, two silhouettes of cloaked and hooded figures stealthily approach the cathedral on foot through the swirling sand storm.

Raphael glances sideways at his three companions and says in a lowered voice, "This looks like the usual cloak-and-dagger stuff with storm clouds and wild winds, as in some mock-up stage play. That owl sitting on the bell tower is the standard ill omen."

"Adonai and Yeshua Messiah are well aware of Augustine's Replacement Theology to discredit the Jews and Israel, and of the Vatican's plan to take possession of Jerusalem. Nothing is hidden from the God of Heaven." Michael explains, "Tonight we will witness the agenda for the closure of this age."

After the two dark figures are ushered into the darkened doorway of the Catholic cathedral, Raphael anticipates the angelic response. "We're moving into this hole? Yes?"

Michael nods. "However, we will enter through the star-gate in our usual hyper-dimensional cover."

Before they make a move, two other figures suddenly swoop down from above through a demonic portal and enter the building right through the cathedral wall.

Looking almost amused, Michael lowers his voice to a chilling whisper, "I recognize those two. That's Satan herself and her side-kick Sonneillon. This must be some high profile meeting to have those two devils attending. Let's move in and observe."

The angelic foursome glides down a narrow staircase and into a darkened cellar. The entry door with its huge metal hinges and iron security bars indicates that this is no ordinary room. The irregular stone walls have no windows. At the far end of the large rectangular room is another narrow door leading to a second staircase leading up to ground level.

In the center of the room and huddled at a round table are the two dark sinister-looking figures that were seen entering several minutes earlier. Also seated at the table are two cloaked Augustinian monks who are not part of any monastery as they are domiciled in the Catholic Cathedral. In the center of the table are three glowing flickering candles.

The foursome seated around the table is unaware of the presence of Satan and Sonneillon who are hovering over them. The high ceiling disappears into a black void that emits an undulating, oppressive red glow that could be mistaken for reflections of the candle flames. Both Satan and Sonneillon are cognizant of the presence of the angelic God Squad along the opposite wall. The hostile energy waves streaming between the two opposing camps of angelic and demonic forces cause the candle flames to distort into bizarre whipping patterns.

The four dark figures at table are mesmerized by the candle flames. Rather than focusing upon each other, all eyes are fixated upon the dancing flames between them. All four participants are aware of the spirit powers at play around them, but none is aware to what degree or extent.

Raphael sniffs the air with a shocked look and exclaims, "I smell burned flesh. I smell death. This is a dungeon. Look at those manacles attached to that stone wall near the ceiling. That's fresh dried blood all over the wall. This is a torture chamber. Somebody died here painfully, and not long ago. This is a Roman Catholic cathedral. There should not be a torture chamber in it. Before we entered this pit of hell, I noticed a fresh grave in the large cemetery outside."

"Look at the shelf in the left corner," points Uriel. "I see the butt ends of two coiled whips. Why would whips be needed in a cathedral?"

"Nothing new here," Michael adds. "This Roman Catholic Cathedral has had an on-going secretive inquisition in one form or another from its very beginnings. It's about extracting confessions and denials. Those who don't break down under torture will die. Adonai told me that the Vatican's campaign of violence will continue for another twelve hundred years. The Catholic Church of the Vatican stands as the colossal nemesis of the Coptic Christians and of all true believers."

"It's about the conflict between the Vatican and the Coptic Christian Churches, which will not adopt or bow down to Rome's pagan beliefs." Gabriel adds a bit of history, "Worst yet is what the Augustinians represent. As the father of Replacement Theology, it was Augustine who promoted hatred against the Jews, and who labeled the Jews as the murderers of Jesus. It was Augustine who set the pattern for the Roman Catholic Church, which promoted the hatred of the Jews, which continues to be the Vatican legacy. We are here tonight to observe the continuing fallout of Augustine's toxic hatred toward the Jews which is being translated into Vatican action."

"What is this Replacement Theology?" inquires Uriel.

"Replacement Theology is about the Vatican teaching that the Jews are no longer God's chosen people and that the Roman Catholic Church in Rome has replaced the nation of Israel in regards to God's plans and promises." Gabriel continues, "It's about the Vatican's arrogant distortion of Scriptures stating that because the Jews had rejected Jesus Christ and had Him crucified under the Romans, the promises given to Abraham, to Isaac and to Jacob have been transferred to the Roman Catholic Church.

It is Rome's desperate ploy to be seen as the New Jerusalem. Augustine was an exceptionally brilliant theologian who was held in high regard throughout the Roman Catholic Church." Gabriel exposes and concludes, "For these reasons, and for reasons of credibility, the Vatican delegated Augustine to create an unchallengeable treatise excluding the Jews from further participation in God's plans and blessings. It's about delegitimizing Israel and the Jews."

The wind rushing down the staircase and through the wide crack underneath the door whistles and whines in undulating eerie wailing. With each wind gust, the candle flames flicker and gyrate erratically as they cast ominous dancing shadows onto the rough stone walls around the room. Gray and orange patterns of light sweep the black ceiling.

At the table, an Augustinian monk emanating a salacious aura with one eye permanently half shut, stammers with authoritative pomp and snarl, "I have been given my marching orders from the Vatican, from none other than the Holy Father himself. This is a matter of high priority. Your cooperation is not an option. Here are the problems the Vatican is facing this very night. The Orthodox Coptic Christians of Alexandria will not submit to Rome, and they will not acknowledge the Pope's authority. Besides, these upstart Copts are denying and violating our Babylonian traditions passed on to Rome. How dare they defy the Vatican and the Holy Father! The Holy Father is really upset and wants the Coptic Christians and the Jews annihilated. The big question is how to achieve these ends. That is why we are meeting here tonight."

Inside the cathedral, opposing spiritual powers of the highest orders are present. Outside, the entire cathedral is surrounded by myriads of demons and angelic beings. Both enemy camps are represented in equal numbers. This meeting, on this particular night, is a cosmic focal point with unimaginable future consequences. The stakes couldn't be higher. All four individuals at the table are aware that this particular Augustinian meeting room inside the Catholic Cathedral in Mecca is a torture chamber and an execution cell for enemies of the Vatican.

Turning smugly to the two cloaked figures, salacious monk barks out abrasively, "The Holy Father has instructions for the two of you."

With trembling voice, the lone female shrinks back into her chair in fear. "I will do whatever the Holy Father requires."

Addressing her, salacious monk now calls her by name. "Khadijah, His Holiness, the Pope, wants you to find a young, clever, ruthless, and uneducated man, marry him and train him up for our purposes. Because of your wealth, your influence, and your power, you will be able to control him and to groom him to suit our ends. We need to punish those arrogant Orthodox Copts! We will create a competing religion for these desert Ishmaelites. And this young man in your future will be their prophet. All the Catholic monasteries have been ordered to proclaim a coming Ishmaelite messiah and to prepare mentally all the desert tribes to anticipate his arrival."

Salacious monk now turns to the second hooded figure. "Okay, 'Cousin' Waraquah, last week we explained that because of your theological training you will be the teacher of this coming prophet. You and I together will be his advisors. We will write the new Arabic bible, which we will call the Quran. We will call this new religion 'Islam.' Allah of old will be the god of Islam. This Allah is the well-known moon god from the Babylonian times of Nimrod who had three daughters. The followers of Allah, we will call Muslims. Your immediate job is to help to find a young stud for Khadijah. The Vatican will reward both of you richly for your future successes. But in the meantime, while we are waiting for this Mr. Right for Khadijah, we will start planning and writing our new holy book for the Ishmaelites. As you can see, I have a secretary who is ready to take notes." Salacious monk points to his skinny Augustinian partner.

Squinting with his good eye, salacious monk nods enthusiastically, "Islam is a good choice of name because it means 'submission.' We want these ignorant desert caravan marauders to submit on their knees and with their foreheads touching the ground. We want them to hate the Coptic Christians and to hate the Jews. Given Ishmael's seeds of hatred passed on to his descendants, this should prove to be an easy sell. We need to do everything we can to discredit the Orthodox Christian Copts and their religion in the eyes of the Arabs. But at the same time, we want the Ishmaelites to be sympathetic to the Roman Catholic Church and to protect our many Churches and monasteries here in North Africa, Egypt, Palestine, Arabia, Syria, and Turkey. We want the Ishmaelites to see the Roman Catholic Church as their friend."

The expressions on Waraquah's face spell enthusiasm. "Your choice of the name 'Islam' is terrific. The word *Islam* is a variation of the word *Salem* which means peace, except that Islam will bring anything but peace for the Jews and for the Copts."

Salacious monk expands upon his intended version of Islamic peace. "There will be peace when Islam eradicates the Jews and the Coptic Christians whom we will call *Infidels* or *Kafirs*."

With a fiendish grin and with his good eye glazed over, salacious monk is bubbling over with enthusiasm. "We will want these new Arab converts to fight for us. The Holy Father in Rome desperately wants Jerusalem. This is his first and foremost goal, and he will do whatever it takes to achieve this end for the Vatican. By any standard, this is a tall order. But just how can we persuade the Ishmaelites to fight for Rome? How can this be orchestrated? Waraquah, what are your ideas?"

Outwardly, Waraquah appears as one who is confident and self-assured in his new role as prophet-maker. With his eyes fixated in a trance-like gaze upon the flickering candle flames, Waraquah proclaims, "We need to look for a candidate who is uncertain about himself and who lacks self-esteem. He must have a vicious streak of hatred. He should be the manner of person whom we can work like a lump of clay. A good measure of instability in him would serve our purposes well. He should be someone who will let power go to his head. If he is not on hashish, we will find ways to get him hooked on this mind bender. Then he will have dreams and hallucinations which we will interpret for him."

My cousin Khadijah has many business contacts and lots of experience dealing with all manner and all types of personalities. In time and with my help, Khadijah will find a willing stooge as this future King of Clay whom we will mold and manipulate."

With a bounce in his chair and with a look of satisfaction, salacious monk pushes his agenda. "We need to flesh out some details. How do we get these sandblasted Arabs to fight for the Vatican? What incentives can we dangle in front of their eyes so that they will be willing to die for Allah?"

There is nothing innocuous about salacious monk's request. This insecure piece of work has a face which even a mother could not love. Multiple scars surround his droopy eyelid, obviously from a horrific confrontation somewhere in his deep, dark past. As a known sexual deviant, everything about salacious monk screams dangerous being. His missing and rotting teeth add to his repulsive image. The pentacle hanging from his neck adds to the disturbing aura which surrounds him. Nature worship? Venus worship? Devil worship? and inside a

Catholic cathedral? a great choice in keeping with the objectives of the Vatican!

"First and foremost, a core and foundational belief of Islam must be the blatant denial of Christ as the Son of God. That's a given. No Son of God! No dying on a cross! No shed blood! and No resurrection! In Islam, believing in the divinity of Christ will be made to be a far worse crime than committing murder. Frying in Hell will be the reward."

Casually, Waraquah leans back on his stool. "We need to understand the driving principles and the emotions behind human behaviour and apply them to our problem. These basic emotions are fear, hatred, greed, and love. By far, the strongest of these emotion is fear or self-preservation. Hatred comes in as a close second. The beautiful thing about hatred is that it can fester for thousands of years as it is passed down from generation to generation. Hatred is an intense driving force. We need to capitalize on past hatreds and imagined hatreds which we will massage and engineer, and make them work for the Vatican. We need to make fear and hatred work for the Vatican. We need to construct the Quran so that it is driven by hatred against Christians, hatred against Jews, and by the fear of Hell. If we promote it correctly, Ishmael's hatred of Abraham's wife Sarah and his hatred of Adonai will work wonders for the Holy Father in Rome."

As he weighs Waraquah's words, salacious monk is intrigued by what he has heard. "You sound like the repository of the knowledge of good and evil. Did you also have a bite of Eve's apple in Eden?"

It is apparent from Waraquah's facial expression that he is highly flattered by

> "They contrived, and Allah contrived. Allah is the supreme contriver."
>
> - Quran 3:54

this metaphor. Pumped up, Waraquah launches into his thesis. "First, this new Arabic bible must be designed so that many decades from now after the Copts have been blotted out and the Vatican controls Jerusalem, Islamic scholars and the whole world will come to realize just how stupid and contradictory this Quran is. Once future generations of Arabs get educated, they will discard this Islamic silliness. Then the Arabs will gravitate to the Vatican and the Holy Fathers will win again.

In the meantime, we get to play children's games of pretend and to write fairy tales or jinn tales for the gullible sand Arabs."

Salacious monk likes what he hears. "Your words sounds good to me. You're the Bible expert. So let's hear your strategies."

"To achieve our ends," explains Waraquah, "we have to make the case against Jesus and reduce his credibility to less than zero. Then we will set up the Quran to focus on attacking the integrity and the credibility of the Bible. At the same time, we will need to feed the hatred towards the Orthodox Copts and toward the Jews so that the Vatican can take control of Jerusalem. Finally, we need to put the fear of Allah into every living soul. We will give the Arabs no choice. It's either, 'Submit to Allah, or burn in Hell.' To raise the level of fear, Muslims will call Allah the 'God of the Sword' and Islam as the 'Religion of the Sword.'"

Salacious monk nods approval. "It sounds like good strategy. We want to design a scorched-earth war zone for the Copts and for the Jews. However, the first step must be to deny and to break the cross. Historically, it cannot be challenged that Jesus was nailed to a cross. However, Islam must deny this most central event of redemption. At all cost, Islam must deny the crucifixion of Jesus Christ as the Son of God. Muslims must be taught that Jesus never died on the cross in the way the Christian world has been led to believe. Muslims must be taught that it was Allah who allowed Jesus to die and that it was Allah who took him away to Paradise. This is a stretch and it's going to be a hard sell, so let's put this verse near the beginning of the Quran as verse 3:54 as, 'They contrived, and Allah contrived. Allah is

> "They said, 'We have put to death the Messiah Jesus, son of Mary, the apostle of Allah.' They did not kill him, nor did they crucify him, but they thought they did. . . . They did not slay him for certain. Allah lifted him up to Him. Allah is mighty and wise. There is none among the People of the Book but will believe in him before his death, and on the Day of Resurrection he will bear witness against them.'"
>
> *- Quran 4:157–158*

the supreme contriver. Allah said, 'Jesus, I am about to claim you back and lift you up to Me.'"

"If we can pull off this Quran verse with the Arabs, then we will have it made. Muslims must be told that Allah intentionally fooled the people. How do you think it will go over to tell these goat herders from the sand dunes that Allah is one monstrous liar and that he can't be trusted? If the Arabs believe this Quranic line of stinking camel dung, then it will be open season on the truth the next time we meet to weave more Allah fiction."

The ideas are starting to flow as this gruesome threesome gets into the swing of it. Waraquah lifts his gaze to the dancing lights on the ceiling, "I agree that the Quran 3:54 verse may turn out to be a hard sell. Why don't we stick in several verses to diffuse the issue and muddy the waters, somewhat like a dust storm in the desert? I have an idea. How's this for a duo of verses at Quran 4:157–158?"

"They said, 'We have put to death the Messiah Jesus, son of Mary, the apostle of Allah.' They did not kill him, nor did they crucify him, but they thought they did. . . . They did not slay him for certain. Allah lifted him up to Him. Allah is mighty and wise. There is none among the People of the Book but will believe in him before his death, and on the Day of Resurrection he will bear witness against them.'"

"How's that for creating confusion and obfuscating the issue? These caravan bandits aren't smart enough to figure this out."

With his eyes closed, salacious monk tries to get a mental image of what he has just heard, "Fantastic! Fabulous! Sounds excellent to me. Just as their goats swallow grass without thinking, these unschooled, desert goat-herders will swallow this dung without questioning it.

"Waraquah, in your list of basic drives, you forgot one overriding persuader, and that is the promise of sex. Young desert studs can be motivated by sex rewards. We need to consider how to use sex in the Quran."

> "We will burn him in the fire of Hell: an evil end. . . . . Allah will not forgive idolatry. . . .
> He that serves other gods beside Allah has strayed far indeed."
>
> — Quran 4.116

"Eternal sex sounds like a terrific idea. We will think about it, but in the meantime, let's drive a few more nails into the Orthodox Coptic coffin. Let's fashion a commandment of the highest order, and let's call it 'Shirk.' We'll construct a verse of the Quran that makes believing in the divinity of Christ to be a much greater crime than murder. *Shirk* or polytheism will forbid associating partners with God. In other words, Islam will not allow any of this Father-and-Son heresy. Let's raise the temperature even higher. We'll make violating *Shirk* to be punishable in the fires of Hell. Believing in God the Son will be a one-way ticket to hellfire. We'll choose another random location in the Quran for this verse. How about at Quran 4:116? It will read, 'We will burn him in the fire of Hell: an evil end. . . . . Allah will not forgive idolatry. . . . He that serves other gods beside Allah has strayed far indeed.' Here's another knife between the ribs of the Coptic Christians. Quran 2:193 will read, 'Fight against them until idolatry is no more and Allah's religion is supreme.' In other words, our Allah does not forgive association with Him. Associating partners with Allah will be punishable with hellfire."

"Praise be to Allah who has never begotten a son; who has no partner in His kingdom. Quran 17:111. "Never has Allah begotten a son, nor is there any other god beside Him.

- *Quran 23:91*

Salacious monk continues, "What will this mean? In Islam, it will mean that believing God is the Holy Spirit also is the unpardonable sin. On both counts, we've got the Orthodox Coptics backed into a corner." Hooting and cheering follow. The candleholders bounce in response to the pounding on raucous response. "See, we're making it absolutely clear that God has no son."

With a smug smile, Waraquah picks up the reins of the discussion. "Why not add more insult to injury? Let's write into the Quran that whoever believes that Allah is Jesus the son of Mary commits a terrible blasphemy and is cursed by Allah. Let's put this verse at Quran 5:17 and let's make it read, 'They do blaspheme who declare: "Allah is Messiah, the son of Mary."' Or we could word it slightly different, 'Verily, they are disbelievers and infidels who say

"The Messiah, son of Mary is God."' Either version will work for us. Let's create several more verses showing that God has no son. We'll make Quran 17:111 read, 'Praise be to Allah who has never begotten a son; who has no partner in His kingdom.' At Quran 23:91, let's write in, 'Never has Allah begotten a son, nor is there any other god beside Him.'"

Visibly distressed and angry, Khadijah interrupts, "You are urinating on my God. You are spitting into the face of Yeshua Messiah! It is you who are blaspheming. It is you who blaspheme. The Quran is turning out to be a book of blasphemy."

Waraquah tries to calm the waters and soothe Khadijah, "It's *not* about what *we* personally believe. I don't believe a word of what I am writing into the Quran. It's what the Holy Father in Rome wants us to do. It's all for the common good. Just remember the end justifies the means." Khadijah is hesitant, but for the moment she appears to be pacified.

Waraquah continues as if he hadn't heard a single word of Khadijah's opposition. "We need to stick in a couple of verses somewhere at random which read that even Jesus himself directs worship to Allah." Waraquah spends a minute scribbling on a parchment and then blurts out his new twist. "In Quran 5:72 I have written, 'They do blaspheme that say: "Allah is the Messiah, the son of Mary."' In Quran 5:73 I have written, 'They do blaspheme that say: "Allah is one of three." There is but one God. If they do not desist from saying, those of them that disbelieve shall be sternly punished.' How is that for confusing God with Allah and confusing Allah with God and muddying the waters? These Arab sand-dwellers will never figure this out."

Salacious monk is well pleased, "These two mischievous verses will go a long way."

As if they were programmed by an invisible force, all four conspirators shout and lift their beer mugs skyward, almost in unison. However, Khadijah's arm is the last to join the other three. Reluctance is written all over her face.

> "They do blaspheme that say: "Allah is the Messiah, the son of Mary."
>
> - Quran 5:72

Salacious monk is elated, "The Holy Father will be pleased with our progress. To continue our war against Jesus, let's deliver another good punch to the head and another swift kick to the Coptic butt. Quran 19:88–92 will threaten gross blasphemy with serious consequences: 'Those who say, "The Lord of Mercy has begotten a son," preach a monstrous falsehood, at which the very heavens might crack, the earth split asunder, and the mountains crumble to dust. That they should ascribe a son to the Merciful, when it does not become the Lord of Mercy to beget one!'"

> "Those who say, 'The Lord of Mercy has begotten a son,' preach a monstrous falsehood, at which the very heavens might crack, the earth split asunder, and the mountains crumble to dust. That they should ascribe a son to the Merciful, when it does not become the Lord of Mercy to beget one!'"
>
> —Quran 19:88-92

Salacious monk continues in the same theme, "Let's stick this next verse at the very end. Quran 112:1–4 will say, 'Allah is One, the Eternal God . . . He begot none, nor was He begotten. None is equal to Him.' Here's a good Fire and Brimstone verse. Quran 3:149 to Quran 3:150 will threaten, 'We will put terror into the hearts of the unbelievers. They serve other deities besides Allah for whom He has revealed no sanction. The Fire shall be their home; evil indeed is the dwelling of the evil-doers.'"

Warquah's twisted mind is working overtime. "We need another clincher to summarize and to seal this Allah issue once and for all. How's about this? Let's invent a perverted Jesus for Islam. Instead of writing it into the Quran, let's have a verse inserted into separate book called Islamic Traditions of the Prophet, where we will say that when Jesus returns he will declare himself to be a Muslim. Let's have him deny all his claims of being God. Let's write that if they do not convert to Islam, Jesus will condemn them and be a witness against them on the Day of Judgment. How does breaking the cross and punishing the Christians sound to you? This new verse will read, "Jesus the Son of Mary will break the cross, kill the pig and abolish jizya, and on the Day of Judgment, he will be a witness against them."

With intense resolve and emotion, Waraquah continues to impress his cohorts, "This verse will be just another knife stuck between the ribs. Jesus will be a witness against the Christians. We will write that when Jesus returns, he will kill all Jews and Christians who did not convert to Islam, and he will lead the invading enemy armies against Israel. And so you so-called 'people of the book,' you Coptic Christians and you Jews, beware, because you all are headed for hellfire."

The room is filled with thunderous applause, shouting, back-slapping, and more pounding on the table. To an observer, it would appear as if this threesome were possessed. And so they were. Without any doubt, the added crescendo was provided by Satan and Sonneillon. However, in this last round, Khadijah is not a participant in this undignified frivolity. She remains silent as she repeatedly winds and unwinds her rosary around her left forefinger. Khadijah is visibly angry as she stares coldly into the far corner of the darkened ceiling. The fire in her eyes sends a warning. Her tightly pursed lips restrain an imminent explosion.

After the revelry and the silliness die down, the dam breaks as Khadijah launches another objection. "There you go again. You are defiling my Christ Messiah. You are blaspheming Jesus with these Quranic verses. These verses are all blasphemy, blasphemy, blasphemy against Jesus! This Quran fraud which we are perpetrating is one monstrous blasphemy against Christ the Messiah. This is all degrading blasphemy. I don't want to be part of it!"

Salacious monk heaves a loud sigh, slaps his thigh, and launches into a long tale of looming woe. "You're a long way from Rome. You're insulated in your home and in this Roman Catholic Cathedral, and you don't understand the turmoil, the politics and the dangers swirling around the Vatican. It's been 117 years since the Western Roman Empire fragmented in AD 476 and was lost to the barbarian Huns. Today, the power of the Western emperors is long gone. The Vatican is stepping into the breach and trying to restore some order. Now, the Vikings are making raids on the northwest coasts of Gaul. The Mongol hordes in the east are stressing China. At some point, they will turn west and make incursions into Europe. Then there are the marauders from Turkistan moving west into Turkey. And let's not forget the Magyars. They're stirring in the Urals as they point westward and towards the Black Sea. It's not *if*, it's *when* they will move against us. Then there are the Tatars heading west towards Ukraine. And in their on-going string of conflicts, we know only too well that the nineteen-year Byzantine-Parthian-Persian War ended last year. But those unpredictable Parthians could move west against us any time soon. With the collapse of Rome in 476, all stability was gone. Now the Germanic tribes are pressuring the Catholic Church for control. Europe has been in a cauldron of unpredictable flux. Today, the big concerns for Rome are the ravaging Lombards who are fragmenting Northern Italy. And then there are the Ishmaelite Arab hordes in the south and all around us. Living in desert sands, the Arabs are hungry, restless, and unpredictable. Wouldn't it be better if we tricked them to fight for us rather than to fight against us? Forget about morals and scruples. We are living in desperate times. Of necessity, principles and conscience must be thrown out the window for a short time. Better still, divorce your conscience for a time! A little bit of harmless lying is this Quran is a small price in the sight of God. This end definitely justifies the means."

Salacious Augustinian monk has painted a grim and convincing picture of the compulsion to bend and stoop low for the Vatican. Waraquah attempts to protect his cousin Khadijah's feelings and her high position in the world of business. Gently he joins the fray between the two contesting forces. Waraquah faces Khadijah, "I understand your feelings. Your anger is justified. The Ishmaelites are being sent to Hell, and your faith is being attacked this very night. However, it is possible that further attacks on Rome could overrun the Vatican itself. It's all about the survival of Rome itself. Our base of support in

"We will put terror into the hearts of the unbelievers. They serve other deities besides Allah for whom He has revealed no sanction. The Fire shall be their home; evil indeed is the dwelling of the evil-doers.'"

- Quran 3:149-150

Rome could disappear over night. Our Catholic monasteries and our Roman Catholic Churches in North Africa and in Arabia could come under attack. All of us will be losers if we don't act now. So we must lie and deceive. We have no choice. A few Hail-Marys by you will make everything right. Do you really have any other choice? I don't see an alternative."

Khadijah looks subdued. In total defeat and with her gaze fixed upon the candle flames, Khadijah's response is curt. "Those poor deceived Arabs. We're making fools out of them. We are releasing a den of cobras into their midst. Worst yet, I feel like Pandora who just has opened the lid on the box. I have this foreboding fear that we will never be able to put this evil genie or this jinn back into its bottle. This so-called Quran, which we are composing, may mean annihilation for millions in the future. Somehow, somewhere, sometime there will be Hell to pay for this piece of Quranic folly and treachery which we are creating tonight. This Quran business in front of us is one gigantic fraud. That's what it is! My better judgment is screaming, No! Is my God ever going to forgive me for what I am creating in this dungeon this very night? Will Mary intercede for me? Or am I on a collision course with God's justice and retribution?"

Waraquah draws a deep breath for a long dissertation. With darkened expression and in a sombre voice to match, he makes a surprisingly different attempt to pacify Khadijah. "All of us are experiencing this prolonged miserable era of cold which began in AD 535. This was and continues to be one of the greatest natural disasters ever. Fifty years ago, we were enveloped by dust and ash from Krakatoa, that super giant volcano of all time. That volcanic monster blast blotted out the sun for eighteen months and left us in darkness and in this frigid cold. The veil of the choking dust was like a funeral shroud. On-going heavy rains turned the ground blood red. The volcanic winter that followed killed a large part of humanity among us and across the world. Many just froze to death. The Justinianic Plague of 541 AD and 542 AD which followed, killed many hundreds of thousands in Constantinople alone. Those who didn't die of disease died of starvation because of food shortages. People were dying so fast and in such overwhelming numbers that there were few left alive who could bury the dead. Many died in the streets. The numbers of dead choked movement and travel of any kind. These were our grand parents. Bodies were stacked in the streets and left to rot, adding to a further spread of rats and disease. This plague continues to cycle through us today. It's this continuing cold weather, drought, flood, famine, and starvation. Europe continues to be overrun with rats. Then there's this black death disease which is being spread by these cursed creatures. This plague is killing millions, causing death within a single day, or within several hours. Victims eat lunch with their friends and family on Earth and have dinner with their ancestors in Heaven or in Hell. They die just so quickly. To make matters even worse, now there are fears of invasions from the East. Food shortages are pushing migrations from Mongolia and central Asia towards us in the west. There is a famine across much of the known world. Now in these desperate times of famine, the dreaded Scythians are on the move in search of pasture lands, food, and water. This is about survival, survival, survival right across the world!"

Springing out of his chair like a scalded cat, salacious monk shrieks, "Scythians!!! Do you realize who they are and what they are? They are part of Magog of the book of Revelation. Yes, Magog! And they're coming our way? Horrors! They're highly skilled with a bow. They are precision marksmen as well as expert cavalrymen. From early childhood, Scythians are trained to kill with super accuracy at full gallop, shooting both forward or backward. The Great Wall of China was built to keep out the Mongols and other horseback terrorists like the Scythians from crossing over into China. These vicious murdering thugs are the ultra-barbarians of the ages. Their archery skills on horseback are unmatched. In the lands which they invade, the Scythians and the Mongols strap screaming children to their left arms and then use them as shields, while they hack their fathers to pieces with swords in their right hands. I know history and I am terrified. In 612 BC, a coalition of Medes, Persians, Babylonians, and Scythians sacked and burned Nineveh and destroyed the Assyrian Empire forever. Because they are starving, the Scythians of today are far more vicious than their forefathers ever were." As he speaks and shrieks, great beads of perspiration roll down the face of salacious monk. "Unfortnately, the Arabs will be collateral damage of the Quran in this great tragic scheme of events. Either they die or we die. Which way do you prefer to go?"

The looks of distress and anguish on Khadijah's face register the need for her to forget conscience and to move forward with this distasteful piece of Quranic evil design.

The volcanic fallout of Krakatoa led to a mini ice age and a survival mind-set around the world. People withdrew into a state of fear and ignorance. Climatic chaos, food shortages, and virulent diseases guided Europe to the fall of the Roman Empire in the West in 476 AD and to the Dark Ages which followed.

After a few moments of hesitation, Waraquah continues, "These are desperate times which call for desperate measures. And the Vatican is desperate, very, very desperate. Rome and the Vatican are at high risk of being overrun again, but this time by an assortment of much more threatening hordes from the east. And we four are in a position to make a difference." Reluctantly, Khadijah nods agreement.

Suddenly, salacious monk gets up from his chair. He walks briskly around the table returning to his place. Remaining standing, he places both hands on the tabletop and then leans forward putting his considerable weight onto his outstretched palms. Glaring down upon his three cohorts, he makes eye contact with each one sequentially and repeatedly as he speaks, "We need to put some Church history on the table. After Emperor Constantine moved the capital from Rome to Constantinople, the center of Church control also shifted to the east. Some two hundred years ago, the Roman Empire was divided into its western and eastern legs. Since then, the battle of words and threats has been raging and heating up between the Eastern Orthodox Church and the Western Catholic Church. The Eastern Orthodox Church absolutely rejects the primacy of the Holy Father in the Vatican. At best, Constantinople considers the Pope to be only the first among equals. The four of us here have our own personal stake in this spiritual-political mess. We are Augustinians inside this Roman Catholic Cathedral and we are being supported by Rome. But the Eastern Orthodox Church has no use for Augustinian Replacement Theology and it also will not accept Augustine's teaching on original sin or Augustine's position on the Holy Spirit. Since we are Augustinian Roman Catholics, we have our own personal axes to grind, and it's all about our very survival. We cannot afford to sit back and be neutral."

Salacious monk maintains his defiant, rigid pose. His anger escalates as he continues to blast Byzantium at Constantinople. "Only fifty-six years ago, in AD 537, Eastern Emperor Justinian had the arrogance and the audacity to build the largest and the most expensive Greek Orthodox Cathedral in the world. Justinian then added further insult by naming it Hagia Sophia, which in Greek translates to mean the Church of Holy Wisdom. Holy Wisdom? Whose wisdom? What's holy about defying the Holy Father in Rome? This massive Eastern Orthodox Cathedral of extraordinary Greek architecture was an outrageous affront of one-upmanship. While Rome was suffering under the heel of the barbaric Huns, Justinian went on a defiant spending spree, which economically Byzantium could not afford. Hagia Sophia was meant to be Constantinople's thumb-in-the-eye of the Holy Father in Rome and Byzantium's middle finger to the Vatican. Well here's *my* salute to Constantinople!"

While his inflamed words are still rolling off his tongue, salacious monk abruptly fully extends his right arm skywards and repeatedly stabs his middle finger at the ceiling. Like a grape squished under a heavy boot, momentarily, both candle flames flatten and balloon outwards explosively as Satan drops down to possess salacious monk. Only the God Squad sees this extra-dimensional transaction behind the scenes which was hidden in plain view from the four humans at the table.

In his enraged state, salacious monk continues to lash out at Constantinople. His contempt for the Eastern Orthodox Church is palpable. Salacious monk continues his ranting, "It's a continuing battle of divergent claims. The Eastern Orthodox Churches are persistent in rejecting Vatican authority. Then there are the many theological disputes. The schisms between West and East are on-going and unrelenting. The last one called the Acacian Schism ended seventy-four years ago in 519 AD. West and East are drifting apart rapidly. The continuing clashes and hostilities are over doctrine, theology, politics, geographical separation, and over language differences. Latin and Greek don't mix, and they never will. This is a huge disconnect.

Constantinople is on a deliberate collision course with Rome. The Vatican is on alert against Byzantium. Yes, the Vatican has some major scores to settle with Constantinople!"

In this emotionally-charged atmosphere, Waraquah's brittle tone of voice is no less hardened. "Well, here are more insults from Greek Orthodox Constantinople. They believe that Mary the Mother of Jesus is *NOT* the Queen of Heaven. They believe that Mary is *NOT* our mediatrix and that Mary is *NOT* our co-redemptress. This rejection of Mary is heresy and blasphemy, which Rome *must* challenge."

Waraquah pushes future intentions, "That is why we need to massage Islam to be a composite religion based upon convenient portions of Roman Catholicism, emphasis on Mary as Queen of Heaven, emphasis on the New Testament, emphasis on the Old Testament, emphasis on the Egyptian Goddess ISIS, and on worship of the Babylonian Goddess ISHTAR (Venus). And of course, there will be key and major emphasis on ancient Arab worship of the moon god Allah. By making Allah central to Islam, the Arabs will be hooked. Allah must be central."

Regaining his breath and a measure of composure, salacious monk strips off any façade of pretence. "Here's the real scoop given to me by several cardinals. This is privileged information. You're not supposed to know it. It is well understood in the Vatican that there is no hope of future reconciliation with Byzantium at Constantinople. The Pope's decision is to remove once and for all this aggravating resistance and this challenge by the Greek Orthodox Church to Vatican primacy. The only way to do this is to arm the Arabs with Islam, so that they will overrun and crush Byzantium and remove this threat to us."

As evident by her restless hands playing nervously with her rosary beads, Khadijah is visibly in a deep quandary. She is caught up and torn in an internal conflict of clashing spiritual principles. From her squirming and her changing body language, it is obvious that Khadijah is being whipped and whip-sawed in an emotional battle for supremacy of her heart and soul. Which camp will win? Will Khadijah allow herself to continue to be part of this high-stakes political gamesmanship, intrigue, and betrayal? Which of her principles must she sacrifice? Mary is *NOT* the Queen of Heaven? Mary is *NOT* the Mediatrix?? Mary is *NOT* the co-redemptress??? Heresy? Blasphemy? Who is right? Is the

Greek Orthodox Church really correct about Mary? Her long-held spiritual beliefs are being challenged and undermined by this foreign Greek Orthodox religion that is hundreds of miles to the east. Is her own eternal destiny being jeopardized this very night? Like cheese melting under the noonday desert sun, Khadijah's hard-line disposition and resistance are in flux, but mellowing rapidly."

Khadijah treads on dangerous ground as she exposes some of her inner beliefs. "I am very concerned by the Vatican's obsession with Mary. I revere Mary, but Mary did not die on the cross, and it wasn't her blood that was shed. I could get excommunicated for making this statement, but enough said." Much to the chagrin of her partners in crime, Khadijah keeps her decision silent.

During the next 461 years, the conflicts between the Vatican and Constantinople will roil and increase in severity. In a final escalation of hostilities and mutual excommunications, the psychological warfare will culminate in the final and Great Schism of AD 1054, which continues to the present day. The East was behind the Massacre of the Latins in 1185. In revenge and in retaliation for this massacre, in 1204 AD, during the Fourth Crusade against Islam, the Vatican armies sacked and looted the Hagia Sophia Orthodox Cathedral. The Hagia Sophia and other Orthodox Church sites were converted to Latin Catholic worship. However, in 1261, the Greek Orthodox Church wrested back the Hagia Sophia Cathedral from Vatican control. The hatreds became generational. As with Ishmael, hatreds became incorporated into the DNA of the Vatican and into the DNA of the Eastern Orthodox Churches.

In spite of attempts by John Paul II and Joseph Ratzinger to bridge the Great Schism of 1054, today, the Eastern Orthodox Church of the 21st century will **NOT** accept papal primacy, papal supremacy, papal power, papal privilege OR the dogma of the pope's infallibility. Pope Benedict XVI, then Cardinal Joseph Ratzinger, had bluntly stated that none of the maximum solutions offered any real hope of unity between the Roman Catholic Church and the eastern Greek Orthodox Churches. As in 1054 AD, the 21st century Eastern Orthodox Church rejects Roman Catholicism as being heretical and pagan. The East-West schism was and continues to be fundamentally irresolvable without even the faintest possibility of reconciliation.

After a long silence, salacious monk boldly summarizes, "We really have no choice here. So we must move forward." Salacious monk simply ignores Khadijah's words of caution as he pushes his agenda forward aggressively. "Everything follows from these verses which we have documented in this Quran. So, let's restate our position on this new Quran-Allah 'religion.' In the Quran, there will be *NO* Yahweh, *NO* Elohim, *NO* Adonai, *NO* Hashem! There will be *NO* son of god! There will be *NO* crucifixion! There will be *NO* blood sacrifice! There will be *NO* resurrection! There will be *NO* atonement! There will be *NO* forgiveness of sins, except through Allah! These are the basic NOs of Quranic Islam. It's NO! NO! NO! NO! NO! NO! NO! NO! NO! and NO! With regard to Jesus, we're making sure that everything in our Quran is contrary and opposite to the Bible and opposing Jesus Christ whom we assert is *NOT* the Son of God. We must make sure that there is nothing left of Christianity. This way Islam will provide *the* one and only alternative as regards the forgiveness of sins. And that forgiveness will be earned by martyrdom for Allah's sake. How does that sound?"

"Brilliant! Pure genius!" As the master of flattery and persuasion, Waraquah lavishes compliments upon salacious monk who glows with pride. "That should stir up a hornets' nest with the Copts. Inspired! Inspired by God! Simply inspired!"

Salacious monk is ecstatic, "Any more such good lines? Any more Luciferian light?"

Waraquah is on a roll, "Besides herding goats, these Arabs are used to robbing caravans for a living. However, nobody wants to die for somebody else's cause. Even if they get paid with sex, there are limits to risk-taking. After they have accumulated enough sex slaves, they will want to quit and enjoy the spoils. Nobody wants to die willingly, but especially for someone else. So we need to devise some cunning scheme which will insure that these sand-blasted Arabs will actually want to fight for Allah until they die. We want them to *want to die* for Allah. But there must be convincing and compelling reasons why they would *want* to die a violent death.

Salacious monk snorts a hashish and spits out a put-down. "Get real! You're imagining the impossible. Die they must. But nobody but nobody is going to *want* to die willingly for Allah. So what's your game plan, Waraquah?"

Waraquah is only too willing to table his strategy. He takes a big swig of his beer as he raises his mug towards the ceiling. "Have you noticed how our inhibitions were loosened and how our ideas began to flow after our heads began to spin from all this beer? Well, immediately before the Muslims go into battle, instead of beer, we will put them into a drug-induced daze. We'll ply them with plenty of hashish and marijuana and work them up into a murderous fanatical frenzy of rage, so that they will want to kill and want to be killed for Allah. But the key to this is to persuade this would-be Ishmaelite messiah to use hashish and marijuana. We know that these mind-bending plants cause dreams and hallucinations. By using marijuana and hashish upon our future prophet and victim, Khadijah and I will be able to channel this up-and-coming Arab messiah through his visions and hallucinations."

Salacious monk is intrigued by the possibilities of hatching Waraquah's brood of serpents. He is quick to offer his support. "I'm sure that the Vatican will supply you with all the marijuana and hashish that you will ever need. So let's brainstorm further. But first, let's take a short break so that we can think about these tantalizing schemes."

Hashish and marijuana use in the Middle East dates back to the dawn of recorded history, well before the advent of Islam. However, from the times of Muhammad, records reveal the prevalent use of cannabis for spiritual insights. It is known that Muhammad used marijuana and hashish to induce hallucinations and that he had at least one very "bad trip" during his alleged revelations from the Archangel Gabriel. It is on record that in *all* the lands invaded by the Muslims, widespread use of marijuana and hashish followed.

Five minutes later, salacious monk reconvenes the group. His good eye is blood-shot from the stresses of the meeting and from the hashish. He scans the faces of his three partners in crime. "How about these convincing reasons? How about a guarantee of instant paradise for those who die fighting for Allah? If they die in Allah's cause, they will have earned the privilege to become an intercessor for seventy members of their families. That sounds mighty persuasive to me. What do you think?"

Again, salacious monk is on a power trip and he does not wait for a response. "Here are a few compelling reasons how and why a Muslim could be persuaded to give up his life willingly. I want to squeeze in this verse somewhere near the beginning. Quran 2:207 needs to read, 'But there are others who would give away their lives in order to find favor with Allah.'"

Waraquah plays the devil's advocate, "Yes, but what favors will Allah bestow on those who would give away their lives for him?"

> "But there are others who would give away their lives in order to find favor with Allah.'
>
> – Quran 2:207

Salacious monk is quick to respond, "We'll string them along and tease them for a while with another verse. Let's promise them pie-in-the-sky rewards in the hereafter for dying for Allah. How about if we put this gem of trickery somewhere near the beginning. Quran 4:74 will read, 'Let those who would exchange the life of this world for the hereafter, fight for the cause of Allah; whoever fights for the cause of Allah; whether he dies or triumphs, on him We shall bestow a rich recompense.'"

Waraquah is quick to challenge with humor, "And don't forget the wine to go with the pie in the sky." There is a burst of laughter. "Good verse, but what is this irresistible, beckoning rich recompense going to be?"

Visibly, Augustinian salacious monk is frustrated. "I'm thinking. I'm thinking. I'm thinking. Give me some time to figure it out. But in the meantime, here's another zinger that is guaranteed to kill millions of Vatican enemies. Quran 9.111 is a volcanic verse

> "Let those who would exchange the life of this world for the hereafter, fight for the cause of Allah; whoever fights for the cause of Allah; whether he dies or triumphs, on him We shall bestow a rich recompense."
>
> – Quran 4:74

reading, 'Allah has purchased from the faithful their lives and worldly goods, and in return has promised them the Garden (Paradise). They will fight for the cause of Allah, they will slay and be slain. Rejoice then in the bargain you have made. That is the supreme triumph.'"

"Allah has purchased from the faithful their lives and worldly goods, and in return has promised them the Garden (Paradise). They will fight for the cause of Allah, they will slay and be slain. Rejoice then in the bargain you have made. That is the supreme triumph."

- Quran 9.111

Initially looking skeptical, Waraquah is in the face of salacious monk once again. Then he does an about-face. "Supreme triumph? Maybe! Is it a captivating bargain? Maybe! Martyrdom in exchange for Paradise? Well, why not? It's a most compelling verse. It's a good trade-off. Paradise may be the carrot we need. Gaining Paradise is guaranteed to kill many. Sure, why not?"

Little does Waraquah know that 1,418 years later, Quran 9.111 will be the key driving verse that will be the motivation in the take-down of the twin towers of the World Trade Center on 9/11 of 2001. The date September 11, 2001, will be chosen deliberately because of its numeric symbolism to Quran 9.111. During those minutes of infamy on that single day in history on 9/11, Quran 9.111 will snuff out some three thousand American lives in New York City.

Oblivious of the horrific future impact of Quran 9.111, Waraquah gleefully continues with his agenda. "And here's a good supportive verse to go with that previous jewel. At Quran 4:104–05, it will read

"Seek out the enemy relentlessly."

- Quran 4:104-05

as, 'Seek out the enemy relentlessly.' The word *relentlessly* makes it a matter of urgency. I can hear the approaching drums of war echoing in the distance."

Salacious monk picks up this intriguing thread, "We were looking for a compelling reason why Muslims will want to kill for Allah. Well, here it is. Allah will demand fighting because he will make it obligatory. Quran 2:216 will read, 'Slaughtering people with the sword is obligatory for you, much as you dislike it. But you may hate a thing although it is good for you, and love a thing which is bad for you. Allah knows, but you do not.' This verse is a prime instance of how we want to design the Quran so that it lies through its teeth."

Waraquah's ideas continue to flow. "Now here's a permissive option. It leaves the killing open to interpretation. Since the goal is to defeat the enemies of Islamic rule, the end justifies whatever means is imaginable. Quran 17.33 justifies killing for most any reason that one can create, 'You shall not kill any man whom Allah has forbidden you to kill, except for a just cause.'"

Salacious monk grabs onto Waraquah's new twist, "Yes, those words *just cause* permit a whole lot of leeway when it comes to killing Allah's enemies. Anything and everything is allowed!"

> "Slaughtering people with the sword is obligatory for you, much as you dislike it. But you may hate a thing although it is good for you, and love a thing which is bad for you. Allah knows, but you do not."
>
> *– Quran 2:216*

Waraquah is overcome with a sudden brain wave idea, "Here is how we will compel fighting for Allah. We will write verses that will put the fear of Hell into young believers. We will have Allah punish with hellfire if He doesn't get His way. Quran 9:39 is about Allah's punishment for disobedience: 'If you do not fight, He will punish you severely.' Or we can word it differently as follows, 'If you do not go to war, He will punish you sternly, and will replace you by other men.'"

> "You shall not kill any man whom Allah has forbidden you to kill, except for a just cause."
>
> *– Quran 17.33*

> "If you do not fight, He will punish you severely.' Or we can word it differently as follows, 'If you do not go to war, He will punish you sternly, and will replace you by other men."
>
> – *Quran 9:39*

"Now let's seal it inside Quran 6:155 and make certain to connect disobedience of Allah with fear and threatening hellfire, 'Fear Allah, do not disobey His orders that you may be saved from the torment of Hell.'"

Waraquah, the Vatican theologian, is all fired up as he continues on a roll, "How's this for our Islamic Doctrine of Holy Hatred? Let us have Quran 9:38–39 make it abundantly clear that peaceful Muslims are hypocrites who are destined for Hell, 'Believers, why is it that when you are told: "March in the cause of Allah," you linger in the land? If you do not go to war, He will punish you sternly, and will replace you.'"

> "Fear Allah, do not disobey His orders that you may be saved from the torment of Hell."
>
> – *Quran 6:155*

"Let's insert two more verses to put the fear of Hellfire into hypocrites who refuse to fight and to kill for Allah. Quran 33:60–62 curses the hypocrites who want to sit on the sidelines, 'If the hypocrites and those who have tainted hearts …do not desist, we will rouse you against them. Cursed wherever they are found, they shall be seized and put to death without mercy.'"

"We will make war foundational in Quran 9:73, 'Prophet, make war on the unbelievers and the hypocrites and deal rigorously with them. Hell shall be their home.' How's that for brain washing? Do these verses create enough fear of Allah and fear of Hell?"

The foursome breaks out into hilarious laughter, as they wildly thump the table and raise high their mugs of beer. "It sounds like marvelous brain washing! Absolute fear, that's the big breakthrough! Well done, Waraquah. Well done!" shouts salacious monk.

Almost immediately, with his forehead furrowed in a worried look, salacious monk raises a serious concern. "We must take precautions so that all this killing will not be directed against our monasteries or against our Catholic Churches. Khadijah, do you have any ideas?"

> "Prophet, make war on the unbelievers and the hypocrites and deal rigorously with them. Hell shall be their home."
>
> – Quran 9:73

Khadijah gives a blank nod as she shifts her gaze from the candle flames and fixates her eyes upon the Venus pentacle dangling from the neck of salacious monk. "The goddess figure has long been in the traditions of the Roman Catholic Church going all the way back to Babylonian and Egyptian times. The Ishmaelites are heavy into goddess worship, a tradition which goes back to Egyptian ISIS and the three daughters of Allah. As Catholics, we worship Mary, the Mother of Jesus, and we pray to her. As ISIS was the Egyptian Queen of Heaven, so Mary is the Catholic or the Vatican Queen of Heaven. Why not use Mary the Mother of Jesus as the bridge between the Roman Catholic Church and this new religion which we decided to call Islam? Instead of ISIS worship or Venus worship, why not Mary worship and Queen of Heaven worship, as we Catholics do? Why not use the feminine deity in the Quran to protect the Muslim Arabs and the Catholic Churches? Why not write a chapter about Mary and put it in the Quran? We will want the Ishmaelite Arabs to hold our Mary in high esteem. The Mary connection will protect our monasteries and our Churches and cathedrals from attacks by Islam. After they have finished killing the Jews and the Orthodox Copts, this chapter on Mary will be the key to bring Islam under Vatican control."

Salacious monk is ecstatic and beaming, "Fabulous! Fabulous thinking! Fabulous idea! Simply fabulous! Now there's a splendid and powerful idea! Ninety-eight verses about Mary will do the trick."

Salacious monk shifts his attention to Waraquah and requests, "Waraquah, in the next few days, put together a chapter which we will call 'Mary: In the Name of Allah, the Compassionate, the Merciful' and include Mary in the Quran at chapter 19."

> "They shall sit with bashful, dark-eyed virgins."
>
> – Quran 37:48

In a confident tone, Waraquah goes one better. "Terrific! I will get on it first thing tomorrow morning. Now, since we're using goddesses, how about adding unlimited sex with heavenly virgins that Allah will provide as a reward in Paradise? The prospect of heavenly sex for an eternity will be strong motivation for any young Muslim stud. So let's provide them with a lot of diversity of fancy and fantasy. How about providing seventy-two heavenly virgins for each martyr for Allah's cause? Seventy-two dark-haired virgins will give them lots to dream about. But wait, for variety let's provide a few blonde virgins. At least one of these incentives ought to work. How about enticing potential male converts to Allah with a sample of free sex here and now? With all the women and girls whom they will capture from the caravans, there will be no shortage of sex slaves and free sex. Let's give the Islamic prophets and Islamic martyrs special privileges in Islam's Paradise. Let's give them up to one thousand virgins each."

Once again, all four conspirators break out into whoops of laughter as they pound the table top with their fists, sending the pitcher of beer flying off the table.

With a grin that suits him, salacious monk strokes Waraquah's ego, who then elevates this Quranic nonsense. "All right, let's begin creating this trail of sex rewards in Paradise. We'll insert a number of verses throughout the latter part of the Quran. First we discredited Jesus as the Son of God. We discredited the Jews. Then we discredited the Bible. Then we put the fear of Allah into everybody. We made martyrdom a priority to get to Paradise. Now we get to slather the sex icing on this cake to hide the poisons inside. It's good psychology to put sex rewards in the middle of the Quran and to scatter the verses widely for about twenty chapters. We will tease the sex-obsessed Muslim boys with Quran 37:48: 'They shall sit with bashful, dark-eyed virgins.'"

Gleefully, salacious monk bounces up and down on his stool. Yes, blinking and winking, bashful dark-eyed virgins running naked in Allah's Paradise, and Muslim martyrs with perpetual erections chasing them all around Paradise! We will give them a broad hint that sexual intercourse will be permitted and promoted in Paradise. Let's ignite their dreams and their passions with Quran 41:32, 'Rejoice in the Paradise you have been promised. . . . There you shall find all that your souls desire and all that you can ask for: a rich provision from a forgiving and merciful Allah.' The Christian Bible says that there will not be marriages in heaven. So why would any young virile Muslim male want to go to Christian Heaven when Allah's Paradise is an eternal whorehouse? These sex-crazed Arab boys will just be killing and dying to get to Allah's whorehouse in the sky as fast as they can, so that they can lie with these 'bashful virgins.'"

Archangel Gabriel is annoyed, angry, and exasperated with these goings-on, "This gathering of sickos doesn't stop. It goes on and on and on from one perversion to the next. We've heard more than enough! Why don't we bring down a fireball from Heaven on this piece of hell? I could use my neutron laser and leave this Catholic Cathedral standing, or I could use my mini-atomic laser and leave a giant smoking hole in the ground."

> "Rejoice in the Paradise you have been promised. . . . There you shall find all that your souls desire and all that you can ask for: a rich provision from a forgiving and merciful Allah."
>
> – Quran 41:32

Michael is sympathetic with Gabriel, but again he cautions restraint. "Let these four sickos unfold the rest of their subversions against these poor Arab Ishmaelites. We need to listen in so that we can prepare. The poor Arabs don't deserve what's coming at them from the Vatican."

Waraquah is not aware of this verbal exchange within the angelic star-gate. He continues developing his demented intrigues, "Sex could be the tipping point to push young Muslims males over the brink to become martyrs for Allah. Muslim males will need no incentives to rob caravans, to kill, and to rape. Nothing succeeds like repetition. It's called brain washing and indoctrination. Quran 56:22 and the preceding verse will stir up lust and tantalize the Arab boys as beckoned by Allah's dark-eyed virgins, 'They shall incline on jewelled couches face to face, and there shall wait on them immortal youths. . . . . And theirs shall be the dark-eyed virgins, chaste as virgin pearls.'" Pushing his sex incentives further, Waraquah continues, "Quran 56:35 is more of the same, 'We created the houris and made them virgins, loving companions for those on the right hand.' We'll leave this sex topic on a swelling high note in Quran 78:31–33, 'As for the righteous, they shall surely triumph. Theirs shall be gardens and vineyards, and high-bosomed maidens with swelling breasts for companions: a truly overflowing cup.'"

> "As for the righteous, they shall surely triumph. Theirs shall be gardens and vineyards, and high-bosomed maidens with swelling breasts for companions: a truly overflowing cup."
>
> – Quran 78:31-33

"Yes, high-bosomed maidens with swelling breasts, and lots of wine, in pottery cups or maybe in brassieres cups. We will leave this to their imaginations." Another burst of laughter and table thumping follows."

With a boast of superiority Waraquah continues, "There! Finally! We've slipped in 'dark-eyed virgins' into five different verses. We're making sure that Allah's message is loud and clear. Eternal sex will be the martyr's reward in Allah's Paradise. This is about arousing their sexual desires and their resolve to do anything and everything possible to reach this kind of sex Paradise."

Unfortunately, Waraquah isn't quite finished. He goes down a darker alley saying, "And for the Ishmaelite sodomites and pedophiles—since it's well known that Ishmaelite men seek out young boys for anal sex—let's indulge them and gratify their perversions. The Quran will promise them young boys in Paradise. Here are several verses for these sodomite bastards that will fire up their fantasies. We'll create this as a Quranic version of Sodom and Gomorrah. Quran 52:24 will throw in a few Sodomite twists as, 'and there shall wait on them young boys of their own, as fair as virgin pearls.'

"Quran 56:10–17 will throw in some young boys and immortal youths as in, 'They shall recline on jewelled couches face to face, and there shall wait on them immortal youths.'"

"Finally, in Quran 76:19, we'll slip in, 'They shall be attended by boys graced with eternal youth, who to the beholder's eyes will seem like sprinkled pearls.'"

Khadijah frowns and grimaces. "Vatican or not, Pope or no Pope, Holy Father or no Holy Father, I am drawing a red line in the desert sands on your last three verses. These are depths of immorality, chicanery, and debauchery to which I will not crawl. Sodomizing young boys is absolutely wicked in my books. It may be acceptable for Allah in his Paradise, but not here on my Earth it isn't! Here are two of my verses that I want inserted to counter what you guys just wrote. In Quran 7.81 write, 'You lust after men instead of women. Truly, you are a degenerate people. . . . Banish them from your city.'"

"In Quran 26:166, write, 'Will you fornicate with males and eschew the wives whom Allah has created for you? Surely you are great transgressors.'"

Waraquah backs down gracefully. "Okay! Okay! Okay! Cousin, we'll insert your two verses. Actually, this will work out well for us. It suits our purposes to erect conflicting verses in the Quran. This way we can contest or defend either side of the argument as the situation calls. We will fabricate such opposite views as often as possible. Splendid!"

The skinny monk has been taking notes feverishly. Sitting expressionless, salacious monk rocks back and forth on his stool, nodding approval as he stares at the candle flames. "Waraquah, that's quite the depraved load of iniquity which you've dumped upon us. Not bad for a theologian. Seventy-two heavenly virgins for every martyr for Allah? Martyrdom in exchange for eternal sex in Allah's Paradise? An eternal whorehouse in Paradise with Allah's blessings? Recycled or renewed virgins out of thin air? Sodomy and pedophilia in Paradise? My, oh, my! You have constructed this Luciferian Allah to be one perverted bastard! Now I can understand why the Holy Father chose you to be our advisor. I hate to admit it, but you are very creative and very cunning to boot. I'm beginning to appreciate you. You're a man after my own heart, you wicked devil, you!"

A sudden violent blast of wind swirls through the wide crack under the entry door and over the tabletop as it sweeps outward through the crack underneath the exit door. The haunting turbulence in its wake ruffles the parchments on the table sending them flying, upsetting the ink well and spilling its contents onto the table. The candle flames sway wildly as one candle is blown out. The explosive whoosh of the moaning wind is like the dying gasp of a tortured soul. There follows a string of profanities and loud cursings from the skinny monk, who relights the candle and proceeds to clean up the spilled ink. Unnoticed by the four conspirators at the table, Satan scowls in her anger and rage. However, the four Archangels do notice.

Michael comments to his companions, "How dare salacious monk give credit to Waraquah when it was Satan who whispered these devious ideas into Waraquah's ear? Nobody upstages Satan without future retribution. Never, never, never does anyone talk in that manner to a female or about a female who is in a position of wielding cosmic power as does Satan!"

Raphael's head snaps backward in disbelief, "Satan is a female? I've been suspecting that for a while."

Gabriel returns to his long-standing negative views on deviant human sexuality. "There! We've heard it. Twelve Quranic verses are being dedicated openly and shamelessly to perverted sex with the intent to inflame the senses. Worse yet, sex is being used as a reward and as a weapon for entry into Paradise. In addition to fear and hatred, wanton sex is being used as the third significant driving force in the Quran. This twisted sex theme continues to slither its way through human history."

The minutes drag as the skinny monk cleans up the mess and refills the ink well. With his head cocked towards his left shoulder while impatiently drumming his fingernails onto the top of the table, salacious monk needs someone to blame for this delay. His anger is visible and palpable as his droopy eyelid twitches repeatedly.

"And there shall wait on them young boys of their own, as fair as virgin pearls."

- Quran 52:24

Khadijah joins in on this disgraceful display. "Seventy-two heavenly virgins for each Allah martyr? This will cause some questionable problems for Allah. Recycled virgins won't do for Islamic martyrs. But how are these virgins going to be renewed from a previous encounter?

With this high demand for chaste virgins and eternal sex, there will be a virgin shortage in Allah's Paradise. We'll have to come up with an explanation as to Allah's source of this unlimited supply of virgins."

There is more laughter, more applause, and more table thumping as the glassy-eyed trio starts to slur their words. "Let's have another round of beer."

After Waraquah brings a measure of decorum to the meeting, he summarizes their progress, "Now let's encapsulate the main points of this Quran which we are engineering. God is *NOT* our Father. Jesus is *NOT* God. Jesus is *NOT* the Son of God. Jesus did *NOT* die on the cross. Jesus was *NOT* resurrected from the cross. Jesus did *NOT* atone for our sins and Allah is *NOT* pleased with the words of Jesus, his prophet. Allah will reprimand Jesus. Minutes ago, we had itemized the basic *NOs* of Islam. Now we have the six-plus-one basic *NOTs* of Islam."

"We need to forge some competition for the Jesus Messiah. So, here's another way-out head-banger. Islam will have Jesus descend from heaven and promote the cause of his own replacement as the Islamic messiah whom we will call the Mahdi." The skinny Augustinian secretary drops his writing quill, bends over in laughter and rolls off his stool and onto the floor in a convulsive fit of derision.

Amused by the skinny monks's antics, salacious monk can hardly contain his exuberance over this exotic and irrational brainwave. "It's going to be open season on Orthodox Christian Copts and on Jews. I have a feeling that we are about to enter a new era, an era and a geographic region that will be known as the Islamic Killing Fields. Waraquah, you may get your wish to be elevated to a cardinal. I will write to the Holy Father recommending a promotion for you. Waraquah, in my mind's eye, I can picture you in the robes of a cardinal."

With a superior look of satisfaction, salacious monk concludes, "Haven't we done a marvelous job of discrediting the Son of God? Hasn't the Quran performed an excellent demolition by defecating and urinating all over Him and all over the Bible? His Holiness, the Vicar of Christ at the Vatican will be highly pleased with our dedication to the Roman Catholic Church."

> "They shall recline on jewelled couches face to face, and there shall wait on them immortal youths."
>
> - *Quran 56:10-17*

Waraquah interjects, "Not so fast. We have forgotten one major insult. We will have Archangel Gabriel to be the messenger from Allah to our lucky Muslim candidate. We will say that it was Gabriel who brought the dreams and revelations to our chosen prophet. And of course, our Augustinian candidate will declare that it was Archangel Gabriel who dictated the Quran to him."

There is a final explosive outburst of hilarity which is cut short by a sudden powerful blast of wind as the entry door at the top of the stairs swings open abruptly, slams violently against the wall, tearing itself off its hinges, shaking the building, and blowing out all three candles. In the dark, there follow loud cursings from the Augustinians and a dull thud as the portrait of the Holy Father slams to the floor shattering its frame and ripping the Pope's face down the middle.

Gabriel smiles at his three companions. "They have a lot of audacity framing me. There, I did it. I just smashed the unholy father's frame. I couldn't restrain myself any longer. It's a brusque closure which those four Augustinian thugs didn't expect." The smile disappears and in a harsher tone Gabriel continues, "Instead, justice demands that this place be reduced to smoke and a heap of ashes."

Somber-looking Michael summarizes his perspectives of the meeting. "In the last several hours, we have witnessed an exposure of the dark side and the dark side yet to come. The Vatican is creating wicked Islam for the express purpose of using it as a sword against the Orthodox Coptic Church and against the Jews. The Vatican doesn't have the manpower to carry out its nefarious warfare in Arabia and against Jerusalem. Instead, the Pope is using the unsuspecting Arabs to carry out the doctrines of Rome, under the guise of a new religion. The Ishmaelites are about to fall for the biggest and the most evil fraud in all of human history. Islam is being constructed to be a Vatican proxy war, now and far into future generations. By design, the Vatican will appear at arm's length in order to look innocent to the outside world, while its surrogate Arabs will do the killing and the senseless dying for them. The Vatican 'Holy Father' of the Catholic Church is turning the Roman Empire upside down and on its head."

With fists clenched Gabriel is in great distress. "The Quran is being brewed in Hell's kitchen. Yes, we just have witnessed the most heinous recipe imaginable straight out of Hell's kitchen with Allah the chef presiding. Poor Arabs! Poor Ishmaelites! No peoples and no nations deserve the horror that is being unleashed upon them on this very night by the Vatican."

> "They shall be attended by boys graced with eternal youth, who to the beholder's eyes will seem like sprinkled pearls."
>
> *- Quran 76:19*

Michael summarizes, "The Vatican had enlisted Augustine with his Replacement Theology to discredit Israel and the Jews. Then three centuries later, the Vatican enlisted the Augustinian monks to create the Quran and to discredit Jesus Christ and the Christian Church."

Symbols of the crescent moon are found within the heralds of Catholic items. On the coat of arms of the national Catholic University of America, the crescent moon straddles the crossbeams of the crucifixion cross. The crescent moon is in the foreground taking precedence over the crucifixion cross, which is in the background. The Catholic Church justifies the crescent moon as representing Mary, the mother of God. There is this mysterious and strange correspondence between the Vatican and Islam, which goes back to its roots in that Augustinian dungeon inside the Roman Catholic Cathedral of old.

Throughout two thousand years of Church history, more Christians were slaughtered for their convictions under the papal Roman Empire than under any other religion. Historians have written that Christianity has proved to be "the most murderous religion there has ever been." Today, by official Vatican II doctrine, the Catholic Church treats Muslims as being saved on the same level as Christians. The Vatican reason for recognition of Islam is that Islam worships one god. Vatican Roman Catholicism recognizes Allah as the God of the Bible. In 1985, Pope John Paul II declared to an audience of thousands of Muslim youths stating, "Christians and Muslims, we have many things in common as believers and as human beings----We believe in the same

God, the one and only God, the living God." This false and audacious Vatican declaration by Pope John Paul II was his fist smashing across the face of Adonai and across the face of Yeshua Messiah.

Unofficial estimates show that since its inception more than fourteen centuries ago, the teachings of the Quran have promoted the butchering of 300,000,000 lives. The Quran blasphemes the Holy Trinity and denies the divinity and the Son-ship of Jesus Christ. On May 14, 1999, inside the Vatican, YouTube video shows Pope John Paul II bowing to the Quran and kissing the Quran in front of Shiite and Sunni leadership. On May 14, 1999, fourteen centuries after the Roman Catholic Augustinians had launched the Quran in secrecy, the Vatican confirmed Islam publicly in front of the watching world. When the Pope kissed the Quran, it all came full circle from the Vatican, to the Augustinian dungeon in the Roman Catholic Cathedral in Mecca and back to the Vatican. From its clandestine launch inside that seemingly insignificant Roman Catholic Cathedral in the desert sands of Arabia, the Quran was acknowledged and validated with a kiss by its creator source within the Vatican on May 14, 1999. This Vatican Judas Kiss, which was seen and heard around the globe and across the cosmos, was yet another thunderous slap by the Vatican across the face of Adonai and across the face of Christ the Messiah. Vatican deceptive hatred is the ultimate Fraud of the Ages, for which there will be Divine retribution.

CHAPTER 7

THE LIFE OF MUHAMMAD

Years after Sarah had evicted Ishmael and Hagar from Abraham's tents, Isaac married Rebeccah who gave birth to Esau and Jacob. Through collusion with his mother Rebeccah, Jacob defrauded his brother Esau of his birthright. To escalate the family hatreds, Esau married one of Ishmael's daughters. Now both partners of this Esau-Ishmael marriage were hurt by Abraham's women. This fanned the flames of hatred even higher. The hatreds generated by Jacob's theft of Esau's birthright are present even today. Furthermore, this Esau-Ishmael consolidation raised the hatred levels a double portion. It was far, far more than just an acrimonious family snit fest.

The year is AD 610. The place is Mecca, Arabia. Satan and her junior devil Sonneillon are hovering around, over and through a male figure tossing and turning on his bed. Expressions of emotional upheaval and pain intensify in this tortured figure as both devils are provoking and distressing his dreams with whisperings, shrieks and flashes of light.

The four angelic sentinels are at their viewing watch posts observing Muhammad's every move. Archangel Michael summarizes his recent instructions, "Adonai has directed the four of us to monitor this guy without let up. Muhammad is positioned to be the major deceiver of mankind. Muhammad is destined to shake up all of civilization from this time forward. Muhammad's plans are unfolding according to his own wicked ambitions, according to Vatican ambitions and according to Satan's designs. Muhammad has opened the doorway to Hell itself. Through his marijuana and hashish use, he not only is influenced by

Satan, but he is possessed by a legion of demons. There is Satan and her understudy Sonneillon in control of Muhammad's body and mind."

"Just observe Muhammad," points Gabriel. "Look at him writhing and convulsing in his sleep. He's having brain seizures. His dreams are straight from Hell. There, see, he has just been jolted from out of one of his demonic nightmares. Look at his eyes and that wrinkled and distorted face. He looks disturbed and terrified like a cornered animal. I can hear his heart pounding. Look at his heaving chest and the sweat rolling off him. His bedding is soaked. Do you see his neck muscles twitching with terror? Can you hear that loud whistling and roaring in his ears? It's called tinnitus and it's driving him even more mad."

Raphael moves closer to observe Muhammad's wretched convulsions. "I have witnessed thousands of cases of demonic possession but none as chilling as this one. Now he's talking to his wife Khadijah. Let's draw nearer and listen."

Muhammad is all choked up and barely able to get the words out of his mouth, "O Khadijah, I see lights and I hear sounds. I fear that I am mad. I'm afraid I'm going out of my mind. I feel that I am possessed by an evil spirit. I have been meditating throwing myself from a mountain crag."

Khadijah consoles and reassures Muhammad. She tries to calm him down, "Don't be so suspicious. It is Allah who is speaking to you."

The band of Archangels is on high alert paying careful attention to proceedings. Very much intrigued by unfolding events, Gabriel shakes his head from left to right to left. "You've just heard Muhammad admit that he was demon possessed. He's told his wife, his family, and his friends that he is demon possessed. Raphael, you're the psychiatric expert. Are these demons just visiting or have they taken possession of Muhammad?"

"Three demons have taken up permanent residence. The person who's possessed by demonic spirits knows it. Muhammad is well aware that he is being controlled by the spirit world."

Gabriel draws back in revulsion to the safety of his companions. He points at Muhammad. "I recognize those three spirits. One is the demon of lust, the second is the demon of hatred, and the third is the demon of murder."

"That's ominous in more ways than one," shudders Raphael. "The locals know that Muhammad had an encounter with a spirit in the cave of Hira. Muhammad had admitted to a violent confrontation in the dark with an 'angel' who had choked him until he began reciting what this spirit was telling him. Muhammad was terrified by the spirit that almost strangled him. He believed that he was possessed by demons, and he became suicidal. Muhammad was quoted as saying: 'I will go to the top of the mountain and throw myself down so that I may kill myself.' Look at him, his neck muscles are twitching with terror."

> "For when they were told by Muhammad that, 'There is no deity but Allah,' they replied with scorn: 'Are we to renounce our gods for the sake of a mad poet?"
>
> – Quran 37:36

"Prior to Muhammad's time, Arabs believed that great poets were inspired by the demon of poetry," exclaims Gabriel. "Many who knew Muhammad believed that his revelations came from demons and that he was demon-possessed. In Quran 37:36, Muhammad recorded that those around him thought that he was a 'mad poet.' Quran 37:36 reads, 'For when they were told by Muhammad that, 'There is no deity but Allah,' they replied with scorn: 'Are we to renounce our gods for the sake of a mad poet?'"

"It is well known in Muhammad's community that he is addicted to marijuana and to hashish." Gabriel continues, "People around Muhammad thought that he was crazy and possessed by demons. In Quran 44:14, Muhammad had written that those around him had said that he was a 'madman.' Quran 44:14 reads, 'But how will their new faith help them, when an undoubted apostle did come to them and they denied him, saying: 'A madman, taught by others!' Either Muhammad was demon possessed, or he had epileptic seizures, or both."

"Going forward in time, there exists a long history of cannabis use and its spiritual use in the Islamic world, but especially among the Sufis and the Ismailis." Medical historian Raphael is well aware of the backlash of marijuana/hashish addiction. "Although booze and opium are forbidden, cannabis is not forbidden in the Quran. For at least six millennia, Arabian people had used cannabis in healing medicine. From its ancient past, hashish has been of accepted importance in Persian mysticism. Muhammad's alleged flight to Mecca was an out-of-body experience that was enabled by hashish. It is well known today that occultic mystics channel spirits while under the influence of hashish. Some cannabis users will experience the same mental aberrations as did Muhammad. If intelligent Muslims know that Muhammad was a hashish addict who was demon possessed or that he was very ill, and if people read Quran 37:36 and Quran 44:14, and they still adhere to Islam, then there is no other earthly logic which will prevail."

"Say, just look behind us." Raphael continues, "The hood partly covers the face. But isn't that Sariel, the Angel of Death? Doesn't she keep tabs when there is demonic possession and when the wicked kill each other? I hate to say it, but Sariel is like a circling vulture waiting for the kill."

"But how will their new faith help them, when an undoubted apostle did come to them and they denied him, saying: 'A madman, taught by others!'"

- Quran 44:14

Michael confirms Raphael's analysis. "The last time when I saw Sariel in action was during the tenth plague of Egypt. At that time she was commanded to kill every firstborn in Egypt, but she passed over the houses with blood on the doorposts. Her presence can only mean that there will be much slaughter about to take place shortly. Without fail, Sariel's presence has always been associated with much bloodshed and death."

Gabriel is visibly ill at ease as he shrinks back. "Because of her job description, I'm uncomfortable to be around her. I'll keep my distance from her. I've never dared to follow her to see where she takes her spirit prisoners. Michael, what really happens behind the scenes with Sariel?"

As supreme military commander who coordinates all heavenly operations, Michael explains Sariel's role. "Her job is not pleasant. Spare yourself the curiosity and the anguish. Poor Sariel. She must have nightmares regularly. But then again, she's doing penance for screwing up. Sariel's job is to escort the unwilling to their eternal destination in Hell. The closer she gets to the pit of Hell, the hotter it becomes. Suddenly, the disembodied spirits wake up to their new reality. And they do not want to go there. Many had been deceived during their lifetimes. During their final dark journey, many realize that paradise with virgins and eternal sex is a lie and a cruel hoax. They see the spirits of their angry victims whom they had murdered. Often Sariel has to chain her spirit prisoners and to drag them tugging, screaming, and shrieking all the way to their timeless prisons. I don't envy her."

Rather hesitantly and with a visible tremor Raphael asks, "Is it true that Sariel is one of the fallen rebel angels who has been redeemed? How did that come to be?"

With considerable trepidation, Michael paces back and forth. He replies with slow and deliberate words, "Sariel was one of the two hundred Watcher Angels who had descended upon Mount Hermon. There are rumors flying around in the heavens, but no one is really sure. Is she a she or is she a he? No one knows that either. There is just so much innuendo about her or him that I get goose bumps just talking about it. But I do know that Sariel is on a special mission. However, Adonai has not spoken to anyone about it. How about you Gabriel? What do you know? Adonai usually tells you first when it comes to women."

"Well, He did provide some background," shrugs Gabriel.

Hesitantly, Raphael ventures, "I would feel more comfortable if she or he, whichever, did not join us. Besides, I would be stuck for knowing what to say to her or to him."

With boldness in his voice, Gabriel throws out a challenge, "Now just hold on a moment. Don't write her, or him, off so quickly. I'm prepared to give her or him the benefit of the doubt. It's true that Sariel was the leading angel who lusted after the daughters of men. However, it is not for her rebellion that she was thrown out of Heaven. It was for her indiscretion that Sariel was sent to Earth. Now she has been given the unwelcome job of paying for her bad judgment when she broke Adonai's celestial law. She failed to remember that angels must not fall in love with mortals. It's the Nephilim problem all over again. However, in her case, I do not consider that to be rebellion. Apparently, neither does Adonai. He has given her an opportunity to redeem herself. Remember that on a number of occasions Sariel did work alongside all three of you. Give him or her a break. Besides, we need all the support which we can get."

"Hey, listen up! Muhammad is talking to his wife Khadijah." Michael hushes the others. "Listen, he is saying to Khadijah, 'It's the Archangel Gabriel who is bringing messages to me from Allah.'"

Upon hearing these words, Gabriel is incensed and on the verge of losing his cool. Gabriel draws his laser, but his fellow angelic combatants quickly restrain him.

"What? Me? Bringing messages from Allah to Muhammad? That low-down murderous sex pervert! He's maligning me and ruining my reputation. Lies from Lucifer!" laments a visibly angry Gabriel. "I don't bring messages to Muhammad *ever*!"

Michael understands Muhammad's strategy to undermine Adonai's plans. Michael reviews past history with Gabriel. "It was you who had brought the good news to Elizabeth about John the Baptist. It was you who had brought the good news to Mary about the birth of Jesus. It was you who had brought the word that Christ the Messiah was the Son of God, as the Son of Adonai."

Gabriel stomps his foot and clenches his fist. "Yes, but now this liar, this deceiver, this madman, and this murderer is bent on denying all of that. And he's attributing it to me? Why me? What is this Islam business all about? And who's this Allah pretender? Is Allah a senior devil or is Satan masquerading as Allah?"

Reluctantly, Michael brings more bad news to Gabriel. "I don't know the answer to some of your questions. I do have to check in with Adonai, but it does appear that Satan is masquerading as Allah. And it gets worse. I regret to tell you this. Satan, a.k.a. Allah, is using your name to justify Muhammad's misdeeds. I call it a smear campaign to discredit the Christian Church. Raphael attempts to bring a measure of solace to Gabriel. "For generations, Allah, the moon god has been worshipped by Muhammad's tribe. There is nothing new or different here. Muhammad knows the history behind Ishmael's humiliation and he has adopted it personally to be his humiliation as well. Ishmael's radical hatred has become Muhammad's radical hatred. This is all about hatred, revenge, power, and political gamesmanship. Muhammad is attempting to convince the local tribes that there is a new celestial plan afoot as Allah's decree. However, Islam is nothing more than a continuation of this moon god worship. Gabriel, you have the right to be upset. I would be angry too. Over the last several years, this nut job has attempted suicide a number of times. For years he has been plagued with doubts that maybe Satan is pulling his strings. There is no denial. Satan is controlling Muhammad's destiny. This very night, we have witnessed the demonic aura around Muhammad. Arabs in Mecca know all about Muhammad's suicide attempts. It's unthinkable that someone possessed by Satan, and bent upon suicide would be considered to be a great spiritual leader under divine guidance."

Raphael looks him in the eye as he questions Gabriel. "Have you considered why Muhammad has chosen you as his target angel? He could have chosen Michael or Uriel, or me, or even Sariel. Why would Muhammad choose you?"

Shrugging his shoulders and venturing a guess, Gabriel puzzles, "You know that I understand female psychology better than any male angel can. I understand the cycles of the moon. I know how the moon influences the ocean tides and the menstrual cycle of many females. I will always be associated with water and with the moon. Maybe Muhammad is making a connection between Allah and me because of my association with the moon."

Cocking his head to his left, Raphael replies, "It sounds like a logical association. However, you should be thankful that you have had no contact with this low-life thug. Even with your extra-terrestrial powers, this guy would not hesitate to try to sodomize even an archangel. Muhammad has entertained thoughts of attempting a physical union that is the opposite of the Nephilim creation. Instead of fallen male angels having sex with earthly females, Muhammad as a male would go out of his way to have sex with a heavenly angel or to sodomize a male angel. Muhammad is the sex pervert of the age. Muhammad has boasted that in paradise, he will marry Mary the mother of Jesus and force intercourse with her. Clearly this is demonic intent. Muhammad has no shame, no decency, no morals, no scruples, and no respect for any man or woman dead or alive. His sword is the extension of his penis."

Uriel brings to memory a distant event. "Twenty-five-hundred years ago, we heard Gabriel bring Adonai's message to Hagar that Ishmael would be 'a wild ass of a man.' As a descendent of Ishmael, Muhammad's radical behavior is the exaggeration of Ishmael's description. Muhammad also is that 'wild ass of a man, his hand against every man and every man's hand against him.'"

As the legal expert, Archangel Michael comes to the defence of Gabriel and provides a different perspective. "All of Heaven knows your special place with Adonai. He has given to you an understanding of women about whom the rest of us males know almost nothing. You are a great man of God but Adonai has given to you the sensitivity of a woman. You are His Messenger Archangel of Communication. He had sent you to deliver His messages to Daniel. Adonai chose you to be His messenger to Elizabeth and to Mary. So please forgive the rest of us guys when we are just a little bit jealous of your special status with Adonai. We know that you are more of a man than the rest of us."

Michael now proceeds to reveal to the God Squad the depths of Satan's strategy and her tactics of war. "The choice of Gabriel is clear and necessary for Muhammad's wicked designs. Muhammad is using Gabriel to validate and to justify his fabrications and his distortions. Gabriel is Muhammad's mantle of credibility. Indirectly, by choosing Gabriel, Muhammad denies Gabriel's previous message made more than six hundred years ago to Mary the mother of Jesus. The Vatican's choice of Gabriel, and Muhammad's choice of Gabriel raise doubts and shakes the very foundations of the Church. In one swoop, Muhammad and Satan are attempting to destroy Christianity through Gabriel. Very clever! This cunning ploy is designed to raise all manner of doubts and questions about Adonai, questions such as why did Adonai change His mind? Are Adonai and Allah the same Person? Why would Gabriel bring a contradictory message six hundred years later? By promoting Muhammad, Gabriel thereby would reduce Jesus to just another prophet of a lesser stature. In front of the eyes of the world, Muhammad's fraud strips Adonai of having a Son. It negates Jesus' blood sacrifice. It negates His atonement for sin. And basically, it really discredits Adonai and makes Him out to be a liar. You, Gabriel are the central and the key figure of Islam. The entire Quran stands or falls upon your messages to Muhammad. You have been chosen by Muhammad to provide him with the flawless and perfect cloak of legitimacy. At the same time, Muhammad is mocking you and crapping all over you Gabriel. Muhammad is telling you that he hates you. Muhammad's Quran is a message of Satanic hatred designed to undermine Adonai and to destroy the Christian Church. In this context, you, Gabriel, stand defiant and stand tall!"

With slow and deliberate words, Michael continues, "Remember, that we are not fighting a man. We are up against Allah, a.k.a Satan, and all the powers of Hell." Michael, the legal beagle intones as he expands upon his previous words, "Gabriel, this is a devilishly clever and wicked strategy by Satan to use you and to accuse you falsely as Allah's mouthpiece. This Satanic ploy is designed to tell the world that Adonai had lied to you, that Adonai had lied to Mary, that Adonai had lied to the world, and that Adonai has changed his mind and that Jesus is not his Son. By Islamic construct in the Quran, all of a sudden, Adonai does not have a Son."

Gabriel searches the heavenly database for Muhammad's writings. Because angels move freely back and forth across the time dimension in many cases, Gabriel is able to retrieve Quran 4:171. Gabriel quotes from the Quran. 'The Messiah, Jesus son of Mary, was no more than Allah's apostle and His Word which He cast to Mary: a spirit from Him. So believe in Allah and His apostle and do not say 'Three.' Forebear, and it shall be better for you. Allah is but one God. Allah forbid that He should have a son.'"

"Do not say, 'Three.' 'Desist!' Clearly, that's outright denial. In Islam, to believe in the deity of Christ is an unforgivable sin. However, legend has it that although Allah the moon god has no son, Allah does have three daughters. Where are Allah's daughters? What are his daughters doing? Are they co-rulers with Allah?"

Raphael considers the verse, 'Allah is but one God. God forbid that He should have a son,' and is visibly stirred. "The Quran makes references to the Old Testament, but Muhammad conveniently forgets about the book of Isaiah and the psalms. **Isaiah 7:14** reads, 'a young woman shall conceive and bear a son and shall call his name Immanuel.' It's difficult to miss that Immanuel is the Messiah. **Psalm 2:7** reads,

'You are my son, today I have begotten you.' It's even more difficult for Islam to miss that Adonai does have a Son. How is Islam able to ignore these revealing verses?"

Michael, the legal specialist, answers Raphael from a historical perspective. "The Quran is twisted revisionist Biblical history. Waraquah, Khadijah, and Muhammad modified and twisted the books of the Bible to suit their purposes. They rejected verses that they could not falsify. Instead, they attributed these verses to corrupt Jewish and Christian scholars whom Islam accuses of distorting the Bible *after* Muhammad had written the Quran. However, the overwhelming weight and frequency of diverse ancient manuscripts, which predate the Quran by more than six-hundred years, do not support Islam's falsifications. Instead, ancient historical records which predate the Quran by many centuries expose the Quran for the deception and the fraud that it is."

Gabriel is clear when he summarizes Muhammad's counterfeit Quran. "It's obvious that the Quran is a frontal attack upon Adonai and upon the Christian Church. Clearly, the god of Islam and the God of the Bible are not the same power."

As a brilliant military strategist, Michael does not underestimate the power of his adversary. "We've seen that this cunning murderer is also a clever military schemer. Now we are hearing that Muhammad is insisting that he is Allah's prophet and that the whole world must submit to Islam and to Allah, or die."

In a raised voice, Michael echoes and mocks Muhammad's declaration. "If the world does not submit to Allah willingly, then they must be forced to bend their knee at the point of a sword. If they do not submit and if they refuse to acknowledge Allah as supreme and Muhammad as his prophet, then they shall die by the sword. Those are the words of Muhammad. Submit to Allah or die. Make no mistake, the real and final battle is between Adonai and Satan-Allah."

The year is AD 623. The place is Mecca.

The four Archangels known as the God Squad are monitoring Muhammad's activities. Gabriel is the first to notice a shocking event.

"What's he doing with that little girl? She looks to be no more than six years old. Does anyone know her name?"

"I do," replies Raphael. "Her name is Aisha. I'm appalled by what I'm seeing. It looks like a marriage ceremony. This guy is fifty-three years old. Aisha is six years old. Muhammad is saying to Aisha that Allah told him to marry her?"

Gabriel looks at each of his three companions. "Should we take this pervert out now before the marriage to this child proceeds?"

In a chorus, the answer is a fearful "No!"

Raphael points in the direction of the chimney. "Whom do you see behind the chimney?"

"Whoa! That's Satan with twelve other devils. I'm not ready for that kind of confrontation just yet," replies Michael, the cautious strategist. "Let's withdraw but let's keep these thirteen pedophiles in constant view."

Lurking in the shadows of the chimney, Satan points to the four Archangels as she addresses Sonneillon. "No secrets here. We see them, and they see us. There are thirteen of us and only four of them. Just ignore them. They wouldn't dare to make a move against us. What's important is that we have the big prize. I've been a long time looking for this murdering sex-crazed Ishmaelite. Muhammad is our ultimate weapon. And of course, Sonny, Muhammad is so full of hatred that you will enjoy working with him. Ambition and hatred driven by extreme violence, sex addiction, and hashish addiction are the ideal combination for our purposes. Remember the fun that you and I had with Abraham, Hagar, Ishmael, and that piece of work Sarah? It was all about forbidden sex way back then, and it's still about sex today. Finally, after fourteen-hundred years, I have found the perfect weapon against Adonai. Muhammad will shake the world."

The year is AD 624. The place is near Badr, Arabia. Muhammad leads an unprovoked and vicious attack upon a caravan. After killing forty males, Muhammad plunders its riches. He takes the women and children as slaves. He rapes whomever he desires. Muhammad then murders twenty-five Meccans who had opposed him. In cold blood, he beheads an old enemy whom he has just captured. Muhammad puts all prisoners to the sword. As recorded in Quran 8:67, through gritted teeth Muhammad hisses, "A prophet may not take captives until he has fought and triumphed in the land."

"A prophet may not take captives until he has fought and triumphed in the land."

- Quran 8:67

As the Archangel of health and wellness, Raphael is sickened to see the unspeakable evil and savagery of Muhammad and his legions of radical killers for Allah. Raphael turns his face away from the ruthless slaughter of innocents in front of him and laments, "Assassinations, murder, cruelty, torture, and beheading of prisoners all in the name of Allah. Just hear Muhammad's murderers boast about their deeds of fearlessness. Killing for Allah is a badge of honour that is justified by the Quran."

The four angelic sentinels scrutinize events from their watch stations. Michael strains to look at the horizon. "See that figure in the distance. That's Sariel proceeding to her call of duty. She will dispatch the souls of the slaughtered to their final destinations. Today is but a small indication of the ruthless bloodshed of millions that will soak the sands of Arabia blood red. Sariel will be a very busy Angel of Death."

Uriel, who is usually the silent one, makes some astute conclusions about Muhammad's dysfunctional family origin. "The roots of Muhammad's radical hatred go back to the tragic events which broke up Abraham's household. Islam is the spectre that forever haunts the alienated members of Abraham's clan. Their hatreds have smoldered in the sands of Arabia for many generations. This driving obsession to redress their shame of being expelled from Abraham's tents continues today. When the Jews rejected Allah and Muhammad as his prophet, the heat of ancient murderous passions flared up. We are witnessing those raging fires of hatred in front of us this very moment. Unfortunately, this Islamic drive to dominate the world is the consuming fire storm of the ages."

"Well spoken, Uriel," quips Gabriel. "Being in charge of the sun and galaxies, you would know all about flames and fire storms."

Uriel continues to provide his galactic viewpoint. "Yes, it's easy to control the behavior of the sun. The sun is perfectly predictable. Controlling the fires of Hell is unpredictable and nearly impossible. It's the flames of hatred which have driven Islam to be obsessed with exterminating Israel, the Jews, and the Christians. Islam has embraced the hate-driven spirit of Ishmael. Muhammad has chosen to enshrine violence in Islam forever by making a religion out of hatred, vengeance, and killing. Muhammad is making the Quran into a book of sex and slaughter. The Quran threatens death and damnation against every infidel-kafir."

Uriel refers to his palm computer. "The Quran database speaks of the killing of Jews and infidels. Here's a quote, 'May Allah destroy them,' and another quote, 'Seize them and kill them wherever you find them.' Quran 9:5 commands to 'slay the idolaters wherever you find them. Arrest them, besiege them, and lie in ambush everywhere for them.' Quran 2:191 through to Quran 2:193 command Muslims to, 'Slay them wherever you find them… put them to the sword.' There is nothing left to the imagination. Killing infidels, Christians and Jews is a core command in the Quran. Enshrined in the Quran, the exhortation to kill is not open to question or to misinterpretation."

"At my last count, there are 112 verses in the Quran which command Muslims to chop off heads, arms, legs, and fingers, to make war, and to kill non-Muslims," adds Gabriel.

> "Slay them wherever you find them… put them to the sword."
>
> - *Quran 2:191 through to Quran 2:193*

Michael, the cosmic legal beagle, intervenes with the hard evidence. "There are more than fifty separate references in the Quran on the duties and the demands of fighting Holy War. The Quran commands Allah's followers to spread Islam by force of arms throughout the entire world. Killing infidels as Christians and Jews is never an option. Killing Infidels and Jews is an Islamic duty. Failure to kill for Allah or failure to martyr oneself is punishable by Hellfire. Masquerading as a religion, the Quran is a political manifesto for world domination. At this very moment, as we are observing on this field of blood and slaughter, Islam is being spread at the point of the sword.

Severed heads roll in the dirt and in the bloody mud. In shrieks of pain and anguish, infidel flesh is being crushed, splattered, and spattered under the hooves of horses. As we are witnessing the inhumanity and the depravity before us today, infidel blood and minced flesh will continue to flow ankle-deep until the end of this age. In Muhammad's Quran, threats of Islamic Hell await Muslims who do not partake in this Holy War against the Jew, against the Christian, and against other infidels."

The year is AD 626. The place is Mecca. Three years have elapsed. Once again, it is Gabriel who is at the forefront. "Aisha is nine-years-old. There's Aisha playing with her dolls and her three friends."

Raphael observes Muhammad in Aisha's bedroom. "Yeah, and there's that sexual predator making ready to penetrate nine-year-old Aisha."

Aisha's mother brings Aisha into her bedroom and makes her sit on Muhammad's lap. All the adults leave the house. They don't want to be part of this shameful betrayal by Aisha's family.

With a painful look of anger and disgust, Gabriel erupts. "Everyone's aware of Muhammad's violent and bloody history. It is reckless suicide to deny Muhammad his every wish, but especially when it comes to sex. And just like that, he's penetrated Aisha! This fifty-six-year-old Muhammad prophet has just raped nine-year-old Aisha. This is grotesque and heinous. He has no morals, no scruples, no principles. This guy is a sexual deviate and a total sex monster. Aisha is innocent enough that she may not realize what he just did to her. See, she's going back to her dolls and her three friends again. Look by the chimney. There's Satan and her dirty dozen whooping it up in approval."

The four children continue swinging and playing with their dolls as if nothing happened. However, Aisha says nothing to her three friends, but clearly she is not participating in her former joyous manner. The distant look in her eyes tells the real story unfolding inside. Without blinking her eyes, she sits and stares at the horizon. Her childhood innocence has been ripped away. Psychologically, the damage is irreparable. Years later, Aisha's anger will boil over. Standing at a distance and shaking her head in utter disbelief, is twenty-one-year-old

Fatima looking upon Aisha who now is her nine-year-old stepmother and who still is playing with dolls. Fatima understands the utterly twisted transaction which has just been perpetrated by her father upon a nine-year-old child.

Raphael correctly predicts, "The seeds have just been sown for future warfare between Aisha's followers and Fatima's followers. Another war of the women is in its infancy."

As Gabriel lunges forward towards Muhammad, he shouts, "Let me at him! Let me at this slimy scoundrel! Just let me at this perverted child molester!"

Michael moves quickly to grab Gabriel's right arm while Raphael takes hold of Gabriel's left arm. Uriel swoops in front of Gabriel to block his forward momentum. With much difficulty, the trio of Archangels is barely able to restrain Gabriel.

It takes many minutes before Gabriel regains his composure. It takes even longer for him to stop shaking. After a further time of silence, he warns the trio, "Sometime in the near future, when you least expect it, I will put an end to this life of salacious debauchery."

Michael, Raphael, and Uriel are quietly supportive and sympathetic. Michael, who is aware of the public views in Mecca, volunteers the commonly held feelings. "Muhammad's family, his neighbours, supporters, and his enemies are all agreed that he is mad and demon-possessed. That's in keeping with Muhammad's own assessments of himself. He is deeply troubled and tortured. Neither incest nor rape nor murder is a moral deterrent for Muhammad. Nothing but nothing can stand in the way of his unbridled lust for power and for sex. Everyone but everyone is afraid of crossing this guy. No one dares to turn his back on Muhammad. No one wants to take on a violent bully with an army of crazed sex fanatics carrying swords. Gabriel, the three of us are as distressed with Muhammad as you are. We are trying desperately hard to keep our impulses in check with this piece of Hell on Earth. This Muhammad thug makes up the rules to suit his deviant pleasures, and then he writes them in his book as revelations from Gabriel. His Quran 2:223 entry reads, 'Women are your fields: go, then, into your fields whence you please.'"

"Women are your fields: go, then, into your fields whence you please."

– Quran 2:223

"Muhammad treats women with contempt." Gabriel cuts to the chase, "This fornicator of all time will take sex willingly or force it at any time, at any place and with no restrictions, even as to age."

In the shadows and in the enveloping smoke from the chimney, the demonic thirteen are celebrating another victory. The Islamic Hadiths record that Aisha took her dolls with her to Muhammad's house. Whenever Muhammad was not having sex with her, the child in Aisha needed to play with her dolls. Was this her psychological regression to a time of innocence? Was it a protective denial of a horrible reality that was forced upon her? Will this poison explode from her later in life? Yes, it will, and in a manner that has killed and is killing millions of lives.

The Bukhari Hadiths record that this debauched sexual glutton "used to visit all of his wives in a round, during the day and night and they were eleven in number."

Leaving his three Archangel companions, Gabriel is away on assignment. Raphael uses this opportunity to probe the deeply disturbing issues set in motion by Muhammad's marriage to Aisha. Raphael who understands mental health issues is puzzled by Muhammad's dangerous obsessions. "Unbridled sex, hatred, violence, and hunger for power make for a deadly combination indeed. We know the roots of Muhammad's radical hatred. His preoccupation with sex is unrivalled. Records show that Muhammad had sex with sixty-six women. This monster Muhammad has distorted sex and made it into a religion. Just check out the place of women in his Quran. The Quran records sex on demand, 'Women are your fields, go into your fields as you please.' Today, Muhammad has sex with anyone he pleases, whenever he pleases, and wherever he pleases.

The year is AD 629. The place is the Battle of Khaibar. The four Archangels are looking on as the Jews are defeated by the Muslim army. The Jewish leader is tortured and beheaded.

In the aftermath of the bloody slaughter, Raphael comments, "More of the same! Muhammad kills the Jewish leader and takes his beautiful wife Safiyah. While the battlefield blood is still running with her husband's blood, Muhammad forces sex upon Safiyah."

Several days later, "He won't be ravaging her for long." Gabriel is pleased to say as he watches Safiyah cook a sheep which she has laced with poison. Gabriel watches as Muhammad and his companions partake of their just reward. Gabriel thinks to himself, "Eat hearty, you murderous, rapist scoundrels."

Muhammad and everyone around him know that he has been poisoned. For the next three years Muhammad suffers from terrible pains inflicted by the toxin. There is no question that Muhammad was poisoned. But is this the poison which finally killed Muhammad three years later?

The year is AD 630. There is an air of suspense and anticipation within the angelic God Squad. Michael makes an announcement. "There are rumors that Aisha is cheating on Muhammad with a young Arab called Safwan. There is bound to be a major crisis if Muhammad finds out. Let's keep Aisha under observation while Muhammad is doing battle. Aisha has just left the armed campsite pretending to go to the loo. Now she's talking to Safwan in the shadow of that sand dune to our left. This is no accidental meeting. It appears that this encounter was pre-arranged."

Muhammad's raiders defeat the Jewish tribe of Bani Al Mustalik. As usual, the men are butchered and their women and children are taken captives. One of the captives is Juwayreya, wife of the chief of the Jewish tribe. She is stunningly beautiful. With his cloak beginning to bulge, Safwan whistles in low tones as he observes Juwayreya. "She has got to be the most beautiful woman in Arabia. I can hardly take my eyes off her."

Aisha moans, "Stop lusting after her. Just look who's taking her as his slave, my husband Muhammad. I already hate her. First, he'll fornicate with her if he can and then he will take her as his wife. Just watch. He's done this before. Muhammad doesn't need all that booty from robbing caravans. He's after all those young girls. He'll butcher their fathers and their husbands just so that he can capture the women and the young girls and rape them. It's all about sexual gratification for him. His penis rules his entire life. Muhammad is Allah's Phallic Prophet."

Safwan questions, "Why do you allow him to marry so many women? I hear that Muhammad does all his wives in a round within a single night. Is that true? No man in his sixties can manage to do this. How does he manage to perform such physical feats?"

"Don't believe a word of it," Aisha sneers. "Since he was poisoned, there's no such performance. It's only empty boasting. This guy is an unbelievably smooth liar. Since that Jewess Safiyah poisoned him, Muhammad hasn't been able to have an erection. All that he can do now is to lick the female parts. I've asked a few of his other wives, and that's all that he does with them. He certainly can't satisfy me. I need a young stud who can perform and penetrate."

With some hesitancy, Sufwan ventures sheepishly. "I'm sure that I could meet your expectations on both counts."

Aisha squeals gleefully, as she bounces off the camel's back and follows Sufwan behind a sand dune.

Blushing, Gabriel addresses his companions, "Okay, okay. It's time for tea. Let's go."

Two hours later, an exhausted Safwan and a satisfied Aisha ride into Mecca on his camel. Aisha is sitting behind Safwan. Gabriel looks on in disbelief. "Look at the crowd with their mouths open, staring at those two. You can almost hear what they're thinking. A married woman in the company of a man who is not her husband is an absolute no-no. Muhammad is absolutely livid! There's Muhammad's daughter Fatima clucking and shaking her head in disbelief and shame. The hostile expression on her face makes it clear that another chapter of female intrigue is unfolding."

Seven minutes later, Aisha dismounts the camel in front of her home. Two minutes later, with pounding hoof beats in a cloud of dust, Muhammad pulls his Arabian steed to a sharp halt. In a furious rage, he dismounts abruptly and stomps to the door.

Once inside the house, Muhammad lets loose with invectives. "You little slut! You've humiliated me in front of hundreds of Meccans. Did Safwan screw you?"

"I'll never tell." Aisha snaps back. "But I will tell you that I could see by the tilt of his cloak that he had an erection. Too bad that's something that you aren't able to do any more since Safiyah poisoned you."

Defiantly waving her fists, Aisha screams at Muhammad, "You raped me when I was still playing with dolls. You stole my childhood, you pervert. And now you accuse me when all the while you kill men and rape their wives and their children. Weren't you getting enough sex from me that you needed all those others? You abandoned me to have sex with Juwayreya, your new sex slave. I am jealous of her! I am very angry, and I hate her."

With his eyes radiating hatred, Muhammad screams at Aisha. "Allah has given me his permission for doing sex with slaves."

Aisha screams back with sarcasm, "Allah, shmallah! How convenient for you. You're just farting through your teeth, you scoundrel! Your Allah is just too willing to bend to your every sex wish. Anything you want, Allah gives to you. You see a beautiful woman and Allah gives you permission to fornicate her. Or is Allah just a convenient fabricated excuse, you $*#!% liar?"

"You think that you're so superior that you have the right to kill anyone who doesn't bow down to your Allah. Then you make up terrifying verses like Quran 8:12 where you threaten to cut off the heads and fingertips of those who disbelieve."

Gesturing wildly, Muhammad fingers his sword as he approaches Aisha. When he is nose to nose with her, he points in the direction of the animal enclosure. "Anyone who doesn't submit to Allah is like those goats that can be killed without a second thought. If they don't bow down to Allah, they're not even human. They're lower than your goats. With a clear conscience, they can be robbed, enslaved or beheaded."

"And you say that Allah's Hell is full of women? You have nothing but contempt for women." Aisha snarls, "It's more than obvious that you are full of Ishmael's hatred for women. Adonai was right when He said that Ishmael would be an ass of a man with his hand against every man and every man's hand against him. You too are an ass of a man and you kill everyone who disagrees with you."

In a fit of rage, Muhammad becomes unhinged. As he screams out, he slams his sword across a wooden stool sending pieces of it flying towards Aisha, "Enough! Who is this Adonai? There is no God but Allah!"

Aisha is not intimidated as she screams back, "Like Ishmael, you too are that ass of a man!"

"Enough! Enough!! Enough!!! I will wait one month. If you don't bleed, I'll cut your head off with this sword. One way or another, there will be blood. You send word to me when you are having your period."

With those words, Muhammad storms out of the house slamming the door behind him.

Aisha thinks to herself, "Either Safiyah didn't use the right poison or she didn't use enough of it. But I will see about that."

One month passes. Once again Muhammad rides in on pounding hooves and in a cloud of dust. Once inside Aisha's house, he doesn't waste any words. "Prove it, bi*ch! I want to see for myself," Muhammad hisses through clenched teeth.

Aisha throws herself onto her back on her bed. She lifts her dress above her head, revealing her south end which silences Muhammad. She bends her knees towards her breasts and spreads her legs wide. Muhammad does a double take. She thrusts her hips provocatively, "Have a good look, you salacious sex addict, but don't touch! There! Are you satisfied now? And it isn't rooster blood either. It's menses blood, my blood."

After staring at her tempting southern exposure, Muhammad realizes that his insatiable sexual urges are aroused. He is mesmerized. However, he turns abruptly and leaves coldly and rudely in the same manner with which he entered.

Uriel expresses his wonderment. "Now there's a feisty thirteen-year-old teenager who is not afraid to challenge the most barbaric sex tyrant of all time."

The next day, Muhammad advertises to everyone he meets, "The Archangel Gabriel brought me word from Allah that Aisha is innocent of any wrong doing. Accidentally, Aisha was left behind when the army moved on. Safwan found her and brought her back. Nothing else happened."

Recorded history reads otherwise.

Uriel, who usually is preoccupied with celestial matters, mockingly asks, "So why did Allah wait a whole month before declaring that Aisha was innocent? What took her so long before Allah broke her silence? But of course, we know the truth. However, no one in Mecca believes Muhammad's version of his 'truth' either. Safwan did have sex with Aisha. By boast or by accident, Safwan blurted out to his friends about his sexual tryst with Aisha. It's no secret. Tsk! tsk! tsk! Allah! Allah!! Allah!!! You need to pay attention instead of spending time with your 'young boys as fair as virgin pearls' up there in your paradise, you perverted sodomite. And Muhammad maintains that Allah told Gabriel that Aisha did not have sex with Safwan. It's good that Gabriel is not here to listen to another of Muhammad's insults. Gabriel would be greatly distressed and angry to hear his name being defamed and slandered again."

"Rumors of Aisha's adultery and Allah's one month of silence have spread throughout the city and surrounding areas." Michael is most reluctant to review this salacious conduct. "Silence from Allah for a whole month means that Aisha is guilty. Because Aisha is a young and spoiled teenager, the gossip has exploded with accusation and innuendo which have discredited Muhammad's claim to being a prophet of Allah. This highly suspicious, scandalous, and infamous encounter in the desert between Aisha and Safwan has demoralized Muhammad, has undermined his integrity, has created doubts about Allah, and has split the Islamic communities asunder. This gossip is disintegrating into bitter internal Islamic backlash."

From this point forward, internecine Islamic wars have continued for over fourteen centuries, having killed hundreds of thousands of Muslims. It's Aisha versus Fatima and Sunni versus Shiite.

Because of the prevailing culture, there is a great deal of head shaking within the God Squad. Raphael reveals further shattering disclosures, "In Muhammad's military campaign against the Jewish Tribe of Bani Al Mustalik, one of the captives was Juwayriya (Juwayreya). Islamic sources claim that she is one of the most beautiful, glamorous, and eloquent women in Arabia. Juwayreya is a cultured princess of class and splendour, whom Muhammad promptly has promoted from sex slave to wife."

It is well documented by reliable Islamic historical sources that Aisha had admitted that she was jealous of Juwayreya because of her stunning beauty. Aisha has admitted that she hates Juwayreya. Muhammad's marriage to Juwayreya elevated and intensified the warfare between Muhammad's wives. There is more than enough hatred and warfare within Muhammad's clan of Islam. This internal warfare validates Daniel's vision of Nebuchadnezzar's statue with toes of iron mixed with clay, which will not adhere to one another. These disintegrating toes speak of civil war within Islam which has been the pattern for fourteen centuries."

Raphael continues the painful exposure. "The gossip is rampant. Aisha was deeply offended during the Bani Al Mustalik military campaign that Muhammad had abandoned her in order to spend time with Juwayreya his new sex slave. Furthermore, the talk of Mecca and Medina was that Allah knew that Aisha had an affair with Safwan and that Allah was waiting to see if Aisha would miss her menstrual period. In other words, quite unlike Adonai, who is the omniscient God of Heaven, Satan-Allah does not know the future."

Well, it gets worse, a whole lot worse, and a whole lot sicker. Not many days later, Muhammad overhears Aisha yelling at his daughter Fatima saying, "By Allah, O daughter of Khadijah, you feel that your mother was better than us?"

As Muhammad is entering the house, he hears Aisha continuing to shout at and berate Fatima. When Fatima sees her father, she begins to cry. Muhammad asks Fatima, "What makes you cry, O daughter of Muhammad?"

Fatima rats out on Aisha as she sobs to Muhammad, "Aisha degraded my mother and caused me to cry. Aisha is nasty to me, and I don't appreciate her unkind words to me."

Michael and company are on hand to observe this unfolding crisis and the future conflicts that will escalate throughout the centuries. "From this confrontation forward, there will be no reconciliation and no love lost between Aisha and Fatima. As his only biological daughter, Muhammad has shown and continues to show great love and kindness toward his daughter Fatima. However, because Muhammad shows favoritism toward Fatima, Muhammad's wives resent her and hate her intensely. They are envious of Fatima and they plot against her. Now, this hatred and plotting are embodied within Aisha who becomes the ringleader of some of the wives against Muhammad."

"Quite bluntly," exclaims Michael, "Islam is the single biggest fraud of all time. For the gullible, Allah's and Muhammad's paradise is a pie-in-the-sky fantasy dream which will turn into a bitter cosmic nightmare. Their sexual paradise is a figment of Muhammad's distorted and psychotic imagination. Pure and simple, Islam is polygamy. At any one time, Muslim males can have up to four wives and any number of concubines or slave girls. However, with four wives at a time, faithfulness to one's wife is meaningless. Wives don't have equal rights. Without pretence, women are baby factories and the means of gratifying their husbands. Founded by the schizophrenic, psychopathic, criminal, false 'prophet' Muhammad, his Allah is the fictional head of the mafia cult of Islam with political ambitions of world conquest."

Archangel Raphael complements Michael's perspective. "Muhammad has no respect for women or for his wives. Gabriel and the three of us have heard him say that women simply are toys to pleasure men and that all women are intellectually inferior. Muhammad states repeatedly that the majority of dwellers in Hell are women. Muhammad's extremely low opinion of women is an affront to half of humanity."

Trying hard to keep a straight face, Raphael mischievously continues. "But if Hell is full of women, then I just don't understand where Allah is getting these countless numbers of virgins. Is there a virgin factory somewhere in the universe? Is Allah the mother of these virgins? And just how does Allah recycle a deflowered virgin? It sure beats me how Allah does it!"

The trio of Archangels breaks into refreshing heavenly laughter at the absurdity of these mindless fairy tales out of Muhammad's whorehouse paradise. From a clear blue sky, Heaven echoes a rolling thunder of applause. And with that applause, Gabriel is welcomed back from his secret assignment. There is a happy reunion of the Heavenly God Squad.

The year is AD 632. The place is Medina.

The God Squad of Archangels watches as Muhammad drags his feet while he is being escorted by two men supporting him under each arm. As the threesome approaches Aisha's house, Gabriel strains to understand this sight, "Muhammad will not be long among the living. It appears that death soon will be upon him. But look at the tilt of his cloak."

Uriel interrupts, "He is dying but he still manages to have an erection. Sex is always on his mind."

The Angelic God Squad is there to hear Muhammad's last threats and his dying words to his favorite wife, Aisha. While in his death throes, the venom of Muhammad's radical hatred pours out. "O Aisha! I still feel the pain caused by the food I ate at Khaibar, and at this time, I feel as if my aorta is being cut from that poison." As he writhes in pain like a snake, his sweat soaks the bed sheets. Muhammad rails against Safiyah, his Jewish wife who poisoned him three years earlier. "The Jews mean to kill me. If I die of this poison, then I will have died as a martyr. For assassinating me, you must punish the Jews forever until you wipe them off the face of the earth." During pangs of pain, Muhammad makes dire pronouncements about the destiny of the Jews. Both Sahih al-Bukhari and Sahih Muslim wrote in their Hadiths and quoted Muhammad's dying threats as, 'The last hour will not come before the Muslims fight the Jews and the Muslims kill them. In that day Allah will give voice to the rocks and the trees and they will cry out, 'O Muslim, there is a Jew hiding behind me. Come and kill him!'... Even as he is dying, Muhammad is spewing hatred."

After hearing Muhammad's threats and curses, all four Archangels are visibly distraught. Muhammad's curses and exhortations are found in his Quran and in the Hadiths. With an air of despair, Michael warns of ominous events to follow which will bring closure to this age. "Muhammad is using any and every excuse to blame the Jews. Adonai and Yeshua Messiah have warned me and prepared me for this moment. It pains me greatly to say it, but Christians and Jews in North Africa, Europe and India soon will feel the point of the Islamic sword. From this moment, blood-bath massacres of hundreds of millions loom on the horizon, and all in the name of Allah! As this Islamic plague spills violently out of Arabia, both Christians and Jews will be butchered together."

On June 8, 632, two hours later, Aisha watches as Muhammad dies an extremely writhing and agonizing death unfit for any prophet of god. Uriel quickly exits on a fact-finding assignment.

The three remaining members of the God Squad huddle for a solemn consultation. Michael addresses Gabriel, "It's a fitting end for the most evil and murderous sex scoundrel of this age. Muhammad spewed poisonous hatred and he died of its poison. He lived by his sword and by his penis and he died in prolonged poisonous agony."

What kind of poison takes three years to finish the job? How can Michael be so sure? Was Muhammad poisoned progressively in small doses, or by one massive dose of poison? There are too many unanswered questions.

The three remaining Archangels watch as Muhammad's body is being prepared for burial. Gabriel is embarrassed as Raphael, the health and medical guru, explains the rising action. "What you are seeing is a long-known medical phenomenon called the death erection. Most often it is called Angel Lust or priapism. Yes, it is ironical that it should be called Angel Lust! The Lord God of Heaven certainly has a sense of humor. It is recorded that victims of hangings and victims of violent deaths by poisoning get what is known as a post-mortem erection. It is undeniable proof that Muhammad the Prophet of Allah was poisoned by a massive dose of wife-justice. Did Allah know about the poison in advance? Was Allah away on assignment with his virgins in his paradise? Or was it because Allah does not know the future?"

As his family and associates prepare his body, attempts are made to cover Muhammad with triple shrouds to hide his embarrassing pubic bulge. Their efforts are futile. Aisha is in despair as she expresses her concerns, "The last thing we want for everyone to know is that the Prophet remained erect unto his death, and beyond." To prevent public embarrassment and humiliation for Aisha and Muhammad's other wives, a public viewing of his body is denied. With an erection, Muhammad is buried quietly in the same house in which he died.

"Muhammad's Islam has perverted sex as one of God's greatest gifts to mankind," Gabriel laments.

Uriel returns hurriedly from his investigative assignment. "I've got late-breaking news that's shocking! First, there are all manner of rumors circulating around Mecca and Medina. Suspicions are rife that it wasn't the Jewess Safiyah who had administered the lethal dose of poison. It also is rumored widely that it was his two wives, Aisha and Hafsa who had poisoned Muhammad on the orders given by their fathers Abu Bakr and Omar. But then there are other rumors that it was his adopted son's beautiful new bride, Zaynab. Muhammad lusted after Zaynab. His adopted son stepped aside, divorced her and let Muhammad marry Zaynab. The Meccans condemned this marriage as being incestuous. Now all these other relational poisons are in the mix to make future sectarian Islamic warfare inevitable."

With a hint of sarcasm in his voice, Gabriel takes the high ground. "It's beneath our dignity to travel back in time to see who really did the world a great service. But it's easy to understand why some manner of justice was necessary and inevitable."

Raphael volunteers his vast knowledge on psychiatric health issues, saying, "Aisha bint Abu Bakr was nine years old when Muhammad began forcing sex on her. The innocence of her childhood was stolen from her by Muhammad. She was compelled to join his harem of wives when she was still a child playing with dolls. Sexual abuse like that causes serious long-term psychological devastation. Aisha was livid and emotionally explosive with Muhammad's wife-collecting spree, but especially marrying the stunning beauty named Juwayreya whom Aisha hated with a passion. It is small wonder that Aisha was the most rebellious of Muhammad's wives. Aisha's immature and petulant behavior made certain that Muhammad's harem was a den of division and vicious in-fighting. Muhammad's wives were divided into two warring camps with Aisha leading one group. Today, Aisha has not recovered from Muhammad sexual assaults. Just look at her right now. Her face certainly is not that of a grieving wife. For a fifteen-year-old, her face is hardened with strife, revenge and hatred."

Gabriel, who understands the depths and breadths of female psychology, supports and echoes Raphael's insights. "Another special favor from Allah to Muhammad was followed by yet another wife for his Prophet. Another wife was just the last straw that broke the camel's back and broke down Aisha's self-control. By the well-worn cliché, 'Hell hath no fury like a woman scorned' Aisha was that woman scorned. Aisha's fury was Hell-bent as she had reached for the poison."

"However, Aisha does have a window into Muhammad's life which no other human has had. As the 'Mother of Believers,' it is Aisha who speaks of Muhammad doing black magic and his being controlled by the Devil. Is Muhammad's Allah actually Satan in disguise? The four of us certainly know this to be true. Whatever Aisha's inner upheavals were, her firsthand testimony about Muhammad cannot be disregarded."

"Truly, truly, Aisha is the many faces of Eve. Aisha is an experienced young teenage woman in great turmoil and in a deeply troubled state of mind. From all appearances, Aisha's life is an ongoing tragedy. Aisha will yet shake the world around her."

And shake the world she did. Once Muhammad was dead, massive and widespread killing inside Islam began. The killing has never stopped. Aisha conducted the first civil war in Islamic history led by a woman. Aisha commanded an army against Fatima's husband Ali who was the elected fourth Muslim Caliph. In the war known as the Battle of the Camel, Aisha's leadership led to the bloody slaughter of twenty thousand Muslims. Today, the Shiites proclaim that as punishment to avenge the death of Muhammad's daughter Fatima, the Twelfth Imam Mahdi, will bring Aisha back to life and whip her publicly. Aisha's psychotic hatred launched the ongoing Sunni-Shiite wars which continue into the 21st century. Where was Allah in this cosmic split of Islam which was engineered by a woman filled with hatred driven by sexual abuse inflicted by Muhammad?

Michael proceeds to address a different reality. "Finally, Gabriel, you will meet your accuser face to face."

In an instant transformation, Gabriel's smiles turn to frowns of shock and distress. With visible fear and with an expression of horror, Gabriel recoils, "Meet Muhammad? Meet this murderer and sex scoundrel who has smeared my name and who has maligned me?"

As commander of the heavenly forces, Michael tries to detach himself from his emotions. "I regret to bring this bitter assignment to you. For just this one occasion, Adonai wants you to assist Sariel, the Angel of Death. You need to deal with Muhammad's assault upon your angelic position, upon your character, and for his assaults upon your psyche. Muhammad had attributed all of his Quran as your words from Allah. We feel your deep pain and anguish. This unpleasant job is a necessary step for your inner healing. After you escort Muhammad to his place of punishment, you will never have contact with him again. Unfortunately, in order for you to be set free, you have to deal with his demonic spirit."

An LED turns on inside Michael's head, "Waaaaaaaaaaaait a minute! For the last three years, the three of us have been having some questions and doubts about you Gabriel. And I've just had a revelation! Was it Safiyah the Jewess who poisoned Muhammad? Was it Aisha and Hafsa? Was it Zaynab? Was it Juwayreya? Or was it you who poisoned Muhammad? Was it? Or did you help his wives? Well, Gabriel? Please, tell us! Did you poison this monster? Is that why Adonai wants you to finish the job and drag Muhammad to his just reward? Six years ago, you did warn us that you would take him out. Tell us so that we can celebrate this occasion together."

Gabriel doesn't answer but turns his face away. The three Archangels exchange glances of uncertainty. Did Gabriel or did he not make good on his threat against Muhammad? Michael whispers to Raphael and Uriel, "We'll get to know sometime in eternity."

Gabriel is in no mood for any celebrations. He is crestfallen and appears to be frightened and terror-struck. He does not want to cross paths with his archenemy. "I do not want to face Muhammad and to drag him to the Pit. But I will do what Adonai wills." He sits down upon the trunk of a fallen tree to gather inner strength for the looming trauma. In the distance, Gabriel sees his distasteful and fearful assignment, the disembodied spirit of Muhammad. On the opposite horizon, Gabriel observes Satan-Allah and her dirty dozen. That satanic sight adds to Gabriel's fears. Will they challenge Gabriel as he carries out his assignment? Once again, will he need assistance from Michael? Oh, but wait. Approaching him, Gabriel sees Sariel, the Angel of Death. Gabriel rises to meet Sariel to convey Muhammad's spirit to the pit of Hell.

CHAPTER 8

ISLAM AFTER THE POISONING DEATH OF MUHAMMAD

The year is AD 632. The place is Medina, Saudi Arabia. Muhammad has been poisoned by his wives. The news of his death spreads like a wildfire burning across the hot desert sands of Arabia. Most of Muhammad's Islamic followers dump his Muslim teachings and turn their backs on Allah and upon Muhammad as Allah's psychotic and murderous sex-crazed prophet.

Twenty-six centuries before Muhammad had spread his cancerous hatreds throughout the Middle East, Ishmael's and Esau's venomous hatreds had percolated within the veins of the Arab peoples. In the face of Muhammad's accusation of complicity in his Quranic revelations, Gabriel continues his self-vindication in self-defence, saying, "The hatred of the Syrian hordes as they slaughtered the Jews in the Jerusalem Temple in AD 70 was testimony to the lethal legacies in the dysfunctional families of Abraham, Sarah, Hagar, Ishmael, Isaac, Rebeccah, Esau, and Jacob."

Michael assesses the political whirlwind in and around Islam. "Much of Islam has just heaved a big sigh of relief. There is widespread rejoicing that this megalomaniac madman is dead. Few want anything to do with Muhammad's version of Allah, whom they know to be a female goddess. However, Aisha's father, Abu Bakr will have none of this turning away apostasy. The Islamic sword rules again. Abu Bakr butchers seventy thousand backsliding Muslims. Arabs kill Arabs. Muslims behead former Muslims. Abu Bakr's slaughter is rightly known as the Wars of Apostasy. Abu Bakr's sword is active decapitating all apostates. Abu Bakr is re-establishing Islam in Arabia."

In this horrible cauldron of treachery, murder, and iniquity, we see all of Muhammad's wives who, except for Aisha, now are disinherited and thrown out onto the street." Gabriel is sympatheic to their plight. The wives are seeking support, and they look to Muhammad's daughter, Fatima, and to his widow Aisha for assistance. Aisha vehemently opposes Fatima. Aisha is only too willing to bring the wives on her side. She is acutely aware of the hatred being directed towards her by Fatima's supporters. Knowing that her own life is in danger from Fatima and Ali, Aisha encourages help from all the allies she can enlist. In similar fashion, Fatima knows that her own life is in danger from Aisha's father, Abu Bakr and from Omar. For self-preservation from these two gangsters, Fatima and Ali bond in marriage. A confrontation to the death is in the works. The Wars of Succession have begun in all seriousness. The gloves are off, the swords will play, and heads will continue to roll on the sands of Arabia.

There is uncertainty about Fatima's exact date of birth. Fatima was Muhammad's only daughter through Khadijah. Almost religiously, Muhammad showed extreme fondness for Fatima. Some believe that Fatima was born five years before Muhammad's first encounter with the 'Gabriel' apparition. An age difference of twelve years made daughter Fatima considerably older than her father's wife Aisha, who became Fatima's stepmother. This awkward age differential triggered stress, resentment, and jealousy between daughter Fatima and wife Aisha. Fatima is suspicious that Aisha may have poisoned her father. In the Intrigue of the Wives and without her father Muhammad to protect her, Fatima meets her demise just months after Muhammad was poisoned. Aisha was the prime suspect, but it could have been any of the wives or even Aisha's father. The Intrigue of the Wives was a toxic and venomous battle to the death with the daughter of Muhammad. Many Muslims of the Twelfth Imam Shia division believe that Fatima was murdered by Umar (Omar) while she was trying to defend her husband Ali against Abu Bakr. In a final show of disrespect and contempt towards Fatima, she was buried in an unmarked grave. Today, no one knows where Fatima is buried. Many Shia of the Twelfth Imam branch of Islam carry fourteen centuries of hatred towards the Sunni Muslims who revere Abu Bakr and Umar. The Genesis prophecy about Ishmael's warfare with every man, and Daniel's feet and toes of iron mixed with clay, began many centuries before Muhammad was poisoned by his wives. The Islamic battles between Muhammad's wife Aisha and his daughter Fatima have been fought for fourteen centuries. The hatreds and the battles between the Shiites and the Sunnis continue to be fought today. The War *OF* the Women of fourteen centuries ago, continues as the War *AGAINST* the women of the 21st century.

The Islamic Wars of Succession have a striking parallel with the Booze Wars of the 1920s and the 1930s when Al Capone ran the Chicago mafia in a continual bloody battle with rival gangs vying for territorial control. In terms of character, morals, and principles, there was no difference between the murderous thugs of the 1930s and the murderous thugs who had run Islam from its beginnings and those who run Islam in the present. But compared to the magnitude of the Islamic Wars of Succession, the St. Valentine's Day Massacre was just a single drop of blood in a giant swimming pool of Islamic bloodshed. The enormity of the treachery and the butchery in the Islamic Wars of Succession has no parallel in human history. The deadly conflicts following the poisoning death of Muhammad set the tenor for fourteen centuries of internecine warfare which will last until the end of this age.

Gabriel reminds his companions, "Recall that some 4,000 years ago, in **Genesis 16:12**, Adonai the God of Heaven spoke through me and prophesized to Hagar that her son Ishmael would be 'a wild ass of a man, his hand against every man and every man's hand would be against him.' Today, Arabs are butchering Arabs, Aryans are butchering Arabs and Arabs are butchering Aryans. Muslims will continue to betray and murder each other. Sunnis and Shiites will continue to slaughter each other. Sariel, the Angel of Death, is not getting a moment's rest escorting these Islamic killers to the fires of Hell."

Michael provides a disturbing view of the future. "Until the end of the age, death is Allah's judgment which awaits all who turn away from

Islam and who reject Islam. In particular, this will continue to be the genocidal killing of Christians and Jews."

The year is AD 638. The place is Jerusalem. The Angelic God Squad is observing from the Mount of Olives as the Ishmaelite armies approach the city. Mounted on a prancing Arabian steed, Caliph Omar rides into Jerusalem. Michael remarks, "Look at the smugness on his face. Omar is relishing every moment of his superiority and his position of power."

The Jewish inhabitants are outside their homes to view another calamity over-running their beloved city. When Omar's horse stops on the Temple Mount near the scattered stones of the second temple, Omar addresses the defeated Jewish remnants. "More than twenty-six-hundred years ago, that bitch Sarah sent young Ishmael into the desert to die. Today, Ishmael's descendants are here before you. Now, it's Ishmael's turn. Guess where you and your children are going? Into the burning desert!" Omar turns around and gallops back down the Mount as his armies take over the city. Today, the Mosque of Omar stands on the site of the destroyed Second Temple.

The year is AD 656. The place is Basra, Iraq. The Battle of the Camel is in progress. The Angelic God Squad is at their observation post. Archangel Michael provides a synopsis of the continuing slaughter. "It's been twenty-four years since Muhammad's wives poisoned him. The bitter slaughter within Islam continues. We've just witnessed the assassination of Caliph Uthman. Rumor has it that Ali, cousin and son-in-law of Muhammad, is mixed up in Uthman's murder. Now we are observing the vengeful fires of hell raging from Aisha. There she is on her camel in the middle of the battle. This woman has no fear. Just look at that fierce expression on her face. I see hatred written all over it."

As Aisha leads the charge, her forces are allied with those of several other of Muhammad's widows. The widows are challenging the armies of Ali, the new Caliph. The War of the Wives, also called the War of the Mothers of the Believers, has exploded from within Muhammad's bedrooms and into a war for the very heart of Islam. Aisha's rebellion is directed against Islam itself.

Mounted on her camel, Aisha swings her sword left and right. Heads roll in the desert sands. As Aisha butchers fellow Muslims, she directs a storm of accusations and curses at Allah, "You #&%$ jerk! You think that women are intellectually inferior to men, do you? How about those three studs whom I just ran through with this sword? Who's inferior now? And you say that Hell is full of women? Not now. Just today, I sent seven of your martyrs to join you in the flames, you scum! Look around you, Allah. This is no Paradise, and I'm not one of your recycled virgins. No sex here and no smoke-and-mirrors either, just your Hell of dust and blood." Looking upward into the sky, Aisha points her extended middle finger at the moon as she spits upon the ground.

"Did you see what Aisha just did?" asks Gabriel in a voice ringing with utter disbelief. "She just saluted Allah with her middle finger of contempt. In the past, she's shown scorn for Allah by letting her goats chew on many pages of Muhammad's radical Quran. Those pages of hatred are gone forever. It's no wonder that the Shiites want to whip her for being an apostate."

As the expert in psychology, Raphael digs back into his memories to earlier conflicts in time. "Islam's second-class citizens are in revolt. Aisha is thirty-nine years old, and she's leading a war? In thirty years, she has gone from the innocence of dolls and swinging on a tree limb, to the brutality of swinging a sword across the necks of her enemies. Aisha is the widow in black, but she's not in mourning for her husband. She is grieving for her lost childhood, which that son from Hell had stolen from her. The independence and the rebellion of this Aisha woman remind me of Lilith's rebellion against her husband Adam in the Garden of Eden. Aisha's domineering and her aggressiveness also remind me of Abraham's Sarah. But Aisha's destructive ambitions are those of a Cleopatra. Unfortunately, I also see a streak of a Jezebel in her. She's unsettled and torn apart by a conflict within herself and with the world. Childhood rape and her harem servitude have twisted Aisha's mind into a dangerous psychotic state beyond recovery. Her mind is a captive of her childhood. Muhammad's bedroom legacy is one of unleashing the hurricane forces of Hell itself. And Muhammad is being worshipped as a prophet of Allah to be admired and copied?"

After 110 days of carnage, the Battle of the Camel comes to a bloody end. After the slaughter of ten thousand on each side, Aisha's forces are defeated. Aisha withdraws to Medina.

The four Archangels have monitored Aisha as closely as they had monitored Muhammad. Raphael, the health and wellness guru, comments, "As close as Aisha was to Muhammad and to his Allah stooge, she wants no part of either of them now. Aisha hated Muhammad and his fictitious Allah with a passion. She knew that Allah was Muhammad's mirage and the tool of his convenience. And she wasn't about to chase his mirage across the desert sands. As messed up as she is, even while moving in virulent revenge, Aisha is not deceived. She sees through the smoke and mirrors. Did she poison Muhammad?"

Gabriel expresses his concerns for Aisha and for Muhammad's other harem wives. "These few women of Islam have taken back their lost ground. But are they going to be punished for their rebellion?"

Michael who has the inside track on future events, provides a depressing outlook. "There is no question that in general, future women will be punished and subdued severely by Muhammad's Islam. I'll tell you what spells bad news for all Islamic women. It's the Shiite threat to resurrect Aisha and to whip her when the Twelfth Imam returns. Unfortunately, the women of Islam will be forced to submit to much harsher depths of mistreatment. Captured infidel women and children will be sold for sex until the curtain comes down upon this age."

The bloody warfare inside Islam continues. Succeeding Caliphs are murdered in succession as Sunnis and Shiites vie for power.

The year is AD 691. The place is the Mount of Olives in Jerusalem. Umayyad caliph Abd al-Malik completes the Dome of the Rock on the Temple Mount. It stands where once stood the Temple of Solomon, and the Second Jewish Temple which was destroyed by the Romans in AD 70.

From the Mount of Olives, the angelic foursome surveys the site and this majestic Islamic structure. Michael laments, "The Dome of the Rock stands on the pinnacle of Mount Moriah, the very site of the <u>Holy of Holies</u> during the <u>Temple era</u>. The Dome is a symbolic festering boil which will fester and inflame all future generations of

Christians and Jews, until this boil is lanced. Indeed, this Muslim shrine was intended to be a great humiliation for the Jews and for the Christians, and it continues to be just that. The Dome stands on the rock where Abraham prepared to sacrifice his son Isaac. That's four thousand years ago. This Islamic shrine is a provocative challenge to Adonai. As in the days of King Nebuchadnezzar, an Ishmaelite insult of this significance will be met in cataclysmic fashion. Once again, the finger of God will write, but this time it will be upon the very walls and upon the ceiling of the Dome of the Rock."

With reluctance, Raphael reviews history which rips rather than heals. "So sorry, Gabriel, but the Dome of the Rock on the Temple Mount represents Islam's final assault upon you as well. According to Quran 17, the Temple Mount is the rock from which Muhammad's alleged winged horse leapt into the sky as you accompanied him on his Night Journey into Paradise."

Through gritted teeth, Gabriel sets the record straight. "Winged horse? Winged camel? How about the Winged Nut instead? It was just another flight of fancy and another Muslim fairy tale for the gullible. Muhammad's final Night Journey was his one-way trip to the flames of Hell, and it wasn't upon his magic carpet either. On that night in June of 632, after Muhammad was poisoned, together with Sariel, I chained the spirit of that sex-addicted mass murderer. That was one awesome struggle. Finally, Muhammad got to meet me, the real messenger, face to face. And I got to tell Muhammad where I was taking him. In a continuous battle on his journey to Hell, I dragged that shrieking coward to the great sulfur pit. Upon arrival, all the other prisoners were unchained, but Muhammad was chained and will remain chained inside the gates of Hell for all eternity. In a never-ending procession of torchbearers, Muhammad will receive hundreds of millions of Muslims whom he had deceived and butchered. I wonder where those riotous throngs in Hell will shove their torches?"

Having the foreknowledge imparted to him by Adonai, Michael reveals, "This rock, this very foundation stone of the Temple Mount is destined to shake the very foundations of earth and Hell. Before that terrible day of Armageddon and the Second Coming of Christ the Messiah, the Dome of the Rock is prophesied to be replaced by the third and final Temple. Those will be fearful times indeed."

Opposite the Mount of Olives, Satan-Allah and and her partner, Sonneillon, observe the activity taking place on the Temple Mount. Strutting around like peacocks, these two devils gloat over their recent victory as they watch the completion of the Dome of the Rock, and its defying erect penis minarets. Satan-Allah boasts triumphantly, "For many centuries to come, our Dome of the Rock will tear into the hearts of the Jews and Christians, but especially into Adonai. Maybe the Dome will stand forever. Hey look, Sonny, there are our four adversaries. They are one sad-looking bunch of whipped dogs. Adonai and his gang have lost the most significant psychological war of all time. The Dome of the Rock is our political statement that Islam is proceeding to win the war of religions and to win the war of civilizations. The Dome of the Rock is my insult of the millennia to Adonai. The Dome also is shaped perfectly to be my personal crown and my crowning glory. Once it's clad in pure gold, I will wear it forever. Nothing less than gold will do for the Queen of Heaven! And I am the Queen of Heaven! There will be no third Temple on the Temple Mount, not ever. I am very thankful for Sarah's stupidity. Without Sarah there would be no Dome of the Rock."

Satan-Allah continues, "Gabriel can lament until Hell freezes over. It won't do him any good. Once a lie has been repeated thousands of times, it becomes gospel truth. For all generations, Gabriel will be known to be Allah's and Muhammad's angelic stooge."

In the early years of the eighth century, to add insult to insult, the Umayyads built a palace which they attached to the end of the Temple wall. Intended to be a slap in the face for the Jews, the Umayyad Palace was built to appear as a scar on the Temple wall and so it has remained until today.

By brutal conquest which spills the blood of many tens of millions, Islam will be spread at the point of the sword from China all the way to France and across North America.

The year is AD 712. The place is Debal, Western India (modern-day Pakistan). The Angelic God Squad has followed the wide swath of Muhammad's Islamic blood-soaked paths out of Arabia. Michael expresses the emotional anguish of his companions, "I am sickened and depressed by all this senseless slaughter, decade after decade after decade. Islam's jihadist martyrs hope to murder their way into Allah's Paradise. Syria, Egypt, North Africa, Persia, Armenia, Damascus, Antioch, entire cities are put to Allah's sword. Sixteen thousand Christians were butchered in Antioch where one hundred thousand were sold into slavery. The Christians of Damascus were decapitated after they had surrendered. How can these Islamic Arabs whoop it up and sleep after a day of shrieking terror and after sloshing around in ankle-deep blood? Just this very day, Islam extinguished more than one hundred thousand men, women, and children who were living in peace. In all of history, these horrific Islamic massacres in India are unparalleled in numbers and in brutality. What are these Muslim Arabs doing in India? Killing their way into Allah's favor? Where is conscience?"

Gabriel weighs in to address this ruthless inhumanity. "Conscience? Muhammad's Islam strangles conscience as we know it. Then the Quran redefines conscience. Only Muslims are innocent. All others are criminals in rebellion against Allah. It is Allah who commands his followers to commit plunder, rape, violence, and massacre to advance his cause. All who do not bow down to Allah must be killed in any imaginable way. I need a break. I'm going to assist Sariel after which I will try to bring comfort to the surviving locals."

The date is October 8, 732 AD, one hundred years after the poisoning death of Muhammad. The place is the forests of Tours-Poitiers, France. As supreme commander of the angelic hosts, Michael has been observing the formations and the strategies of two armies as they converge. "The Christian Franks have positioned themselves directly in the path of the advancing Islamic Saracens and the Barbary Coast Islamic killers. However, the Franks are badly outnumbered and outclassed. They have no cavalry. The Umayyad forces enjoy the advantage of having heavy cavalry. Their entire forces are mailed and armored horsemen. Infantry alone cannot win against cavalry. Without the elements of surprise, diversion, and strategic location, but especially without Divine intervention, the Franks cannot win."

While not understanding the fine points of military tactics, Gabriel is aware of the spiritual battles behind the scenes. "Yes, but the advantage in numbers and horses will not win this battle for the Muslim forces. Thanks to you Michael, in dreams and in visions, I have relayed your military strategies to Charles Martel of the Frankish forces. He is taking these dreams as a revelations from God, and he is arranging his forces according to the dreams I have given to him. As I had intervened with Daniel in dreams some thirteen hundred years ago, so too have I intervened with Charles Martel."

The date is October 10, 732 AD, exactly one hundred years after Muhammad's poisoning trip to Hell. The place is the forests of Tours-Poitiers, France. The Arab armies are caught completely off guard. While the Franks are cold-weather ready, the Arabs are not at all prepared for cold weather. As Divine fate and destiny would have it, an advancing Arctic cold snap forces the Ishmaelite-Saracen king to attack. Umayyad King Abdul Rahman Al Ghafiqi is killed in battle. Under Charles Martel, the Franks win a decisive victory against the Umayyad forces of Islam. After massive losses and a complete diversionary rout on the battlefield, the surviving Umayyad armies beat a hasty retreat in the night. In their state of sheer panic, the Muslims abandon even their tents and booty. Reminiscent of Gideon of old, the Arabs flee in fear of the unknown. Many Christians consider this victory to be a miracle of Yeshua Messiah and of Adonai the God of Heaven.

Visibly pleased, Michael congratulates Gabriel for his dream interventions. "The elements of surprise and diversion were absolute keys for this overwhelming military victory. Mounted charges in the forest trees were impossible. The Ishmaelite heavy cavalry was a disadvantage and a liability among the forest trees."

Gabriel throws out several bouquets. "Ah yes, but first you should thank Uriel for engineering that unusual cold snap in the weather. Keep in mind that more than forty-five hundred years ago, I had instigated the wars among the Nephilim giants, those children of the Watcher Angels. Remember that I am Adonai's messenger angel. But sometimes my messages are meant to be deliberately misleading and just plain destructive to the enemy. I made sure to give the Ishmaelite Umayyad king pleasant dreams of victory. He was so confident that he failed to scout ahead. Tsk! Tsk! Tsk! Costly mistake, Kingo! But Allah could have warned King Abdul Rahman of Charles' armies hiding in the forest. Allah did not. Perhaps Allah was asleep, or out to lunch. Or maybe once again, she was forcing sex upon the young boys in her paradise."

Following the miraculous victory at Tours, the Archangels come to some startling conclusions. Michael is amazed at how Gabriel barred Allah from snooping through the forests of Tours.

Uriel pushes the ludicrous take, "Inside their hashish clouds of smoke, the Islamic forces are living inside a dreamlike fairy tale world complete with virgins suspended from clouds like ornaments."

On the opposite side of the battlefield, Satan and her dirty dozen are in shock and in despair. They had expected an easy slaughter of the Franks. Satan-Allah was caught with her pants down, and her image took a terrible beating. Three consecutive and major military defeats cooled the Islamic conquest of Europe.

As the four Archangels observe their satanic adversaries, Michael comments, "Tails between their legs, a depressed looking bunch, aren't they? But let's not gloat. It isn't over till it's over. And it won't be over for many, many generations."

Within a few years, the Umayyads pull out of France all the way south across the Pyrenees and back into Spain.

The year is AD 750. The Umayyad Dynasty has collapsed. In their first expansionist downturn, the Ishmaelites and their Muslim allies absorbed a resounding defeat with massive losses at their second siege of Constantinople in AD 718. Then, in 721AD the Arabs took a severe beating at Toulouse in France. Finally, the crushing defeat at Tours in 732 brought the curtain down upon the Umayyads. The Battle of Tours proved to be the single most important battle and the most decisive battle in the history of the world. In both east and west, the Arab invasions of Europe had been stopped dead in their tracks, and rolled back. Europe had been rescued from the Muslim Saracen swords. All of Europe breathed sighs of relief, for a while.

Gabriel summarizes the significance of the Arabic setbacks. "The Muslim defeat at Tours saved Europe for Christianity. It also saved the Jews from extermination for it provided them with a European refuge from the Ishmaelite swords."

Michael has the final word. "Unfortunately, there are more Islamic blood bath massacres yet to come, many, many more."

The initial expansionary wars of the Arab Muslims were funded by the Vatican on agreement that Rome would be given possession of Jerusalem. However, after the battle between Aisha and Fatima, the Battle of the Camel, and the Wars of Succession, the caliphs reneged and broke their agreement with the Vatican. As a backlash and in revenge, Rome engineered the long-running Crusades which failed to secure their centuries-long Vatican dream of possessing Jerusalem.

The year is AD 1453. Constantinople has fallen and the massacres of Christians begin. The Muslim armies have just completed building their phallic minarets and placing the crescent moon onto the giant Hagea Sophia Greek Orthodox Cathedral, which they converted into an imperial mosque. The Muslim advance into Eastern Europe was stopped at the Battle of Kosovo in 1389. The Muslim armies were defeated at the Battle of Vienna in 1529 and in 1683, at the Great Siege of Malta in 1565, and at the Battle of Zenta in 1697. Muslim atrocities continued during the Turkish genocide of Armenian Christians in 1915–16. The Israeli-Arab Six Day War in 1967 was a replay of the Battle of Tours in AD 732. After nineteen centuries, victorious Israel took full possession of Jerusalem.

The time is June 1967. The place is Jerusalem. The Six-Day War has ended. The God Squad reconvenes at the top of Golgotha, known as Calvary. Raphael inquires, "I know much about the Quran, but what are these Islamic Sunnah and Hadiths about?"

"The Sunnah," explains Gabriel, "refers to the precedents set by Muhammad." As recorded by Muhammad's companions, the Sunnah are about what Muhammad said, what Muhammad did, and what Muhammad approved. As recorded in the Hadiths, the Sunnah are the very foundation of the Muslim faith which is enshrined in Islamic law known as Sharia Law."

"In many ways the Hadiths within the Sunnah take precedence over the Quran." Michael voices information that is largely unknown by the Western world. "By intentional design, the Hadiths may contradict the Quran and the Quran may contradict the Hadiths. It is convenient, it is clever, and it is deliberate deceptive design, for it allows opposing challenges to any argument. On their own, the Hadiths are shocking reading."

"There are two renowned, high-profile, and highly-revered Muslim authors who had assembled and recorded Muhammad's words and deeds." Gabriel proceeds to go to some depths of revelation, "The versions of Sahih Bukhari and Sahih Muslim are deemed authentic and are the most canonical Hadith collections on record."

"I will proceed to expose just seven of the most troubling Hadiths in Islam." Michael takes over the reins of throwing light upon these obscure and dark corridors hidden from the unsuspecting world. "In the first of these seven, as reported by Abu Musa, Muhammad claimed that Muslims will be spared Hell-fire by Allah if they force Jews to take their place and be thrown into Hell instead of them.

"In Book 037, Numbers 6665, 6666, 6667, 6668, Sahih Muslim recorded, 'When it will be the Day of Resurrection, Allah will deliver to every Muslim a Jew or a Christian and say: 'That is your rescue from Hell-fire.'"

"In Volume 9, Book 84, Number 59, Sahih Bukhari wrote, 'Allah's Apostle (Muhammad) said, "I have been ordered to fight the people till they say: 'None has the right to be worshipped but Allah.'"'"

"In Volume 4, Book 56, Number 791, Sahih al-Bukhari recorded that Abdullah bin Umar heard Allah's Apostle [Muhammad] saying: 'The Jews will fight you, and you will be given victory over them so that a stone will say, "O Muslim! There is a Jew behind me; kill him!"'"

"In Book 041, Numbers 6981, 6984, and 6985, Sahih Muslim stated that Abu Huraira reported Allah's messenger as saying, 'The last hour would not come unless the Muslims fight against the Jews and the Muslims would kill them until the Jews would hide themselves behind a stone or a tree and a tree or a stone would say: Muslim, or the servant of Allah, there is a Jew behind me; come and kill him.'"

After doubling over with hilarity, Gabriel regains his composure saying, "Consider the logic offered in defence of this Hadith by Muslim scholar Ali al-Faqir who had written, 'Sir, it has been proven scientifically that the trees and the stones have a language of their own. But we don't have the ability to invent the instruments that will convey the tree's voice and the stone's voice to us.' This is the ultimate stretch of the bizarre of all time. In this Islamic Silly Season, Islam assumes that those who are not Muslims are more gullible than kindergarten children who will believe this fantasy tripe."

"Without blinking or blushing or any hint of shame, Muslims are telling us that stones talk." Michael joins Gabriel in mockery, "This stretch of absurdity would work well in a children's fairy tale. And in Volume 3, Book 43, Number 656 of his hadith, Sahih Bukhari had documented that Abu Huraira had recorded Muhammad to have said, 'The Hour will not be established until the Son of Mary (Jesus) descends amongst you as a just ruler, he will break the cross, kill the pigs (Jews), and abolish the Jizyah tax.'" Sahih Bukhari completes this circle of shocking hatred stating, "Muhammad's dying words included a curse on the Jews and on the Christians. As narrated by his widow Aisha and by Abdullah bin Abbas, Muhammad had said, 'May Allah curse the Jews and Christians for they built the places of worship at the graves of their prophets.'"

"Islam certainly was concocted and brewed in Hell's kitchen," announces Gabriel. "Today Islam is intoxicated from drinking this brew straight out of Hell."

CHAPTER 9

ISLAM
IN THE TWENTY-FIRST CENTURY

The year is 1988. Ayatollah Khomeini is in power in Iran. Iraq and Iran have been at war for eight years. The place is the marshes separating Iraq and Iran. The Angelic God Squad is positioned in the middle of a battle with bullets flying all around them. Muslims have been killing Muslims for fourteen centuries. This is a racial battle as much as a War Against Women. Distinct from the Arabs, Iran is not Semitic. Iran is an Aryan race. The Kurds are an ethnic community that is not Arabic. Turkey is only partly Arabic. In these marshes, with Allah's blessings upon both sides, Muslim Arabs and Muslim Aryans are killing each other. After four thousand years, Adonai's prophecy given to Hagar by Gabriel holds true today. Ishmaelites continue to be at war with each other and with their neighbors. The major schism in Islam, which was provoked by Muhammad's poisoning death by his wives, split Islam into two warring groups: Sunnis and Shiites. Within a few years after Muhammad's murder-poisoning death, more than a hundred thousand Muslims had been slaughtered by fellow Muslims. As a participant in the bloodiest empire in history, Saddam Hussein and his fellow Sunnis gassed and murdered untold hundreds of thousands of Kurds as their Muslim opponents. After fourteen centuries, the Sunnis and the Shiites continue to kill each other today. Islamic justice was, and continues to be, through murderous revenge. Fueling these Islamic fires of hatred is the racial divide.

Michael summarizes some foundational history, saying, "Only Iran adopted the schismatic concept of the Twelfth Imam Shiism as their state religion. Sunnis reject the Twelfth Shiite Imamate. Nor do Sunnis believe in the return of the Hidden Imam. Sunni Muslims do not follow religious leaders as the Iranian Shiite ayatollahs. In total contrast, the imamate is the central aspect of Shiite Islam. Sunni scholars state that the Twelfth Imam never existed, but that he was designed as a myth to keep the Shiite cause from disappearing. In the Sunni-Shiite divide, the Sunnis want an earthly ruler while the Shiites look for a spiritual ruler to establish his kingdom of Heaven on earth. The deadly battle of who should have succeeded Muhammad as leader of the Islamic faith, had irreparably polarized these two perpetual deadly rivals. Following Muhammad's murder by poisoning, the Muslim majority accepted Abu Bakr as the first Caliph, but a small minority wanted Muhammad's son-in-law, Ali as the Muslim leader. After Abu Bakr died, Umar became the Caliph. Umar hardened the Sunni-Shia division when he decreed that a non-Arab could not inherit from an Arab unless that heir was of Arabian birth. His decree excluded Iran at square one. Umar's hard-line put the Arabs on a permanent collision course with Shiite Iran. Now, that is racial and national warfare."

"Sunni scholars speculate that the Twelfth Imam never existed and never went into hiding," Gabriel reinforces. "Sunni scholars are emphatic that the Twelfth Imam occultation is a myth which was designed to keep the Shiite minority alive."

Michael jumps forward fourteen centuries saying, "Today, Sunni Saudi Arabia is in deathly fear of Shiite Iran to the point of colluding secretly even with its archenemy Israel, so as to prevent Iran from developing nuclear weapons. Saudi Arabia wants the U.S. and Israel to bomb Iran's nuclear underground installations. Through ancient Jewish prophecies, Saudi Arabian rulers of today know that Iran will use their nuclear weapons against the Saudi oil fields and set them on fire to burn forever. Keep in mind that Iran is the world's biggest Shia country."

"In his infamous nuclear agreement with Iran of November 23, 2013, U.S. President Barack Obama launched a new nuclear weapons race in the Middle East." Gabriel is most distressed with this unexpected and irresponsible turn of events, "In his reckless agreement with Iran, the American President pushed Saudi Arabia to strike a deal with Pakistan. Saudi Arabia is seeking to purchase off-the-shelf, ready-made nuclear bombs from Pakistan. In their knee-jerk reaction, Sunni Saudi Arabia, is running scared. Besides cooperating with Israel, on December 29, 2013, the Saudis pledged $3-billion dollars of military aid to Lebanon's Sunni Muslims in order to protect Sunni Arabia from Iran's Shiite Hezbollah. Saudi dollars are intended to buy French weapons for the under-equipped Lebanese military which is fighting Hezbollah. Earlier in 2013 and for similar purposes, Saudi Arabia granted Sunni Egypt a $5 billion grant to oppose Iran."

As usual Uriel brings some comic relief to a very serious discussion. "Just as in the days of Nebuchadnezzar and Belshazzar when the 'loins of kings were loosened,' the Saudi king and his myriad of princes are crapping their drawers every day in fear and in panic over Iran."

"There you go again, Uriel. What would we do without your smelly humor?" Raphael laughs.

"In the twenty-first century, Shiite Muslims believe that after Fatima's husband Ali, there were to be only twelve Imams. The Shiites believe that the twelfth and last Imam, known as the Mahdi, is still in hiding since the ninth century."

Uriel can hardly disguise his mischievous grin. "You mean that young kid who disappeared down a well, or was it down a rabbit hole, in his desperate escape from Sunni hit men?"

There is a long burst of laughter from the Angelic foursome until Michael finally soberly interjects, "The imamate is the central and foundational Shiite doctrine which sets it apart from Sunni Islam. Quite unlike the secular Sunni Imams, the Shiite imams are considered to be spiritual leaders who transmit Allah's mystical aspects to humanity. This group known as the Twelvers represent the majority of Shiite Muslims."

Gabriel motions to the group that he has important background information on Iran. "The Shiites in Iran are split into a number of conflicting factions with moderate to major doctrinal differences between them. In some cases, the differences between the Twelvers and some of the Shiite splinter groups are severe enough to influence a complete doctrinal breakdown. Not only is there total animosity between the Shiites and the Sunnis, but the Shiites can't agree even among themselves."

Raphael goes back to book of Genesis, "Yes, even after four thousand years, Gabriel's prophecy that Ishmael would be 'a wild ass of a man, his hand against every man' is still valid today. Ishmael's legacy of divisiveness and conflict has metastasized like a cancer spreading from Semite to Aryan."

Michael picks up the threads of the Twelfth Imam saying, "These Twelvers believe that their final imam known as Muhammad al-Mahdi will return on the Day of Judgment when the entire world is in extreme chaos. The Mahdi's return to crush the Christian and Jewish forces is the central feature of Shiite Islam. Twelvers believe that it is their sacred duty before Allah to create as much unrest, destruction and anarchy as possible in order to hurry on the coming of their Twelfth Imam. Detonation of nuclear weapons over Israel, over Saudi Arabia, and over the United States fits the Shiite concepts of maximum pandemonium to bring Mahdi out of his rabbit hole. A nuclear-triggered electromagnetic pulse (EMP) over the United States will facilitate the Shiite Day of Judgment which will follow the Mahdi's return and the final apocalyptic battle of all time."

Raphael, the health and wellness expert, ventures into the thick of the lethal smog of the war zone between Iraq and Iran. After a time, Raphael shouts to his partners. "I can hear you, but I can't see you through this heavy fog of poison gas. There are hundreds of rotting corpses all around me. These two neighbors have used hundreds of tons of nerve gas on each other. In the last eight years, Allah's holy warriors have killed a million Muslims, including thousands of young boys."

"Slay them wherever you find them"

- Quran 2:192.

In the distance, Michael shouts back, "It's all clear where we are." After a few minutes, Raphael joins the group. Michael continues, "Look in the distance and see that long line of young boys holding hands as they walk towards us. They're sweeping the field of land mines. Further back, you can see hundreds of military personnel, motorized vehicles, and weapons of war. The army is just waiting and observing the unfolding martyrdom of these young children. The army and the armaments are not expendable. However, when not used for sex, these young boys are expendable for Allah. In Islam, the most important act of sacrifice is jihad as in dying for the cause of Allah."

As Michael speaks, several blasts produce tiny volcanoes of sand, leaving behind small craters. A solitary shriek pierces the air. When the dust settles, one young body moans and writhes in the dirt. At each of the other land mine craters, there is no movement from three other crumpled young human forms. Each tiny body is collapsed into a small crater.

At random times and locations on this large field, similar scenes are repeated in various sequences. As one array of boys is annihilated, they are replaced with another wave and another wave and another wave of young boys. When an entire wave of boys reaches the safety of the road in front of the Archangels, all the land mines have been detonated. Then and only then do the military personnel, motorized vehicles, and armaments follow. No one is in any hurry to assist the maimed children. There is no respect for human life in Muhammad's Islam. All life is expendable for Allah. This is Muhammad's Islam which is coming to Western democracies.

"As in Nice, France, where a jihadist used a large transport truck to mow down and kill adults and children, ISIS now is calling its supporters to attack children specifically." In high sarcasm, Uriel mocks, "Allah is such a benevolent and loving god!"

> "Seek out your enemy relentlessly"
>
> - Quran 4:104.

"After fourteen hundred years of observing the brutal Islamic slaughter of innocents, I should be hardened to all this human carnage, but I'm not." Raphael's face and body language express his revulsion and distress. "In the last eight years of this war, I've seen these same deadly sequences replayed far too many times. Many thousands of young boys have been fooled and sacrificed to clear mine fields for the Muslim troops who follow.

"Why would these boys throw away their young lives? It's the same old trickery, same old trickery. It's the same Muhammad lie that works every time with Muslims. Using unspeakably cruel brainwashing, Muhammad's warnings of hellfire and promises of unlimited sex in paradise always succeed in convincing his young followers to do his bidding. The same indoctrination works equally well with today's jihadist terrorists and suicide bombers. Young Muslim males beg and plead to be allowed to die for Allah."

"The younger the teen, the higher the testosterone level and the more driven he is to satisfy his sexual urges," Raphael continues. "For young boys, the promise of an unlimited number of dark-eyed virgins is irresistible. Day and night, they dream about the delights of Paradise. They kill for sex, and they're dying to get into Muhammad's brothel in the sky. Young Muslims have an unshakeable conviction of their beliefs in martyrdom and in its promises of sex in the afterlife. These core beliefs translate into Muhammad's Islam of observable, foundational doctrine committed to and destined for world conquest."

"Turn into detested apes."

- Quran 7:166.

After a brief period of silence, Gabriel mutters, "Islam is one very sick society. From its very beginning, Muhammad's sex-crazed murderous, slaughter campaigns demonstrated his moral bankruptcy and depravity. The moral and ethical compass of Muhammad's radical Islam was broken in the seventh century and remains broken today."

Within audible range and within full view of the God Squad, Satan-Allah and Sonneillon are ecstatic over the success of Islam. They transport themselves into the midst of the four Archangels.

Satan mocks Gabriel, "Sick or not, Islam is kicking your butts. Hey, Gabby, you forgot to mention some of the juicier parts of Allah's recyclable virgins. His Paradise whores don't menstruate, don't urinate, and don't defecate. And they have yummy, yummy appetizing vaginas. My paradise is just one eternal sexual orgy."

Both devils double over with laughter and roll in the dirt.

But while he is still rolling hilariously on the ground, Sonneillon gets a tail-curling jolt in the rear end from Michael's lightsaber. With his horns smoldering and sparking from the intense heat of the cosmic laser, Sonny lets loose with one long shriek. Instantly, in a trail of smoke, both devils withdraw in silence.

Hours later as the four Archangels sit around in a circle, Michael, the cosmic legal and doctrinal expert muses, "I want to read some peaceful quotes from the Islamic Book of Tranquility." With a copy of the Quran in his hands, Michael reads from Quran 2:192: "'Slay them wherever you find them.' Quran 4:104 is just plain predatory: 'Seek out your enemy relentlessly.' Quran 7:166 reads: 'And when they scornfully persisted in their forbidden ways, We said to them: "Turn into detested apes."' Quran 7:166 is blatant hatred. Quran 8:12 doesn't leave anyone alive except Muslims, 'I shall cast terror into the hearts of the infidels. Strike off their heads, strike off the very tips of their fingers.'"

> "I shall cast terror into the hearts of the infidels. Strike off their heads, strike off the very tips of their fingers."
>
> – *Quran 8:12*

Archangel Gabriel blows off the cover on another of Muhammad's hateful missiles. "Quran 8:14–8:16 spews more of Muhammad's hatred: 'Believers, when you encounter the infidels (Christians and Jews) on the march, do not turn your backs to them in flight. . . . . If anyone on that day turns his back on them. . . . . He shall incur the wrath of Allah and Hell shall be his home: an evil fate.'"

"We have much to anticipate as 'peaceful' Islam spreads across Europe and America cutting off heads and chopping off finger tips." Michael delivers, "Quran 8:12 is all about the Islamic sword and the more than 300 million lives which Islam has slaughtered in the last fourteen centuries."

> "Believers, when you encounter the infidels (Christians and Jews) on the march, do not turn your backs to them in flight. . . . . If anyone on that day turns his back on them. . . . . He shall incur the wrath of Allah and Hell shall be his home: an evil fate."
>
> – *Quran 8:14–8:16*

"Ouch!" Gabriel recoils, "I am depressed and sickened by this senseless killing by Islam—century after century after century. Quran 8:59 and Quran 8:60 brings to memory the nightmares of 9/11 commanding, "Terrorize them. They are your enemy and Allah's enemy.'. . . 'Strike terror in the enemies of Allah.' Quran 9:5 doesn't leave anything to the imagination, exhorting to 'Slay the idolaters wherever you find them.' Radical Islam means to kill with a clear conscience. War is foundational to the Quran. Quran 9:73 leaves no uncertainty in Islam's obligation to kill: 'Prophet, make war on the unbelievers and the hypocrites and deal rigorously with them. Hell shall be their home.' Quran 9:123 is more and more of the same: 'Believers make war on the infidels that dwell around you.' The Islamic sword swings again in Quran 47:4, directing Muslims to 'Strike off the heads of the disbelievers making a wide slaughter among them.'"

"In Volume 4, Book 56, Number 791," reveals Michael, "The famous hadith tradition as documented by Sahih al-Bukhari reads: 'The Jews will fight you, and you will be given victory over them so that a stone will say, "O Muslim! There is a Jew behind me; kill him!"'"

Archangels usually are not known for sarcasm, but there are limits to their restraint. Uriel throws out another stinger, "Enough already, enough already. All of these peaceful Islamic exhortations are making me drowsy. Okay, okay. We're convinced. President George W. Bush was right. Islam is a religion of peace. Yuk!"

A serious looking Michael redirects the conversation and takes it to a philosophical level. "In the face of satanic terror, sometimes sarcasm is the only weapon left. All four of us are frustrated. What I have read is but a short list of Quranic exhortations to kill for Allah. There are one hundred twelve other such war verses urging the killing of infidels, but primarily Christians and Jews."

> "Slay the idolaters wherever you find them."
>
> - Quran 9:5

"All this mindless killing is performed by testosterone-driven young males who are brainless enough to have to be instructed about which shoe to put on first," says Raphael in frustration. He continues with sarcasm, "Is it the right shoe first or the left shoe first? In their Hadiths, Sahih al-Bukhari and Sahih Muslim wrote to start with the right side of the body when putting on shoes and washing hands. A

Muslim will put on the right shoe first and then the left shoe. When shoes are taken off, the Muslim is instructed to take off the left shoe first. When unable to use both hands, a Muslim will start by washing the right side of the face first and then the left. Likewise he is instructed to wipe the right side of his head before the left. Blowing the nose and removing filth should be done with the left hand. No Muslim shall eat with his left hand or drink with it. Of course, there is the foot washing ritual, and then there is the mouth washing ritual with the middle finger all the way to the back of the throat. When entering a place of respect, such as a mosque, Muslims must enter with the right foot first. Entering places of lesser respect such as a lavatory, Muslims enter with the left foot first. The hadiths show that Islamic law compels every minor detail of human life to occupy and imprison the mind. All this silliness is Islamic control for the sake of control. If this isn't mindless stuff, then what is it?"

The year is 2001. The place is Hamburg, Germany. In a local mosque, Muhammad Atta listens as a Muslim imam preaches "Christians and Jews should have their throats slit." The same hatred of Christians and Jews is being preached worldwide in many other mosques. This is Muhammad's real radical Islam.

> "Strike off the heads of the disbelievers making a wide slaughter among them."
>
> – Quran 47:4

The year is 2001. The day is September 11. The place is Manhattan, New York. Muhammad Atta, Egyptian leader of the nineteen terrorists, pilots his plane into the World Trade Center Towers. 9/11 is Muhammad's Islamic hatred in action. In the manner of Muhammad who took great joy in the brutal slaughter of his enemies, today's radical Islam is following in Muhammad's footsteps. It shows itself to be a shameless regime which takes pride in brutal, barbaric killing. This is the unmasked, real Islam of Muhammad.

September 11, 2001, is a most distressing day for the Angelic God Squad. In the bedlam of the collapsing World Trade Center towers,

Michael addresses his three fellow combatants, "9/11 is not a random date. It has special significance. By the calendar, Quran 9:111 is the Islamic call for the 9/11 slaughter. September 11 has special significance dating back from the Great Siege of Malta of 1565, from the Battle of Vienna of 1683, and from the Battle of Zenta of 1697."

From their vantage point on the steps of the New York Stock Exchange, Raphael thumbs through the Quran. He finds verse 9:111 and reads it out loud, "'Allah has purchased from the faithful their lives and worldly goods, and in return has promised them the Garden. They will fight for the cause of Allah, they will slay and be slain. Such is the promise which He has made them in the Torah, the Gospel and the Koran.'"

> "Allah has purchased from the faithful their lives and worldly goods, and in return has promised them the Garden. They will fight for the cause of Allah, they will slay and be slain. Such is the promise which He has made them in the Torah, the Gospel and the Koran."
>
> - Quran 9:111

"Yes, Quran 9:111 is the key verse to fight, to slay and to be slain. Fighting, slaying and being slain is not the Gospel of Jesus Christ. Quran 9:111 is a revisionist perversion of the Torah and the Gospel. There is no such exhortation in the Torah or in the Gospels to fight, to slay and to be slain. This is ultimate perverted Islamic lying."

According to official records, radical Islamists from Saudi Arabia intentionally piloted two passenger planes to slam into the Twin Towers of the World Trade Center. After fires erupt at the points of impact, the Angelic foursome hear screaming. They see bodies leaping off the top floors of the Trade Center and hitting the pavement in front of them. The God Squad realizes that they are seeing the words of Quran 9:111 being translated into actions.

"Were the persons who hijacked and commandeered those two passenger jets Muslims?" Who were they? Raphael is visibly shaken by the sights in front of him. "I hear many loud blasts coming down the twin towers as they are collapsing in front of us." Seven hours later,

World Trade Center 7 collapses into a pile of debris. An hour later, Raphael asks. "Why is there so much molten steel running all over at the bottom of these smoking heaps?" People reported hearing a series of multiple explosions which followed the floors down as they collapsed sequentially. What does it all mean?"

Raphael returns attention to the liquid metal at the bottom of heaps of rubble. "Before September 11, 2001, some individuals knew that the WTC towers were coming down. Mysteriously, FEMA arrived on September 10. How convenient! Then there was the enigma of World Trade Center 7. Funtionally, WTC Building 7 was the command center for the WTC complex. It housed the giant diesel backup and the oxygen supply. But WTC 7 was far and away more than just the physical control center. WTC 7 housed the Department of Defense, the Secret Service, the CIA, the IRS Regional Council, high profile insurance companies, brokerage firms and banks, and the NYC Office of Emergency Management. WTC 7 was the heart, the very nerve center and the brains of America complete with a bombproof bunker. WTC 7 housed the Securities and Exchange Commission." Raphael continues to raise concerns of potential treason, "Most significantly, it is baffling and most curious that on September 11, 2001, Mayor Giuliani and his entourage had set up camp in a different headquarters. Why did he relocate in advance of the cataclysms? It is more than apparent that those in supreme authority in America knew of the sequence of events which were programmed in advance."

"No airplane hit WTC 7." Uriel, the physical sciences specialist, is deeply puzzled. "Collapse of the North Tower caused some damage and some small fires in WTC 7, but it is baffling that at 5:20 PM WTC 7 was burning like a torch and collapsed into a heap. This forty-seven-story skyscraper folded neatly onto its own footprint in just 6.5 seconds. Engineers are baffled by the collapse WTC 7. Portions of its steel members had been partly evaporated. Partly evaporated??? The collapse of WTC 7 was a classic implosion which followed the blow out of its central columns so that WTC 7 fell in onto itself without damaging other buildings just feet away."

"WTC 7 was a steel-framed building," Uriel continues. "The laws of physics say that a weight dropped from a height of four hundred meters would hit the ground in nine seconds. However, at four hundred meters, the South Tower hit the ground in ten seconds. The speed of the collapse of the towers was almost at free-fall speed. The resistance of the undamaged floors below the point of impact should have slowed down the rate of collapse, but it did not. Even Nobel Prize–winner Dario Fo questioned the rapid rate of descent saying that 'There is something that's inexplainable about the rate of fall by the WTC towers.'"

"But there's more, much, much more. Weeks after the collapse of the towers, inspectors found pools of molten metal underneath the debris of all three buildings. Portions of the steel girders had melted, but the temperatures inside the buildings were too low to melt steel or even to soften the steel. Federal Building and Fire Safety Investigation and Underwriters Laboratories also determined that the steel did not soften and did not collapse."

"How was it determined that the temperatures were not high enough?" Gabriel questions.

"It's all about the color of the flames," explains Uriel. "As with the 2005 Madrid super fire in the Windsor Tower skyscraper, white flames indicate lots of oxygen. However, the flames from the WTC towers in New York were dark red with lots of black smoke indicating oxygen-starved fires of low heat. History shows that steel towers do not collapse due to fires. Of great concern, there was laboratory evidence that showed the presence of substantial quantities of a material that should NOT have been present. This chemical agent came from military thermate or thermite that is a mixture of aluminum powder, iron oxide, sulphur, and barium nitrate, which when ignited creates temperatures at one thousand degrees. That is hot enough to melt steel in just seconds. Radio-controlled ignitions fired the thermite implants sequentially, cut through the steel columns, and brought down the WTC towers with precision. These were controlled demolitions that were heard by many firefighters, emergency medical workers, and people escaping from the towers. Numbers of individuals saw brilliant flashes and heard, 'Boom! Boom! Boom! Boom!' That is why there were pools of molten metal weeks after September 11. Dust collected blocks away from the towers contained metal droplets and toxic barium. Necessarily, the explosive charges would have been placed *before* September 11."

"When no plane hit WTC 7, then why was this tower targeted for takedown?" asks Raphael.

"Simple!" adds Uriel. "In just 6½ seconds, thousands of Securities and Exchange Commission files were lost. These files detailed investigations of massive corporate frauds, which included financial giants Enron and Worldcom. Also destroyed were files on market manipulations in the colossal California Electricity Swindle. There were numbers of influential individuals who had escaped prosecution because of the destruction of records in WTC 7. Was that reason enough to bring down the WTC towers in this gigantic fraud that snowed the American public until today?"

"But there is more to this smoke screen stage show," Gabriel advances. "Allegedly American Airlines Flight #77 crashed into the Pentagon. However, there was no evidence on the ground of an impact by a Boeing 757 or by any other plane. Video surveillance crash sequences taken from eight-six different camera locations were confiscated by the FBI, but revealed zero visualization of any passenger aircraft. Flying at six meters above the earth was aerodynamically impossible for a Boeing 757. This was an absurd story concocted by government sources."

"Here is more official government fantasy. American Airlines Flight #77 was a Boeing 757 with a wingspan of thirty-eight meters (or 125 feet) and a height of 13.5 meters, but the hole in the wall of the Pentagon was circular and only five meters in width. As a bedtime story for gullible children, the Boeing 757 simply shrank to fit the hole." Uriel doubles over in derisive laughter. After he regains his composure, he continues. "There should have been hundreds of disintegrated and scattered airplane parts, but there were none. There were no seats and no luggage retrieved. Neither the wings nor the Boeing indestructible titanium engines were recovered."

"Uriel, don't be silly. The wings and the two engines simply vaporized from the intense heat of this dreamland folly," Gabriel joins Uriel in hilarious levity. Several minutes of silence elapse.

Uriel continues in mocking tones, "This intense heat defied and repealed the laws of physics. The heat was intense enough to incinerate and to vaporize the entire Boeing 757 in the explosion, but photographs revealed that it was not hot enough to set fire to office furniture, desks, computers, and books sitting undisturbed right next to the sheared off walls. Sham! Sham! Sham! Lies! Lies! Lies! Treason! Treason! Treason! Why is the American public not screaming out?"

"It has been proven beyond a shadow of a reasonable doubt," Raphael explains, "that the Pentagon was not hit by an airliner but by a missile. The passengers on Flight #77 are on airport videotape. They did exist. These passengers did not vanish into thin air. The uncomfortable question, which begs an answer, remains. Where is Flight #77 now? Where are the passengers and the crew? There were no bodies, no body parts, and no DNA ever recovered from within the Pentagon. Were these passengers and crews murdered to silence them? What happened to their bodies which have never been found for sixteen years? Was this a secret government black operations project to convince the world that 9/11 was Muslim terrorism?"

"Why would the American government go to such extremes as to annihilate its own citizens? What were they trying to cover up that required three thousand lives to be extinguished and sacrificed when the twin World Trade Center towers fell?"

Michael, the cosmic judge and sheriff of the universe, rides in with shattering news. "Here are a few headlines. On September 10, 2001, Secretary of Defense Donald Rumsfeld had announced that $2.3 trillion had gone missing. The timing of this disclosure was just one day before 9/11. The missile strike at the Pentagon conveniently destroyed all those records. Was the mysterious loss of 2.3 trillion dollars reason enough to bring down the three WTC towers and to missile strike the Pentagon? $2.3 trillion was one quarter of America's national debt. Was there another reason for this cover-up?"

Gabriel, another galactic sheriff, declares, "You know how I feel about Muhammad, that murderous, sex-pervert, and you know what I think about his Quran and his moon god Allah. However, justice must be served. There are major discrepancies within the 9/11 airport surveillance videos! At least four pilots of Middle Eastern descent were wrongly identified as the hijackers. As claimed by the FBI, the seat numbers occupied by the alleged hijackers did not correspond with those of the hijackers. News media reported that the hijackers used fake or stolen IDs using the names of real people who were living in Arab countries in the Middle East." Gabriel delves deeper into this monumental treasonous fraud which forever changed the destiny of America, "The *Wall Street Journal, BBC News* and *CNN* were party to reporting on this apparent misinformation. Because the hijackers used fake and stolen IDs, the truth could not be known as to who they really were and for whom they had worked. At least seven of the alleged hijackers were alive *after* 9/11. It is understandable why the Muslim world in the Middle East has been gravely and aggressively hostile toward America since the 9/11 accusations."

"The night before September 11, 2001, the alleged hijackers got drunk in public bars and did everthing possible to attract negative attention. They used credit cards and driver's licenses issued in their false names. They sent multiple emails boasting that they were going to hijack airliners and crash them into the World Trade Center towers. It is obvious that those who planned the 9/11 attacks and the airline hijackings were trying to make their Middle Eastern Arabic origins known. It is obvious that these were attempts to deceive and to link Saudi Arabia as the primary homeland of fifteen of the nineteen hijackers. The trail of concocted evidence left behind was wide and most deliberate, so that everyone would know who was to blame for 9/11. But for what purpose and to what end? That remains the speculative unknown."

Uriel inserts one of his usual one-liners, "I have heard it said and it has been written that the official government version of 9/11 is the mother of all lies."

"It is a fact," shares legal and military expert Michael, "that the official explanation for the collapse of the WTC towers is false because 9/11 was an orchestrated inside job involving many influential individuals at high levels of authority in America. Within the prison at Huntsville, Texas, at least one high profile political figure should be strapped to a gurney for execution by lethal injection." A round of heavy Angelic hand-clapping follows.

"As we know," continues Michael, "September 11 was an ominous date in Islamic history going back to the Great Siege of Malta in 1565, to the Battle of Vienna in 1683 and to the Battle of Zenta in 1687.

The symbolism of 9:111 and 9/11 is undeniable. It's unmistakable. It's intentional. Wittingly or unwittingly, Islamic scholars aided and abetted 9/11. Quran 9:111 is the language of terrorism. It's Allah's command. Quran 9:111 is Allah's marching orders. As high terror for its own sake, 9/11 was the opening assault upon America. Unfortunately, Americans don't know what's in the Quran. And they are not about to listen or to find out either. Soon they will have a catastrophic refresher experience with Quran 9:111."

"Quran 9:111 is the highway to Allah's Paradise Whorehouse in the sky." Michael's perspective provides a much broader view of both the past and of the future. "For the last fourteen hundred years, Quran 9:111 has driven millions of Islamic martyrdom-seekers to slaughter of up to 300 million people. I regret to give you this wakeup call, but 300 million are but the down payment to Allah. Before long, that number will run into the billions."

"Of course, let's not forget the most infamous and diabolical verse of all which Uriel just read. Quran 9:111 pressures the Muslim to kill for Allah. Within a single verse, Quran 9:111 ranges from one extreme to another, from hilarious sex nonsense, to murder and terrorization. Muhammad's Islamic driving force is fear, fear of hell in the Muslim believer, fear of terror in the infidel, and the promise of eternal sex for Islamic jihadists. On 9/11, Quran 9:111 brought down the World Trade Center towers. 9/11 is about Quran 9:111."

Uriel is quick to point out a discrepancy, "It's very close, but 9:111 doesn't look exactly like 9/11."

Michael returns the argument. "Remember that this event is taking place in 2001. Take the "1" of 2001 and tack it to the end of 9/11, and it becomes 9/111. So Quran 9:111 is 9/111 is 9/11. The date and the verse correspond. Muslim scholars planned this event years earlier. September 11 was not a random date. September 11 has a long history of Islamic defeats."

It took a number of seconds for the other three Archangels to weigh the gravity of these two sets of numbers. The four Archangels huddle for a brainstorming session. For the last fourteen hundred years, Gabriel has suffered immensely from Muhammad's false accusations and his psychological assaults upon Gabriel's conduct and character. Gabriel is always on the defensive and always ready to challenge Muhammad's defamations. "Just listen to what this low-life scoundrel wrote concerning me. In Quran 2:98, he defamed me saying, "Whoever is an enemy of Allah, His angels, or His apostles, or of Gabriel or Michael, will surely find that Allah is the enemy of the unbelievers (Jews),' I was no messenger to Muhammad, and I am no supporter of this murderous thug who was murdering Christians and Jews." Gabriel shows relief after venting his ire against Muhammad.

"Consider the words of Tafsir Ibn Kathir. He's Islam's scholar and authority of the fourteenth century. Kathir parroted Muhammad word for word. In Allah's Paradise, the martyred male will be able to have sex with a hundred virgins in one day. One hundred virgins a day is full-time employment. And when sex is finished, the dark-eyed whores will return pure and virgin again. Yes, their hymens are restored for the next Islamic martyr sex assault. The restorative magic of Muhammad's Islam is breathtaking." Raphael doubles over in derision. "How can intelligent people in the twenty-first century believe this laughable, unspeakable, brainless folly?"

> "Whoever is an enemy of Allah, His angels, or His apostles, or of Gabriel or Michael, will surely find that Allah is the enemy of the unbelievers (Jews)."
>
> – Quran 2:98

"These beliefs are just silly, laughable and ludicrous nonsense!" Holding this bizarre Islamic theology in high contempt, Gabriel continues to dismember this lunacy. "With boldness and without a hint of shame, the words of these commentators and 'theologians' speak to the depravity and the moral bankruptcy of the Quran and of Muslim scholars. It is no wonder that the imams warn against criticising the Quran as they scream 'Islamophobia!' The imams know that the Quran cannot be defended at any intellectual level."

"Allah's Sexual Paradise of recycled virgins," explains Michael, "is comedic nonsense which is seen to be a highly exaggerated, metaphoric, cosmic version of Hugh Heffner's Mansion of Playboy Bunnies. It is hilarious fantasy that even Muslim imams blush at Muhammad's 72 paradise virgins as being downright silly. Their only defense is the

Quran. By Islamic standards, if the Quran says it, and the Hadiths say it, then it is a fact. That's the end of the story and the case is closed. Therefore, go kill for Allah and get eternal sex in Paradise with 72 virgins. Muslims across the globe are so ashamed of the writings of this book that they are agitating to make laws that forbid discussion of their Quran even by infidels."

After a long pause, Archangel Raphael continues to review recent Muslim history. "Four thousand years after Ishmael and in retribution and revenge for the injustices inflicted upon Ishmael by Sarah, the Ayatollah Khomeini of Iran escalated the subjugation of women by many degrees. Starting in 1979, Ayatollah Khomeini used the resurgence of Islam in Iran to strip women of their rights and dignities. He reduced women to medieval slavery. Muhammad beat his wives and Muhammad's companions beat their wives. In Quran 4:34, Muhammad had written, 'Men have authority over women because Allah has made the one superior to the other. As for those women from whom you fear disobedience, admonish them, forsake them in beds apart, and beat them.'"

> "Men have authority over women because Allah has made the one superior to the other. As for those women from whom you fear disobedience, admonish them, forsake them in beds apart, and beat them."
>
> - Quran 4:34

"Under Iran's Ayatollah Khomeini's Sharia Law, husbands were allowed, and even encouraged, to beat their wives," Gabriel bemoans. "Sharia Law is the law of Islam. Even in Sunni schools, as further punishment of females under Sharia Law, female circumcision is practiced with a vengeance. But it gets worse, much worse. Back in the 1980s, Iran's Ayatollah Khomeini had given his consent for having sex with female infants. Yes, sex with female infants. How much sicker and more evil can it get? This is depravity and monstrosity straight out of Islamic hell. And this unparalleled licentiousness was ordained by the supreme religious cleric of Iran! To consent to sex with infants far exceeds the sins of Sodom and Gomorrah. To consent to sex with infants, speaks of barbaric hatred toward females that is demonic. If these sexual perverts in Iran lived in America or in Canada, there wouldn't be enough jails to contain them. In this light, Iran's hatred of Israel is better understood as demonic and right from the pit of Hell.

As Yasser Arafat's PLO was being driven out of Lebanon, his Allah-directed Holy Muslim fighters left behind one hundred thousand young pregnant girls in their wake. Muslim boys want only virgins. But Yasser's boys were impatient. They were not about to wait for sex in Paradise. They deflowered Lebanon's virgins in the here and now. Muhammad's Islam is driven by sex and slaughter, but actually and primarily, Muhammad's radical Islam is driven by the promise of eternal sex in Paradise."

Raphael, the health and wellness specialist, presents his medical perspective regarding these abnormal social and psychological distortions. "After the Fall of Adam and Eve in the Garden of Eden, human genetics were corrupted. Adonai made that clear. We also know about the damage done by incest, which cripples the mind and corrupts the DNA. We also know that Ishmael had molested Isaac. When Sarah witnessed this scene, she went livid. With Adonai's approval, Sarah had Ishmael thrown out into the desert together with Hagar his toxic mother. Ishmael's gross misconduct and his punishment twisted his mind and corrupted his DNA. You know the old saying 'Mind over Matter.' Well, I say to you, 'Mind over Genes.' Islam has spread this genetic corruption to other cultures. Just consider Loosey Goosey Saudi Arabia today. King Ibn Saud had 120 wives. Ibn Saud was the father of all the Saudi kings who are living in the luxury of oil dollars. Today, King Abdullah has had more than thirty wives; a great example coming from the head of the Saudi Nation. For four thousand years, the Ishmaelite male has been ruled by his penis. It is sexual indulgence without parallel. Islamic Paradise is more and more sex with more and more virgins."

Within earshot and in plain view of the God Squad, Satan and Sonneillon close the distance hurling abuse and insults as they approach. "How about some honesty from you four angels? How dare you put down King Abdullah and Muhammad?"

Satan now is nose-to-nose with Michael, wagging her index finger at Michael. "Your King David killed the husband of the woman he impregnated. Fine example he was not and a murderer no less. How was King David better than Muhammad? His son, King Solomon was no standard of morality either. Three hundred wives, seven hundred mistresses and an unknown number of children. He couldn't remember all of their names. At least Muhammad could sex all eleven of his wives in a single night. At that rate, it would have taken Solomon more than three months to complete a single round of his women. And you are condemning Muhammad? You finger pointers! How dare you!" Satan-Allah has worked herself up into a feverish pitch.

Michael, the cosmic legal authority on all matters of morals and justice, addresses his adversaries. "Satan, your future is in the fires of Hell. None of us four Archangels would defend David or Solomon or Samson. And look at the destruction which each of them brought down upon his head, upon his family, and upon the nation of Israel. We see the results of King David's folly. It was kingdom civil war with his son Absolom seeking to kill his own father. Absolom humiliated his father publicly by having sex with his concubines. And David's son Solomon? His foreign wives and their gods brought his kingdom into captivity after he died. What can be said in defense of Samson? His lust cost him his eyes, his freedom, his dignity, and his life."

With visible discomfort, Michael continues, "These three men were bad examples to the generations which followed. Muhammad had chosen death. This very moment, he is chained in Hell waiting the final judgment to join you in the flames, Satan-Allah."

It is apparent that Satan is burning up with hatred towards the four Archangels. Speechless and without a defence, she and Sonneillon slink off into the shadows.

Minutes later, Gabriel changes the direction of the conversation and presents the woman's perspective. "It took ten-year-old Nujood Ali to elevate the depravity of Islam onto front and center world stage. In her book, *I am Nujood: Age 10 and Divorced*, Nujood exposes an ugly secret which for centuries has destroyed the lives of Islamic girls who are traded like commodities. As an eight-year-old, Nujood was given in an arranged marriage to a man three times her age. Her husband abused and beat her until she ran away. As a third-grader, Nujood was the first child bride to win a divorce in Yemen. Nujood is just another Aisha."

Gabriel continues, "It takes a Muslim woman who has abandoned Islam to pull back the veil on the polygamy of Muhammad's four-wife legacy. Although Muhammad was 'permitted' by Allah to have twelve wives, he allowed and encouraged only four wives for other Muslim males. Muhammad knew full well of the seething jealousy, animosity, and warfare between his multiple wives. While he controlled men with his sword, he controlled his wives with polygamy. The wives were so occupied fighting each other that they did not have time to cause distress for him. The four of us have seen the pain and the anguish inside these pentagon marriages.

Polygamy was never Adonai's plan for man," adds Uriel. "Now, in her two books, *Infidel* and *Nomad*, Ayaan Hirsi Ali, an apostate Muslim woman, has let the world see the devastations inside and behind the burkas, the niqabs and beyond."

"But now we are getting deeper than just outward clothing." Gabriel presents the woman's perspective. "Ayaan Hirsi Ali speaks of the uncertainty, distrust, envy, and jealousy that run rampant within these wife quadrangles." Because of his female sensitivities, Gabriel empathizes with Ayaan and with Muslim women in general saying, "In addition to forced genital mutilation, there is nothing of security, safety, predictability, and happy family living in these polygamist wife quads. These marriages are the breeding grounds for power struggles and emotional distresses triggered by suppressed jealousy and hostility. Within these poisonous relationships, the wives become mean, angry, and erratic. Often they explode into violence. Honor killings are but one bizarre outcome. The children of these marital wreckages bear the brunt of the misery inflicted upon their mothers."

"It all goes back some four thousand years ago, to that vicious marital triangle unleashed upon the world by Abraham's wife Sarah." Michael reminds them. "Abraham had set a terribly bad example for his son Ishmael by having two wives; as Hagar his mother and as Sarah the mother of Isaac. Ishmael was given every reason to distrust and to hate women. In revenge, Ishmael determined that he would trample upon women. His taught his sons and their descendants to subdue and to crush women."

Michael summarizes the history of Islamic women, "Twenty-six centuries after Ishmael, and in his revenge on behalf of Ishmael, Muhammad permitted male dominance against all women. In his spirit of vengeance, retribution, and lust, Muhammad doubled the number of permissible wives to four. Muhammad sets the pattern for fourteen centuries of female domination and exploitive sex."

Archangel Gabriel provides supporting insights and perspective. "Crush the female is what Ishmaelite males have done over the ages. By genital mutilation, Muhammad and his generations made sure that they deprived the female even of sexual pleasures while inflicting maximum pain during this barbaric clitoral butchery. To ensure chastity, the opening of the vagina was sewn together. The psychological trauma inflicted upon young girls by this physical deformation lasts a lifetime. This is Muhammad's Islamic discrimination, humiliation and violence against women. It was all about Muhammad's Islamic control of women and control of their sexuality."

"According to Ayaan Hirsi Ali, it's no different today." Gabriel continues, "Medically, genital mutilation is considered to be invasive maiming. Polygamy was and continues to be another means of suppressing females. The women born into Islam are silent about their pains, their tensions, and the double-mindedness of polygamy. Just as he had promoted child marriage, Muhammad enshrined polygamy inside his Quran."

Dr. Raphael expounds the origins of marriage, "Monogamous love was built into our genetic survival code in **Genesis 2:24** as spoken by Adonai, 'Therefore a man shall leave his father and his mother and cleave to his wife, and they shall become one flesh.'"

"We are neurologically hard-wired *not* to face life alone. Dependable, secure attachment to a mate makes for healthy and happy lives for both partners. Loneliness, loveless marriage, emotional isolation, and social isolation raise stress cortisol levels, increase blood pressure, depress the immune system, and raise the risk of strokes, heart attacks, and all manner of other sickness."

"Islamic marriages of four wives to one husband do not fulfill the psychological bonding for which people were designed." Raphael continues, "People crave and need emotional balance which never can be found within Muslim polygamous marriages. People function at their best when they are partnered up and bonded in a stable relationship on which they can count. The strife of competition among four wives promotes stability for none. Emotionally, it is the women who suffer the most in these dysfunctional pentagon marriages, which never can be anything other but dysfunctional. The wives in these arrangements are the most emotionally isolated and stressed of all women."

"In the manner of the continual confrontations between Sarah and Hagar, these toxic Muhammad-pentangles degrade into jealousies, emotional upheavals, and vicious physical fights between the four female opponents." Gabriel presents his perspective: "Suppressed emotions eventually explode. Call it 'The Muhammad Dysfunctional Marriage Syndrome.' The foundational example of this marital turmoil was found within the circle of Muhammad's multiple wives. Finally, the plotting, the scheming, the divisions, and the strife were directed at the perpetrator when his wives poisoned Muhammad. After his justified poisoning death, the plotting, the scheming, the divisions, and the strife continued in the Intrigues of the Wives. After Muhammad's poisoning death, all boundaries of restraint were violated and trampled under foot. All manner of warfare was unleashed by his wives in the Battle of the Camel, in the Battle of the Wives, in the War of the Wives and in the War of the Mothers of the Believers."

"The moral rot of gender oppression and gender suppression translate into the intentional death of intimacy." Raphael exposes more of the psychiatric damages, "Both sexes lose, but the wives are the major losers. This helps to explain why Islam and the Muslims within it are so messed up in enigmatic ways. Like the suicide gear which they carry, suppression of Muslim females eventually erupts into one or another form of violence. We see it again and again. Muslim women are becoming more and more aggressive and more and more daring."

"In the volatile Muslim provinces of the Caucasus, another round in the deadly battle of liberation from Russia exploded in Volgograd on December 29 and 30, 2013." Gabriel shifts to the violence exploding out of Muslim women, "The Muslims are fighting a psychological war for the independence of Chechnya and Dagestan. Their aims are to raise anxiety, to create a state of insecurity, to cause carnage, and to disrupt the winter Olympic Games in the Black Sea resort city of Sochi. In these mass killings, it was determined that one of the suicide bombers was a female. Bomber Lady was the widow of two successive husbands, both of whom were rebels and both of whom were killed by Russian forces in the Caucasus. She was one of many in the string of female suicide bombers who have been dubbed as 'black widows.' The bottled up anger and hatred inside these black widows is being unleashed."

"Within this context, Muhammad enshrined Ishmael's distrust and his hatred of women inside the pages of his Quran." Projecting back to the days of old, Michael summarizes, "Ishmael and Muhammad made sure that there would never be another Sarah or another Hagar in their midst. If their wives or their daughters defied them, then an honor killing would eliminate this threat. Over many centuries since Muhammad, honor killing of women has been the rule. Hundreds of years after Muhammad, his followers raised the level of male affliction upon their women whom they forced to become faceless and shapeless black ravens inside their burkas and niqabs. Because of Arabic shame, anger, and hatred, neither Hagar nor Sarah is mentioned by name in Muhammad's Quran. However, enigmatically and in stark contrast, Mary the mother of Jesus gets a whole chapter devoted to her in the Quran."

"Devoting chapter 19 of the Quran to the mother of Jesus, raises multiple questions of authorship and intent." Raphael reviews the events of that clandestine meeting on that fateful night in the Catholic Cathedral in Mecca, "All four of us heard Waraquah, Khadijah and the Augustinian monk making plans to include Mary in the Quran. This is the stamp of undeniable collusion in its construction by the Vatican."

As the angelic role model for women's justice and equality, Gabriel is at the front line of this battle for gender equality. Gabriel speaks in a voice with tones of anguish but with obvious determination. "Female Muslim authors and journalists are beginning to take a stand. Now hear what the past president of the Muslim Canadian Congress had to say. As the author of *Islam, Women and the Challenges of Today*, Farzana Hassan pulls no punches. Farzana stated that the niqab symbolizes 'deep-rooted sexism, patriarchal control and misogyny...'The niqab is 'the most pernicious symbol of female subjugation which greatly stigmatizes and marginalizes women in society. The niqab is a means of control over women's bodies, travel, and activities.'"

"I'm in agreement that Islam does not require women to cover their faces," Michael pitches in from the legal point of view. "The niqab is merely a political declaration of Islamism. Farzana leaves nothing to the imagination when she accuses a society that permits the marginalization of women to be a dysfunctional society which Canadian courts must discourage."

"Dysfunctional society?" Gabriel echoes. "Now those are fighting words for the ayatollahs. But there is much more here that must be understood. There are a number of different female dress wares which range from a burqa to a chador to jilbab to an abaya to a hijab and to a niqab. However, besides marginalizing women, these dress wares are Islam's political-religious fist at the world that walks among the people and flaunts its defiance. The niqab serves the same purpose as the phallic minarets around the mosques. It's the middle finger to Christians and to the world. The niqab silently spits upon Yeshua Messiah. The burqa, the chador, the jilbab, the abaya, the hijab, and the niqab silently declare to the world that Christ is *NOT* the Son of God, that the blood of Christ was *NOT* shed on the cross, that Christ did *NOT* die on the cross, that Christ was *NOT* resurrected, that atonement for sins did *NOT* happen and that Christ is coming back as Allah's servant *to kill Christians and Jews.* Four phallic minarets around the perimeter of a mosque dome are the Islamic middle fingers screaming out that the penis overrules women, that the penis rules Sharia Law and that the penis rules Islam. The presence of phallic minarets at every mosque is indisputable proof that even moderate Muslims endorse the penis-controlled Sharia Law."

Raphael has been patient and polite waiting for a pause in the conversation. "For centuries as the Angel of health and wellness, I have observed the fallout and the mental suffering of the children of these distorted and perverse marital arrangements. Consider Ayaan

Hirsi Ali's father. He had four wives and six children. Three of the children suffered severe incapacitating mental illnesses, one of whom had psychotic episodes of manic depression. Does polygamy invite emotional instability, mental instability, and madness?"

From his position of maturity and wisdom, Michael responds with his overview. "You are the medical authority and you are asking me? My answer to your question, Raphael, is a resounding 'Yes.' Four thousand years ago, we witnessed what happened to Ishmael. Sarah and Hagar inflicted upon Ishmael the same mental and emotional distresses and distortions of which Ayaan Hirsi Ali speaks today. Ishmael was damaged and warped emotionally. Although polygamy predated Islam, Muhammad raised it to a higher level and made it a law. Today the world is paying the high price for the folly of those two warring females inside the tents of Abraham, and for the folly of Muhammad's Quran.

"Islam has defined defiance of male control of women to be equivalent to defying Allah," Michael continues. "An independent vocal woman is anathema to Islam and to male family domination. An independent and defiant woman tarnishes a male's reputation and shames the family. Because they defied their father, three Muslim sisters and one wife died in an honor killing after intentionally being drowned inside their car which was deliberately submerged in the Rideau Canal in Ottawa by male members of their family. *Murdered* is the better word. In 2007, in Mississauga, Canada, sixteen-year-old Aqsa Parvez was strangled by her Pakistani father and her brother because she refused to wear a hijab."

"What happened at the local mosque makes Aqsa's killing death even more serious," interjects Gabriel. "Aqsa's classmates agreed that she had brought her murder upon herself. Even the imam of the mosque sanctioned and agreed with the honor killing. Now that's great cause for concern in Canada when the Islamic community supports an honor killing. Canadians should be extremely concerned that Islam can use Sharia Law to inflict honor killings on Canadian soil."

"To stop this family killing, a well-known female Muslim journalist, Irshad Manji, had taken up Aqsa's cause and her cry for help. Irshad called it "Aqsa's Law." In her book, *The Trouble with Islam Today*, Irshad Manji has become the critic of traditional mainstream Islam.

Even Tarek Fatah, a fellow Canadian Muslim, agreed with much of her memoir. It comes as no surprise that Irshad Manji had received numerous death threats from Muslim groups."

Cosmic lawyer Michael brings the discourse back into the legal fold. "Honor killings simply are symptomatic of the inner cancer. The *National Post* revealed, 'Muslim governments pressing UN to root out Islamophobia in Western countries.' Muslims want to muzzle freedom of speech worldwide so that there will be no criticism of Muhammad and of Islam. Muslim governments know that Islamic ideology cannot withstand the test of scrutiny. They know that that Islam is a political system for world domination. They want to head off all criticism before the whole world realizes that the Quran and Islam are a manifesto for world conquest. Muslim governments are running scared of exposure of their indefensible political doctrines for world domination."

"Just in case there are any doubts about the minds of Muslim males, let me remove those doubts from *your* minds with just one instance." Archangel Gabriel reveals the event, "A Western woman traveling alone in the North African country of Morocco must be fearless, crazy, or both. Her bodily integrity is constantly at risk. Across Muslim North Africa and throughout the Muslim Middle East, from Morocco to Egypt to the borders of India, sexual harassments and sexual assaults make daily news. In these lands, an unveiled female tourist is met with leering glares. Female journalists living in Casablanca tell of living under constant 'eye-rape.' This is the male-dominated world of Islam with no moral scruples and no pretences."

Raphael raises these Islamic assaults upon women and girls to the highest levels of backlash and to the potential of civil unrest. "With the recent massive migrations into Europe by Muslim refugees from Syria and North Africa, 'eye-rapes' have morphed into vicious physical rapes on a massive scale by Muslim males who are defying all authorties with impunity while European governments are helpless and paralyzed in fear.

"Gabriel, just recall your message to Hagar four thousand years ago." Michael takes them back in time. "For forty centuries, Ishmael's hand has been against every man and every man's hand has been against him. Generational hatred, violence and war are Islamic genetic predispositions of conscience. Polygamy, rape of captives, sex slaves, anal sex, incest, rape of young girls, and even sodomy of young boys are the dark evil of 'holy' Islam. Muhammad did it all in spades. In the Hadiths, Muhammad is the prime offending Muslim example. And what a wickedly sorry example of a 'holy' prophet Muhammad had turned out to be."

"But hey, the Roman Catholic Church has its pedophile priests doing sodomy on young boys." Gabriel uncovers more slime, "With regard to pedophilia, the Catholic Church is in a crisis of credibility. Is it all in their genes or is it only in their jeans?"

"Now, I do have a substantial grasp of genetics," says medical expert Raphael who uncovers the depths of behaviors controlled by genes. "As with selective breeding of behavioral patterns in dogs, this is an issue of genetics and DNA. As the descendants of the wolf, the mildly aggressive but highly intelligent Border Collie has a visibly different behavioural pattern from that of the dangerous Pit Bull terrier. It's all in the DNA. Ishmaelite aberrant behaviour of sex, violence, and warfare is more than cultural. It's about genetic degradation of the mind-set. Four thousand years of sexual misconduct, sexual perversion, and slaughter have corrupted the Ishmaelite Y-chromosome. It's more than cultural. Are Ishmaelite males wired differently? By spiritual heredity, it's the sins of the fathers that are passed down to their sons for generations. As stated in Exodus 20:5, "For I the LORD your God am a jealous God visiting the iniquity of the fathers upon the children to the third and fourth generation of those who hate me.' Gabriel, you know that. Adonai's words from you to Hagar were foretelling that Ishmael would be 'an ass of a man with his hand against every man and every man's hand against him.' Between the lines, your message to Hagar about Ishmael said as much that it was in Ishmael's DNA. The world has yet to recognize this spiritual genetic fact."

"But it gets worse." Michael exposes horrific Quranic teaching in Middle Eastern Muslim communities. "In Islamic schools, grade 7 students are taught that unbelievers, both Jews and Christians, as the People of the Book, shall burn forever in the fires of Hell. Muslim children are taught that Christians and Jews are the vilest of all creatures. Yasser Arafat initiated his Campaign of Children Suicide

Bombers. Palestinian children were being sent to blow themselves up against Israeli civilian targets. Saudi Arabia funds kindergartens in Palestine. How noble of the Saudis. But the Saudis have an agenda. Saudi money buys control. The Saudis direct the curriculums in their madrassas. Palestinian children are taught to play-act the attacks of suicide bombers. These small children are forced to wear military uniforms and mock explosive belts. Palestinian children are trained to use imitation Kalashnikov rifles. It's preparation for the real weapons and their trip to Sex Paradise. Saudi and Palestinian children are taught that killing Jews while blowing themselves up is Allah's perfect will. Today, textbooks in Syria repeatedly drum it into young minds that all Jews must be annihilated. Arab children suck hatred with their mothers' milk."

Michael asks a rhetorical question, "What triggered the Second Palestinian Intifada? Yasser Arafat was looking for any excuse, and inadvertently, Ariel Sharon provided it when he visited the Dome of the Rock in Jerusalem. The Final Intifada and Armageddon will be launched when Israelis move to replace the Dome of the Rock and to rebuild the Third Temple. Make no mistake, the Dome of the Rock will be one of the central stumbling blocks leading to World War III."

"As recorded by Sahih al-Bukhari in Volume 4, Book 52, Number 176 and by Sahih Muslim in Book 041, Number 6981, is a quote of Muhammad's dying words, 'The last hour will not come before the Muslims fight the Jews and the Muslims kill them. In that day Allah will give voice to the rocks and the trees and they will cry out, 'O Muslim, there is a Jew hiding behind me. Come and kill him!' Other versions include the threat, 'May Allah curse the Christians and Jews.' Yes, Christians and Jews will hang together, or be butchered together."

The year is 2003. The place is Palestine. The Palestinian Authority has distributed Hitler's *Mein Kampf*. It's an eye-opener which exposes that there is much equivalency between and Muhammad's Quran and Hitler's *Mein Kampf*. Both books are about killing Jews and Infidels.

Uriel fills in with other supporting details and ways in which Muhammad

> "If you do not fight, He will punish you sternly."
>
> – *Quran 9:38-39*

used to frighten young Muslims with the threat of the fires of Hell. "Muhammad surely knew how to work the male psychology angle. He played his psychological triple sequence to perfection. First Muhammad offered the gift of eternal sex in Allah's paradise. Secondly there was the expectation and the demand to kill for Allah. Thirdly, if Muslims refused to kill, then came the threats of punishments of hellfire. Quran 9:38–39 threatens that, 'If you do not fight, He will punish you sternly.' It is about punishment for disobedience. It's about cruel and unconscionable brain washing that works to perfection. Quran 6:155 exhorts and threatens to 'Fear Allah, do not disobey His orders that you may be saved from the torment of Hell.' This verse makes certain to connect refusal to fight for Allah with disobedience of Allah and hellfire punishment."

Gabriel takes these Quranic verses right to the very pit of Hell. "Every serious Muslim is driven by the fear of Hell. Every Muslim thinks, 'How many do I need to kill to guarantee Paradise for myself? If I kill five infidels, is that enough? What if I kill fifty infidels? Will killing a hundred be enough? Even after killing a hundred infidels, I still can't be sure of Paradise.' By the words in the Quran, every peaceful Muslim is a hypocrite destined for Hell. By Muhammad's Quran, a Muslim is not permitted to be at peace. The fear of Hell which drives Islam, makes every Muslim a potential terrorist. We just don't know which neighbor of ours will turn out to be a terrorist. He may be another Major Hasan at another Fort Hood near you."

Always the objective observer who usually keeps his distance, Uriel gives a few carefully crafted conclusions. "In the clearest language possible, Muslim leaders are declaring that Israel must be annihilated, no matter what the human cost. Islam's unchangeable goal is world conquest. There cannot be peace until the entire world is under Allah's heel. The Arabs and Iran see themselves as nations created by Allah, not for life, but for death."

Raphael quotes Quran 33:60-62 which curses the hypocrites with death threats, 'If the hypocrites and those who have tainted hearts . . . do not desist, we will rouse you against them. Cursed wherever they are found, they shall be seized and put to death without mercy.'"

"So true, Raphael," chimes in Michael. "It's Jihad and sex with virgins in paradise, *or* the fires of Hell. Under the pretence of religion, the Quran is a political manifesto to commit mass murder for Allah. The Quran is a book of extremist Islamic doctrine."

"Fear Allah, do not disobey His orders that you may be saved from the torment of Hell."

– Quran 6:155

"As twisted as the Communist Manifesto was, at least it had a semblance of earthly logic that appealed to the intellect." Raphael continues his line of exposure, "Only the harsh reality of experience brought communism crashing to its knees. However, Muhammad's Islamic manifesto in the Quran is not open to any earthly challenge. Under threat of Hell, the Quran commands to do Allah's will. For the Muslim, Allah's command is the only defense needed. End of story. Pass the explosive vest."

"There is no earthly way to stop someone from killing himself or herself." Gabriel interjects, "All day long and much of the night, these young studs have visions dancing in their heads of full-breasted dark eyed virgins lying on couches, winking and blinking and beckoning. Testosterone-fired-up Muslim males are begging Allah to provide them with a martyr moment. The world is confronted by an enemy that is hell-bent on killing, hell-bent on being killed, and hell-bent on being martyred in any battle for Allah."

It takes a highly trained medical mind to analyze Muhammad's cunning and the cunning of the Augustinian monks who wrote the Quran and who were aided and abetted by input from Muhammad's wife Khadijah and from her cousin Waraquah. Raphael presents his objective psychiatric analysis. "Morbid fear of Hell and promises of eternal sex in paradise are two extreme but mutually supportive driving forces which aid and abet irrational slaughter. The combination of excessive fear coupled with intemperate sexual rewards rip the mind apart. This lethal psychological cocktail becomes an irrational and psychotic obsession against which there is little defence. In this conflicting mix, Muhammad did not allow the hypocritical option of refusing to fight for Allah. By demonic design, death as a jihad martyr is the only way a Muslim could be certain of attaining paradise. In a swirling battle for control of the mind, compelling and overwhelming emotions overrule and bypass the brain. In this reflexive and neurological short-circuit when the fear of Hell is spiked with high levels of testosterone and lust, this mental cocktail is explosive and lethal." With nods of approval, Raphael's evaluation resonates with his three companions.

"If the hypocrites and those who have tainted hearts . . . do not desist, we will rouse you against them. Cursed wherever they are found, they shall be seized and put to death without mercy."

– Quran 33:60-62

As the medical authority, Raphael presents other psychiatric drivers of this aberrant suicidal behavior, saying, "A prolonged and intense emotional response to deep-seated fears wreaks havoc upon mind and body. Churning thoughts, feelings and emotions disrupts the sleep cycle. Sleep deprivation is known to create unpredictable psychiatric disturbances. The response pattern of sleep deprivation resembles Post Traumatic Stress Disorder. Gene expression is modified. Over a period of months, the physiology of the body and the levels of hormones and neurotransmitters do change. Levels of cortisol, serotonin, and dopamine will fluctuate unpredictably. Muhammad was a masterful artist in manipulating young males. This manner of brainwashing continues today. On this emotional neurotransmitter roller coaster, often the choice for a would-be terrorist is either performing a plain vanilla suicide or becoming a suicide bomber. Proverbs 23:7 states that, 'As a man thinks, so he is.'"

As the deep thinker and the political theorist of the Angelic God Squad, Michael gives his worldview of history. "Together with the input of mind-bending drugs as marijuana and hashish, the Islamic curtain of the mind is more rigid and more impenetrable than the Soviet Iron Curtain ever was."

The year is 2007. The place is the White House in the USA. President George Bush addresses the American Nation saying, "Islam is a religion of peace."

It takes unusual circumstances to see Archangel Michael shaken up. "What!? A religion of peace!? Did I hear it right? Islam is a religion of peace? Not in this universe! We are aware that most young Americans do not know their own history. Americans are ignorant of what Islam did fourteen hundred years ago in Arabia and in the rest of the world since then. Is this Bush tongue-in-cheek gamesmanship? Is it politically correct posturing? Is it blithering ignorance? Is the U.S. president trying to indoctrinate Americans that Islam is benign? Or is America running scared? Fourteen centuries of Islamic religious discrimination which has caused the suffering and the deaths of up to 300 million is called peace and tolerance? A religion of peace!?"

Michael's three companions are taken aback by his reaction. Gabriel expresses his amazement. "Michael, you're usually cool, calm, and collected. It's been almost a hundred years since I saw you so upset. Not since the Armenian Genocide by the Muslim Turks. But you're right. Blatant deceit by an American president shows his contempt for the intelligence of the American people. But then, America cannot afford to offend its Muslim allies or the oil-rich Saudis. A dishonest attempt to be politically correct puts off the recognition of reality for another day."

The date is November 29, 2009. The place is Switzerland. The referendum to stop the construction of minarets on Islamic mosques was passed by a 55 percent margin. The four Archangels are monitoring the political waves in Switzerland and in the rest of Europe. They are sitting around in a circle reviewing the significance of these events.

"Why are the Swiss so upset with the minarets?" Uriel inquires.

"Just as the rest of Europe, the Swiss know the historic dark resonance of Islam," replies Raphael. "It goes back to the butchering of Christians at Constantinople by the Muslim Turks in 1453. When they conquered Constantinople, the Turks erected a minaret on top of the Hagea Sophia Cathedral. Until then, the Hagea Sophia was the world's biggest Christian Greek Orthodox Church. Then came the genocide of Turkey's Christians in Armenia in 1915. Armenian Christian survivors recorded more than three million murderous deaths by the Ottoman Turkish Muslims. All of Europe was wounded and aggrieved by those losses. Today, Europe is resistant to forgetting Islam's violent and murderous history. Can anyone blame them? Today, there is a deep insecurity fomenting inside the European conscience. As Muslim minarets scream rebellion, the imams boldly preach jihad under their domes. Europeans know that many mosques in the West are centers for jihadist training. Western Europe is now the battleground in the war on terror."

"It is well known that the minarets are phallic symbols of defiance," Uriel digs deeper. "But there is an alternate metaphor. I have heard it said that in 2003, Recep Tayyip Erdogan, now President of Turkey, had boasted that 'the mosques are our barracks, the domes are our helmet, the minarets our bayonets and the faithful our soldiers.' In comparable language, the Muslim Brotherhood logo and its motto shout out 'Allah is our objective. The Prophet is our leader. The Qur'an is our law. Jihad is or way. Dying in the way of Allah is our highest hope. Allah Akbar!' Yes, Erdogan is the new prophet of Allah."

"Europe is aware of the Muslim Brotherhood logo and motto," explains Michael the political heavy weight. "The peoples of Europe remember the Turkish massacres inside Europe five and a half centuries earlier. Europeans painfully remember the unspeakable Turkish cruelties, atrocities and the brutal extermination of Christians by Muslims throughout the old Byzantine Empire. To this very day, Bulgarians and Serbs hate the Turks and the Bosnian Muslims." Michael wades into this fomenting and evil-smelling brew of hatred. "It's far, far more than being wounded. Hatreds never die. Many Europeans view the minaret as the symbol of Islamization and the Islamic symbol of victory. The Turks had used the minaret as the visible symbol of political power, contempt, defiance, dominance, and superiority. After they slaughtered the inhabitants, they erected minarets around every Byzantine Church, which was converted into a mosque with a crescent moon on top. It was one-upmanship in 1453, and it's one-upmanship today. The Muslims raise their minarets to be taller than surrounding buildings so that they dominate the landscape. They're saying, 'We are better than you and we will govern you eventually.' The minaret is the 'architectural scream' of defiance that Islam is supreme in the land. Much of Europe knows that the minaret is the Islamic middle finger to the world. Europe remembers that one hundred years ago, by conservative official body counts, Muslim Turks brutally slaughtered at least one and a half million Christian Armenians. Their grandparents lived in those dark days of the Armenian Genocide of 1915. Memories of those brutalities are passed down the generations from father to son, from mother to daughter. These Ottoman Muslim atrocities continue to haunt the memories of their grandchildren. Europeans remember the great 1915 massacre when Turkish women were given daggers so that they could deliver the dying stab to wounded and disabled Armenians. By delivering the final stab to Armenian Christians, the Turkish Muslim women were participants in killing for Allah. These acts were unimaginable depravities enacted on a massive scale. By these acts of cruelty, Muslim women were taught that they would gain Allah's approval for having killed a Christian. Europeans remember the Turkish destruction of Christian Smyrna in September 1922."

Gabriel inserts some statistics which are not on the official records. "Local Christian survivors and their descendants in Armenia says that the number of Armenian Christians slaughtered by the Ottoman Turks was up to four million."

Uriel the silent keeper of the sun informs, "Today in Turkey, the mushrooming Islamic movement has incited interest in Hitler and in his book *Mein Kampf*. It's a reaction against the Jews and against Israel's actions in Palestine. Turkey wants to gain EU membership, but it has been denied entry. Because of that rejection, Turkey is introverting into Islam and into the *Mein Kampf*. The galloping popularity of the Hitler cult is Turkey's middle finger to Israel. Turkey is saying, 'Up yours, Europe and up yours, Israel.' It's just more bad news for Israel."

In 2002, an imam in Saudi Arabia had said, "we will control the land of the Vatican; we will control Rome and introduce Islam in it." These kinds of threats erect further barriers to Turkish entry into the European Union. "But why does the Bible not speak about the destruction of Rome and pagan Roman Catholicism?" asks Gabriel.

Michael provides the answer, "As the imam of Saudi Arabia had said, the Muslims will have destroyed or taken over the Vatican *before* the final battle begins."

On the opposite side of the street from the polling booth, with their tails dragging, Satan-Allah and Sonneillon are licking their wounds. "Sonny, we can't win every battle, but we are winning the big war. Besides, it ain't over until the fat lady in the hijab sings." The two devils burst into bizarre convulsive laughter while thumping their tails in a ritualistic drumbeat.

The date is January 1, 2010. The place is Jerusalem. In a museum near the Temple Mount is a special room with all the utensils and furniture that will be needed to outfit the Holy of Holies of the future Third Temple.

The Angelic God Squad surveys the scene as Michael reviews historical events. "The ancients of Abraham's day and of Moses' day knew that the Promised Land of Israel would be the epicenter of the world. They knew that Jerusalem would be the epicenter of Israel and they knew that the pinnacle of Mount Moriah would be the epicenter of Jerusalem."

"Four thousand years after the fact, the truth of Adonai's words is so obvious today," Gabriel pronounces. "The eyes of the whole world are focused upon Jerusalem, but those eyes are not loving eyes. They are the eyes of hatred. Only Canada, under Stephen Harper, has stood alone in its support of Israel."

Obviously on a mission, Gabriel continues, "But the world should be focused upon Mount Moriah. It's the Temple Mount on the pinnacle of Mount Moriah that is the real focal point. Four thousand years ago, the four of us were present right here when we saw Abraham prepare the altar to sacrifice Isaac. Four thousand years ago, catastrophic history began to unfold right in front of where we are standing today. It's upon this same Rock that King Solomon built the first temple."

With his defiant adversaries in view, Michael expands upon Gabriel's historical perspective. "The Temple Mount is the epicenter of all of civilization. A key date is 1967. It marked the first time in nineteen hundred years that the Temple Mount came under Jewish control. Satan and the Dome of the Rock straddle the Temple Mount. Their desecration of the most sacred piece of real estate on earth stands as a continuing insult to Adonai. You see the entrance to the Dome of the Rock where Satan and Sonneillon are thumbing their noses at us? To fulfill prophecy, the Dome of the Rock must be replaced and will be replaced by the Third Temple, which *is* to be erected, and which *will* be erected."

Archangel Gabriel zeroes in on the root of imminent Divine Retribution quoting Rabbi Yochanan who wrote that, "The First Temple was destroyed because of the sins of idolatry, licentiousness and murder." The Rabbi also wrote that the Second Temple was destroyed "because there was baseless hatred" and that "the punishment for baseless hatred is immense."

"Yikes!" screams Uriel. "There's that ugly word again. It's called '*HATRED*' and it's in the title of this book, waiting for Divine '*RETRIBUTION*.'"

The date is March 2, 2010. The place is the White House in the Washington, DC. Turkey throws a diplomatic temper tantrum as it warns the U.S. Congress against approving the Armenian Genocide Bill.

As usual, the Angelic God Squad is in the thick of proceedings. Archangel Michael comments on the sequence of events. "Eleven NATO allies acknowledge that the Armenian Genocide did happen. However, Barack Obama, the American President, is making every effort to submerge the Armenian Genocide censure before the Washington legislators. Barack Obama, Hillary Clinton and Joe Biden are doing everything possible to prevent a full vote by Congress."

With a look of impatience and disgust, Gabriel lets fly, "This is just more of George W. Bush. It is politically incorrect to challenge Muslim killers, or even to call them terrorists. The terms *Islamic extremism, radical Islam* and *Islamic jihad* have been banned by the Obama administration. The new forbidden word in the White House is *terrorist*. Fear of offending Muslims is the new dynamic and the new paradigm."

The date is March 5, 2010. The place is the American Congress in Washington, DC. A U.S. congressional committee has voted to approve a resolution recognizing the World War I killing of Armenians by Turkey as "genocide."

Michael fills in the details. "By ultra conservative official counts, during 1915–1916, the Ottoman Turks starved and massacred one and a half million Armenian Christians. This was an organized campaign of race extermination and genocide to wipe out the Christian minority in Turkey."

The date is March 25, 2010. The place is the White House in Washington, DC. U.S. President Barack Obama has just lowered the boom on Israeli Prime Minister Benjamin Netanyahu saying, "Stop building settlements in East Jerusalem, or else." Prime Minister Benjamin Netanyahu is ordered to withdraw all forces from the West Bank. President Obama has denied Israel all airport landing rights to refuel in Turkey and in all USA bases in the Middle East.

"Is it true that President Obama humiliated visiting Prime Minister Netanyahu by making him come through a service entrance to the White House?" Uriel quizzes Michael. "And that he didn't even offer him a cup of tea? Did President Barack Obama leave Benjamin Netanyahu to sit alone while he left to have supper with his family?"

"Yes to all three questions," responds Michael. "Barack Obama's actions were insulting and disgraceful. It was an unprecedented show of contempt to a foreign dignitary representing a friendly government. By his actions, President Obama has made it clear that the United States no longer supports Israel's self-defence. Clearer still, Barack Obama is no longer a friend of Israel or of the Jewish people. President Obama now refers to Jerusalem by its Arabic name of al-Quds, another monstrous insult to Israel."

Michael is rocked by the seriousness of the event. "The American President has just thrown Israel under the bus. Did the American President forget that for the last century, the Jews have formed a majority in Jerusalem? And now do they need American approval to build houses in Jerusalem? This reversal in support from America is another step in the fulfillment of another prophecy."

Gabriel's file on Barack Obama is extensive. He has done his homework on Barack Obama as he launches into his history. "Barack Obama was born to a Muslim father," announces Gabriel with thick sarcasm. "By birth Barack Obama is a Muslim. It had been reported that his birth certificate reads August 4, 1961, Mombasa, Kenya. It had been reported that his paternal grandmother is firm that she was present at Barack's birth. However, there's another birth certificate with the same date. It reads Honolulu, Hawaii. It has no official embossed seal of Hawaii and no official border. It appears not to be a real birth certificate of the United States. Is it real or isn't it? Barack Obama's birth certificate continues to be a question mark in the minds of millions of Americans. Barack's mother remarries. Barack Obama's stepfather is a Muslim. Because Indonesian law does not permit dual citizenship, Barack Obama is a citizen of Indonesia. Barack Obama attended two schools in Indonesia. Both school registrations state that Barry Soetoro, alias Barack Obama is Muslim. Barry Soetoro studied Islam two hours a week and attended a mosque. Barry Soetoro was given a Muslim upbringing. These are the hard facts on the ground. Before he was killed, Colonel Mu'ammar Qadhafi, the Libyan Arch-Terrorist, stated repeatedly that Barack Obama is a Muslim. It takes one to know one."

Tension among the four Archangels rises and the air is electrified as Gabriel continues his exposé. A faint glow pulses from the angelic group. "It was with delight that Barack Obama quoted from the Quran. As the American President, he praised and glorified Islam and said that he has a 'deep appreciation for the Islamic faith.'"

With more than a hint of sarcasm in his voice, Gabriel is on a tear, "No Christian with biblical knowledge could make that statement without cringing. Deep appreciation for the Islamic faith? Faith in what? Faith in whom? Barack Obama voices pride over Islamic cultural achievements of the past but he avoids any mention of fourteen centuries of massive Islamic slaughter and the murder of 300 million. Barack Obama refuses to bow before the Queen of England, but he bows low before the Islamic Saudi King of Arabia?"

Raphael expresses his indignation, "Bowing down before a murderous Saudi thug? For an American President, this is a bad precedent. It's an ominous sign of what will be required of all infidels. Christians and Jews will be kissing the feet of Islamic killers. Fifteen of the 9:111 or 9/11 suicide assassins were from Saudi Arabia."

"Christianity is as far removed from Islam as Heaven is from Hell," booms Gabriel. "A Christian cannot extol the virtues of Islam. Barack

Obama professes to be a Christian but he says that there are many ways to God. Many ways to God? To which God is he referring? Allah? For Christians, there is one way to God and only one way. It's the Way of the Cross through Yeshua Messiah. Then there is Barack Obama's hostility toward toward the land of Israel."

Michael, always the cautious diplomat, tries to lower the emotional levels in the God Squad. He reaches back to the time of Abraham. "The world forgets Adonai's promises and His legal transactions of all time. Before Isaac was born, **Genesis 15:18** states that Adonai had made a covenant with Abram saying, 'To your descendants I give this land, from the river of Egypt to the great river, the river Euphrates.'"

"That promise is four thousand years old, and it has never been withdrawn." Michael continues, "Adonai's promise and His covenant still are valid today. His Promised Land includes all of Jerusalem. Ishmael was not yet conceived when Adonai identified the descendants of Abraham who would inherit the land. In **Genesis 15:13**, Adonai had said to Abram, "Know of a surety that your descendants will be sojourners in a land that is not theirs, and they will be oppressed for four hundred years.'"

"This four-hundred-year period of history had never happened to the children of Ishmael," Michael says emphatically. "At that time of the Egyptian captivity, Ishmael's descendants were not in Canaan but in the Arabia. Historically, the Arabs have no part whatsoever in these prophesies."

"The four of us were present to hear Adonai's promise to Abraham. Notice the significance of this message. It was very different from all the many other messages which Gabriel had delivered. In this case, none of us were intermediaries. It was a direct revelation, from God to man, from Adonai to Abraham."

"Okay! We were there to hear the words of Adonai to man." Gabriel poses a challenging perspective, "But has man himself acknowledged and recognized the right of Israel to its land and the right to exist today?"

A pregnant pause follows. Michael's face tells the story, but keeping them in anticipation he is slow to announce, "The UN General Assembly Partition Resolution of 1947 reinforced Israel's legitimacy and its right to its lands."

"You say that the Partition Resolution of 1947 *reinforced* Israel's legitimacy?" Gabriel arches an eyebrow as he asks, "Reinforced? Reinforced what? Reinforced when?"

Slowly and deliberately, Michael supplies the missing links. "Recall the San Remo Conference of Italy in April 1920. None of you attended it, but I was present to monitor these events. I was on assignment for Adonai."

"Did you read in the *National Post* on June 12, 2010, what historian Conrad Black had to say about the San Remo Conference of 1920?" There was only deep silence from Archangels Gabriel, Raphael and Uriel.

"Historian Conrad Black had said that Israel's legal rights originated in San Remo, Italy, at the San Remo Conference of April 1920, where the Supreme Council of the Allied Powers exclusively adjudicated the territory hitherto known as 'Palestine' to the Jewish people. The Supreme Council based their decision on their historical connection to the land as the grounds for reconstituting their national home there. The San Remo Resolution launched the Mandate for Palestine, thus entrenching the acquired rights of the Jewish people in international law and making them valid to this day.'"

"Yes, the legal rights of Israel and the Jewish people were entrenched in international law." Michael continues, "In the sight of the God of Heaven, the world, at its peril, chooses to ignore the epic decisions and confirmations by the San Remo Conference."

Gabriel raises an important question. "Didn't the San Remo Conference include the entire Balfour Declaration?"

"You're quite right, Gabriel. Obviously, you've paid attention to politics," remarks a surprised Michael.

"Just what was the Balfour Declaration?" Raphael inquires.

Gabriel proceeds with the explanation. "Following the collapse of the Turkish Ottoman Empire, Britain administered its territories in the Middle East. The British Government wished to see the creation of a state in Palestine for the Jewish people. This position was expressed in the Balfour Declaration of November 2, 1917. It was a simple statement of intent by the British Foreign Secretary, Arthur James Balfour."

"But isn't it true that all members of the Supreme Council of the Principal Allied Powers approved the San Remo Resolution?" quizzes Uriel who monitored the technical advances during the war."

Speaking to his three companions, Michael is only too pleased to supply the additional information. "It is true that all five victorious countries of World War I were present at San Remo. It was Britain, France, Italy, Japan, and eventually the United States who were agreed unanimously. Later, on July 24, 1922, the San Remo Resolution was unanimously accepted by the League of Nations. This was international law at its best. Today, the San Remo Resolution remains valid, legally binding, and irrevocable. But the world chooses to ignore this monumental international law that is carved into history."

Gabriel cocks his head at an angle as he inquires, "What were the boundaries that were approved for Israel?"

Once again, Michael, the historian and the legal expert, supplies the details of this critical international agreement: "The San Remo Conference granted the right under international laws for Jews to settle *anywhere* in western Palestine. This is the area between the Jordan River and the Mediterranean Sea."

"Amazing! Entrenched in international law!" Gabriel is clearly pleased as well as clearly angry. "Well, thank you, Michael, and thank you, Conrad Black, for bringing this historical information for the world to read and to hear, again. The Palestinians of today do not have a legal leg on which to stand. Ninety years after the San Remo Resolution, why is the Western world deaf, dumb, and blind to these legal international facts? Where is the media on this issue? The San Remo Resolution gives legitimacy to Israel. Now it's carved in stone by man and by God. To ignore the San Remo Resolution is to violate international law and to slap the face of Elohim, the God of Heaven."

"The world is ignoring it, and it will continue to ignore it." Michael continues, "But wait. Recent world-shaking events are coming to a head. On April 19, 2010, Israel celebrated its independence. The same day on April 19, 2010, President Barack Obama announced from the White House that the United States would no longer stand automatically with Israel on UN Security Council decisions.

For the first time in history, the United States had turned its back on Israel."

The implications of this withdrawal of US support have shaken the God Squad visibly. Gabriel assesses the damages, "In effect, President Barack Obama and the United States are denying Israel's legitimacy, Israel's right to its territory, and Israel's very existence."

Michael reviews the legal precedent set almost a century ago. "Keep in mind that on April 19, 1920, exactly ninety years ago to the day, the San Remo Conference had convened to justify Israel's very existence. This act of denial by President Barack Obama was a history-changing decision. Then, on April 20, 2010, the very next day, British Petroleum's Deep Water Horizon drilling platform exploded in the Gulf of Mexico. The Macondo Well started to spew millions of gallons of crude. Adonai's judgment upon the United States was swift and devastating. It was a shot across the bow and a warning of worse to come for America under Barack Obama. But very few knew that this was judgment against America for the sins of their President."

"This explosion and the massive hemorrhaging of oil into the Gulf of Mexico created the worst environmental disaster in U.S. history, which was greater than the Exxon Valdez oil spill in Alaskan waters." Raphael, the health guru, understands the magnitude of this disaster upon the aquatic birds and upon all marine life in the Gulf waters.

Gabriel hangs out the query, "Is this coincidence, or is it the judgment of God?"

Continuing in their tight conference circle, Michael states emphatically, "These crisis events in the Gulf of Mexico have been unfolding since the Bush Administration, but they have escalated in frequency since the Barack Obama's election in 2008. Barack Obama's decisions opposing Israel have put the United States on a collision course with the God of the Universe. In **Genesis 12:3**, Adonai's words to Israel and to the world are a clear warning: 'I will bless those who bless you and whoever curses you I will curse.'"

"In answer to your question, Gabriel, the explosion in the Gulf was no coincidence. After 9/11, it is the beginning of the next phase in God's judgment upon America. The curses from the God of Heaven will increase in frequecy and in severity, including catastrophic weather disasters which will batter the U.S. Eastern coast with heavy rains, hurricanes, and massive storms. Western America will reel from water shortage, severe droughts, blinding sandstorms, and raging firestorms followed by massive flooding as further punishment of Obama's America. Now comes the hard part." Archangel Michael proceeds to deliver the very heavy-duty revelations, "The prophecy of **Zechariah 12:2–3** is coming to pass before our very eyes, 'Lo, I am about to make Jerusalem a cup of reeling to all the peoples round about . . . and that day I will make Jerusalem a heavy stone for all the peoples.' Which nation today does not find Jerusalem to be burdensome and a stumbling block? Now, even America under President Barack Obama has shifted to the other side of the ledger. President Barack Obama's hostility towards Israel is ominous for America, but there are but few who realize this. However, America will know this after Obama is gone from office."

"And now comes the very scary part. The prophecy in **Zechariah 14:2** states, 'For I will gather ALL the nations against Jerusalem to battle.' That word *all* is frightening. With the White House decision of March 25, 2010, this prophecy looms as more than possible and soon. What was unthinkable yesteryear is now in process. It's all about the word *all*. In 2014, only Canada remains on side with Israel. Muslim denial of the right for Israel to exist adds additional credibility to Zechariah's prophesies. The only question is *when* will Zechariah's prophecies be fulfilled?"

"On March 25, 2010, President Barack Obama isolated Israel from the rest of the world. Israel's only remaining major ally now has gone Muslim and Palestinian. America is in the process of withdrawing from Israel. In his intense hatred of Israel, a page has been turned and a new chapter is being written by U.S. President Barack Obama. The wheels of destiny under Zechariah's prophecies are now starting to spin out of control."

Future history shows that President Donald Trump stops Israel's forced descent into the abyss under Barack Obama.

The date is June 15, 2010. The place is the White House in Washington. With intensifying hatred toward Israel, President Obama states that it is the intention of the United States to support a U.N. investigation of Israel's action against the Turkish ship attempting to run the blockade of Hamas-controlled Gaza.

"Layer by layer, President Barack Obama is disrobing Israel of its support and of its dignity." Michael is chagrined, "This is President Obama's virtual war on Israel. At some future date, will America actually do physical battle against Jerusalem? Or will America just stand back and watch Israel's enemies proceed to try to destroy her? Zechariah's prophesy says yes. Therefore, it is important to look at Israel through the third lens of Bible prophecy."

"Here is "rule of law" Barack Obama who is a former constitutional law professor." Michael takes his perspective from the scriptural laws of the ages. "Unfortunately, Barack Obama's vision is narrow and shortsighted. He has spent too much time reading the Quran. Instead, he should acquaint himself with the books of Genesis, Daniel, Zechariah, and Revelation."

"Muslim fanatics murdered three thousand Americans on 9/11." Gabriel adds his bit of flame to this exposure. "Building a mosque called Cordoba House near Ground Zero is a defiant statement of contempt. Historically, Cordoba was the capital city in Andalusia, Spain. Cordoba was once the high profile symbol and seat of Islamic power, of Islamic dominance, and of the Islamic Caliphate. By backing the plan to build the Ground Zero Mosque in what once was the shadow of the World Trade Center, Barack Obama attempted to perform a fundamental re-organization of America by stealth."

"Barack Obama's support for the Cordoba Mosque pales in comparison to what he had done to Israel," Michael steers the conversation back to Israel. "Barack Obama is the most anti-Israeli president in American history. How appropriate an ending that a Muslim-sympathetic American President should be the last straw to break Jerusalem's back. Barack Obama is the modern day Judas Iscariot. Barack Obama's insults are directed not only against Prime Minister Netanyahu and at Israel but against Adonai Himself. Withdrawal of American support now puts the United States on a frontal collision course with Adonai the God of Heaven who oversees Israel."

"Russia is arming Iran with long range missiles and nuclear technology." Gabriel lists the four key players in the Battle of Armegeddon soon to come. U.S. Barack Obama has all but abandoned Israel. Turkey has turned its back on Israel and has allied itself with Iran and with Russia. Radical Iran is looking for that one operation, that grand finale which will cripple Israel and cripple America once and for all."

Michael projects the discussion toward end-time events saying, "U.S. law makers and persons in high authority are betraying America. As dean of the Harvard Law School, Elana Kagan had become the champion of Islamic Sharia Law. Allowing Sharia Law to penetrate American capital markets is the thin edge of the wedge to destroy the U.S. from within, and that is what the Harvard Law School's Islamic finance project eventually will accomplish. Elana Kagan was appointed by Barack Obama to sit on the Supreme Court."

"You're way over my head on the economics front." With a quizzical look on his face, Gabriel probes, "We do know that Sharia Law is a barbaric and totalitarian code that Islam is seeking to impose upon the world. We do know that Sharia Law requires and mandates engagement in civilizational jihad."

"Civilizational jihad? What is civilizational jihad??" asks Raphael.

"Civilizational jihad," exclaims Michael, "is the non-violent form of jihad better known as stealth jihad promoted by the Muslim Brotherhood. It's the fifth column in America." Michael is taken aback that his companions do not know. "With creeping subtle invasion, its intent is to battle on every possible front of American society. That includes the laws, the schools, the media, politics, and culture. The aim of civilizational jihad is to eliminate and destroy Western civilization in slow degrees from within by sabotaging its culture. Its goals are exactly the same as those of al Qaeda. Those goals are none other that forcing worldwide Sharia Law and restoration of the Caliphate."

Worried looks creep across the faces of the four Archangels. The most anxious is Gabriel who continues to dig deeper asking. "Who and what is this Muslim Brotherhood?"

' With a pained expression, Archangel Michael proceeds to flesh out the details, "The Muslim Brotherhood is the dominant and visible front of mainstream Islamist ideology. Their job is to promote Sharia Law as innocent Muslim culture. Sharia Law is supremacist ideology."

In response, Gabriel comments, "It would take a lot of money to influence such a cunning shift in Western thinking."

"You're absolutely correct," adds Michael. "And this surreptitious sabotage is being funded by the Saudis right under the noses of Americans and Canadians. If this isn't willful blindness, then nothing is. The majority position of hundreds of millions of Muslims is to convert free and Western societies into Sharia societies. This is not a fringe position. Muslims who migrate to America do not integrate. They don't intend to integrate. Terrorism aside, the only disagreement among Muslims is about tactics. The bottom line and the common Islamic line is the Allah-ordained mission of world domination through the spread of Sharia Law. And yes, it's domination under Allah who makes the rules. Establishing Sharia Law is the bedrock tenet of Islam."

As usual, Uriel, who has been listening silently in the background, presents the militant side of Sharia Law. "In Muhammad's Islam, there is no such thing as freedom of conscience. Any Muslim who turns away from Islam can be killed."

"I don't get it," responds Gabriel, who directs the conversation back to finances. "I see that bucket loads of money are needed to fund this treachery. But how is this money being channeled and laundered?"

"It's very simply done," Michael adds almost casually. "It's through the sanitized legal hocus-pocus known as Sharia-Compliant Finance. Through a fancy title such as the Islamic Law Section of the Association of American Law Schools, Prince Alwaleed bin Talal of Saudi Arabia kicked in a $20 million donation in appreciation of Harvard's support."

As Adonai's messenger of the ages, Gabriel voices the clincher. "Now that's a mouthful of words that could choke a horse. Barack Obama's choice of Elena Kagan now sits on the Supreme Court."

It is more than obvious that a deceived, wounded, and financially bankrupted America is limping down its home stretch as Republicans battle Democrats in 2016 for the presidential office. Republican Donald Trump is running against Democrat Hillary Clinton. Donald Trump does win the American presidency.

Michael has a parallel but bleaker perspective as he says, "If America is limping down its home stretch, then so is Europe. Europeans are entering a time of great unrest. Finally, though, they are beginning to wake up to what Islam is about and where Islam is taking Europe. Increasing numbers of non-Muslims are running scared. Switzerland lowered the boom on the minarets. Now the Dutch are reacting by swinging hard to the right. This Geert Wilders politician has just pulled off a spectacular electoral breakthrough victory as the anti-Muslim Freedom party. Wilders wants to end immigration from Muslim countries as well as to ban new mosques and ban the Quran."

Gabriel is shocked as he questions the direction taken by Wilders' political party. "Geert Wilders has equated the Quran with Hitler's *Mein Kampf.* Isn't that a bit extreme?"

Michael expresses relief rather than shock. "Finally, someone has had the courage to forget about political correctness and to call a spade a spade. Muhammad and his Quran are about hatred and the killing of Christians and Jews. It's a fair statement to say that the Quran and Hitler's *Mein Kampf* complement each other. Both books spew hatred towards the Jews. But the Quran also spews hatred against Christians."

"Well, here's another brave and fearless soul," interjects Gabriel. "On August 19, 2010, on CNN, Reverend Franklin Graham said that 'Islam is a religion of hatred.' Before the eyes and ears of the world, Reverend Graham stated, "The God of Islam is not the same God of the Christian or the Judeo-Christian faith. It is a different God, and I believe a very evil and a very wicked religion." Even his father, Billy Graham once referred to the Muslim faith as that 'evil religion.'"

"You know that most days I have been monitoring the newspapers closely." Gabriel states a fact that is well known by his three friends," On December 2, 2013, Muslim journalist Sheema Khan wrote an article in the *Globe and Mail.* She summarized the Global Gender Gap Index, which was published by the World Economic Forum in 2013. Sheema Khan wrote that women in Muslim countries are severely restricted and marginalized. Here is what she had to say, 'Statistics on female empowerment were provided in the areas of health, education, economy, and politics. The lowest ranking countries surveyed were North Africa, the Middle East, and South-Western Asia. Ten of the bottom twenty-seven countries have majority Muslim populations while eighteen countries having a minimum Muslim population of 75 percent. In the arena of political participation, the Muslim countries of Brunei and Qatar had a female political empowerment sub-index of zero or dead last in the world. Other Muslim countries fared no better, as political rule is almost completely controlled by males. In Muslim countries at the national level, the average political empowerment gender gap rating was just a mere seven women for every one hundred men in positions of political power. Pakistan and Yemen ranked near the bottom of the education sub-index. In Afghanistan, the Taliban discourage female participation in education by throwing acid in female student's faces or by burning down their schools. Across the four areas of health, education, economy, and politics, the female empowerment data in many Muslim countries is grim.'"

"These dismal female participation statistics would make proud any Ishmael or any Muhammad," Michael sadly proclaims. "Female participation in true democratic process is anathema to Islam. Female participation in true democratic process are destined never to meet in Islam."

Gabriel proudly states, "I also monitor the *Jerusalem Post* and the *Jewish World Review,* and I always read articles by Caroline B. Glick. Caroline Glick is the senior Middle East fellow at the Center for Security Policy in Washington, DC, and the deputy managing editor of the *Jerusalem Post.* On November 27, 2013, Caroline Glick wrote in the *Jewish World Review* that she felt that President Barack Obama's goal and foreign policy are not to prevent Iran from becoming a nuclear power but to weaken the State of Israel."

"And I monitor anything and everything to do with flames, uranium, and nuclear weapons," vaunts Uriel. "I subscribe to the Flame Hotline e-alerts. On December 03, 2013, Flame Hotline published that the Iran uranium enrichment deal was an 'ill-begotten devil's bargain.' They said that Iran was allowed to retain its vast enrichment capabilities with its centrifuges. Under American pressure, the international community allowed the continuation of Iran's heavy water reactor in Arak. There were no limits imposed upon Iran's nuclear threat. The United States shredded the six-member United Nations Security Council Resolution that would have ordered Iran to abandon all enrichment reprocessing capabilities. The only red line in the sand was the one drawn in front of Israel by Barack Obama. Where was the United States Congress to allow an imperial executive-order-driven president to run roughshod over America's strategic interests and undermine Israel?"

"The Ayatollah Khamenei of Iran made the public threat 'to wipe Israel off the map,'" Gabriel reads. "On December 06, 2013, in the *Jewish World Review*, Caroline B. Glick wrote on the politics of subversion stating that secretary of state John Kerry and 'the Obama administration as a whole lost all credibility when they negotiated the uranium enrichment deal with Iran last week.' Caroline Glick went on to say that PLOs chief negotiator Saeb Erekat speaking to foreign supporters said that the 'Palestinians will never accept Israel's right to exist.' Their entire existence as a people is predicated on denying Jewish rights and nationhood. As Erekat put it, 'I cannot change my narrative.'"

And as Michael phrases it, "The Iranian threat 'to wipe Israel off the map' is the Muslim Middle East Peace Plan summarized in a nutshell— an explosive nutshell and an End Time Nutshell."

"Verbal threats of extermination of Israel from high-ranking Muslim leaders cannot be ignored." Gabriel hypothesizes, "But Israel can defend itself. On the contrary, Christians in Muslim countries are defenseless. In two separate bombings on Christmas Day 2013, thirty-eight Christians in Baghdad were massacred. These massacres of Iraq's Christian minority are an uninterrupted and continual record of persecution and killings. ISIS is making a statement by selectively killing Christians. It is obvious that Christians and Jews will be butchered together."

In 2014, 2015, and in 2016, it is apocalyptic that radical ISIS is slaughtering their way across Syria, Iraq, Paris, California, Indonesia, Burkina Faso, Nice.... Out of this Islamic cauldron, there is a broad rising tide of anti-Semitism in Europe. Increasingly, elites in Europe are talking about de-legitimizing Israel and stripping Israel of her territory. Random acts of killing and bloody violence against Israelis are applauded as heroic acts by Islamic Palestinians. Middle East anti-Jewish fervor has spread across Europe at frightening speed. As with a metastasized cancer, anti-Semitic hatred has gone viral and systemic across Europe. European Jews are escaping hatred by emigrating to Israel.

The United Nations has acknowledged that within and across the Muslim world, Christians are the most persecuted group in the world. Rounding out the jihadist war against Christians and Jews, the 2016 Islamic Easter slaughter of Christians in Lahore, Pakistan, was born of Muhammad's horrific, virulent hatred.

The **Revelation 13:1–15** prophecy states, "And I saw a beast rising out of the sea, with ten horns and seven heads. . . . . It was allowed to make war on the saints and to conquer them . . . and to cause those who would not worship the image of the beast to be slain."

"In 2015 and in 2016, ISIS is making war upon the Christians in the Middle East, conquering them and killing them." Michael is chagrined, "Under the murderous hands of ISIS, the dark shroud of Muhammad's radical Islamic Quran is choking and slaughtering the lives of the populations of Syria and Iraq and propelling the exodus of millions of Muslim refuges into Europe, into America and into Canada."

"ISIS is butchering Christians who refuse to bow down to Allah." Archangel Gabriel wrings his hands as he grieves for the suffering and the dying, "Muhammad's ISIS is hardwired to facilitate and to provoke the Apocalypse."

"If life were a game of baseball, it would be the bottom of the ninth inning with the bases loaded and ISIS at bat." In another of his extreme analogies, Uriel throws another curve ball right out of the book of Revelation, "The Beast of the East is rising from the deep and the Mahdi as the Twelfth Shiite Imam is approaching the batter's box."

"Thanks for the bone-chilling metaphor, Uriel," exclaims Michael. "The March 22, 2016, Islamic terrorist slaughter in Brussels and the truck-mowing slaughter of young children in Nice, France on July 14, 2016, are the new normal in Europe. But unfortunately, there is no path for Western democracies to win against the Caliphate of Muhammad's ISIS because it has metastasized broadly across the globe. The Islamic massacres in Paris, San Bernardino, Brussels, Nice, and Turkey leave no doubts that the world is into a new paradigm and into a different kind of global war. The objectives of ISIS are the enslavement of women and the obliteration of democratic freedoms across the world."

"As Muhammad had executed in the darkness of the seventh century, the massive indiscriminate butcheries by his understudy ISIS are the psychotic manifestations of hatred executed by the lowest of minds and by the darkest of souls." Gabriel struggles to continue, "ISIS is the escalating, virulent disease of violent, radical Islamic jihadism."

"Because of sophisticated encryption, Western governments have lost the social media war to ISIS, making it difficult to impossible to track Islamic terrorists." As the physical sciences authority, Uriel has the inside track on electronics and social media. "When a terrorist goes dark on social media, then government tracking of him also goes dark. It is vital and absolutely urgent to engage Silicon Valley as soon as possible to regain the encryption high ground."

"The complaints and shrieks of 'Islamophobia' by 'moderate' Muslims do not stand up to scrutiny." Michael raises his voice in frustration, "The silence of 'moderate' Muslims who refuse to oppose Muhammad's radical Islamic jihad, also does not stand up to scrutiny. There is no such middle ground, and no such 'moderate' Muslim. The choice is clear and without option. Muhammad's Quran dictates to kill the Kafirs if they don't fall to the ground and worship Allah. A 'moderate' Muslim is an apostate because he or she is denying the multiple exhortations and the commands within the Quran and the Hadiths to kill non-Muslims. The 'moderate Muslim' lie is obvious because all Muslims are clamouring for the institution of Sharia Law, tenets of which are the enslavement of women and the eradication of democracy. A 'moderate Muslim' is the oxymoron of this age."

"Terrorists in Brussels were attempting to blow up a nuclear facility to provoke a Fukushima-style nuclear meltdown." In an avalanche of emotions, Uriel raises the stakes to nuclear levels, "Shock of shocks. Others of these ISIS killers were attempting to obtain fissionable material to create dirty bombs."

"Now the world is witnessing the creation of a continent-wide network of Islamic terrorist cells targeting Europe." Michael pulls back the European economic curtain exposing financial disaster, "With an economy in crisis, a threatened banking collapse, a drain on resources by the massive refugee influxes, and the escalating Islamic terrorist attacks, the European Union is unravelling, hanging by a thread, and on the brink of collapse. In the count-down to disaster, Brexit rang the first European bell."

"Fears of ISIS attacks are heightened across the European continent." Psychiatrist Raphael understands the raw emotional stresses of waiting for that next shoe to drop. "In palpable panic and hysteria, Europe is experiencing the transitioning from the seventh-century world of barbaric Islamic tyranny to the 2017 world of indiscriminate barbaric terror through the use of weapons of mass destruction. Nuclear events by ISIS in Europe are unthinkable, but probable. Today, Europe is terrorized into a continent-wide powder keg of raw emotions while waiting for that next event, which may come soon in the form of a nuclear blast from a suitcase bomb."

"How's this for fear? In St. Peter's Square, inside the Vatican, worshippers were subjected to very tight security on Easter Sunday 2016," states Archangel Michael.

"Many Muslims contend that ISIS is not Muslim." Gabriel passionately disagrees, "This position is a pretence and an absolutely misleading denial! ISIS is following in the murderous footsteps of Muhammad. ISIS is fundamental, orthodox Islam in Muhammad style."

"Look! There in the distance I see Sariel the Angel of Death. What's all that commotion around her?" questions Michael.

"I'll scoot over and talk to her." Gabriel is more than curious. After talking to Sariel for several minutes, there is more commotion. Gabriel returns in an agitated state blurting out, "Sariel is escorting to the pit of Hell the spirits of those two suicide bombers who killed fourteen people in Brussels. They were giving Sariel a very hard time. The el-Bakraoui brothers thought that Sariel was taking them to Allah's paradise to begin a round of sex with all those dark-eyed virgins. But they were dead wrong! Ibrahim and Khalid el-Bakraoui became extremely violent when Sariel told them that there was no such place as Allah's paradise, that Muhammad had lied, that there would be no virgins waiting for them now or ever, and instead of an eternal flame within their genitals, they were facing the flames of Hell. I had to subdue both of these deranged spirits with a laser blast."

"Speaking of flames and fires, let's go back fourteen centuries to Muhammad's military campaign against the Jewish Tribe of Bani Al Mustalik." In an abrupt change of topic, Archangel Gabriel paces back and forth before his Angelic colleagues saying, "Rumors of Aisha's adultery with Safwan and Allah's inexplainable one month of silence had spread throughout Medina like wildfire. Aisha's alleged adultery laid the groundwork for the Sunni-Shiite split. From this Sunni-Shiite split, the Islamic family has been at war now for over fourteen centuries. Hundreds of thousands of Muslims have been killed over that split. If Allah knew that Aisha had an affair and if Allah is God, why did he have to wait for evidence? Since it was proved that Aisha wasn't pregnant, then it also was proved that Allah is not God because she could not foretell the future. The outcome of Aisha's sexual misconduct with Safwan totally discredited Allah. Why then are twenty-first century Muslims continuing to be duped by Muhammad's fraudulent Quran and by his concocted Allah?"

"Here is more shocking evidence of Muhammad's humiliating and abusive conduct toward his wives." Raphael states, "At the very least, there is evidence that Muhammad had slapped Aisha with 'an open palm.' In her hadiths, Aisha had narrated that Muhammad had done far worse in that, 'He struck me on the chest which caused me pain.' The inconsistency of this disclosure by Aisha should shatter the credibility of any prophet of any god. In Book 004, Hadith Number 2127, Sahih Muslim also wrote that Aisha had said, 'He struck me on the chest which caused me pain.' There is enough suspicion to indicate that something untoward had transpired between Muhammad and Aisha."

"In Volume 7, Book 72, Number 715, Sahih Bukhari had written that Aisha had said, 'I have not seen any woman suffering as much as the believing women. Look! Her skin is greener that her clothes!' In other words, her skin was green because of bruises from blows. Here is more. In Volume 8, Book 82, Number 828, Sahih Bukhari wrote that Aisha had narrated, 'Abu Bakr came towards me and struck me violently with his fist. . . . But I remained motionless as if I was dead lest I should awake Allah's Apostle although that hit was very painful.'" Visibly Raphael becomes exceedingly angry declaring, "Abu Bakr, who became the first caliph, was Aisha's father. How deplorable for Abu Bakr to beat his own daughter with his fist! When Sharia Law is made the law of the land, American women and Canadian women beware! Your skins will become green all over from repeated beatings by your fathers, by your husbands or by your brothers."

It has been said that Muhammad's greatest miracle was sex. It has been written that Muhammad's greatest miracle was his unmatched prowess for lovemaking because Allah gifted him with the libido of thirty men. Yes, at the age of sixty plus, Muhammad could make love to eleven young women in a single night. In Volume 1, Book 5, Number 268, Sahih Bukhari had written, "The Prophet used to visit all his wives in a round, during the day and night and they were eleven in number. The Prophet was given the strength of thirty (men)."

"On this related note, it is easy to assume that Aisha and Muhammad's other wives were sexually deprived." As the expert on matters of physical health, Raphael explains, "Simple logic makes it obvious that eleven wives could not be satisfied by one old man. When Sharia Law is made the law of the land, American women and Canadian women beware! You will be but one of four wives, and you will be emotionally and sexually deprived. However, your time will be taken up fighting the other three wives. So much for romance, ladies!"

In Volume 4, Book 52, Number 74, Sahih Bukhari had written that Allah's Apostle said, "Once Solomon, son of David said, '(By Allah) Tonight I will have sexual intercourse with one hundred women each of whom will give birth to a knight who will fight in Allah's cause.'"

"Yes, one hundred women in one night was another flight of fantasy by Muhammad. Why does the modern Muslim world subscribe to this utter fictitious trash?" muses Gabriel.

After reading Sahih Bukhari's fantasy, the four members of the God Squad look at each other in a round of disbelief. Raphael shakes his head, "Invoking Solomon, and in one single night to have 'sexual intercourse with one hundred women' and then each woman to 'give birth to a knight'? This reads like stories out of One Thousand and One Nights by Scheherazade. This is just so over the top and off the scale. How much hashish does one have to smoke to believe this tripe?"

As the medical authority, Raphael speaks from rock-solid ground, "Aisha had narrated more of Muhammad's hadiths than his other wives. Most of Aisha's hadiths describe the blushing, intimate sexual performances of Muhammad which comprised half of Muhammad's religion. Aisha described in detail Muhammad's techniques of fondling her when she was menstruating. Aisha applauded Muhammad for his ability to constrain his ejaculations. These were stupendous audacities which Aisha had made available for public consumption. It is understandable why the ayatollahs of Iran are insisting that when the Mahdi arrives, he will resurrect Aisha and have her whipped in public. And in the context of Muhammad's embarrassing and humiliating public sexual exposures by Aisha, why are Muslims still killing themselves and slaughtering others?"

In twenty-one words Archangel Michael encapsulates the Quran: "The Quran was structured around sex and slaughter, and driven by the fear of Hell for disobeying Allah the Moon god." Michael continues, "The year 2017 is not the era of Muhammad when the moon was held in awe and worshipped. In this day and age of sophistication, when men have walked upon the moon and have walked upon Allah up in the sky, to worship Allah as the moon god is infantile, nonsensical, and unintelligent."

CHAPTER 10

THE QURAN AND HADITHS PROMOTE HATRED AND THE KILLING OF CHRISTIANS AND JEWS

*D*abiq, the latest issue of the ISIS magazine aimed at Christians, has dictated to its followers to "break the cross by the sword." The sword is Allah's law. The goal of ISIS is to discredit Christianity. ISIS calls upon jihadis to attack Christians and to destroy Christianity, declaring that Jesus was a slave of Allah. Islam began in the tents of Abraham. His wife Sarah had evicted Hagar and her son Ishmael. Ishmael's hatred toward Sarah and Adonai, the God of Heaven, continues to burn hot today in Muhammad's Quran as practiced by **ISIS**.

Four thousand years ago, as recorded in **Genesis 16:12**, Gabriel brought Adonai's message to Hagar proclaiming, "Behold, you are with child and shall bear a son; you shall call his name Ishmael... He shall be a wild ass of a man, his hand against every man and every man's hand against him..." **Genesis 16:12** speaks of Ishmael's hatred which was adopted by Muhammad.

"Here is shocking detail that should turn the Muslim world onto its head," quips Gabriel. "**Quran 3:54** summarizes, encapsulates and puts into stark perspective the entire Quran. **Quran 3:54** reads, *'They contrived, and **Allah contrived. Allah is the supreme contriver**.'* Yes, Allah contrived. Yes, Allah is the supreme contriver and the supreme liar of all time. The entire Quran is contrived fiction. In **Quran 3:54**, Muhammad destroyed the credibility of the entire Quran."

> "They contrived,
> and Allah contrived.
> Allah is the supreme
> contriver."
>
> - Quran 3:54

Raphael laments, "Islamic websites avoid these words as if they were the very plague. They absolutely avoid the words *Allah contrived.* and *Allah is the supreme contriver* as if these embarrassing words are a pestilence. Muslims are deeply ashamed of this verse and they run and hide from it because these words show who Allah is and how Allah operates."

"Here are definitions of the meaning of the word *contrive*," Gabriel reads from his tablet. "To contrive is to plan with evil intent, to devise, to invent, to scheme, to concoct, to fabricate, to plot, and to plan with cleverness. Islamic scholars are extremely offended by this verse. They run from it in panic as though retreating from a war zone or running from death itself."

"Michael explains, "Islamicists are taking serious offense to this verse. Hostility is directed at anyone who dares to search the web for Quran 3:54. Islamic commentators compare the exposure of Quran 3:54 to Salman Rushdie's *Satanic Verses,* as being worthy of a fatwa."

With a tone of deep concern, Raphael explains, "What Salman Rushdie wrote in his *Satanic Verses* was as benign as milk toast compared to what Jeremiah Stone has written. So what grief is waiting for Jeremiah Stone?"

With a determined look, Gabriel firmly declares, "Not to worry! I am looking out for him. Jeremiah has a destiny to fulfill."

"Quran 3:54 leaves Muhammad's Islam and Muhammad's Allah shamed, discredited, and absolutely defenseless with her back to the wall and with no rat hole down which to crawl," Uriel burns the bull's-eye with another one of his arrows."

"With Quran 3:54, Allah has been unmasked for the whole world to see," adds Archangel Raphael. "Quran 3:54 has undressed Muhammad's Allah. The arch contriver and the arch liar is left stark naked. The sight is not pretty. This embarrassing self-inflicted wound is terminal for the Quran."

Archangel Gabriel summarizes this 3:54 Quranic debacle, "As Allah is the arch deceiver of all time, so too is Muhammad and his Vatican-

Augustinian-concocted Quran. Quran 3:54 leaves all Muslims with their pants down at their knees. Because there is no defence for Quran 3:54, Islam has been pushing the UN to outlaw criticism of the Quran as being Islamophobia and blasphemy against Muhammad and against Allah."

ISLAMIC HATRED IN THE QURAN DRIVES THE KILLING OF CHRISTIANS AND JEWS

The following verses from Muhammad's Quran and from his Hadiths speak of hatred toward Jews and Christians.

1. **Quran 2:63–65** of the Children of Israel: "*You will be changed into detested apes.*"

2. **Quran 2:98**: "*Whoever is an enemy of Allah, His angels, or His apostles, or of Gabriel or Michael, will surely find that Allah is the enemy of the unbelievers* [Christians and Jews]."

3. **Ishaq** had written, "*Allah totally approves of the killing of the Jews, enslaving the women and children.*"

4. **Quran 2:191–192**: "*Slay them wherever you find them.*"

5. **Quran 2:193**: "*Fight against them until idolatry is no more and Allah's religion is supreme.*"

6. **Quran 2:194**: "*If anyone attacks you, attack him as he attacked you.*"

7. **Quran 2:207**: "*But there are others who would give away their lives in order to find favour with Allah.*"

8. **Quran 3:59**: "*Jesus is like Adam in the sight of Allah. He created him* [Jesus] *from dust and then said to him: 'Be,' and he was.*"

9. **Quran 3:85**: "*To Him we have surrendered ourselves. He that chooses a religion other than Islam, it will not be accepted from him and in the world to come he will surely be among the losers.*"

10. **Quran 3:140**: "*Allah may test the faithful and annihilate the infidels* [Christians and Jews]."

11. **Quran 3:149** to **Quran 3:151**: "*We will put terror into the hearts of the unbelievers* [Christians and Jews]. *They serve other deities* [Adonai] *besides Allah for whom He has revealed no sanction. The Fire shall be their home; evil indeed is the dwelling of the evil-doers.*"

12. **Quran 4:36**: "*Serve Allah and associate none with Him.*"

13. **Quran 4:48**: "*Allah will not forgive those who serve other gods beside Him.*"

14. **Quran 4:74**: "*Let those who would exchange the life of this world for the hereafter, fight for the cause of Allah; whoever fights for the cause of Allah, whether he dies or triumphs, on him We shall bestow a rich recompense.*"

15. **Quran 4:89**: "*Seize them and put them to death wherever you find them.*"

16. **Quran 4:116**: "*We will burn him in the fire of Hell: an evil end . . . Allah will not forgive idolatry. . . . He that serves other gods beside Allah has strayed far indeed.*"

17. **Quran 4:124**: *"nor shall it be as the People of the Book* [Christians] *desire...But the believers* [only Muslims] . . . *shall enter Paradise."*

18. **Quran 4:157–158**: *"They said, 'We have put to death the Messiah Jesus, son of Mary, the apostle of Allah.' They did not kill him, nor did they crucify him, but they thought they did. . . . They did not slay him for certain. Allah lifted him up to Him. Allah is mighty and wise. There is none among the People of the Book but will believe in him before his death, and on the Day of Resurrection he will bear witness against them.'"*

19. **Quran 4:171**: *"People of the Book, do not transgress the bounds of your religion. Speak nothing but the truth about Allah. The Messiah, Jesus son of Mary, was no more than Allah's apostle and His Word which He cast to Mary: a spirit from Him. So believe in Allah and His apostles and do not say: 'Three.' Forbear and it shall be better for you. God (Allah) is but one God. Allah (God) forbid that He should have a son!"*

20. **Quran 5:17**: *"They do blaspheme who declare: 'Allah is the Messiah, the son of Mary . . . who could prevent Allah, if so willed, from destroying the Messiah, the son of Mary."*

21. **Quran 5:33**: Kafirs *"shall be slain or crucified or have their hands and feet cut off on alternate sides."*

22. **Quran 5:51–52**: *"Believers, take neither the Jews nor the Christians for your friends."*

23. **Quran 5:58–59**: "*People of the Book* [Christians and Jews]... *those whom Allah has <u>cursed</u> and with whom He has been angry, transforming them <u>into apes and swine</u>.*"

24. **Quran 5:64**: "*The Jews... May they be <u>cursed</u> for what they say.*"

25. **Quran 5:72–73**: "*They do blaspheme that say: 'Allah is the Messiah, the son of Mary, For the Messiah (Jesus) himself said: 'Children of Israel, serve Allah, my Lord and your Lord. . . . . They do blaspheme that say: 'Allah is one of three.' There is but one God.'... If they do not desist from saying, those of them that disbelieve shall be <u>sternly punished</u>.*"

26. **Quran 5:115**: "*Then Allah will say, 'Jesus son of Mary, did you ever say to the people: 'Worship me and my mother as gods besides Allah?' / 'Glory to You,' he will answer, 'I could never have claimed what I have no right to.*"

27. **Quran 6:155**: "*Fear Allah, do not disobey His orders that you may be saved from the torment of Hell.*"

28. **Quran 7:166**: "*And when they scornfully persisted in their forbidden ways, We said to them: '<u>Turn into detested apes</u>.'*"

29. **Quran 8:14** to **8:16** spew more of Muhammad's hatred, "*Believers, when you encounter the infidels* (Jews and Christians) *on the march, do not turn your backs to them in flight... If anyone on that day turns his back on them.... He shall incur the wrath of Allah and Hell shall be his home: an evil fate.*"

30. **Quran 8:39**: "*Make war on them until idolatry* [worship of Yeshua] *shall cease and Allah's religion shall reign supreme.*"

31. **Quran 9:5**: "*Slay the idolaters* [worshippers of Yeshua] *wherever you find them. Arrest them, besiege them, and lie in ambush everywhere for them.*"

32. **Quran 9:29**: "*Fight against such of those to whom the Scriptures were given as believe in neither Allah nor the Last Day.*"

33. **Quran 9:30**: "*Christians say the Messiah is the son of God. Allah confound them! How perverse they are!*" Other versions say, "*May Allah destroy them..*" "*Allah assail, curse, them...*"

34. **Quran 9:36**: "*fight against the idolaters* [worshippers of Yeshua]."

35. **Quran 9:63**: "*Are they not aware that the man who defies Allah and His apostle shall abide for ever in the fire of Hell?*"

36. **Quran 9:73**: "*Prophet, make war on the unbelievers and the hypocrites and deal rigorously with them. Hell shall be their home.*"

37. **Quran 9:111**: "*Allah has purchased from the faithful their lives and worldly goods, and in return has promised them the Garden (Paradise). They will fight for the cause of Allah, they will slay and be slain... Rejoice then in the bargain you have made. That is the supreme triumph.*"

38. **Quran 9:123**: *"Believers make war on the infidels that dwell around you."*

39. **Quran 10:68–70**: *'They say: 'God (Allah) has begotten a son. God (Allah) forbid!...Surely for this you have no sanction...for their unbelief We will make them taste the grievous torment.'*

40. **Quran 12:106–107**: *"...believe in Allah only if they can worship other gods besides Him. Are they confident that Allah's scourge will not fall upon them, or that the Hour of Doom will not overtake them unawares, without warning?"*

41. **Quran 17.8**: *"You shall again be scourged. We have made Hell a prison-house for the unbelievers."*

42. **Quran 17.33** *"You shall not kill any man whom Allah has forbidden you to kill, except for a just cause* [whatever reason you want]*."*

43. **Quran 17:111**: *"Praise be to Allah who has never begotten a son; who has no partner in His kingdom."*

44. **Quran 19:88–92** *"Those who say, 'The Lord of Mercy has begotten a son,' preach a monstrous falsehood, at which the very heavens might crack, the earth split asunder, and the mountains crumble to dust...That they should ascribe a son to the Merciful, when it does not become the Lord of Mercy to beget one!"*

45. **Quran 23:91**: *"Never has Allah begotten a son, nor is there any other god before Him."*

46. **Quran 31:13** exhorts and threatens, *"Serve no other deity besides Allah, for idolatry is an abominable sin."*

47. **Quran 47:3–4**: *"When you meet the unbelievers* [Christians and Jews] *in the battlefield strike off their heads."*

48. **Quran 48:13**: *"As for those that disbelieve in God (Allah) and His apostle, We have prepared a blazing Fire for the unbelievers"*

49. **Quran 112:1–4**: *"Allah is One, the Eternal God…He begot none, nor was He begotten. None is equal to Him."*

Driven by overwhelming Islamic hatred, the following verses of extreme violence in the Quran are about stern unforgiving punishment and ruthlessness, cursing Christians and Jews, using swords, making holy war, inflicting grievous punishment, harrowing scourging, fighting, invading, making war, destroying, slaughtering, striking terror, terrorizing, obliterating faces and turning them backward, striking off heads, melting skins with scalding water, lashing with rods of iron, burning with fire, jihad killing in the way of Allah, and casting into the fires of Hell.

1. **Quran 2:216**: *"Fighting is obligatory for you, much as you dislike it. But you may hate a thing although it is good for you, and love a thing which is bad for you. Allah knows, but you do not."* (The Arabic version says *"Slaughtering people with the sword is obligatory for you… "*)

2. **Quran 2:242–244**: *"Fight for the cause of Allah."*

3. **Quran 3:56:** *"The unbelievers shall be sternly punished in this world."*

4. **Quran 3:167:** *"Come, <u>fight</u> for the cause of Allah."*

5. **Quran 4:47–49:** *"before we <u>obliterate your faces and turn them backward,</u> or <u>lay Our curse on you.</u> . . . Allah will not forgive those who serve other gods beside Him."*

6. **Quran 4:70:** *"<u>fight</u> for the cause of Allah."*

7. **Quran 4:74–76:** *"The true believers <u>fight</u> for the cause of Allah."*

8. **Quran 4:95:** *"those who <u>fight</u> for the cause of Allah with their goods and their bodies…Allah has exalted the men who <u>fight</u>…"*

9. **Quran 4:104:** *"<u>Seek out</u> your enemy relentlessly."*

10. **Quran 8:12:** *"I shall <u>cast terror</u> into the hearts of the infidels . . . . <u>Strike off their heads,</u> strike off the very tips of their fingers."*

11. **Quran 8:59–60**: *"Muster against them all the men and cavalry… so that you may <u>strike terror</u> into the enemy of Allah and your enemy."*

12. **Quran 8:65:** *"Prophet: rouse the faithful <u>to arms</u>."*

13. **Quran 8:67**: *"A prophet may not take captives until he has <u>fought</u> and triumphed in the land."*

14. **Quran 9:14:** *"<u>Make war</u> on them: Allah will <u>chastise them</u> in your hands."*

15. **Quran 9:20:** *"the man who believes in Allah . . . and <u>fights</u> for Allah's cause."*

16. **Quran 9:21:** *"Those that . . . <u>fought</u> for Allah's cause. . ."*

17. **Quran 9:39:** *"If you do not <u>go to war</u>, He (Allah) will punish you sternly, and will replace you by other men."*

18. **Quran 9:86:** *"Believe in Allah and <u>fight</u> alongside His apostle."*

19. **Quran 9:88:** *"A woeful <u>scourge</u> shall fall on those of them that disbelieved."*

20. **Quran 9.111:** *"Allah has purchased from the faithful their lives and worldly goods, and in return has promised them the Garden (Paradise). They will <u>fight</u> for the cause of Allah, they will <u>slay and be slain</u>. . . . Rejoice then in the bargain you have made. That is the supreme triumph."*

21. **Quran 17:16:** *"When we resolve to raze a city. . . . We <u>destroy</u> it utterly."*

22. **Quran 21:44:** *"We <u>invade</u> their land and diminish its borders."*

23. **Quran 22:19:** *"<u>Garments of fire</u> have been prepared for the unbelievers . . . <u>scalding water</u> shall be poured over their heads, <u>melting their skins</u> and that which is in their bellies. . . . They shall be <u>lashed with rods of iron</u>."*

24. **Quran 25:52:** *"Do not yield to the unbelievers, but <u>fight</u> them vigorously."*

25. **Quran 33:60–62:** states, "*If the hypocrites and those who have tainted hearts . . . do not desist, we will rouse you against them. Cursed wherever they are found, they shall be seized and put to death without mercy.*"

26. **Quran 40:43:** "*The transgressors shall be the inmates of the Fire.*"

27. **Quran 47:35:** "*unbelievers shall not be shown forgiveness by Allah.*"

28. **Quran 48:29:** "*Muhammad is Allah's apostle. Those who follow him are ruthless to the unbelievers.*"

29. **Quran 50:26:** "*Cast into Hell every hardened unbeliever... Hurl him into the harrowing scourge.*"

30. **Quran 61:4:** "*Allah loves those who fight for his cause.*"

31. **Quran 61:9–12:** "*fight for Allah's cause with your wealth and with your persons.*"

32. **Quran 65:10:** "*Stern was Our reckoning with them, and harrowing was Our scourge. . . . Allah has prepared a grievous scourge for them.*"

33. **Quran 66:9:** "*Prophet, make war on the unbelievers and the hypocrites, and deal sternly with them. Hell shall be their home, evil their fate.*"

ISLAMIC HATRED IN THE HADITHS DRIVES THE KILLING OF CHRISTIANS AND JEWS

1. **Sahih Bukhari in Book 1, Volume 1:35**: *"Allah's apostle said, 'The person who participates in (Holy Battles) in Allah's cause . . . will be compensated by Allah."*

2. **Sahih Bukhari in Book 1, Volume 3:125**: *"Allah's apostle said, 'He who fights so that Allah's word (Islam) should be superior, then he fights in Allah's cause."*

3. **Sahih Bukhari in Book 1, Volume 8:387**: *"Allah's apostle said, 'I have been ordered to fight the people until they say, 'None has the right to be worshipped but Allah'"*

4. **Sahih Bukhari in Book 4, Volume 52:65**: *"Allah's apostle said, 'He who fights that Allah's word should be superior, fights in Allah's cause."*

5. **Sahih Bukhari in Book 1, Volume 52:73**: *"Allah's apostle said, 'Know that Paradise is under the shades of swords.'"*

6. **Sahih Bukhari in Book 4, Volume 52:177**: *"Allah's apostle said, 'The hour will not be established until you fight with the Jews..."*

7. **Sahih Bukhari in Book 4, Volume 52:220**: *"Allah's apostle said, 'I have been made victorious with terror.'"*

8. **Sahih Muslim in Book 1, Volume 1:30**: *"that the Messenger of Allah said, 'I have been commanded to fight against the*

people so long as they do not declare that there is no god but Allah.'"

9. **Sahih Muslim in Book 1, Volume 1:33:** *"that the Messenger of Allah said, 'I have been commanded to fight against the people till they testify that there is no god but Allah, that Muhammad is the messenger of Allah.'"*

10. **Sahih Muslim in Book 19, Hadith Number 4294:** *"Fight in the name of Allah and in the way of Allah... Fight against those who disbelieve in Allah...Make a holy war."*

11. **Sahih Muslim in Book 20, Hadith Number 4645:** *"There is another act which elevates the position of a man in Paradise to a grade one hundred (higher), and the elevation between one grade and the other is equal to the height of the heaven from the earth. He (Abu Sa'id) said: What is that act? He replied: Jihad in the way of Allah! Jihad in the way of Allah."*

12. **Sahih Muslim in Book 20, Hadith Number 4696:** *"One who died but did not fight in the way of Allah nor did he express any desire (or determination) for jihad died the death of a hypocrite."*

13. **Sahih Muslim in Book 31, Hadith Number 5917:** *"Allah's Messenger, on what issue should I fight with the people? Thereupon the Prophet Muhammad said: 'Fight them until they bear testimony to the fact that there is no god but Allah and Muhammad is his messenger.'"*

14. **Sahih Muslim in Book 31, Hadith Number 5918:** "*I will fight them until they are like us.*"

15. **Sahih Muslim Traditions No. 10–14–15:** "*A great slaughter of the Jews will ensue and every one of them will be annihilated. The nation of the Jews will be exterminated.*"

16. **Sahih Muslim Traditions No. 9–15–21:** "*At the proclamation of truth by Christ* [Islamic Christ], *the Christian religion will become extinct* [Traditions No. 1-2-4-6]"

17. **Tabari 7:97:** "*Kill any Jew who falls under your power.*"

18. **Tabari 9:69:** "*Killing unbelievers is a small matter to us.*"

19. **Muhammad bin Ishaq wrote:** '*Christ was not crucified. Allah took Jesus up directly to him and will refute those who say that he was crucified and was resurrected. On the final day, the Day of Resurrection, those who follow Christ but do not believe in his divinity, will be blessed. Those who insist that Christ is God, part of the Trinity, and reject true faith, will be punished in Hell,*"

20. **Mustadrak Hakim wrote:** "*Jesus* [Muslim Jesus] *destroys the Antichrist, exterminates the Jewish people . . . will break every cross.*"

21. **Sunan Abu Dawud in Book 37, Number 4310:** "*The Prophet said that Jesus will descend to the Earth . . . wearing two light yellow garments. . . . He will fight the people for the cause of Islam. He will break the cross, kill swine. . . . Allah will*

perish all religions except Islam. . . . He will destroy the Antichrist [Christian Christ]."

22. **Sahih Muslim wrote**: "*Certainly, the gates of Paradise lie in the shade of swords.*"

23. **Sahih Bukhari wrote:** "*Be aware that Paradise lies under the shadow of swords.*"

24. **Sahih Bukhari wrote:** "*Muhammad punished the men of the Uraina tribe by cutting off their hands and feet and letting them bleed to death.*"

25. **Sahih Bukhari wrote:** "*Muhammad ordered that their hands and feet be cut off and their eyes gouged out with hot pokers. They were thrown on jagged rocks, their pleas for water ignored and they died of thirst . . . who abandoned Islam. . . . Death is the sentence for apostasy, leaving Islam.*"

26. **Sahih Bukhari wrote:** "*Allah's Apostle (Muhammad) said, 'I have been ordered to fight the people till they say: 'None has the right to be worshipped but Allah.'*"

27. **Sahih Muslim wrote:** "*When it will be the Day of Resurrection, Allah will deliver to every Muslim a Jew or a Christian and say: 'That is your rescue from Hell-fire.'*"

28. **Sahih Bukhari wrote:** "*The Hour will not be established until the Son of Mary (Jesus) descends amongst you as a just ruler, he will break the cross, kill the pigs (Jews), and abolish the Jizyah tax.*"

29. **Muhammad's dying words:** "*May Allah curse the Jews and Christians for they built the places of worship at the graves of their prophets.*"

30. **Sahih al-Bukhari and Sahih Muslim wrote:** "*The last hour will not come before the Muslims fight the Jews and the Muslims kill them. In that day Allah will give voice to the rocks and the trees and they will cry out, 'O Muslim, there is a Jew hiding behind me. Come and kill him!'*"

31. **Ali al-Faqir wrote:** "*Sir, it has been proven scientifically that the trees and the stones have a language of their own. But we don't have the ability to invent the instruments that will convey the tree's voice and the stone's voice to us.*"

Today in the Middle East, Muslims chant "**KILL JESUS!**"

CHAPTER 11

JESUS CHRIST, YESHUA MESSIAH, YESHUA HA MASHIACH

A rchangel Michael addresses the God Squad trio stating, "As dictated to him by Satan-Allah, in his Quran, Muhammad repeatedly claimed that Allah has no son." Michael emphatically declares, "Here are nine references from the Torah of the Old Testament to reveal undeniably that the God of Heaven with many names as Yahweh, Elohim, Hashem, Adonai . . . has a Son."

Genesis 1–2 reads, "*In the beginning God created the heavens and the earth . . . and the Spirit of God was moving over the face of the waters.*" Michael details the awesomeness of what he had observed. "Yes, the four of us were privileged to witness this most magnificent spectacle of creation of all time. Note that two members of the Godhead are the forces mentioned; both God and the Spirit of God as the power behind creation."

Genesis 1:26 exposes who He is, "Then God said, 'Let *Us* make man in *Our* image, after *Our* likeness; and let them have dominion over...'" Michael continues, "Three times in one statement, the reference to God is to the plural name Elohim as in '*Us*,' as in '*Our* image,' and as in '*Our* likeness.' However, it is exasperating to see how some humans obfuscate and deny the plural name of Elohim.

"Now listen to **Proverbs 30:4** which reads, 'Who has ascended into heaven and come down? Who has gathered the wind in his fist? Who has wrapped up the waters in a garment? Who has established all the ends of the earth? What is his name, and what is his son's name?'

Only the God of Heaven has the power to 'gather the wind in his fist' and to 'establish all the ends of the earth.' Yes, this mighty creator God has a Son. His Son is the second Person of the Godhead as in the plural name Elohim. These words about God's Son were written at the time of King Solomon which was almost one thousand years before the earthly birth of Yeshua Messiah the Son of God."

"In **Daniel 7:13–14**, Daniel wrote: 'I saw in the night visions, and behold, with the clouds of heaven there came one like a son of man, and he came to the Ancient of Days and was presented before him. And to him was given dominion and glory and kingdom, that all peoples, nations, and languages should serve him; his dominion is an everlasting dominion, which shall not pass away, and his kingdom one that shall not be destroyed.' Gabriel asks, "To whom would the Ancient of Days give dominion, glory, all peoples, all nations and languages to serve him, and an everlasting kingdom as well? With whom would the Ancient of Days share His authority, His dominion, and His sovereignty? Of course, this *'son of man'* would be no less a Being than the Ancient of Days Himself."

"In **Daniel 3:25**," explains Gabriel, "just read the words of Nebuchadnezzar, the Babylonian king of the ancient world, who had bound and thrown Daniel's three friends into the fiery furnace and then had said: 'But I see four men loose, walking in the midst of the fire, and they are not hurt; and the fourth is like a son of the gods.' Yes, as King Nebuchadnezzar had said, 'like a son of the gods!' This fourth man was Yeshua Messiah. Who but the Son of the Ancient of Days could walk through the fiery furnace with His three friends and with their hair unscorched by the blast of the furnace flames? Who?"

"Certainly, it was not Muhammad, that serial fornicator who had burned himself out indulging in sexual trysts with his twelve wives and with countless captured slaves. Certainly, it was not Muhammad who was scorched and flamed out by his wives who had poisoned him. Certainly, it was not Muhammad who died an ignoble death with his corpse displaying a shameful, a disgraceful and a humiliating poison-induced rigor-mortis-erection which he took into the eternal fires of Hell!"

"Shock of shocks! Now hear **Isaiah 9:6–7** which declares, 'For to us a child is born, to us a son is given; and the government will be upon his shoulder, and his name will be called 'Wonderful Counselor, Mighty God, Everlasting Father, Prince of Peace.' It is an amazing and a staggering enigma that this Child also was addressed as the 'Mighty God, Everlasting Father, Prince of Peace.' Think of it. This Child as the Son also is called the 'Mighty God' and the 'Everlasting Father.' What? 'Everlasting Father?' How can that be? But it is! Who on earth can figure out how it is that this Child also carries the identical name of 'Mighty God' and 'Everlasting Father?' Many humans have gone apoplectic in their vehement denials of the reality of the Son of God, while others get mental hernias just trying to interpret this enigma of all time."

Michael continues to expose the earthly suffering of this child, this son, this 'Mighty God' and this 'Everlasting Father' in **Isaiah 53:1–12**, "But he was wounded for our transgressions, he was bruised for our iniquities; upon him was the chastisement that made us whole, and with his stripes are we healed . . . and the LORD has laid on him the iniquity of us all . . . like a lamb that is led to the slaughter . . . he was cut off out of the land of the living, stricken for the transgression of my people . . . when he makes himself an offering for sin . . . because he poured out his soul to death, and was numbered with the transgressors; yet he bore the sin of many and made intercession for the transgressors.'"

"Yes, this Child, this Son, this 'Mighty God' as this 'Everlasting Father' 'was cut off out of the land of the living,' 'poured out his soul to death' and was 'made intercession for the transgressors.' Michael advances his claims, "Yes, it's all about death! Elohim is one Being in three Persons. For Muhammad's Islam, there can be no weaseling, no evading, no twisting, no denying and no escaping Genesis 1:2, Genesis 1:26, Psalm 2:7, Psalm 22:16, Proverbs 30:4, Daniel 7:13–14, Daniel 3:25, Isaiah 9:6–7, and Isaiah 53:1–12, most of which were written a thousand years before Muhammad's Quran. Elohim has a Son! His name is Jesus Christ as Yeshua Ha Mashiach. It's pure and simple. There is no rat hole down which Muhammad's Quran and Muhammad's Islam can crawl to escape these nine Old Testament verses which give testimony to the Son of God and to His intercession death on a cross."

CHAPTER 12

THE QURAN, THE HADITHS, THE SIRA, AND SHARIA LAW

The date is the latter part of the second decade of the twenty-first century. The time is July 2017. The place is inside the Babylonian palace of King Nebuchadnezzar and upon the exact site of its ancient ruins which have been in restoration since Saddam Hussein began its rebuilding in 1983. Repeatedly, the God Squad has made the Babylonian palace their home base.

"The greater part of the Quran," states Michael, "is about the kafirs and most of the Sira is about Muhammad's battles against the kafirs."

"Tell me more about this Kafir business," Uriel questions.

"A Kafir is the lowest form of life, an outright scum, a most disgusting, wicked, and evil human."

Archangel Gabriel expands upon this portrayal. "It's Islam's ugliest form of contempt possible to describe non-believers. Muslims can cheat them, deceive them, lie to the Kafirs, and with Allah's permission, it is proper to enslave, to torture, and to kill a Kafir."

"The greater part of the Quran is about the Kafir and most of the Sira is about Muhammad's battles against the Kafirs. The Sira documents the warfare directed by Muhammad against the Jews, which takes up a very large part of the Sira. The Hadiths and the Sira together are known as the Sunna. The Hadiths call this 'holy war' as 'fighting in Allah's Cause.' In Quran 48:13, Allah told Muhammad, 'We have prepared a blazing Fire for these kafirs who do not believe in Allah and His Messenger.' The threat of Hellfire speaks of the Muslim mind-set."

"We have prepared a blazing Fire for these kafirs who do not believe in Allah and His Messenger."

– *Quran 48:13*

"It's the dual ethics of Islam," Archangel Michael proceeds deeper. "Islam is about treating Muslims one way, and treating Kafirs in a radically different way. Islamic authority and historian Sahih Bukhari had written that on his deathbed Muhammad had said, 'First, drive the Kafirs from Arabia.' Sahih Bukhari also wrote that Muhammad had said, 'I have been directed to fight the Kafir until every one of them admits, "There is only one god and that is Allah."'"

"Muslims are taught that no death is too painful for the kafir and that for eternity, Allah will be even more cruel to them in Hell." Gabriel cringes in horror as he speaks. Muslim historian Sahih Bukhari had written, 'Muhammad punished the men of the Uraina tribe by cutting off their hands and feet and letting them bleed to death.' Sahih Bukhari wrote, 'Muhammad ordered that their hands and feet be cut off and their eyes gouged out with hot pokers. They were thrown on jagged rocks, their pleas for water ignored and they died of thirst . . . who abandoned Islam. . . . Death is the sentence for apostasy, leaving Islam.' Cutting off the hands and feet and letting them bleed to death were extremely cruel tortures and prolonged, agonizing deaths. These monstrous barbaric tactics terrorized the surrounding Jewish tribes far and wide. This was Muhammad's and Allah's blood lust and hatred. This was Muhammad's radical Islamic terrorism. This was Muhammad's Reign of Terror which ISIS is duplicating, and which has been surging across Iraq and Syria today into 2017 when Donald Trump is the American President."

"From its Quranic roots out of Muhammad, Islam continues to be a political-religious ideology and a martyrdom-death-cult whose goal is the suicide killing of kafirs," Michael summarizes. "Muhammad's Islam is a political totalitarian philosophy ruled by barbaric murder and terror whose goal is to enslave the entire world."

"Out of the Syrian civil war, ISIS, which re-named itself as Islamic State, is the most brutal killing machine on earth. ISIS is using terror to achieve its political aims. The Pope had called it piecemeal World War

III. American President Trump is changing that dynamic by taking the battle to ISIS in the Middle East."

"As murderous as these radical Islamic terrorists are, they only are following the instructions in the Quran, Muhammad's teachings and his actions in the Hadiths and in the Sira. The Quran, the Hadiths and the Sira scream of Muhammad's undeniable, rampaging, jihadist Islamic reign of terror. This is Muhammad's radical Islamic slaughter and terrorism. The Quran, the Hadiths and the Sira make it absolutely clear that the killing of kafirs, but particularly the killing of Christians and Jews, is mainstream Muhammad radical Islamic theology."

"Al-Qaeda has a 2004 field manual," explains Gabriel, "which is called *The Management of Savagery*. This manual promotes jihad as the holiest of endeavours when it recommends all manner of crudeness, violence, treachery, terrorism, and massacring. This manual instructs and encourages Muslims to create as much mayhem and murder as possible with butchering and with deadly car bombs, so that the world will spin down into global chaos."

"Following the Paris massacres, French President François Hollande stated that, 'It was the French who killed other French.' Just what were the deeper, underlying reasons why French Muslims perpetrated the Paris massacres?" inquires Raphael.

"Following the end of the Algerian colonial war in 1982, thousands of Algerian refugees had moved to France. However, assimilation failed, which today has exploded into a generation of alienated young Muslims in Paris," Michael picks up this French theme.

"Another great concern is the Paris massacre backlash which has descended into shockwaves of anti-Muslim retaliations which are washing over the world and escalating this crisis." Raphael understands the psychology of fear, hatred, and retaliation. "These young Paris Muslims identify themselves neither with Algeria nor with France. They are 'morally outraged' at what they see as worldwide persecution of Muslims. In the Islamic philosophy of 'a tooth for a tooth,' they are taking their revenge by becoming holy warriors for Allah."

Gabriel abruptly interrupts Raphael with astounding history. "The September 11 attack on Benghazi was an extension of 9/11 as 9/11/11. It was another fulfilment of Quran 9:111. As we have talked about it, the compelling forces behind September 11 had been seared into Islamic consciousness for more than five centuries. It was on September 11, 1565, that Sultan Suleiman the Magnificent attempted to conquer Rome. On September 11, in the Great Siege of Malta, his huge armada was trounced by the Knights of Malta. The Battle of Vienna began in earnest on September 11, 1683. It was intended to vanquish Europe and to crush Christendom. Grand Vizier Mustafa celebrated September 11 by chopping off the heads of thirty thousand Christian captives. However, the next day, Polish King Jan Sobieski smashed the Ottoman Turkish armies of Mustafa. The Battle of Vienna was one of the most decisive military campaigns ever because it stopped the three hundred-year armed conflict by the Muslim Ottoman Turks to subjugate Europe. Again, on September 11, 1697, the Ottoman Muslim Turks were defeated in the Battle of Zenta after which the Ottoman Turks surrendered Croatia, Hungary, Transylvania, and Slavonia to Austria. Since the Great Siege of Malta, the Battle of Vienna, and the Battle of Zenta, the date of September 11 has remained the day of infamy in the Muslim conscience, the day of Islamic hatred for their triple defeats, and the day for Islamic revenge against Christianity. There was no provocative video as the cause of the Benghazi killings. Quran 9:111 continues to be the driving verse behind the September 11 attacks."

"Great insight, Gabriel! To continue to fulfill Quran 9:111, expect more 9/11 attacks on U.S. interests. ISIS is using the shock value of barbarous beheadings, crucifixions, and even the murder of women and infants. In the same fashion as Muhammad had performed, the goal of ISIS is to strike fear and terror into their targets, showing that the Caliphate is fearless and that it is willing to stop at nothing to impose Muhammad's Islamic ruthless control."

"ISIS is following in the footsteps of Muhammad by raping, murdering, and terrorizing their way across Syria and northern Iraq." Raphael, the medical expert, weighs into this ISIS sexual cesspool of hatred. "Perpetrating genocide against the Yazidi people in the northern Iraqi province of Nineveh, ISIS terrorists repeatedly have raped Yazidi women and girls as young as nine and then complained that nine-year-olds were 'too old.' In their atrocities, ISIS killers have raped Yazidi girls as young as six years of age. What manner of depraved monsters are these Muslim males? Hell isn't quite hot enough for them! ISIS is imitating Muhammad. Like teacher, like student!"

"ISIS is following this *Management of Savagery* manual's recommendation in using all distortions of fear, brutality, and terror. Muhammad set the example, and ISIS is following suit. It is mainstream fundamental Islam. Savagery is at the very heart of Islam."

"The Muslim Brotherhood has its own manual and its own war mantra which reads, 'Allah is our goal, the prophet is our model, the Quran is our Constitution, jihad is our path and death for the sake of Allah is the highest of our wishes… Allah-Akbar! Allah-Akbar!' Michael states, "Yes, jihad and death are their highest goals. This is the Muslim Brotherhood and the ISIS war logo. This is Muhammad's radical Islamic imperialism for world conquest."

"The Muslim Brotherhood and ISIS are longing for jihad and for martyrdom. They want to die as desperately as kafirs want to live. The description of their treachery is worldwide terror."

"The home-grown terrorist known as the Boston Marathon bomber had written a suicide note saying, 'Know that you are fighting men who look into the barrel of your gun and see heaven,' Raphael confirms and amplifies the Muslim Brotherhood war chant at the jihadi level. "However, what the Boston Marathon Bomber was seeing were dark-eyed virgins winking and blinking at him as they lay on couches in Allah's paradise, beckoning to him to hurry up and join them for sex."

"The terrorist group called Hamas was founded by the Muslim Brotherhood," Michael reminds them. "All of the jihadi murderous thugs track their roots right back to the Muslim Brotherhood. What is the Muslim Brotherhood doing in America?"

"ISIS uses verses such as Quran 8:60 which goads them to 'Muster against them all the men and cavalry at your command, so you may *strike terror* into the enemy of Allah and your enemy.' Except that their cavalry are American tanks and guns which they had stolen from the terrified, retreating, cowardly Iraqis. To strike terror is to imitate Muhammad. Striking terror is exactly what ISIS has been doing, that is, until Donald Trump became the U.S. President."

"Muster against them all the men and cavalry at your command, so you may **strike terror** into the enemy of Allah and your enemy."

- Quran 8:60

"We are witnessing the merging of al-Qaeda and ISIS," Gabriel supplies unpublished details suppressed by the mainstream media. "Stirring this toxic cauldron with his Iran Nuclear Deal, President Barack Obama has just enabled Shiite Iran to develop nuclear weapons and to re-create the Persian Empire of old."

"Although his enabling of Iran might appear to be a dumb mistake, make no mistake. Barack Obama is neither stupid nor incompetent. Barack Obama's world is unfolding beautifully according to his plan." As the military leader of the ages, Michael knows battleground tactics. "By pulling American troops out from Iraq, Barack Obama opened the door to the explosive growth of ISIS and the refugee crisis out of Iraq and Syria."

"In this wicked stew of broiling hatred, both Shia and Sunni extremists revile each other as much as they hate the West and Israel. Even Sunnis are fighting Sunnis. Sunni Egypt is fighting Sunni Islamic State." In a state of high anger, Gabriel repeats, "Once again, **Genesis 16:12** is being fulfilled daily before our eyes. Remember that four thousand years ago, it was I who had brought Adonai's message to Hagar proclaiming that Ishmael would be 'a wild ass of a man, his hand against every man.'"

"With the threat of a nuclear Iran, now Sunni Saudi Arabia is running scared of its deadly Shiite archenemy of fourteen centuries. To protect themselves against rising nuclear Iran, the Saudis are acquiring 'off-the-shelf' atomic weapons from Pakistan." In humor Uriel inserts himself, "Yes, daily the Saudi rulers are crapping their drawers in fear of being nuclear-fried. It appears that the only question is who will get fried first. Will it be Iran or Saudi Arabia?"

"In **Isaiah 34:9–10**, here is what the prophet wrote about Esau's Edom, which is today's Saudi Arabia, 'Her land shall become burning pitch. Night and day it shall not be quenched; Its smoke shall go up forever.' Events will unfold so quickly that the Saudis will not have the opportunity to crap their drawers until after their oil fields have been set ablaze."

"It sure reads and sounds as if the Saudi oil fields will be nuked and set on fire by Iran." Nuclear physicist Uriel launches Isaiah's prophecy over Saudi Arabia. "And with all that nuclear radiation, nobody will be able to get near those oil wells to put out the fires, which will burn forever."

"What about high justice for Shiite Iran who is the chief supporter, promoter and exporter of terrorism against Israel and across the globe?" queries Gabriel.

> "Muster against them all the men and cavalry at your command, so you may *strike terror* into the enemy of Allah and your enemy."
>
> – Quran 8:60

As the administrator of justice, Archangel Michael eagerly responds, "Major catastrophic judgment is coming to Iran. In **49:35-38, Jeremiah** had prophesied, "Thus says the LORD of hosts: Behold, I will break the bow of Elam, the mainstay of their might; and I will bring upon Elam the four winds from the four quarters of heaven; and I will scatter them to all those winds, and there shall be no nation to which those driven out of Elam shall not come. I will terrify Elam before their enemies, and before those who seek their life; I will bring evil upon them, my fierce anger, says the LORD, I will send the sword after them, until I have consumed them; and I will set my throne in Elam, and destroy their king and princes, says the LORD."

"Wow! Who is this Elam and where is this Elam?" begs Raphael.

As the physical sciences expert, Uriel responds, "Elam is Persia of old or present-day Iran. Iran is the center of Shiite Islam which is determined to destroy Israel and to conquer the world for Allah. Elam is located along the west coast of Iran at the very northern end of the Persian Gulf. Elam includes Bushehr Province with its capital city of Bushehr. Of supreme military significance, Bushehr is critically important today because it is the vital location of Iran's nuclear facility. It is feared that Iran is using this plant to build nuclear weapons to destroy Israel and to threaten other nations. It is very likely that Israel will attack Iran to destroy this nuclear complex at Bushehr. This preemptive attack could be the catalyst that will launch World War III. Amazingly and apocalyptically, Iran sits on major fault lines. In recent years, ominously, Elam has suffered several devastating earthquakes. In 2003, Elam was hit by a devastating 6.6 magnitude quake."

Michael delivers his apocalyptic vision, "The God of Israel has put Iran on notice that the Bushehr nuclear reactor is a target of His judgment."

"After fourteen centuries of hatred and fighting between themselves, both the Sunnis and the Shiites are calling upon their Allah and upon his messenger for help against the other side. In Quran 5:33, Allah terrorizes them threatening, 'The recompense of those who wage war against Allah and His Messenger and do mischief in the land is only that they shall be killed or crucified or their hands and feet cut off on the opposite sides or be exiled from the land.' Poor Allah is not sure whether to help the Sunnis or the Shiites." In his constant state of high anger toward Muhammad for his defamations of him, Gabriel constantly reviews his archenemy's false accusations of bringing Allah's messages to construct his Quran.

"Fighting is obligatory for you.' In Quran 4:89 Muhammad commanded, 'seize them and put them to death wherever you find them.' In Quran 9:36 Allah exhorted to 'fight against the idolaters."

- Quran 2:216

"Yes, Muhammad's Allah is telling them to kill, to crucify, and to cut off the hands and feet on the opposite sides, OR instead to use a car bomb which will cut off many hands and feet and many heads in a single blast." Raphael is stressed out by the constant slaughter of innocents. "This macabre brutality was Muhammad's radical Islamic terrorism of the most extreme kind. The radical Islamic terrorists of the Paris massacres showed far less brutality than those inflicted by Muhammad in the seventh century."

"Quran 2:216 states, 'Fighting is obligatory for you.' In Quran 4:89 Muhammad commanded, 'seize them and put them to death wherever you find them.' In Quran 9:36 Allah exhorted to 'fight against the idolaters.' This nauseatingly repetitive Quranic brainwashing exasperates Raphael. "Putting kafirs to death is obligatory in the Quran. These are the undeniable words of Muhammad's radical Islamic jihad and terror, which *all* Muslims are called upon to perform. To deny that these commands exist is a Muslim lie. Without exception, for *all* Muslims, holy war is a religious obligation that cannot be dodged or evaded."

"Do any of you read this Muslim author named Farzana Hassan who writes in *The Sun* newspaper?" Archangel Gabriel inquires. Nobody answers.

Gabriel continues, "As usual, it looks as if I'm the only one who reads the newspapers. Farzana Hassan, who is a Muslim, wrote that 'Muslim radicals want to wreak havoc in Western countries and to kill infidels,' and that they are out to get the infidels. The word 'Infidels' is another word for 'kafirs.'"

"So tell us what this Muslim female author says about Sharia Law," probes Uriel.

Gabriel is only too willing to quote from her newspaper articles, "Here are a few excerpts from Muslim Farzana Hassan's book titled *UNVEILED*, which is about the spread of the burka and the niqab and the marginalization and denigration of Muslim women. Farzana wrote: 'Islam clearly discriminated against women . . . polygamy, wife-beating and the segregation of women . . . men with whom these women had allegedly committed adultery not being held to account . . . the medieval notion that men own women. . . . The Quran permits men to use force to make wives to comply with their wishes. . . . Beating was allowed under Sharia . . . burka-clad women, patriarchal control, political Islam. . . . Islam does not even prescribe the face veil . . . sharia law even in its most innocuous form, will systematically discriminate against Muslim women . . . sharia is all man-made . . . polygamy, unequal inheritance shares for women, punishment for adultery, the fact that a woman's testimony is considered half of a man's, the fact that men can pronounce a divorce so readily, and the fact that the custody of children is invariably granted to the father.'"

"That's quite the shocking summary of control of women under Sharia Law. That is not what American and Canadian women want to hear. Fundamentally, Sharia Law is about suppressing and denying the right of free speech." Raphael understands the psychological traumas inflicted upon Muslim women. "Enshrouding Muslim women under burkas and under niqabs is about forcing women to become camouflaged and remain anonymous lumps under the domination of men. Sharia Law is the domain of the Invisible Woman."

"Consider reading another Muslim female named Irshad Manji, who is the controversial author of *The Trouble with Islam Today*," suggests Gabriel, "and consider that the world's major Islamic terror groups named al-Qaeda, Boko Haram, Hezbollah, the Iranian Revolutionary Guard, the Muslim Brotherhood, and ISIS are determined to make Sharia Law to be the law of the land across the globe. It's already happening in London, England."

"Islamic jihad is about the killing of kafirs. As they are admitting, jihad is warfare against non-Muslims, to set up Islam as the only worldwide religion."

> "Fight against such as those to whom the Scriptures were given as believe in neither Allah nor the Last Day.' Another version of the Quran 9:29 reads, "Fight those who do not believe in Allah or in the Last Day."
>
> - Quran 9:29

"Small wonder, Gabriel! Recall that Muhammad wrote that you told him in Quran 9:29 to 'Fight against such as those to whom the Scriptures were given as believe in neither Allah nor the Last Day.' Another version of the Quran 9:29 reads, "Fight those who do not believe in Allah or in the Last Day.'"

With a swing of his arms, Gabriel becomes very animated and indignant. "You know it, Uriel! Muhammad lied about me! I brought no messages to Muhammad, but I did see Satan-Allah whispering into his ear continually. Uriel, you know better and if you keep up that kind of jesting, you just might find yourself on the other side of the Milky Way or maybe inside the Crab Nebula."

Looking distressed, Uriel apologizes. "So sorry, I was just joking. I had better attend to the fires in that galaxy swirling out of control north of the Milky Way."

Michael is quick to regain the focus saying, "Quran 8:39 commands to 'Make war on them until idolatry shall cease and Allah's religion shall reign supreme.'"

Gabriel reveals supportive history, "In his Hadith, the well-known historian authority named Sahih Muslim wrote that Muhammad had been commanded '*to fight* against the kafirs so long as they do not declare that there is no god but Allah'"

> "Make war on them until idolatry shall cease and Allah's religion shall reign supreme."
>
> – *Quran 8:39*

Archangel Raphael draws upon consensus from a respected historian stating, "Back in time, Alexis de Tocqueville wrote that 'there have been few religions in the world as deadly to men as that of Muhammad.' Muhammad's religion of Islam has been about exterminating warfare against the kafirs, but particularly against Christians and Jews."

Archangel Michael echoes agreement with Raphael, "In support of this analysis by Alexis de Tocqueville, Quran 8:60 commands Muslims '*to strike terror* into the enemies of Allah,' and that is exactly what ISIS has been doing in Syria and in Iraq. To strike terror into the enemies of Allah is a command for *all* Muslims to follow without exception. On December 17, 2015, SHOEBAT.com AWARENESS AND ACTION wrote that Muslims in Syria who had kidnapped a Christian pastor told him to, 'Become Muslim or we'll cut your head off.' This is ISIS-Islamic State in action, following in the footsteps of Muhammad and following Muhammad's exhortations within his Quran."

> "*to strike terror* into the enemies of Allah."
>
> – *Quran 8:60*

"Another female writer named Ayaan Hirsi Ali, who is a Muslim, had lived under the intolerable Saudi Arabian regime. Ayaan Hirsi Ali is a women's rights activist and author. She wrote that Sharia Law is 'gender apartheid.' She wrote that 'Islam is not a religion of peace,' and that in the Muslim world, holy war is a duty and a compulsion to convert everybody to Islam, either by word or 'by force.' In the Sharia Law of Saudi Arabia, women are not allowed to drive autos. Marital rape is not recognized. Women are punished in the public square. In her book, *Heretic,* Ayaan Hirsi Ali wrote that a 'reformation' of Islamic doctrine is necessary. In an interview on December 8, 2015, Ayaan Hirsi Ali spoke out saying that the barbaric actions of ISIS and the actions of Saudi Arabia 'are identical.'"

"For a high-profile female Muslim to say that the actions of Islamic State and the actions of Saudi Arabia are identical is a serious indictment of Saudi Arabia. Saudi Arabia is playing a duplicitous role in the fight against Muhammad's radical Islamism and Islamic State. There is just so much pretence and deception surrounding Islam," Michael speaks out in dismay.

Once again, Uriel sounds his warning, "You Edom! also known as Saudi Arabia! Beware! **Isaiah 34:9–10** warns, 'And the streams of Edom [Saudi Arabia] shall be turned into pitch, and her soil into brimstone; her land shall become burning pitch. Night and day it shall not be quenched; its smoke shall go up forever.'"

Saudi Arabia has displayed and continues to display complete disregard for human rights, but especially disregard of the rights of women. Raphael summarizes Saudi Arabia's atrocious human rights record pertaining to women. "Saudi Arabia's treatment of women is vicious and notorious in its exclusion of women, and in its tortures, beheadings and crucifixions. Saudi Arabia is a theocratic, repressive and violent regime with one of the worst Sharia Law human rights records possible."

"It is obvious that Sharia Law and jihad are warfare against freedom of speech and warfare against any manner of freedom," Raphael expounds.

Gabriel continues the same theme, "Quoting Quran 47:4–6, I heard Satan-Allah whisper into Muhammad's ear saying, "those who are killed in the cause of Allah . . . He will guide them . . . and admit them to Paradise.' It's all about Islamic Paradise, and sex with virgins. Radical Muslims are attacking Kafirs because they are driven by a sick ideology that promotes martyrdom over life, that pushes young Muslims to kill for Allah, and which insists that martyrdom will be rewarded with eternal sex in Allah's Paradise."

"But what do Muslim females get as their reward in Paradise?" asks Raphael.

Gabriel hesitates before saying, "Well, there may be very few, if any, females in Allah's Paradise."

"So what happens to the vast majority of Muslim females?"

"Allah may choose to recycle them into virgins of pleasure in Paradise for Muslim males, but the story is much, much worse for most women."

> "Those who are killed in the cause of Allah . . . He will guide them . . . and admit them to Paradise."
>
> *- Quran 47:4-6*

"How much worse can it get?"

"You ask how much worse? In the Hadiths, Muslim historian Sahih Bukhari wrote that Muhammad had said, 'I have seen the fires of Hell and most of its residents are ungrateful women...not grateful to their husband.' Sahih Bukhari wrote that Muhammad had said, 'I have witnessed that most of the people in Hell are women . . . I have never come across anyone more lacking in intelligence or ignorant of their religion than women . . . Is it not true that the testimony of one man is the equal to the testimony of two women? . . . I have witnessed the fires of Hell . . . most of the people there were female . . . because of their ingratitude . . . because of their ingratitude toward their husbands.'"

As the champion of women's rights, Gabriel is livid. "In the Hadiths, Sahih Muslim wrote that Muhammad had said, 'After I am gone, the biggest threat to stability that will remain is the harm done to men by women. . . . Is not the value of a woman's eyewitness testimony half that of a man's? . . . That is because a woman's mind is deficient. . . . After I die, the biggest problem that I leave to man is woman.'"

"By his words, Muhammad had an extremely low and poisoned opinion of women as being ungrateful, as being ignorant, as lacking in intelligence, as being deficient in mind, and as being a threat to man. Muhammad's words speak of extreme contempt and hatred of women. These degrading words of Muhammad directed at females are the very foundation of Sharia Law." Archangel Raphael abruptly rocks backward as he summarizes Gabriel's dismal assessment of the words of Muhammad.

"Within the fog of its smoke and mirrors and diversions, fundamentally, Sharia Law is about the degraded status of women under the control of men. This was female gender apartheid under Muhammad, and continues to be gender apartheid today in all Muslim countries." As the champion of justice, Michael weighs in on behalf of women.

"I'm the authority on mental health," affirms Raphael. "For women who read the Quran, the Hadiths of Sahih Muslim, and the Hadiths of Sahih Bukhari, these words must be most unsettling and disturbing emotionally. I don't understand how Muslim women are handling this kind of denigration with the daily threat of eternal Hell hanging over their heads. I don't understand how they are coping mentally, emotionally, and psychologically. It must be like living in fear under a shroud or under a sword."

"Even with his admitted negative bias and his misogyny, it is shocking that Muhammad had taught that women who had committed adultery should be stoned to death. Today in the Middle East, women who are accused, even without proof of having committed adultery, will be stoned to death. This is part of Sharia Law." Gabriel is compelled by the glaring injustices of Muhammad's words and by the injustices of Sharia Law, "This is such a double standard."

Archangel Gabriel expands upon the travesty of Islamic misogyny. Today Muhammad's Muslims are trying desperately hard to impose Sharia Law upon Americans and upon Canadians. Muslims in America and in Canada are not here to be assimilated. They are here to replace the American Constitution with Sharia Law and the Constitutional Charter of Rights and Freedoms in Canada."

"But *why* was Sharia Law created and by whom?" Archangel Uriel continues to probe for understanding.

"Foremost, it's about male-female relationships. In Muhammad's Quran, which was dictated by the Augustinians and by Satan-Allah, there are clear-cut differences between the rights of men and the rights of women. Quran 4:11 is the rule that women automatically receive less in inheritance. Quran 4:3 allows a man to marry multiple women. Sharia Law permits husbands to have one, two, three, or four wives, to have a mistress, to have concubines and to be granted unfair custody rights of children in a divorce. Quran 2:282 commands that in a trial, one male witness is worth two female witnesses."

"Quran 4:34–35 are two of the most devastating verses for women. These two verses give men total control and total authority over women and provide detailed instructions on how husbands should inflict punishment upon their wives. These two verses read, 'Men have authority over women because God (Allah) has made the one superior to the other. . . . Good women are obedient. They guard their unseen parts because God has guarded them. As for those from whom you fear disobedience, admonish them, forsake them in beds' apart and *beat them.*'"

Yes, you heard it right. "Beat them! Yes, beat them!" scowls Gabriel. "Muhammad and Allah had given to men the authority to beat their wives. In the Muslim world, the view is widespread that women are inferior to men and that wives must be obedient and submissive to their husbands. Many Islamic societies don't allow freedom of expression to women. Suppression of women is the order of the day in Saudi Arabia, in Iran, in Pakistan, and in Afghanistan. Sharia Law is coming to America and to Canada."

> "Men have authority over women because God (Allah) has made the one superior to the other. . . . Good women are obedient. They guard their unseen parts because God has guarded them. As for those from whom you fear disobedience, admonish them, forsake them in beds' apart and *beat them.*"
>
> - Quran 4:34-35

"The fact that Sharia Law permits wife battery in any form, to any degree and for any reason is intolerable!" With a look of scorn, Raphael exclaims, "In this twenty-first century, living under this threat must be most distressing for all Muslim women."

"And it gets worse," expounds Gabriel with indignation. "Islamic historian and scholar Sahih Bukhari had written that Muhammad had decreed that, 'If a woman refuses her husband's request for sex, the angels will curse her through the night.' It's Muhammad's angelic threat for sex on demand."

"Threatening words and beatings are bad, but are there other physical abuses?" inquires Raphael.

"Much more! And of the worst kind. One of the most barbaric tortures ever devised is practiced in the Islamic world. It is female genital mutilation known as clitorodectomy, or female circumcision, an Islamic tradition that is rampant in the many parts of the Muslim world. Islamic laws make clitorodectomy mandatory."

"ISIS is using the Quran to justify these unspeakable horrors which they are inflicting upon the women captured by them. In the areas controlled by ISIS, captured women are so traumatized and so terrorized by these rapes and painful clitorodectomy tortures that they are committing assisted suicides so that they can escape from these appalling, excruciating barbarities. I have witnessed these clitorodectomy atrocities inflicted upon Yazidi females. I have spoken with numbers of them," Gabriel struggles hard to maintain his composure. In Mosul, Iraq, ISIS is performing female clitorodectomies on all girls and women between the ages of eleven and forty-six. By inserting American troops, U.S. President Trump has come to their rescue."

"Shock of shocks, clitorodectomies are being performed surreptitiously by Muslims in the United Kingdom, a democratic country," exclaims Michael in a shaky voice. "The BBC reported over four thousand cases of female genital mutilation on girls between six and fifteen years of age on British soil. British health professionals estimated that in 2013, there were sixty-six thousand women and girls who were forced into gential mutilation. That's a preview and a warning that Sharia Law and clitorodectomies are coming to the United States and to Canada."

"Why do you think Muhammad chose to mutilate women? What was his gain in inflicting this atrocity upon females?" Uriel is perplexed.

"Muhammad encouraged the removal of a girl's clitoris in order to subdue her sexual desires. Removal of the clitoris ensures that a female will not have an orgasm. Clitorodectomies deny to females their right to full sexual pleasure. In his hatred of women and in his Hell-bent revenge against women, Muhammad wanted to cause women as much pain as possible and to deny the pleasures of sex to women. That was Muhammad's justification straight out of Hell," agonizes Raphael.

"Muhammad was driven by hatred for women because Ishmael had been thrown out of Abraham's tents by Sarah who had evicted him and his mother Hagar into the hot desert to die some twenty-six hundred years earlier."

"Today, these assaults against women have spread across the Muslim world." Once again, Archangel Michael is warning all females across the globe. "In 2008, the Egyptian parliament *dropped* the laws making female genital mutilation illegal in Egypt. Secretly, clitorodectomies once again were endorsed in Egypt. Today, 80 percent of Egyptian women endure genital mutilation. Ladies, here is my warning. Very soon, Sharia Law will be bringing clitorodectomies to America and to Canada. Ladies, speak up now while you still have the opportunity."

"Europeans will experience these same atrocities before long. Shortly after Europe falls apart, **ISIS**-Islamic State will be coming to a neighbourhood near you. At this very moment, the Muslim Brotherhood's Trojan Horse is planning his North American Sharia Law debut."

Raphael quotes two famous leaders of World War II; one political and one military. "Winston Churchill had stated that 'Mohammedanism is a militant and proselytizing faith.' General George Patton had spoken of Islam's 'Utter degradation of women.'"

"Muslim historian Sahih Bukhari recorded that Muhammad 'gave us permission to take temporary wives.' Temporary wives? echoes Gabriel. Well, how convenient for Muslim husbands. The temporary marriage is a rather unique tradition of Islam. For an amount of money, a man can sleep with a woman for three days. Shia Islam still has this practice today. This is payment for sex. It sounds like Islamic prostitution by another name. But just how do the wives feel about Allah's cozy arrangement offered to their husbands?"

"Honor killings are the standard form of justice in lands such as Pakistan." Archangel Michael redirects the discussion. "In some Muslim countries, fornication and adultery are punished by stoning or by one hundred lashes, but a blind eye is turned to rape which goes unpunished. It is not the rapist. It is the rape victim who is lashed fifteen times in public. Honor killings are about Muhammad's tradition that men own women. This ownership is enshrined in Sharia Law today."

There are several minutes of cold, uncomfortable silence. Then, once again, Michael exclaims, "Almost twenty-five hundred years after Daniel's vision of Nebuchadnezzar's statue, Daniel's prophecies were fulfilled and are being fulfilled today before our eyes. In a 2015 poll conducted in the United States, more than half of Muslims in America wanted Sharia Law instead of the U.S. Constitution, and about 20 percent of Muslims surveyed agreed that violence was the way to make Sharia Law to be the law of the United States. However, statistics from other parts of the globe are far more disturbing and far more distressing. The majority of Middle Eastern Muslims think that Sharia Law is desirable and should be imposed. From its Muhammadan roots in Medina, Islam has been a political force which today is mushrooming worldwide. From across the Muslim world, there is overwhelming support for Sharia Law to be the law of the land and the ruling ideology."

"Twenty percent of American Muslims is a whole lot of jihadists!" exclaims Uriel.

"Military force alone cannot defeat this insidious treachery. Cutting off the head of the ISIS snake in Syria-Iraq will not stop Muhammad's radical Islam from spreading. Like the nine-headed serpent in Greek mythology, when one head was cut off, two more heads grew in its place. However, in America, the serpents are not recognized as they mingle surreptitiously with the population," Gabriel falls back upon Greek mythology for his metaphor.

"Within the hotbed of terrorism in Molenbeek, Belgium, there roils a disturbingly deep and extremely dangerous undercurrent of radical Islamism. Now, Belgium is jihadi central of radical Islam. In several European countries, Islamic fundamentalism is widespread. Two-thirds of interviewed European Muslims stated that Islamic religious rules were of more importance to them than the laws of European countries and that the appeal and attraction of martyrdom was magnetic and powerful," Raphael elucidates upon the current political-ideological climate.

"The Paris massacres were a watershed moment. Instead of attacking specific targets they attacked anyone within a crowded place," Michael reveals the change in direction of ISIS psychology and ideology. "With that high level of global and international support for Sharia Law, the pattern of the Paris Massacres will continue, but on a much wider scale. Yes, massive killing is the ISIS way to bring in Sharia Law. Just as in the days of Muhammad, fourteen centuries later, nothing has changed. As during the Paris Massacres of November 13, 2015, the Nice, France slaughter of children on July 14, 2016, the ISIS Manchester Arena suicide bombings killing children at the Ariana Grande concert on May 23, 2017, and the ISIS London Bridge Massacre using truck-knives on June 3, 2017, the barbaric jihadist killings will continue and escalate in frequency."

"Sharia Law is the very foundation of Islam. No Sharia Law, no Islam. It's just that simple," Gabriel supports Michael's claim.

"Today, Muhammad's Muslims are determined to provoke a new Holocaust against the Jews," Raphael expresses his horror.

"But there is a difference from the last Holocaust under the Nazis. This Holocaust is going engulf both Jews *and* Christians in the Middle East, and around the world. It's happening right now. Across Egypt, there is on-going Christian genocide. ISIS is conducting Christian genocide and exposing their killings on video before the world. The mainstream media chooses to be silent."

"Today, most Christian persecutions—in the form of loss of home, loss of job, imprisonment, torture and death—occur in predominantly Muslim countries. The top nine most offending countries are Iraq, Syria, Afghanistan, Pakistan, Iran, Somalia, Sudan, Libya, and Eritrea." With visible anguish, Gabriel unfolds this widespread Islamic genocide of Christians which began under Allah's Muhammad in the seventh century.

"On December 20, 2015, I heard on the *Judge Jeanine Pirro Show*, that Christians in the Middle East are in crisis and are facing extinction," Raphael expresses his deep anguish. "Ten years ago, there were 1.3 million Christians in Iraq. Today there are only 300,000. More than 1 million Christians have been killed or displaced from Iraq. They are being persecuted and murdered under Muhammad's Islam. ISIS in Iraq and in Syria, al-Shabaab in Somalia, and Boko Haram in North Africa are killing Christians left, right, and center."

"ISIS leader Caliph Abu Bakr al-Baghdadi had said, 'O Muslims, Islam was never for a day the religion of peace. Islam is the religion of war. Your prophet...was dispatched with the sword...was ordered with war until Allah is worshipped alone.' It pains me to bring Muhammad's murderous sword before you," Gabriel labors emotionally.

Gabriel continues this painful exposition, "Today, ISIS leader Caliph Abu Bakr al-Baghdadi is taking his marching orders from Muhammad's teachings in the Quran, from his Hadiths, and from his Sira. In his Hadiths, Sahih Bukhari exposed how Muhammad had tortured his enemies. He branded their eyes with a hot iron; then he plucked out their eyes. Sahih Bukhari wrote, 'Muhammad ordered that their hands and feet be cut off and their eyes gouged out with hot pokers. . . . They were thrown on jagged rocks, their pleas for water ignored, and they died of thirst' in the hot desert sands. Far and wide, these barbaric, monstrous, excruciating tortures terrorized all the surrounding tribes," Raphael's distorted facial expression mirrors the tortures of Muhammad's dying victims. In 2017, ISIS is duplicating Muhammad's atrocities.

"ISIS is using the same tactics today. When the Islamic State Caliphate takes over the world, no kafir—Christian or Jew—will escape," Gabriel echoes the Angelic consensus of the God Squad.

"But why did Muhammad pick on the Jews?"

"Ancient historian named Ishaq wrote, 'Since Islam is the successor to Judaism, Allah was the successor to Jehovah. It was actually Allah who had been the deity of the Jews and the Jews deliberately had hidden this fact by corrupting the scriptures. For this, Muslims believe, the Jews have been cursed.'"

"Shocking! Simply shocking! What a total distortion! Allah is the successor to Jehovah the God of the universe?? This is Islamic revisionist history! Well of course, Allah is not Jehovah and Allah is not the replacement for Jehovah. This Islamic fraud is just so over the top." Gabriel shrugs his shoulders in amazement, "Muhammad's Islam is about deliberate and false revision of the Bible which predated Muhammad by centuries and by millennia."

"So who was this Ishaq guy?"

"Ishaq, who was born about AD 700, was the most authoritative writer of Muhammad's Sira. This Ishaq guy wrote that 'The Jews' sins are so great that Allah has changed them into apes.' In Quran 2:63–65, Muhammad's Allah wrote of the children of Israel, 'You will be changed into detested apes.' On both counts, this is undeniable racial hatred of the Nazi variety," Gabriel levels this charge against Allah and against Muhammad's shameful prophetic legacy."

"Keep foremost in mind that this preeminent hatred came from the papacy and from the Augustinians who launched the Quran and Muhammad," Michael makes certain to unmask the real perpetrators of the Quran.

> "You will be changed into detested apes."
>
> – Quran 2:63-65

"And those same hateful words are what the Palestinians are teaching their children today. With that depth of psychological poisoning, there can't be any peace in the Middle East," Gabriel proclaims.

"Here is more of Muhammad's hated-filled history against the Jews. Islamic historian Ishaq wrote that after the Battle of the Trench, Muhammad took the captives to Medina where, 'They were forced to dig trenches in the market place of Medina. It was a long day, but eight hundred Jews were beheaded that day. Muhammad and his twelve-year-old wife, Aisha, sat and watched the slaughter the entire day and into the night. The Apostle of Allah had every male Jew killed.' After Muhammad's Jewish victims had dug their own graves, they were hacked down with swords inside the trenches and then covered with garbage and dung." Again and again, Raphael is visibly sickened.

"Beheading 800 Jews was the work of a deranged, maniacal, radical Islamic terrorist. There is a world of difference between killing 130 innocent Parisians with Kalashnikovs and the crude beheadings of 800 men with swords while their wives and children were terrorized as they watched in horror. Most of the 130 murdered Parisians died instantly from a bullet to the head. In contrast, Muhammad was one of history's most vicious, brutal, inhuman, and barbaric butchers of all time, a radical Islamic terrorist and a far more depraved monster than the killers of the Paris Massacre and of the Nice massacre of children," Michael is in continual anguish over Muhammad's butcheries stating, "At the final curtain on this age, justice will prevail from the God of Heaven."

"Warning! Warning! Warning! What Americans and Canadians do not understand is that once Sharia Law becomes the law of the land, the Battle of the Trench is going to be repeated over and over and over on their own soils, " Gabriel is most emphatic in his cautions. "In Syria, ISIS is replaying and repeating the Battle of the Trench right now. And Prime Minister Justin Trudeau is bringing twenty-five thousand Muslim Syrian refugees to Canada. Americans are concerned that these refugees would pose a terrorist threat on their northern Canadian border. However, President Barack Obama had brought far greater numbers of Syrian refugees into America."

Uriel adds, "Prime Minister Justin Trudeau needs to give his head a shake. That's twenty-five thousand *potential* terrorists who have their own versions of trench warfare in Canada. Now I did say they could be *potential* trench terrorists. Time may tell who they really will turn out to be."

"In Muhammad's day, in the town of Khaybar near Medina, there was a community of wealthy Jewish farmers. Muhammad made war upon them and butchered all the men. Historian Ishaq wrote that, 'Among the captives was a beautiful Jewess named Safiya. Muhammad took her for his sexual pleasure. Muhammad always got first choice of the spoils of war and of the women.' In his Hadith, Sahih Bukhari wrote that Muhammad married Safiya. So, here was more proof of Muhammad's uncontrollable and insatiable obsession for sex with beautiful women. Religion was very secondary to Muhammad. Sex drove Muhammad's agenda," Gabriel sneers in a show of contempt.

"This Allah god is quite the killer who seemed to be bent upon satisfying Muhammad's uncontrollable urges for sex, sex, and more sex. So besides having sex with all the beautiful women he had captured, what did Muhammad do with the rest of the women and their children?"

"Historian Ishaq wrote that, "Muhammad took the property, wives and children of the Jews, and divided them up amongst the Muslims... Muhammad took one-fifth of the slaves . . . the women were sold for pleasure. Muhammad invested the money from the sale of the female slaves for horses and weapons.'"

"Muhammad's killing rampages were driven by economics and by personal gain. It is obvious that Muhammad had suffered from a severe psychiatric disorder with delusions of power and delusions of grandeur," Raphael muses.

"According to Muslim historian Ishaq, Muhammad had said that, 'Allah totally approves of the killing of the Jews, enslaving the women and children.' Killing the Jews was about Allah's and Islam's hatred of the descendants of Sarah, of Isaac, of Rebecca . . . but especially hatred of the descendants of Jacob. This obsessive and virulent hatred which began in the tents of Abraham more than four thousand years ago has festered and has metastasized into the cancerous control of the minds and passions of Islamic Muslims of 2017," Michael draws into focus the threads of Muhammad's hatred of the Jews.

"In contrast to this fourteen-centuries-old Islamic hatred of the Jews, stands 'Operation Ezra,' a Winnipeg Jewish community initiative for the rescue and resettlement of Yazidi refugees. Operation Ezra is a comprehensive Yazidi refugee relief project in Canada and in the world, which is sponsored largely by Shaarey Zedek Synagogue leadership and initiative. It is known in Winnipeg that the Yazidis have Islamic roots." Gabriel is only too pleased to challenge Islamic hatred of the Jews.

"Muhammad invented Islam to be a validation of his nefarious sex drive and his greed. Religion was far from his mind. Religion was a convenient cover. Muhammad grew very rich from all his killings, from all his thieveries, and from all his captured slaves which he sold," Michael broadens more exposure of Muhammad's sickening and murderous misconducts.

"On a different but on a related track, and for your information, consider that Bishop Augustine of Hippo (AD 354-430) was a brilliant Roman Catholic theologian. The Vatican directed Augustine to provide a theological basis for discrediting the Jews, on the grounds that the Jews had lost ownership of Israel because of their disobedience for rejecting Christ the Messiah. In doing so, Augustine became a stooge of the Vatican. For purposes of prestige, the Vatican was desperate to take ownership of Jerusalem, to build the Third Temple under Vatican control, and to prove the Bible wrong," Michael reviews Vatican motives.

"I recall some fourteen hundred years ago, when we were secret observers in that clandestine second meeting at the Roman Catholic Cathedral in Mecca, just after Khadijah had died," Archangel Gabriel analyzes the roots of the Quran and Muhammad's Islam. "Satan alias Allah, was hovering with her demonic hordes while Khadijah's Roman Catholic cousin Waraquah was trying to indoctrinate Muhammad on Augustinian theology and on military strategy. Waraquah's assigned role was to corrupt the Old Testament, to pervert it, and to distort it with Augustine's Replacement Theology against the Jews. Waraquah was well-versed in Old Testament theology and the Augustinian mind-set of Replacement Theology."

"About one thousand years after Augustine's Replacement Theology take-down of Israel and the Jews, Martin Luther pushed the hatred of the Jews to higher heights and to lower depths. Martin Luther incited the Christian Churches to burn down Jewish synagogues and to confiscate all Jewish possessions and their gold. However, two days after he had issued this toxic declaration of ethnic cleansing against the Jews, mysteriously, Martin Luther fell desperately ill and died." Michael tables more of the toxic history directed at Israel.

"This was poetic justice! In opposing Martin Luther and in judgment of Luther's hatred toward the Jews, the God of Heaven delivered His instant judgment for the world to recognize." With an expression of victory and in approval, Gabriel raises his arms toward Heaven.

In his book *Mein Kampf*, Adolf Hitler quoted Martin Luther and adopted Luther's hatred of the Jews as his own and as the justification by the Nazi party to launch coordinated attacks upon Jews throughout the German Reich on Kristallnacht in 1938 and beyond. This was the introduction to the Holocaust of Auschwitz. Muhammad's Quran, the Hadiths, and the Sira were far more negative toward the Jews than Hitler's *Mein Kampf.*

"Today the Palestinians are quoting Martin Luther. Many Christian Churches have adopted Augustine's Replacement Theology and Christian Palestinianism, demanding that Israel surrender their ancient lands of Judea, Samaria, and East Jerusalem. Many churches today are demanding to Boycott, to Divest, and to Sanction Israel. The objective of this BDS movement is to eliminate

Israel." Gabriel is appalled by these anti-Israel tactics that fly in the face of Elohim the God of Heaven. "After fourteen hundred years, Islam is growing and threatening the whole world. Islam is like the starfish."

"Like a starfish? Why a starfish?" asks Archangel Uriel.

"When a starfish loses an arm in a fight, it can regenerate a new arm and the severed arm can grow to become an entire body producing an entirely new starfish. After a battle one starfish becomes two starfish. The starfish is about amazing regeneration."

"So then, one starfish becomes two starfishes. As goes that proverbial metaphor, Islam is that indestructible starfish that is metastasizing unstoppably across the globe. The more you kill them, the more they multiply."

"Yes, but this starfish also is killing other starfish. There is this fourteen-hundred-year-old war between the two starfishes of Islam. We continue to see two Islamic worlds locked into a war to the death in the clash of two civilizations of Islam who hate each other as much as they hate Christians and Jews. The Sunnis and the Shiites are the ten toes of iron mixed with clay in the statue in Nebuchadnezzar's dream and in Daniel's dream in Babylon."

"On November 12, 2015, just one day before the Paris massacres, two ISIS suicide bombings hit Beirut in Lebanon killing 43 and wounding 239 others, leaving pools of Shiite blood and broken bodies on the streets."

"But why Lebanon?" queries Raphael.

"It was about the Lebanon-based Shiite Hezbollah which is the military arm of Shiite Iran. With their two bombings, Sunni Islamic State made it clear that there was more to come unless Hezbollah stopped sending fighters to support the Assad Shiite government forces in Syria. In this continuing, fourteen-century-old family warfare, Sunnis aggressively are targeting Shiites. In Nebuchadnezzar's statue, the ten toes of iron mixed with clay continue to crumble."

"This vicious war between Sunni ISIS and Shiite Iran-Hezbollah is just more of the continuing deadly collisions between two Islamic civilizations who want to obliterate each other. Both are trying desperately hard to follow Muhammad's instructions in the Quran, in the Hadiths, and in Muhammad's Sira." Gabriel continues to advance his historical exposure of Islam.

"Not only were Muslims killing each other, they were bent upon killing and destroying the Jews. Here is more of Muhammad's terrorizing bloodthirsty violence from Ishaq. Muslim authority Ishaq wrote, 'Allah totally approves of the killing of the Jews, enslaving the women and children.' Here is another example of Muhammad's depraved viciousness and monstrosity as documented by Ishaq who was the most authoritative writer of the Sira. Ishaq had written that one year after going to Medina, Muhammad began to prepare for war as commanded by Allah. Since the dawn of time, and before Islam was created, the killing of kin and tribal brothers had been forbidden. After the birth of Islam, brother would kill brother, and sons would kill their fathers when fighting jihad in Allah's cause. Yes, if the kafirs don't bow down to Allah, brothers will kill brothers, sons will kill fathers, and fathers will kill sons." Michael laments in disgust.

"Quran 4:89 commands and demands to, 'seize them and put them to death wherever you find them.' I found more of the same in Quran 9:5 which commands and demands to, 'slay the idolaters wherever you find them. Arrest them, besiege them, and lie in ambush everywhere for them.' There is no way for a Muslim of any stripe to dodge Muhaammad's Quran 4:89 and Quran 9:5. Without exception and under threat of Hellfire, every Muslim must 'seize them and put them to death,' and 'slay the idolaters wherever you find them.' A 'moderate Musliim' exists only in the political eyes of George Bush, Barack Obama, and Hillary Clinton. A 'moderate Muslim' is the ultimate oxymoron of the twenty-first century and the greatest snow job by U.S. presidential administrations to blind the eyes of gullible Americans. As Muhammad had commanded in the seventh century, the Paris Massacre, the Nice Massacre, the Manchester Massacre, and the London Bridge Massacre were quite the ambushes, where numbers of idolaters, their children, and infants were ambushed and slaughtered." Uriel prods and mocks Muhammad and three American presidents.

"Seize them and put them to death wherever you find them ."

- Quran 4:89

"These murderous Parisian killers and the lone-wolf murderer in Nice were not aberrant offshoots of Islam as they had been falsely labeled by the imams, by Barack Obama, and by Hillary Clinton. They were following basic grassroots, fundamental Islam with all the details as laid out by Muhammad in Allah's Quran to terrorize and to butcher. Islamic historian Sahih al-Bukhari had written in his Hadiths that Allah's apostle had said, 'I have been made victorious with terror.'"

"Yes, it's about emotional gut-wrenching terror. Muhammad was labeled as the Islamic genie of terrorization and as the Islamic Angel of Death. Islam was about and is about depraved terrorizations with mass hysteria on a national scale and on the global scale." Raphael knows all about emotional gut-wrenching terrorization, which soon is coming to America and to Canada.

"In spite of vigorous denials, protests, and lies by Canadian Muslims and by American Muslims, war and terrorization are documented mainstream, fundamental, supremacist, and totalitarian ideology in the Quran, in the Hadiths, in the Sira, and which are enshrined in Sharia Law. As undeniably exposed by Quran 4:89 and by Quran 9:5, violence with vicious slaughter is the outspoken fundamental theme throughout the Quran, throughout the Hadiths, and throughout the Sira.

Uriel delivers another summary ripping of Muhammad's tyranny, "Jeremiah Stone has detailed eighty-one similar murderous verses from the Quran and thirty similar murderous quotes from the Hadiths which promote and compel exhortations to hate, to torture, to kill, to slaughter, and to send to Hell. Eighty-two murderous hate-filled verses from the Quran and thirty murderous quotations from Muhammad's Hadiths for a total of one-hundred-twelve references of hatred and slaughter are the bull elephant in the Islamic room, which is being ignored by the world. Muhammad exuded hatred from every pore of his body."

"There just is no wiggle room and no rat hole out of this Quran-Hadith-Sira triad of documented historical evidences. All practicing Muslims want Sharia Law. Otherwise, they are apostates, or liars, or both." Gabriel is showing a visible measure of being infuriated with the denials by so-called moderate Muslims.

"Here is the current, indisputable clincher connecting Muhammad to war and the sword. Caliph Abu Bakr al-Baghdadi, as leader of ISIS, had stated that 'Islam is the religion of war.' Abu Bakr al-Baghdadi had said, 'Your prophet… was dispatched with the sword.' It was fitting that under President Donald Trump, Abu Bakr al-Baghdadi was dispatched with a missile." Archangel Gabriel expresses his satisfaction that justice was served.

It was Muhammad who had said, "Certainly, the gates of Paradise lie in the shade of swords," and "Be aware that Paradise lies under the shadow of swords." There is no rat hole to dodge Muhammad's words by Barack Obama and by Hillary Clinton. Islamic authority Sahih Bukhari had written almost identical words that Muhammad had said, "Be aware that Paradise lies under the shadow of swords." Renowned Muslim historian Sahih Bukhari had written, "Muhammad punished the men of the Uraina tribe by cutting off their hands and feet and letting them bleed to death." Undeniably, Muhammad was about cutting off hands, feet, and heads just as ISIS is executing today. As documented by Sahih Bukhari about Muhammad's conduct, was Muhammad a moderate Muslim? Tell us what these words of Sahih Bukhari mean to you, Mr. former President Barack Obama?" prods Archangel Gabriel.

"I had spoken with our friend Jeremiah Stone, who had interviewed three Armenian citizens, who had told him that the number of Armenian Christians butchered by the Muslim Ottoman Turks was more than three million." Archangel Raphael presents unofficial statistics.

"It is so sad that Allah's Paradise turns out to be one of the black holes deep beyond interstellar space. The heat and the gravitational pull from within the black holes are so intense that they prevent anything from ever escaping. Rather than eternal sex, the black hole is the fitting abode and the reward for the Islamic terrorists. Now that's the real description of Hell! And I am the guardian of the gates to these black holes." Uriel stamps his foot with indignation directed at Muhammad's Islam.

Archangel Michael redirects the conversation from black holes in space to a black chapter in the historical roots of America stating, "Because the Arabian Muslims had become skilled in enslavement of their jihadist victims, the slave trade in Africa and out of Africa was run by Islam. For every black slave who was delivered to the American cotton plantations, five died on the way from the outright brutality of war, from the brutality of capture, from illness, and from insufficient food. Out of 130 million Africans who were attacked, captured, and enslaved by the Muslims, only twenty-five million survived en route and reached American cotton plantations. Over the last fourteen centuries, sixty million Christians were butchered in the Islamic jihadi wars. Eighty million Hindus died in the jihadi wars against India. Ten million Buddhists lost their lives to Islamic wars. In a smear of historical facts, former president George Bush had the unmitigated gall to lie to Americans that 'Islam is a peaceful religion.' Hillary Clinton had echoed similar lying words. Barack Obama spoke words of praise for Islam. These were shameful and shameless denials of fourteen centuries of marauding Muslim historical facts and unabashed deceptions of the American people by the monstrous liars who rule America. The fact that these egregious historical statements by George Bush, by Barack Obama and by Hillary Clinton were not challenged by the mainstream news media speaks of the fear of being labeled as Islamophobic. The fact that these outrageous historical statements by George Bush, by Barack Obama and by Hillary Clinton were not challenged by the American public speaks of the shocking American ignorance of Islamic world history which is not being taught in American schools."

Archangel Gabriel is inflamed by this outright lying by American leaders. "Yes, in the face of Islamic lies, denials, and the rhetoric of peaceful Muslim intentions, Islamic extremism is core, mainstream, and fundamental. When Muslim/Islamic apologists are in the public view, they speak of innocent moderates, but when these same Muslim/Islamic apologists are out of public view and behind the backs of the kafirs, they preach a different and harsh militant line. Out of public view and behind closed doors, the Muslim masses secretly and silently endorse and cheer on the Islamic extremists and the Islamic jihadists."

Uriel, the mathematical expert and the statistician of the God Squad, throws out a shocking statistic. "That is just so true. Be aware that today, adherence to Sharia Law and compliance with Sharia Law are generally espoused by the Islamic world. Sharia-adherence or Sharia-compliance can lead and does lead to Islamic jihad."

"Sharia Law is just so fundamental to Muhammad's Islam. There is no Islamic detour around Sharia Law. This silent Muslim Sharia world is so into Muhammad's Quranic mind-set that it simply cannot change and will not change. Sharia Law is fundamental grassroots Islam," Gabriel advances his general analysis.

"Following the U.S-led invasion of Iraq in 2003, ISIS was created by a group of disgruntled Iraqi Sunnis whose intent was and continues to be opposition to Iraqi Shiites and Iranian Shiites. Keep in mind that Sharia-run, Sunni Suadi Arabia continues to oppress and persecute women and that Sunni Saudi Arabia is the secretive driving force behind Sunni ISIS," Michael broadens the analysis of behind-the-scenes Sunni Islam.

Uriel throws out another of his barbed and biting zingers, "This silent majority of the Muslim world is Muhammad's Sharia-hardened die-hards who cannot be dissuaded from their Allah-directed hatred against and toward the kafirs but specifically against Christians and Jews. Metaphorically, in the context of the Quran, the Hadiths, and the Sira, it simply is impossible to domesticate pythons and cobras."

"I agree that the Paris, the Nice, the Manchester, and the London Bridge slaughters were just a small preview of what is coming globally. It is the United States that is high on the target list of **ISIS**-Islamic State jihadists. The world now walks in fear, as though on broken glass. The fear index is over the top and off the scale," Michael speaks his sombre outlook.

"Well, here are the chilling statistics on the Paris Massacre. One hundred thirty were slaughtered and more than 350 were wounded at six different locations. During a rock music event for the young in the concert hall in Paris, multiple dozens of entangled bullet-riddled bodies lay in pools of blood, after being strafed with automatic gunfire. Outside on the sidewalk of the Belle Equipe Restaurant, which was packed with young patrons and filled with life on the Friday night, the terrorists struck in a slaughterhouse massacre. There was more of the same at a soccer stadium. This savagery was a simultaneous, precision series of coordinated attacks against anybody and everybody, but particularly against young Parisians. Two days after the night of terror in Paris, the sound of a blown light bulb at a public gathering sparked a panicked escape in fear and in terror." Gabriel describes the terror of the time.

"In synchronized precision, just eight Islamic terrorists brought all of France into a state of terror and martial law. Just eight Islamic terrorists inflicted the bloodiest extremist attack in France since World War II. With a shrapnel bomb, one ISIS terrorist killed twenty-two children and young adults in Manchester, England."

"ISIS has promised to target Washington and the White House. ISIS has stated that the U.S. is high on their to-do-list. America's turn is coming. In this context, we need to review the conduct of former President Barack Obama," Archangel Michael projects the terror from France to America.

Archangel Uriel delves into the origins of the President, "As the physical scientist, even I know that Barack Obama was born of a Muslim father and that he attended a mosque in Indonesia."

"At the very least, Barack Obama repeatedly has demonstrated that he is a Muslim sympathizer, but especially that he is a friend of the Muslim Brotherhood. In 2009, President Barack Obama was quoted as saying, 'Islam has a proud tradition of tolerance.' What? A 'proud tradition of tolerance?' Where is the proof of Islamic tolerance?" Michael continues in palpable anger and revulsion, "What tolerance? In his unprovoked attacks and at the point of his sword, Muhammad showed no mercy and no tolerance as he butchered the innocents. In 2009, President Barack Obama had invited members of the Muslim Brotherhood to his speech in Cairo, Egypt. In his June 4, 2009, Cairo Speech, Barack Obama had the flagrant audacity to quote Quran 5:32 out of context and to paint a grossly misleading picture promoting the peacefulness and benevolence of Islam quoting, 'whoever saved a human life shall be deemed as having saved all mankind.' However, the very next verse, Quran 5:33 speaks the shocking truth about Muhammad's Islam which commands that they 'shall be slain or crucified or have their hands and feet shall be cut off on alternate sides.' Peacefulness, benevolence and saving all mankind are the extreme opposites of slaying, crucifying and cutting off hands and feet on alternate sides. How convenient for Barack Obama and how flagrantly and provocatively deceptive he was standing in front of the listening world, which was ignorant of the Quran and remained pathetically silent! Quoting from Quran 5:32 to the exclusion of Quran 5:33 portrays Barack Obama for who he really is. Conveniently, Barack Obama had neglected to mention the Islamic killing of 300 million souls over the last fourteen centuries. That was a shocking stretch of Islamic revisionist history of 1400 years. Barack Obama's Cairo address was the catalyst for launching the Arab Spring and ISIS. Barack Obama's Cairo address changed the map of the Middle East."

"Shall be slain or crucified or have their hands and feet shall be cut off on alternate sides."

- *Quran 5:33*

"Two years later, Barack Obama believed that the Muslim Brotherhood is the 'good guy' compared to ISIS. Shortly after that, Muslim Brotherhood leader Muhammad Morsi was convicted and sentenced to death by an Egyptian court for his murderous role in the Arab Spring uprising. Was Muhammad Morsi the 'good guy'?"

"Today, the Muslim Brotherhood is banned in Egypt, but the Muslim Brotherhood is operating at full tilt and unrestricted in the United States. Why?" Raphael is visibly upset by this stunning difference.

"At the time of his Cairo Speech in 2009, the U.S. Justice Department had identified the Muslim Brotherhood as being centrally involved financing the Holy Land Foundation for Relief and Development," explains Michael. "This Holy Land Foundation for Relief and Development was set up by the Muslim Brotherhood which channeled millions of dollars into the bank accounts of the murderous, radical jihadist Islamic Hamas."

"Then there is the Brotherhood's civilizational jihad known as 'financial jihad,'" Michael continues, "which is the hijacking of the financial system, to facilitate jihadist groups such as the radical Islamist

Hamas with their war to destroy Israel." Archangel Michael is infuriated by this injustice which has been hidden from the American public by the Obama administration.

"Here is a shocking revelation from the past," declares Gabriel, "In 1990, in order to spread Sharia Law globally, the Cairo Declaration, which is known as the Universal Declaration of Human Rights in Islam, demanded that there must be 'no crime or punishment except as provided for in the Sharia.' This is universal Sharia Law planned for the entire world. Ladies of America and ladies of Canada pay attention. Sharia Law means enforced clitorodectomies. Female circumcision and the minaret are inseparable."

"Too late!" Medical authority Raphael interrupts, "On May 11, 2017, *FOX NEWS* reported that three Muslim doctors recently performed illegal female genital mutilation (FGM) procedures on two seven-year-old girls here in the U.S. In the *Toronto Sun*, author and journalist Farzana Hassan reported that 'female genital mutilation seeks to suppress, control and eliminate sexual desire in young women in order to keep them submissive.' In a parallel to Muhammad's ISIS, one of the doctors who performed these radical butcheries on the two young girls, justified this abomination on the grounds of it being 'religious practice' which was their guaranteed right under the Constitution... and then this Muslim doctor had the unmitigated audacity to flaunt that disallowing clitorodectomies would be 'religious discrimination.'"

"Islamic 'religious practice' is no excuse for abusive female genital mutilation." Michael contends, "When the long-term happiness and the health of female children are at high risk, then universal human rights always must take precedence over the atrocity of this 'religious practice.'"

"The marauders are assaulting and ravaging the American Constitution." Gabriel lashes out verbally, "Using Sharia Law as a battering ram, the barbarians are storming inside the American House and using 'religious tolerance' to smash and to rip apart the U.S. Constitution. As future wives and mothers in America and in Canada, now seven-year-old Muslim girls are being discriminated against, coerced and caught up in the eye of this ISIS hurricane of clitorodectomies-clitoridectomies-clitorectomies."

Archangel Raphael the medical expert utters a high-pitched "Ouch! It gets much worse! Using infibulation surgery, the edges of the vulva are stitched together to close up most of the vagina to prevent sexual intercourse. And when the Muslim husband wants sex, he will just rip open the vagina.... and then have it sewed up again!...Triple Ouch!!! Now it's open season for clitorodectomies and infibulations on seven-year-old Muslim girls. Muslim or not Muslim, Muhammad's pernicious Islamic depravity is destined for all American and Canadian girls!"

With fire in his eyes, Archangel Gabriel taunts, "When Sharia Law stalks the lands of America, then mothers in the U.S. and Canada, you and your daughters will be compelled to be next in line for clitorodectomies and infibulations. Ladies, are you asleep or are you in disbelief?"

Uriel fires another of his metaphoric flaming arrows to enlighten this wicked darkness, "In a nutshell, this Islamic misogynistic monstrosity concocted by Muhammad is sickening, perverted, depraved and barbaric."

Somber Michael cuts to the chase, "We are looking into the Belly of the Beast. Muhammad's misogyny has no place in America. This Islamic Constitutional challenge must not be allowed to become de facto law."

"In May 2009, together with Egypt, President Barack Obama co-sponsored a United Nations resolution that restrains and condemns 'negative stereotyping of religions' with the specific intent to block 'negative stereotyping of Islam,'" Michael quotes from his tablet. "This move was intended indirectly to enlist United Nations international law to implement Sharia Law which would ban speech that is critical for Sharia Law. It is just a matter of time before this UN resolution is backed by universal force of law, but it becomes especially concerning and grievous when one of America's High Court justices sells out and betrays freedom of speech within her own nation."

"Do you mean Justice Elena Kagan, who was Barack Obama's second appointee to the Supreme Court?" asks Raphael as he continues. "When Elena Kagan was dean of Harvard Law School, she had promoted the Sharia studies program at Harvard University. This

Sharia studies program was funded by Saudi Arabia which is a major promoter of Sharia Law. Elena Kagan had expressed contempt for the value of free speech, saying that certain categories of speech could be suppressed when the government sees fit. What? Suppressng free speech when the government sees fit?"

"It is likely that Elena Kagan was appointed to the Supreme Court because her philosophy on Sharia Law was in keeping with that of Barack Obama. Barack Obama's support of the Sharia schemes is alarming," Archangel Gabriel shakes his head in utter revulsion. "Why was this not front page news?"

"American and Canadian women and girls take note. When the United Nations enforces a ban on speech that is critical of Islam, then free speech will be out and Sharia Law, wife beatings, lashings, stonings, and clitorodectomies will be in!" Raphael delivers his shattering and seismic revelation.

"Since the Muslim Brotherhood has been outlawed in Egypt for their criminal conducts, then why is the Muslim Brotherhood still inside America, and what are they doing in America? The long-term goal of the Muslim Brotherhood is to overthrow all nonMuslim governments and to install Sharia Law across the globe. Sharia Law denies the fundamental right to free speech."

"In the United States, the Muslim Brotherhood controls the Muslim-American groups. The Muslim Brotherhood is encouraging and promoting undercover sabotage and jihad by stealth, all designed to destroy American civilization from within. Bit by bit, the Muslim Brotherhood is forcing creeping Sharia Law into the fabric of American society," Gabriel expands on the criminal treachery of the Muslim Brotherhood. President Donald Trump has stated that he will remove the Muslim Brotherhood from America."

"Islam holds that Sharia Law is incompatible with the American Constitution. Because Muslims of all stripes believe that democracy is un-Islamic, the Muslim Brotherhood is pushing Sharia Law into the American judicial system. The overriding concern for Americans should be creeping Sharia Law and homegrown jihadism. "We are aware that there are sleeper cells of radical Islamic militants inside the United States and inside Canada. ISIS is encouraging jihadists to build terror cells at home in Canada and in the U.S. Evidence discloses that there are ISIS sleeper cells within all fifty states."

"In the *Globe and Mail* newspaper, a former CSIS analyst warns that the jihadi threat to Canada is home-grown. Within his book called *The Threat from Within*, Phil Gurski, who had worked for three decades for Canadian government intelligence, wrote about Islamic religious chauvinism." Gabriel details the Canadian connection.

"Gabriel, we know that you are the only one of us who consistently reads the newspapers. What's the latest after the Paris Massacres?"

"A November 23, 2015, *Sun* newspaper article reads, 'ISIS magazine calls for attacks on Canada. Their publication urges readers to kill Americans and Canadians.' In that issue of *Dabiq*, this Islamic magazine is used as a vehicle to attract terrorist recruits and to encourage Western supporters to launch terrorist attacks in their homelands. Sleeper cells and lone wolves across the world are being instructed to kill in the same geographic area where they live. 'There are at least a couple of hundred serious Canadian radicals.'"

Raphael reaches out to a jihadist convert who had abandoned Islam saying, "In his webmail, Walid Shoebat wrote that <u>Muslims posted this message to the Roman Catholic Church at the Vatican threatening that Muslims 'Will not stop the fighting until we make the Call to Prayer and pray in Rome by Allah's will in a conquest, as a promise from Allah, and Allah does not break his promise</u>.' Radical Islam means to take over its Augustinian author and creator, the Vatican."

"What has Muhammad's radical Islam got planned for Canada?"

"I remember our 2009 meeting with Jeremiah Stone at Keyano College in Fort McMurray, Alberta. Jeremiah warned us about all those eighteen-wheeler truck transports driven by Muslim drivers traveling right past Canadian oil refineries. Eight years ago, Jeremiah Stone cautioned us that Muslim truck drivers have positioned themselves strategically across Canada and across the United States, to wreak synchronized havoc across both countries by delivering potassium nitrate fertilizer bombs to oil and gas refineries, pipelines, gas-storage facilities, hydro plants, hydro-generating dams, water reservoirs, such as Hoover Dam, and to nuclear power plants. There would be multiple continent-wide, Chernobyl-style and Fukushima-style nuclear radiation disasters. All of this was planned out years in advance to bring bedlam and chaos, to bring America and Canada to a standstill and to freeze millions to death in mid-winter. Eight years ago, Jeremiah Stone was ahead of the curve on this one. Gabriel, did you reveal this information to Jeremiah?"

"No, not this time. It did not come from me. Jeremiah Stone has other angelic sources."

"Potassium nitrate fertilizer is easy to obtain in Saskatchewan, Canada, where it is mined. Every crop farmer has fertilizer. Fertilizer bombs are easy to make, and they are undetectable. With countrywide power outages in mid-winter, millions of Americans and Canadians would freeze to death, eventually leading to widespread disease from rotting human and animal corpses. This would be unimaginable ayatollah-fashion apocalyptic catastrophe to bring the return of their Iranian Shiite Mahdi."

"I recall Jeremiah Stone telling us that from 2006 to 2010, Shell Canada had manned their Alberta fuel stations with males from Pakistan. In light of the Paris Massacres, the Nice Massacre, the Manchester Massacre, and the London Bridge Massacre, Canadians should be concerned and alarmed. The Canadian government and security forces should investigate."

"Muhammad's total war on Christianity is continuing today in high gear in the Middle East. Muslim historian Muhammad bin Ishaq had written: 'The Koran tells in detail the true story of Jesus, who is another of Allah's prophets, and that the Trinity of the Christians is Allah, Jesus and Mary…Allah gave the prophet Jesus the power of raising the dead, healing the sick, making birds of clay and having them fly away… Allah gave Jesus these signs as a mark of being a prophet.' Furthermore, historian Ishaq wrote, 'Christ was not crucified. Allah took Jesus up directly to him and will refute those who say that he was crucified and was resurrected. On the final day, the Day of Resurrection, those who follow Christ but do not believe in his divinity, will be blessed. Those who insist that Christ is God, part of the Trinity, and reject true faith, will be punished in Hell.'"

"To summarize Muhammad's satanic hatred, Ishaq wrote that Muhammad had said that there is *NO* Trinity, that Jesus Christ was *NOT* crucified, that He was *NOT* resurrected, that Jesus Christ was but a man who was a prophet of Allah, and that He will return to enforce Sharia Law by killing Christians who refuse to bow down to Allah and send them to Hell. These words from a respected Muslim historian are provocative and inflammatory incentives for all-out Islamic war against Christianity."

"But Jews will be butchered together with Christians. On March 25, 2017, SHOEBAT.COM and RESCUE CHRISTIANS.org reported, 'Imam Calling For Jews To Be Killed In Sermon At Montreal Mosque.' B'nai Brith Canada, filed a complaint with Montreal police." Once again, Archangel Gabriel is infuriated with Muhammad of old.

"Christians should be most concerned about how Islam views Jesus Christ and how it is treating Middle East and African Christians as well as the significance of the burka and the niqab," Gabriel continues to raise alarms.

With a look of extreme distress, Michael responds, "The burka, the niqab and the hijab are making silent political and religious statements. The burka, the niqab, and the hijab are flaunting Islamic ideology that Jesus Christ is *NOT* God, that He was *NOT* crucified, that He was *NOT* resurrected and that Christ the Messiah is Allah's servant. Islam is using the burka, the niqab, and the hijab to spit upon and to urinate upon Jesus Christ in front of the faces of Christians who are afraid and terrified to defend the name of their God."

Raphael exposes events in Africa, "In Nigeria, Boko Haram has murdered thousands of Christians. Boko Haram has taken nine-year-old and ten-year-old girls as sexual slaves. Boko Haram is following the example of Muhammad."

"In 2001, Ayatollah Khamenei of Iran had said, 'It is the mission of the Islamic Republic of Iran to erase Israel from the map of the region.' In 2012, Ayatollah Khamenei had said, 'The Zionist regime is a cancerous tumor and it will be removed.' On September 9, 2015, Ayatollah Khamenei of Iran posted to Twitter that Israel will not survive twenty-five more years. He addressed Israel saying, 'You will not see the next 25 years.' Ayatollah Khamenei added that the Jewish state will be hounded until it is destroyed." Gabriel documents Iran's determination and obsession to destroy Israel.

"Iran despises Israel and the Jews with the hatred of the millennia that was ignited inside the tents of Abraham when Sarah evicted Ishmael and his mother Hagar into the hot desert to die. The culture of hatred toward the Jews that runs deep within the psyche of Iranians is the same culture of hatred which is bred deep into Palestinians, which is fed to their children with their mothers' milk and which is inflamed in their schools and mosques. Bret Stephens, an articulate commentator on the Middle East who wrote for the *Wall Street Journal*, called this virulent hatred the 'Palestinian psychosis.'" Gabriel unfolds the psychotic obsessions scattered throughout Muhammad's Quran and which are embedded in the psyches of all Palestinians.

"Hatred is as the venom of cobras. It's about Muhammad's malignant psychosis which is metastasizing throughout the body of Islam today. This same 'Palestinian psychosis' can be called the 'Iranian psychosis.' Iran's ayatollahs and mullahs see themselves as the earthly agents of their Mahdi, and who will expedite the Mahdi's imminent return. The Mahdi will kill off any surviving Christians and Jews," Michael provides more insights on the venom that leavens the entire Quran.

Michael exposes Iranian Shiite psychosis, "In their mind-set, the Iranian Shiites need maximum earthly chaos for their Mahdi to return. Global mass chaos is the condition necessary for the return of their Mahdi. Multiple nuclear explosions in or over American cities will do the job. During the Soviet era, there was no nuclear war between East and West because of Mutually Assured Destruction or MAD. Both sides wanted to live. However, the Iranian Shiites have stated that they want MAD and that they are striving desperately hard to achieve Mutually Assured Destruction. They want to die so that they can go to Allah's sex paradise. Nuclear war is an inevitable and a necessary requirement for Iran's ayatollahs. Iran is not a country. Iran is a cause with out-of-control hatred."

"This 'Palestinian psychosis' and this 'Iranian psychosis' speak of mental madness. MAD as in deranged, is the proper descriptor for Muhammad's Islamic killer-psychosis," Raphael, the psychiatric specialist, speaks of the Palestinian psychosis and the Iranian psychosis which are determined to drive the world into Allah's abyss.

"Muhammad's MAD Muslims have infiltrated the West. Within the United States, there is unprecedented support for ISIS. There are several thousand known ISIS sympathizers inside the United States. There are nine hundred investigations into ISIS sympathizers, and three hundred recognized ISIS agents under investigation in America. Unquestionably, Muhammad's Islam is the most dangerous and the most egregious Fraud of the Ages ever perpetrated upon all of humanity."

"Recall the *Satanic Verses* of Salman Rushdie. In 1988, Ayatollah Khomeni had issued a fatwa against Salman Rushdie because he had blasphemed Islam. Today, twenty-eight years later, the Islamist-bullying and the Islamist fatwa against Rushie are still in effect. Because of Islamic pressures, democratic India had refused and is continuing to refuse to allow the entry of the *Satanic Verses* into their country."

"Following the Paris massacres and the Nice Massacre, the role of U.S. President Barack Obama had drawn scrutiny. After eight years in office, Barack Obama had never once uttered the phrase *radical Islam*. Even after the November 13, 2015 attacks in Paris, he refused to blame the radical Islamic extremists of ISIS for the terrorizing murders of 130 innocent Parisians. Even after the Paris Massacres and the Nice Massacre, the words *radical Islam* still were forbidden words within the Obama administration. As French President Hollande negotiated with the murderous Russian Vladimir Putin, U.S. President Obama was missing in action. Barack Obama began his presidency in 2009 by running off to Cairo for a major speech aimed at bending his knees before the Muslim world. With bold-faced lying, Barack Obama emphasized that Islam is a religion of peace and apologized for U.S. policy toward the Muslim world. This mockery was performed before and within the hotbed of the monstrous Muslim Brotherhood."

"In the summer of 2015, a poll taken by an American think tank found that one-fifth of the long-term residents of Syrian refugee camps supported ISIS and one-third backed Hamas or al-Qaeda. The Paris massacres made it clear even to the blind, that the world is in a civilizational war against radical Islamists who want to kill all kafirs. French President Hollande named Islamic State as radical Islam while

Barack Obama continued to live in denial in his deliberate fantasy world." Michael the cosmic military strategist shakes his head in protest against Barack Obama's stunning folly.

On December 1, 2015, at the United Nations climate change meeting in Paris, Barack Obama linked the Islamic Paris massacres to climate change. This statement was pure insanity. This linkage was a bizarre stretch of credibility beyond the ludicrous. All four of the Angelic God Squad shake their heads and break out into derisive mockery of this piece of stunning irrationality. President Barack Obama signs the non-binding grossly unbalanced Paris Climate Agreement which would give a ten-year exemption to major polluters China and India, which would cause the loss of six million American jobs, which would cause a major redistribution of wealth in America, and which severely would cripple America economically. The United States would have been required to send one-hundred billion dollars to underdeveloped countries for the next ten years. On June 1, 2017, as he had promised on the campaign trail, President Donald Trump withdraws from the Paris Climate Agreement, and asks to renegotiate this accord.

"Repeatedly, Barack Obama is confident that, once again, he can pull this folly over the eyes of the American people. Make no mistake, there is no fantasy here. The Obama universe is unfolding according to his plan. Through his executive orders and his continuing illegal actions of violating the American Constitution, Barack Obama has amassed overwhelming dictatorial presidential powers. Americans should be alarmed that in the event of a major Muslim terrorist attack within the United States, Barack Obama may suspend the Constitution and declare martial law indefinitely. Barack Obama already has written the executive order to allow him to declare martial law if anything even remotely like a general state of unrest which already *might* be in process. Michael, any excuse will do for Barack Obama to confiscate all guns and then to declare martial law." Gabriel steps boldly into the current political sphere.

"That is my overriding concern as well, Gabriel. Trampling upon the American Constitution and upon democracy would fit the end-time scene." Fortunately for America, President Donald Trump has risen to the rescue.

"Here is more of the same, Michael. On June 24, 2016, Caroline B. Glick who is senior contributing editor of the *Jerusalem Post* wrote in the *Jewish World Review* that U.S. President Barack Obama is demanding that Israel sign a multi-year security assistance deal which is highly dangerous to Israel's survival."

As the leader of the armies of Heaven, Michael is most concerned by this disturbing news from a reputable authority of Caroline Glick's prestige who had written, "In exchange for U.S. military aid, Obama is demanding that Israel surrenders her defensive independence to the White House. The greater majority of Americans support Israel and they expect that Congress will underwrite Israel. However, Obama is maneuvering to redirect this assistance away from Congressional influence and to subject it solely to White House control."

With penetrating insight, Michael unfolds Obama's strategy, "By his conduct, Barack Obama has made it more than apparent that he hates both Israeli Prime Minister Netanyahu and Israel. To prevent congressional support, President Obama is attempting to commandeer an end-run around Congress. Obama's defense assistance agreement is designed to bar the American public and Congress from intervening on Israel's behalf at any time in the future."

Gabriel is irate as he throws up both arms, "It is more than obvious that this agreement would strip Israel of its sovereign capacity to develop and to produce its own munitions, replacement parts, and defense systems. Under Obama's armaments assistance agreement, Israel would be denied the freedom to take defensive-offensive actions without White House approval."

With cold expressionless composure, Uriel evaluates this survival dilemma, "Barack Obama's agreement would be an outright shut-down of Israel's armaments industries and a denial of her intuitive military ingenuity."

In raised voice, Michael wags his forefinger and says, "Congress must not allow this to happen. Israeli technical innovations are the guarantee of Israel's ability to defend herself and to fight wars without White House obstructionism."

"Canceling Barack Obama's hardware aid package and rejecting his highly suspect coercive domination, would greatly benefit Israel because it would ensure Israel's independence and her very survival under a continuing rockets barrage from Palestinian Hamas." Physical scientist Uriel understands the significance of cutting edge innovations in military hardware.

"But there are other White House existential threats to Israel's survival. It is stunning that retired Israeli Defence Force (IDF) general officers have authored position papers agreeing to and accommodating future Israeli withdrawal from Judea, from Samaria and from Jerusalem. This horrifically numbing concession flies in the face of Elohim the God of Heaven Who had bequeathed His land to Abraham and to his descendants. This was not an agreement. In **Genesis 15**, this was Adonai's covenant with Abraham which stands until the end of time." Archangel Michael shakes with shock.

With a look of disbelief, Archangel Gabriel shakes his head in displeasure, "The Israeli Defence Force proposals call for Israel to renounce its claims to sovereign rights over Judea and Samaria, and to divide Jerusalem!"

Michael mutters sadly, "Because of Obama's unrelenting pressures, this blueprint for abandonment by Israel is identical to Obama's position of capitulating to Palestinian demands. Furthermore, U.S. Secretary of State John Kerry is demanding that the Israeli government surrender the Jordan Valley to the Palestinians and to surrender Israeli supervision of the Jordanian border. With this forced surrender to Obama's territorial demands, Israel will become militarily indefensible."

"Recent attacks by Iranian-allied forces against ISIS in Falluja are a stepping stone toward Iran's expansion into Jordan and against Israel. Surrendering Israeli jurisdiction over the border with Jordan will position Iran at the very outskirts of Israel. With Iran's intense hatred of Israel, apocalyptic conflagration will be inevitable." Michael sees Armageddon on the very horizon.

"This foolish and shameless betrayal was supported by Israeli Defence Force generals who have forgotten the prophecy of **Joel 3:2–3** wherein the God of the universe leaves no doubt when He declared, 'I will gather all the nations and bring them down to the valley of Jehoshaphat, and I will enter into judgment with them there… because they have divided up my land.'"

"Yes, it's all about dividing up the land of Israel."

"But the land does not belong to Israel or to the Palestinians. It belongs to Adonai, the God of Heaven."

"Because of Barack Obama's domineering pressures upon Israel to surrender Judea and Samaria, to partition Jerusalem and to surrender Israel's authority over her border with Jordan, because Barack Obama is defying Elohim the God of Heaven in dividing His land, and because Congress has allowed President Barack Obama to run wild with his executive orders in defiance of the U.S. Constitution, then divine retribution upon America will continue through extreme climate upheavals as in the historic one-in-a-thousand-year flooding in South Carolina of October 2015, and the deadly floods in West Virginia in June of 2016. These devastating record-setting floods have continued in southeast Louisiana in August of 2016." Michael understands Divine retribution for breaking Adonai's covenant with Abraham.

"I hear it being said that this is the worst flooding in a thousand years." Uriel exclaims in amazement, "And I know it. I have monitored these events since before Adam and Eve in the Garden of Eden. On the other side of the continent, in diametric contrast, California and the Western states are suffering from record-setting droughts, low water levels, massive fires, and blinding dust storms followed by massive flooding."

A pained expression sweeps across Gabriel's face, "Millions upon millions of Americans support Israel. Americans do not deserve the judgment that is coming down upon their nation because of their reckless President."

"As a constitutional scholar and as a professor who taught constitutional law at the University of Chicago, Barack Obama knows that he is breaking Constitutional laws. Obama is one executive-order-obsessed and lawless President." With trembling voice, Michael expresses, "Hatred and lawlessness bring Divine retribution." What will be President Donald Trump's position with regard to Samaria, Judea, East Jerusalem and the Jordan Valley?

Gabriel details the San Bernardino massacre by Islam, "On December 2, 2015, a husband-wife radical Islamic-jihadist duo went on a murderous killing spree and mass-executed fourteen in San

Bernardino, California. They chose a Christmas party of disabled Christian adults to duplicate the actions of ISIS who are butchering Christians in Iraq and Syria. In unspeakable, well-planned carnage, the jihadi wife had made contact with ISIS, and ISIS had made contact with Jihadi Jane (Malik). Within their wicked web of terror, the husband had made contact with al-Shabaab in Kenya and in Somalia. Then this husband-wife duo left their baby with the grandma while they went on their murderous killing-spree. This husband-wife jihadi couple had thousands of rounds of ammunition and enough bombs to slaughter hundreds. The explosives were al-Qaeda-style pipe bombs. Jihadi Jane was the driving force who, on Facebook, had pledged allegiance to ISIS leader Abu Bakr al-Baghdadi. The father of this jihadi male stated that his son 'was obsessed with Israel' and that he had stated that 'Israel would be wiped off the map within two years.' ISIS-inspired and with hatred toward the Jews, this was Islam versus Christians and Jews. This was Islam bent upon recreating the global Islamic Caliphate. Following the Paris massacres, this Islamic slaughter has been dubbed as the San Bernardino Islamic Jihadi Massacre."

"On December 6, 2015, in his address to the nation, President Barack Obama stated that 'we see growing efforts by terrorists to poison the minds of people.' Barack Obama did not state that these were radical Islamic terrorists and that it was Muhammad's radical Muslim slaughtering campaigns, which were the examples that were poisoning the minds of Muslims today. Without mentioning the words *radical Islam*, the words of President Barack Obama are those of an apologist for Islamic terrorism. On February 3, 2016, as the "defender of Islam" President Barack Obama visited a fundamentalist Baltimore Islamic Mosque. This Islamic Society of Baltimore mosque is known for separating men from women and for reinforcing the Islamic culture that discriminates against American Muslim women. Muslim Farzana Hassan wrote that a reformist in the Muslim movement told *FOX* News that the Baltimore mosque which Obama had visited was 'heaped in Salafism and ideology that is really incompatible with Western identity.' A former imam at this same Baltimore mosque had stated that 'suicide bombings were sometimes justifiable in extreme circumstances.' What? Suicide bombings were sometimes justifiable?"

Raphael finds that Barack Obama's covert and secretive visit to this mosque to be deplorable conduct for a U.S. President.

"In contrast, U.S. President Barack Obama has avoided any mention of the murderous killing deaths of tens of thousands of Christians by Islam in the Middle East today."

In contrast, Gabriel enlists comedic support, "On January 31, 2016, as exposed across the Internet, liberal comedian Bill Maher had said, 'I wish my fellow liberals would show the same 'intolerance' for Muslims that they show for Christians.'"

"As the medical specialist in our group, I state unequivocally that ISIS has exceeded Muhammad's wildest dreams of torturing kafirs. *International Business Times* and Britain's *Daily Mail* reported that on May 19, 2016, in Mosul, Iraq, ISIS killed twenty-five 'spies' by typing them together with ropes. While they were shrieking their lungs out, ISIS lowered them slowly into a large basin of highly corrosive nitric acid until their skins and internal organs dissolved slowly. I know of no other more prolonged and more excruciating death." Raphael is depressed and sickened by the inhuman, depraved, barbaric cruelty of ISIS.

"There are other instances where ISIS slowly lowered their victims into boiling tar. Comparable to ISIS brutality were the ancient Assyrians of Nineveh who scattered the ten northern tribes of Israel. The favorite Assyrian barbaric tortures were to skin their enemies alive and to impale their screaming captives on a stake through the anus until they died many days later."

"This is a shocking and bone-chilling revelation, except that angels don't have bones! ISIS is from the same geographic area of Iraq as were the ancient Assyrians. Nothing has changed. The Assyrian-mimicking ISIS has been cutting off fingers one at a time, cutting off toes one at a time, cutting off the tongue, the penis, one testicle, the other testicle, one breast, the other breast, one hand, one arm, the other hand, then the other arm, one kidney—all over a period of many days so as to inflict maximum, prolonged pain and suffering." Archangel Gabriel dangles frightening and nauseating ancient Middle East history in front of the God Squad, "The people of ancient barbaric Assyria are modern Germany today."

With grimaced expression and voice to match, Gabriel warns, "Americans and Canadians must realize that these barbaric, radical Islamic torturers are coming soon to North American and to Canadian shores."

With anguish in his voice, Raphael announces, "With the continuing Islamic refugee migrations into Europe and Britain—and the Brexit referendum of June 23, 2016—there is a significant upsurge of xenophobia in Britain. Brits are screaming at persons from southeast Asia and other regions, and even at those born in the U.K., to get the hell out of Britain. The predictors of future explosive Islamic upheavals have germinated in Britain. Germinated and in explosive bloom. In 75 days, there have been three Islamic terrorist attacks in Britain; at Westminster Bridge on March 22, 2017, at Manchester Arena on May 22, 2017, and at London Bridge on June 3, 2017."

Michael exposes media coverage, "Following the massacres in Paris, in Brussels, in San Bernardino, in Orlando, and in Nice, and following the Brexit Referendum, Muslim journalist Tarek Fatah wrote in the *Sun* that 'Radical Islam was Brexit's elephant in the room.' In spite of huge opposition by the ruling elites, the British 'working class voted to stop Britain from being swamped by refugees camped on the other side of the English Channel in France.' The Brexit vote was 'to stop the Muslims from coming into this country. . . . Simple as that.' Britons were 'appalled that their country was being reshaped to accommodate medieval values. . . . The ordinary people are angry at Islamism.' The working class Brits are distressed by 'the flaunting of radical Islam on the streets and in the workplaces of Europe's cities.' Once again, Gabriel summarizes the direction of future actions, "With shouts of 'Allah Akbar' before they launch their massive slaughters, we are witnessing the new radioactive age of theocratic, radical Islamic terror against the kafirs."

"It is frightening that there are eighty-eight Sharia courts in Britain which are an extreme irritant for most Brits. This Brexit vote is an European geopolitical earthquake. It's a black swan event with unpredictable impacts upon other EU members."

"But it's also a wake-up call for Americans and for Canadians," Raphael announces indignantly. "Female Syrian refugees who have come to the United States and to Canada are flaunting with defiance their head gear and their ankle-length gowns. Their burqas, chadors, jilbabs, abayas, hijabs and niqabs are a silent but impudent political statement, silent political theatre, a thumb into the eyes of Christians and a middle finger of contempt in the faces of Christians. Their Muslim dress defiantly announces that Jesus is *NOT* the Son of God, that Jesus did *NOT* die on the cross, that His blood was *NOT* shed for humanity, that Jesus was *NOT* resurrected from the dead, that Jesus is Allah's prophet and that Jesus is coming back to kill the Christians and the Jews. In the face of this silent Sharia assault upon Yeshua, the cowardly Christian world in America and in Canada remains pathetically and deplorable silent."

CHAPTER 13

THE KING OF THE NORTH, ARMAGEDDON, AND THE FOUR HORSEMEN OF THE APOCALYPSE

With deep concerns etched across their foreheads, Gabriel echoes God Squad sentiment, "This division in America by race and by color must stop today. The shouts of 'Pigs in a blanket, fry 'em like bacon,' from radical Black Lives Matter is racially divisive and provokes anarchy. Most unfortunately and deplorably, President Barack Obama endorsed and promoted this new chapter of hatred in America when he entertained representatives of Black Lives Matter in the White House. This was divisive and unconscionable conduct by an American President!"

"Barack Obama must stop this widespread, anarchist, antipolice, rhetoric now. The killings of police in Dallas and the ambush of police in Baton Rouge are the continuing fallout of Barack Obama's racially divisive White House folly," Michael warns. In contrast, in 2017, President Donald Trump is trying to coalesce divergent America and to support the police.

"I read the newspapers and I keep my fingers on the pulse of political intrigue," Gabriel displays hard-core evidence. "Here is more high level folly, skullduggery, and disgraceful national deception. Did Saudi Arabia play a role in the 9/11 takedown of the World Trade Center? In 2002, the American Congress revealed its investigations into the 9/11 attacks, but Congress kept twenty-eight pages secret from the public for the last fourteen years. Some of the 9/11 hijackers received assistance from persons who appear to having been associated with the Saudi government. The report indicated that Saudi spies in the U.S. were possibly connected to the Saudi royal family. There were revelations that several months before the 9/11 terrorist attack, imams in U.S. mosques had assisted the hijackers. There were allegations that the hijackers received funding from the Saudi royal family. A CIA memorandum unequivocally revealed linkages between the hijackers and the Saudi embassy in Washington. Yes, for fourteen years, the elected Congress deceived the American public."

With shocked expression, Michael evaluates this stunning exposure. "That's a chilling description of Saudi Arabia's ties and payments to the 9/11 terrorists. It sounds like ultimate betrayal of America by the Saudis. The Saudi betrayal is matched by Washington's betrayal of the American people. In their monstrous lying, Washington misled Americans that there was no foreign national sponsorship of 9/11."

Raphael probes, "But I want to see more substance, more proof, and more facts to verify these revelations."

"Facts? Check out the facts on the Internet and read what investigative journalist Paul Sperry of the *New York Post* had to say about this Fraud of the Ages." Archangel Gabriel dangles his research before the God Squad.

"As the physical sciences specialist, I continue to be utterly amazed by the naiveness of the American public. When two World Trade Center towers fell exactly onto their own footprints, and when a distant third tower, not hit by a plane, also fell onto its own foot print, there was serious chicanery afoot. When three towers collapsed at the speed of gravity free-fall, when explosions were heard all the way down to ground level, and when molten metal continued to flow for many days afterward, the Bush administration fooled the American people into ignoring the law of physics. Instead the American public chose to live in Fantasyland." Uriel spells out the unspeakable fraud that sedated the American public into a national coma since 9/11, a coma which continues today."

"It looked and it sounded like controlled demolitions? But controlled by whom and why?" Raphael asks.

"To raise distrust levels even higher, the Bush administration immediately whisked the bin Laden family out of the country while they covered up the 9/11 evidence for the next seven years. The Obama administration continued this 9/11 cover-up for another seven years until July 15, 2016," Archangel Michael raises suspicions sky-high.

"As these Islamic massacres in the Middle East have continued, they have validated Russia's military intervention in Syria. After Turkey shot down a Russian fighter jet, Russia placed missile batteries within Syria, all within easy access to northern Israel. Well, Gabriel, with the facilitation of Barack Obama, it appears that finally Russian president Vladimir Putin—as 'king of the north'—is in Syria and scripture is being fulfilled before the eyes of the world."

"On December 3, 2015, British Prime Minister David Cameron referred to Muhammad's Islamic terrorists as 'medieval monsters' who are trying to push civilization back to the seventh century and back to the days of Muhammad. On December 3, 2015, Russian President Vladimir Putin said, 'It appears that Allah chose to punish the ruling clique of Turkey by depriving them of wisdom and judgment.' Was this Putin tongue-in-cheek? Yes, through the words of Vladimir Putin, who spoke them worldwide, Muhammad's Allah is in play in this Russian *king of the north*' end-time sequence."

"Yes, it was I who had brought this *king of the north*' end-time message to Daniel in Babylon. In chapter 11 of Daniel's book, I had made seven references to the 'king of the north.' Recall that to reach Daniel, I had fought the demonic Prince of Persia to a draw for twenty-one days, and then you Michael came to rescue me."

"Yes, Gabriel, but this devil was not the Prince of Persia. He is a she, and she was and she is the Queen of Persia. She is better known as the slithering Madonna in the Garden of Eden. I had fought her in Heaven, I had fought her in Persia and very soon, I will fight her for the third and final time."

"Are you saying that the Queen of Persia is the snaky Madonna in the apple tree of the Garden of Eden?"

"Yes, and more, much more. The Queen of Persia is Mary, the Queen of Heaven."

"Wow! Wow! Wow! Michael, in truth, you have just named the Queen of Persia to be Satan-Allah herself."

"And so she is."

"But why would Satan choose to be Queen of Persia when she does not know the future?"

Michael launches into a shocking disclosure: "Satan does not need to know the future. Well before the time of Daniel, Persia was the central figure in the Middle East wars. Adonai's promise to Abraham and your prophecies to Daniel gave to Satan most of the information which she needed to know about future events. The prophecies in **Isaiah 34:9–10** filled in the vital details as, 'the streams of Edom shall be turned into pitch and her soil into brimstone; her land shall become burning pitch. Night and day it shall not be quenched; its smoke shall go up forever.' It was clear to Satan-Allah that the oil fields of Edom, known as Saudi Arabia, would be set on fire and that Persia as Iran would set Edom aflame. From Ezekiel's prophecies, Satan-Allah knows that a nuclear Iran is destined to bomb the Saudi oil fields. Be assured that Barack Obama has been the key figure in facilitating this future nuclear meltdown, which will be triggered by Iran upon Saudi Arabia." This information bombshell sends Gabriel, Raphael, and Uriel reeling. Minutes elapse before Gabriel picks up the threads of prophecy.

"Apocalyptic ISIS as the final caliphate is rampaging through Syria and Iraq. Russia is inside Syria as the '*king of the north*' and as Gog of the land of Magog. In Latakia, Syria, Russia has deployed an S-400 antiaircraft system that is capable of shooting down jets 250 miles away. Today, half of Israel is within its range. Today, the '*king of the north*' is in Syria and on the move toward Israel. Moscow is directly north of Israel. **Ezekiel 38** and **Ezekiel 39** are being fulfilled this very day before our eyes." Gabriel connects his prophecies to Daniel and **Ezekiel 38–39**, events which are unfolding in front of our eyes and before the world today.

As leader of the armies of Heaven, a worried looking Michael expresses his deep concerns and anguish. "Fulfilment of **Ezekiel 38–39** is our concern. In parallel prophecy, **Joel 3:2–3** reads, 'I will gather all the nations and bring them down to the valley of Jehoshaphat, and I will enter into judgment with them there . . . because they have divided up my land.' The world is on the very precipice of Armageddon and the gathering of the nations against Israel in the valley of Jehoshaphat north of Jerusalem. Except for Caroline B. Glick, no other prophet has arisen from within Israel to sound warnings to a nation asleep at the wheel while the 'Philistines' of centuries past a.k.a. the Palestinians of the Gaza of today, are determined to push Israel into the sea while the Persians of today (Iranians) are arming to nuke Israel out of existence."

"Here's a different wake-up call for Americans," Gabriel reveals, "on July 27, 2016, *CHARISMANEWS, CHRISTIAN DAILY, RESCUE CHRISTIANS.org* and *SHOEBAT.com* reported that Muslim **ISIS** terrorists have sent out orders and issued a kill list to slaughter thousands of American Christians in the United States. As the terrorist diaspora spreads from Syria into the Western world, ISIS is targeting the Cross of Christ as they continue their slaughters of Christians. Divine retribution is on its way."

The place is a military air base in Iran. The date is August 16, 2016. The Angelic God Squad is monitoring air traffic.

A worried-looking Uriel shouts out, "Hey! Late-breaking news! Here's a shocker! For the first time, Russian military jets are taking off from Iranian air bases in order to strike ISIS targets in Syria."

"In addition to Putin arming Iran with modern weaponry and long range missiles, Russian war planes are crossing through Iraqi air space on their bombing runs over Syria. That's another poke in the eye of America by the "*king of the north.*' There are up to 100,000 Iranian-backed fighters in Iraq. Radical Iranian Shia cleric Muqtada al Sadr stated that U.S. forces 'are a target for us.' The power Shiite Crescent is now complete. Predominantly Sunni Egypt, Sunni Jordan, Sunni Turkey, and Sunni Saudi Arabia are within the grasp of this Shiite pincer claw enabled by Russia. Because of Barack Obama's folly, Iran and Russia have replaced the United States on the ground and in the air. Events in the Middle East are unfolding at an unprecedented pace." Will President Donald Trump be able to change this dynamic?

"As desperate as events appear to be, things are not falling apart, they are falling into place," Gabriel projects the positive ending.

"The Shiite Twelfth Imam as the Muslim Mahdi, will come back only when there is maximum chaos on Earth." Under this final apocalyptic threat, Michael keeps the God Squad calm and focused. "The Iran Nuclear Deal, which was promoted and enabled by President Barack Obama, has assured that Iran soon will achieve a nuclear bomb, which when exploded above America will create an electro-magnetic pulse (EMP) that will fry all unprotected electronics, thereby sending the United States back to the nineteenth century. That's the kind of chaos Iran and their Mahdi need. As the world's foremost sponsor of terrorism, Iranian Shiites boast that they love death as much as the rest of the world loves life."

"Even though Shiites represent only 15 percent of the Muslim populations, possession of a nuclear bomb by Iran forever would change the equation and the dynamics of power across the Middle East and across the world. Russian support of Shiite Iran tips the scales against the Sunni majority and against Israel. A change in the scale of Russian intervention is imminent. On September 07, 2016, in a hard-hitting speech at Oxford University, U.S. Defence Secretary Ash Carter accused Russia of sowing seeds of global instability by their interventions in Syria. On September 26, 2016, it was reported that Syrian and Russian airstrikes unleashed unprecedented slaughter of civilians in Aleppo. Vladimir Putin is behaving according to the prophecies of Daniel and the prophecies of Ezekiel. Psychiatric thug Kim Jong Un of North Korea is spiralling out of control. With nuclear-tipped, long-range missiles, Kim Jong Un is determined to target the United States. The balance of power across the globe has been changed," exclaims military strategist Michael, who is visibly shaken by recent events. However, by moving an aircraft carrier and submarines near North Korea, President Donald Trump has issued a warning to Kim Jong Un that he will shoot down all missiles leaving North Korean launch pads. On April 21, 2017, in response, North Korea threatened to sink the US aircraft carrier and to launch a super-mighty pre-emptive nuclear strike that will reduce the United States to ashes."

With visible approval, Archangel Gabriel announces, "On April 7, 2017, President Donald Trump ordered US warships to launch 59 Tomahawk cruise missiles at the Alawite-Shiite airbase that was home to the warplanes which dropped sarin gas upon Sunni men, women, and children in Syria. I remember that in Nebuchadnezzar's dream and in Daniel's dream of the giant metal statue, the toes of iron mixed with clay were Islamic Shiites and Islamic Sunnis who have been killing each other for fourteen hundred years. After Muhammad had been poisoned by his wives, Shiites and Sunnis have been butchering each other for fourteen-hundred years and continue their killings today in Iraq and Syria. This is the continuing civil war in Islam. In chapter 11 of the book of Daniel, the '*king of the north*' is mentioned seven times. In my prophecy to Daniel, the Russian '*king of the north*' is the catalyst who is crushing the Islamic toes of the metaphorical metal statue."

"As you said, Gabriel, Islam is at war with itself. With the ever-changing political dynamics, Shiite Iran together with Shiite Hezbollah are locked into a battle to the death against Sunni Saudi Arabia, Sunni Egypt and Sunni Turkey. Shiite Iran and Sunni Saudi Arabia have been archenemies for fourteen centuries. In a mind-boggling political distortion, after the failed coup in Turkey, Recep Tayyip Erdogan has realigned Sunni Turkey with Putin's Russia. What meaning can there be for NATO member Turkey to align itself with Russia, which is enabling Iran and Shiite-Alawite Bashar al-Assad of Syria? Vladimir Putin's armed invasion of Eastern Ukraine and his criminal annexation of Crimea mark the re-emergence of the Russian dictatorship and the Soviet Union. The '*king of the north*' is on the march."

"What do Bible prophecies have to say about Russia?" asks Raphael.

"The book of Ezekiel declares devastating destruction upon Gog as the ruler of the Land of Magog. **Ezekiel 38:1–6** warns, 'Thus says the Lord God: Behold I am against you, O Gog, chief prince of Meshech and Tubal.' The coming War of Gog and Magog and the coming war of **Psalm 83** will be the key events that set the stage for the tribulation. Out of **Ezekiel 38–39**, the Russian '*king of the north*' now looms large in the prophecies regarding Israel. Is Daniel's '*king of the north*' the same person as Gog of Magog?" In his own eyes, the prophecies reviewed by Archangel Michael are compelling as he declares that, "Vladimir Putin is the Darth Vader of the Middle East."

Archangel Michael declares, "It is being said in the media that the forbidden and unholy coalition of Russia and Turkey is an alliance of misfits. The serpentine threads of Daniel's words of prophecy are coming together in the Middle East cauldron today. From the prophecies of **Ezekiel 38–39**, the Antichrist Beast of the Middle East is destined to arise from the area of Syria, or Turkey, or Assyria of old. The Turkish referendum of April 16, 2017, expanded Erdogan's presidential powers away from democratic rule toward one-man rule in establishing a de facto dictatorship to becoming Islam's new caliph. Bible Prophecy is being fulfilled at an unnerving speed. Turkey is declaring that they are 'The Beast Rising Out Of The Dead.' Turkey had decided to resurrect its Ottoman caliphate on Christian Resurrection Sunday by giving Erdogan unlimited powers. His ruling party has declared that all must obey Erdogan as 'Caliph' and as 'God the Holy Spirit.' Yes, you have heard it correctly. Muslim Erdogan has declared himself to be *God the Holy Spirit.* After Erdogan had won his referendum to exercise complete control over Turkey, the first thing he did was to unveil the Ottoman scepter. This scepter is the diadem which is the silk turban or tiara, as the kingly ornament on the head of the caliph. **Revelation 12:3** reveals the 'great red dragon with... seven diadems upon his heads.' Islam is the red dragon." Michael stomps his foot in defiance.

"In this roiling Islamic Middle East cauldron, the Iranians continually scream out, 'Death to America' and 'Death to Israel.' Iranian President Hassan Rouhani and the supreme thug Ayatollah Khamenei have threatened, 'to wipe Israel off the map.'"

Archangel Michael summarizes the Middle East state of chaos. "It is undeniable that pulling American troops out of a stable Iraq ignited and launched ISIS which had set the Middle East and Europe on fire with the exodus and the migration of Muslim refugees. By his opposition to Israel and by his obvious hatred of Israel, Barack Obama's troop withdrawal had encouraged and inflamed Palestinian hatred toward Israel. Barack Obama's troop withdrawal is the undeniable reason why Russia and Iran are in Syria today."

"For his extremely bad conduct, but especially toward Israel, why had Barack Obama not been impeached?" inquires Archangel Uriel.

Gabriel explains. "The Donald Trump election campaign had been a complete indictment of Barack Obama's eight years in the White House. As if he were a god, Barack Obama had shown Olympian disdain for Americans and for the American Constitution. President Donald Trump wants to repudiate and to reverse Barack Obama's climate change policy, all of his executive orders, his ObamaCare, and his Iran Nuclear Deal. However, it is feared that if Donald Trump does not follow Establishment directives, he will end up dead as President John Kennedy."

CHAPTER 14

THE NEW WORLD ORDER
AND THE GATHERING NUCLEAR STORM

"**A**s published on YourNewsWires.com, in *Express*, in the *Mirror*, in the *Sun*, and on news.com.au, here is some late-breaking news that is directly related to the 9/11 takedown of the World Trade Center towers." In a state of high apprehension, Archangel Gabriel spills the disturbing news. "As reported on August 29, 2016, in his deathbed confession, a CIA officer who was riddled with cancer shocked the world with his dying words that the assassination of President John Fitzgerald Kennedy was carried out by CIA secret service operatives."

"An inside job by the CIA operatives who were in Dallas to protect Kennedy?" queries Raphael. "But why?"

"I have known this for more than fifty years," Michael sadly reveals. "Both Adolf Hitler and President Franklin Delano Roosevelt promoted and extolled the virtues of the globalist New World Order. In defiant opposition, Kennedy had given a speech wherein he condemned government secrecy and the New World Order. This speech cost Kennedy his life. But there is more. President Kennedy had fired Allan Dulles as CIA director. Because of its secret operations, it was Kennedy's intention to dismantle the CIA. Did CIA director Allan Dulles order the hit on JFK? Maybe, but the most compelling reason for Kennedy's assassination was his determination to end the power of the Federal Reserve and its control of U.S. money supply. On June 4, 1963, through his Executive Order 11110, President Kennedy began to transfer control and power from the foreign Federal Reserve to the United States Department of the Treasury. Through his Executive Order 11110, President John Kennedy declared that the *privately owned* Rothschild Federal Reserve Bank no longer had the power to loan money at interest to the United States government. Following his Executive Order 11110, on June 4, 1963, Kennedy was a dead man walking. Some of the Secret Service agents guarding President Kennedy's motorcade were ordered to stand down. The decision was made not to have police motorcycle riders alongside the presidential limousine. This allowed unobstructed shots at Kennedy from the grassy knoll. Following his assassination, the wounds to JFK's body and the damage to the limousine were covered up. What followed was the forgery of photographic evidence of JFK's autopsy, which intentionally was conducted improperly."

"There it is! It's the same Lincoln-Kennedy resistance to control America by international bankers. President Abraham Lincoln resisted the Rothschild Bank's financial intervention. During the American Civil War, the Rothschild Bank manipulated the money systems and threatened Lincoln. That threat was the Rothschild gun that led to Lincoln's assassination by their stooge John Wilkes Booth. Ninety-eight years later, Kennedy's bid to "End the Fed" resulted in another stooge named Lee Harvey Oswald supposedly taking out President Kennedy."

"Executive Order 11110?" echoes Archangel Gabriel. "There it is again. That 11110 numeric is ominous. It's that occultic 11:11 connection all over again. That association is absolutely staggering and sinister! Following Kennedy's assassination on November 22, 1963, President Lyndon Johnson appointed Allen Dulles and John J. McCloy to the Warren Commission. John J. McCloy was president of the World Bank. A banker? How convenient! Those two appointments guaranteed that the fix was in and that the commissions results of Kennedy's assassination were lies, lies, lies. It was an inside job."

"And LBJ was an insider," quips Uriel.

"Four to six shots were recorded by the Dallas Police. The first shot which hit Kennedy's throat and which caused his head to snap <u>backward</u>, was fired from 'the grassy knoll' and not from the book depository. But then the plot thickens. On September 11, 1990, in a joint session of the U.S. Congress, President George Bush Senior also extolled the need for a New World Order. Exactly one year later on September 11, 1991, once again, President George Bush Senior continued to express the urgency to create a New World Order. The 9/11 connection is revealing and compelling."

"To the very day, exactly ten years later, the World Trade Towers were brought down on 9/11/2001, exclaims Uriel." What is this obsession with the September 11 date?" asks Archangel Uriel.

"It appears that the Lincoln assassination and the Kennedy assassination are part of a very determined, surreptitious plan to create a New World Order which continues today and which is all about money, power, worldwide control, war, and lots of blood."

"In these troubled times," responds Michael, "look upon the American dollar bill. There is the Eye of Horus, the very symbol of satanic control of America. Rothschild himself had confirmed that, 'Who controls the money controls the world.'"

"Israel has been sanctioned by the United Nations more times than any other nation. The United Nations agenda is to eliminate Israel. The UN is Israel's greatest enemy. The world hates Israel. Jerusalem is one city against the world! Israel is the target in the crosshairs of the end-times. It his speech to the United Nations, Benjamin Netanyahu had said, 'The UN force is the UN farce.' Today, within the context of Muhammad's Islamic worldwide assaults, the most dangerous actions of Barack Obama and of Hillary Clinton have catapulted America onto living on borrowed time."

"Here is the worst!" Gabriel raises the temperature several dozen degrees hotter. "The Islamic Arab Nations have succeeded in changing history and in delegitimizing Israel's holy sites. In late October 2016, under Islamic pressures, the United Nations Educational, Scientific and Cultural Organization (UNESCO) passed a resolution which declared that Judaism has no claim to the Western Wall and to the Temple Mount. Then, through the World Heritage Committee, UNESCO passed another resolution to erase Christian and Jewish ties to Jerusalem. Using the UNESCO declaration, and in their 'attempt to rewrite long-past history,' the Palestinians have sued Great Britain for their ninety-nine-year-old Balfour Declaration. By suing Great Britain, the Palestinians are declaring that 'the whole existence of Israel was a big mistake.'"

Archangel Michael who was present at these historical events reveals, "It was on November 2, 1917, that British Foreign Secretary Arthur Balfour declared his support for the right of the Jewish people to have a state in their ancient homeland of Palestine. Three years later, in an international move, Britain, France, Italy, Belgium, Greece, and Japan ratified the Balfour Declaration in the San Remo Resolution, which was adopted by the League of Nations and enshrined in international law.

Michael the international legal beagle quotes from his sources, "The conference's decisions were confirmed **unanimously** by all fifty-one member countries of the League of Nations on July 24, 1922. The San Remo Resolution was further endorsed by a joint resolution of the United States Congress in the same year. The San Remo resolution received a further US endorsement in the Anglo-American Treaty on Palestine, signed by the US and Britain on December 3, 1924, that incorporated the text of the Mandate for Palestine. The treaty protected the rights of Americans living in Palestine under the Mandate and more significantly it also made those rights and provisions part of United States treaty law which are protected under the US Constitution. The United States Senate ratified the treaty on February 20, 1925, followed by ratification by President Calvin Coolidge on March 2, 1925, and by Great Britain on March 18, 1925."

Archangel Michael continues to quote from his sources, "Britain was specifically charged with giving effect to the establishment of the Jewish National Home in Palestine that was called for in the Balfour declaration that had already been adopted by all the other Allied Powers. It is therefore obvious that the legitimacy of Syria, Lebanon, Iraq and a Jewish state in Palestine as defined before the creation of Transjordan, all derive from the same binding international agreement at San Remo, that has never been abrogated.'"

Gabriel is visibly upset as he reveals disturbing international decisions made in violation of the San Remo Resolution, "In 1947, the United Nations acclaimed the Partition of Palestine by supporting both a Jewish state and an Arab state. What? In the San Remo Resolution, there was not even a suggestion of creating an Arab state. Clearly, the United Nations was in gross violation and abrogation of international law. Why is no one questioning this willful destruction of legal precedent which was carved into history in United States treaty law and globally affirmed and confirmed unanimously by **all** fifty-one member countries of the League of Nations???" Archangel Gabriel is on a high emotional tear. If Gabriel were a man, his sky-high blood pressure would have triggered a brain hemorrhage or an acute aortic dissection. With intense conviction, Gabriel continues, "This illegal decision by the United Nations was followed by war against Israel by the Arab nations in 1948 which continues today. Yes, the barbarians are here. They are inside the United Nations. Today, the Palestinians, the Islamic nations and the United Nations are denying history and violating international law. This defiance of international law was and is a provocative call to Armageddon end-time war."

"In these dangerous and demonic times, in this age of hatred, consider the stunning quotation that reads, 'The white race is the cancer of human history.'" Michael drops a bombshell, and another bombshell, and another bombshell, which shake the God Squad to its very core. "Consider the historic, hateful and murderous quote that reads, 'The best among the gentiles deserves to be killed,' and 'killed without mercy.' Use a search engine to fnd these two quotations, determine their sources, their intention, and their future direction."

Archangel Michael delivers another compelling indictment of the world today, "Just consider the impact of these very public and high profile hatreds which were directed at gentiles. One widely disseminated, toxic quotation dared to vaunt and to taunt that, 'Jesus deserved four more deaths.' Four more deaths???? 'Four more deaths' is a declaration of unspeakable otherworldly hatred in a New World Order directed against Jesus Christ, also called Yeshua Messiah, and against his followers. Muhammad incorporated this hatred against Christians inside his Quran and in the Hadiths as he acted out the Sira. Muhammad acted out this hatred inside his Sira by slaughtering Christians. Muhammad's ISIS is butchering Christians in their drive to break the cross. Directed against Christians, this expressed hatred of 'four more deaths' is the epitome of hatred and evil today. In Canada,

Church pastors are being prosecuted by the Human Rights Commisions for preaching biblical truths on unnatural sexual misconduct as the reason why God destroyed Sodom and Gomorrah."

"Today, across the world, Christians are the enemies of state who are being discriminated against and killed. In the Middle East today, Muslims chant '**KILL JESUS!**' A *USA Today* article read, 'Middle East Christians Need Protection." As stated in Kirsten Powers' excellent column in *USA Today*, 'Christianity is the most persecuted religion in the world.' So asserted German Chancellor Angela Merkel late last year, which caused an international stir. Merkel echoed a concern expressed by then-French President Nicolas Sarkozy, who warned in a 2011 speech that Christians face a 'particularly wicked program of cleansing in the Middle East, religious cleansing.' Dated October 25, 2016, RescueChristians.Org wrote: 'Major UK Children's Charity Says Muslims are Kidnapping White Girls and Forcing Sex Slavery, Using Fake Businesses as Brothels and Transit Houses: Islam and sex slavery are like peanut butter and jelly—you always find the one with the other. Muslims kidnapping vulnerable white girls in the UK and forcing them to be sex slaves has reached an epidemic level according to the UK Charity Barnados.' Christianity is the most persecuted religion on earth. Christianity is living under the Muslim Curtain of Death."

As recorded in **Genesis 15**, the King of Heaven and earth had made a covenant with Abraham that his seed would inherit His Promised Land, but not before they were enslaved for 400 years "in a land that is not theirs." After 430 years of captivity in Egypt, the Angel of Death as the Angel of Judgment passed over the houses with the blood of lambs on their door posts. After this Tenth Plague during which all the firstborn in Egypt were killed, Moses led the Children of Israel out of Egyptian slavery, across the Red Sea, and on their way to freedom in the Promised Land.

Some 3300 to 3500 years later, the pervasive Arab-Muslim slave trade out of Africa enabled the Black slave trade into the cotton plantations of the southern United States. Then Adonai, the God of Heaven, chose another Abraham named Lincoln and made a covenant with him that he would be the second Moses who would lead the Black slaves in America to their escape and freedom from slavery.

As the Minister of cosmic justice, Archangel Michael zeroes in on this devastating upheaval in American society. "This Muslim slave market was about supply and demand economics. Because they had deemed that Blacks had no soul, the plantation owners felt no twig of conscience in owning and abusing Black slaves. Because the White plantation owners were Christians, their crimes against the Blacks and against humanity were much greater than those of the Muslim slave traders."

Michael compares the two Passovers, "As in the Passover and the exodus from Egypt, so it was in this Passover in America that there was much killing and death. It took a divided America, a massive civil war, and much bloodshed to end the captivity of Black America. This Passover from Black slavery to freedom cost millions of American lives. Abraham Lincoln broke the chains of Black slavery and liberated the captives. Lincoln paid for Black freedom with his life. In a parallel to Yeshua Messiah who died on a cross, Abraham Lincoln was assassinated."

Gabriel compares the parallel lives of Moses and Lincoln, "Moses and Lincoln met similar fates. For his disobedience, the first Moses was destined by Elohim, to die in the Sinai desert without entering the Promised Land. As the second Moses, Abraham Lincoln fared much worse. For his obedience, Lincoln was murdered by White America."

Archangel Uriel restates the obvious, "It is more than apparent that without the Muslim slave trade, there would have been little or no African Trans-Atlantic slave market into the southern plantations of the United States."

Michael, the legal beagle, probes deeply into the infamy of the congressional misconducts, which followed the civil upheavals of the war, "The Civil War drained the United States financially and economically, and gave rise to the traitorous **District of Columbia Organic Act of 1871**, which opened the door to control of America by the international bankers. When Congress passed the **Organic Act of 1871**, it created a unified territorial government for the entire District of Columbia. It was signed into law by President Ulysses S. Grant on February 21, 1871. This treasonous Act of 1871 abolished the original constitutional government and created a "**legal fiction**" that forced

Americans to become financially indebted to the international bankers and to be controlled by these international bankers. American citizens are ignorant of the fact that they are enslaved to the international bankers. After the horrific blood bath, America threw off the yoke of Black slavery only to be yoked with surreptitious slavery to the international bankers which continues today."

Michael continues his exposure of the clandestine, murderous conducts by the highest of powers in America, "President John F. Kennedy was determined to reverse this bankster fraud and this high crime against America. On June 4, 1963, through his Executive Order **11110**, President Kennedy began to transfer control and power from the foreign Federal Reserve to the United States Department of the Treasury. Through his Executive Order **11110**, President John Kennedy declared that the *privately owned* Rothschild Federal Reserve Bank no longer had the power to loan money at interest to the United States Federal Government. On November 22, 1963, President Kennedy was assassinated by the highest authorities within America."

Archangel Gabriel redirects the focus to the cancer which is eating at America today, "Instead of being enslaved, Black Africans could have emigrated to America as free peoples. Instead, because of the Islamic slave trade, Black Africans were forced into inhuman and unconscionable slavery. Directly, the Islamic slave trade launched the American Civil War for liberation of the Black slaves under President Abraham Lincoln. Directly, the American Civil War crippled America financially and enslaved America to the international bankers. Directly, the Islamic slave trade led to the racial conflicts and upheavals of the 1960s which continue today as the radical '*Black Lives Matter*' movement. Directly, the Islamic slave trade out of Africa enabled racial politics to be the driving force and the very foundation of American divisive politics today. Directly, America is living under the legacy and under the shroud of the Islamic slave trade of the eighteenth and nineteenth centuries."

Michael encapsulates the racial divide gnawing at the very fabric and at the very heart of America. "More than two hundred years after the Barbary Wars against the Muslims ended, the enemy of America during Jefferson's Presidency is the very same enemy which America faces today. Presently, the mortal enemy of America is Muhammad's Islam, which intends to enslave the entire world."

Gabriel raises strong reservations about the mindset of White America toward the Black communities today. "Are American Blacks still being treated as second-class citizens without a soul? Unfortunately, after 152 years, White America has not removed the ropes which hamper and bind many Black Americans in their state of poverty. However, President Donald Trump has promised to cut those remaining strands which still bind Black Americans, and to create new opportunities in education for them."

Raphael provides his spiritual perspective, "With the intense opposition toward President Donald Trump by the Democrats and by the mainstream media, prayers should be offered up to Adonai, the God of Heaven, to enable President Donald Trump to deliver on his promises to Black America and to all Americans."

"Not seen since ancient times and after being nearly curtailed in many Muslim countries, we are seeing a return to mass slavery in Muslim lands. This is an ominous warning to Christians across the world, but especially to Christians in Africa."

"On September 23, 2016, the *Wall Street Journal* headlined '*The Gathering Nuclear Storm.*' On September 25, 2016, CBS News, *60 Minutes* stated, '*Risk of Nuclear Attack Rises,*'" blurts out Uriel. "In their article the *WSJ* profiled Iran's Ayatollah Ali Khamenei, China's Xi Jinping, Russia's Vladimir Putin, and North Korea's Kim Jong Un. The *WSJ* disclosed that their nuclear brinksmanship and the fast-rising nuclear instability are frightening in the context of considerable unaccounted radioactive material sloshing around the world."

"With nuclear weapons in the hands of psychiatric nut cases such as Iran's Ayatollah Ali Khamenei and North Korea's Kim Jong Un, Americans should brace themselves for nuclear events on U.S. soil." Psychiatric specialist Raphael is most concerned about the aggressive Kim Jong Un whom he views "as being mentally unstable and unpredictably dangerous."

"And don't forget Russia's Vladimir Putin," adds Gabriel. "The ruler of Russia is Daniel's '*king of the north.*' I know because I brought that message to Daniel in Babylon. Ezekiel named him as Gog of the land of Magog.

"The four countries named by the *Wall Street Journal* are the same four countries named in Ezekiel chapters 38 and 39. Rosh is the habitat of Scythia from whom the Russians derive their name. After the invasion and annexation of Crimea, Vladimir Putin has put the nuclear option on the table. It is indisputable that Iran is Persia in **Ezekiel: 38–39** where war against Israel is mentioned eighteen times. **Revelation 16:12** speaks of drying up the Euphrates River to prepare 'the way for the kings from the east.' **Revelation 9:16** numbers the invading army from the east at 'twice ten thousand times ten thousand' which is *exactly* the number of the 200 million-man standing army admitted by Chinese authorities. The number 200 million is amazing prophetic precision written nineteen-hundred years ago." Archangel Gabriel summarizes prophetic utterances.

"Add another unstable factor. Pakistan has threatened to follow Allah's Quran 8:65 to 'rouse the faithful to arms' against India. Pakistan has declared intent to use nuclear weapons to annihilate India. Because of the instability and the chaos which exist in Pakistan's power structure, a state coup by jihadists could result in nuclear weapons falling into the hands of Islamic suicide bombers."

A sombre-looking Uriel makes a bleak announcement, "Yikes! There is another game-changer moving on the Middle East scene. The massive Israeli Leviathan natural gas field discovered in the Mediterranean off Israel's shore and the vast and enormous oil reserves found in the Golan Heights are existential threats to Russia's economic survival. To fund its national budget and its military expansion, Russia is dependent upon its oil and gas sales to Europe. However, the potential export of Israeli oil and gas to Europe and to the Middle East would be a serious assault upon the financial viability of the '*king of the north*.' In light of this imminent existential peril to Russia, Vladimir Putin has declared Russia to be the liberator and the protector of Syria."

> "Rouse the faithful to arms."
>
> *- Quran 8:65*

"Russia's Vladimir Putin desperately needs to control Europe for militaristic and strategic purposes." As the military strategist of the cosmos, Michael explains the psychology that is driving Putin. "Especially in winter, Vladimir Putin's chosen weapons to hold Europe ranson and hostage are Russian oil and gas. Dependence upon Russian oil and gas are the knife to the throat of Europe. For lack of heating fuel, Europe would be frozen meat. NATO would be sidelined. In the chaos of millions of deaths due to exposure, Russia will overrun the Baltic States, Poland, Ukraine all the way down to the Mediterranean. In the dead of winter, any gas shut-down would freeze the European continent into submission, into a downward spiral, and into death." Russia's strategies are transparent to Archangel Michael.

Michael projects and advances prophecy, "The next step will be for the '*king of the north*' to advance on Israel to "reclaim" the Syrian land of the Golan Heights." Gabriel expands upon his Daniel discourse, "As Gog of Magog, the '*king of the north*' will advance over the Israeli border to take the Golan Heights. Immediately, this Russian invasion would overturn the geopolitical dynamics of the entire Middle East, which then would go nuclear."

"The God of Heaven has given no option to Vladimir Putin. In **Ezekiel 38:3–4**, He said to Gog, the '*king of the north*,' 'I am against you, O Gog. . . . I will turn you about, and put hooks into your jaws, and I will bring you forth, and all your army, horses and horsemen.' The vast oil and gas reserves in Israel are the 'hooks into [the] jaws' of Gog as the '*king of the north*.' We soon might be into the two wars of Ezekiel," Gabriel makes this sad pronouncement.

Speaking true to sarcastic form, Archangel Uriel projects the global fires yet to come saying, "James Baldwin was a well-known American novelist, essayist, playwright, poet, and social critic. During the civil rights upheavals in 1963, in the words of his African-American spiritual, James Baldwin prophesied to Americans, '*GOD gave Noah the rainbow sign. . . . No more water . . . the fire next time.*' In 1963, Baldwin had published *The Fire Next Time*."

Archangel Michael summarizes the global fires of Biblical prophetic utterances, "Prophecy cannot be changed. Prophecy is inexorable and Jerusalem is the epicenter of prophecy."

Deuteronomy 4:24 records, "For the Lord your God is a devouring fire." **Hebrews 12:29** says similar, "For our God is a consuming fire."

Isaiah 66:15-16 warns, "the Lord will come in fire. . . . For by fire will the Lord execute judgment." **Psalm 97:3** alerts, "Fire goes before him, and burns up his adversaries round about." **Zephaniah 1:18** foreshadows nuclear war: "in the fire of His jealous wrath, all the earth shall be consumed." **Malachi 4:1** warns, "For behold the day comes, burning like an oven, when all the arrogant and all the evildoers will be stubble; the day that comes shall burn them up, says the LORD of hosts." **Joel 2:3** shocks the reader, "Fire devours before them, and behind them a flame burns." In **Ezekiel 20:47**, Elohim the God of Heaven forewarns the enemies of Israel of intense heat to come, "I will kindle a fire in you... the blazing flame shall not be quenched and all faces from south to north shall be scorched by it." **Joel 2:30** foretells, "And I will give portents in the heavens and on earth, blood and fire and columns of smoke." **2 Peter 3:10** warns of nuclear meltdown, "the elements will be dissolved with fire, and the earth and the works that are upon it will be burned up." **2 Peter 3:12** forewarns of nuclear catastrophe, "the heavens will be kindled and dissolved, and the elements will melt with fire." **Matthew 24:29** confirms that unusual cataclysmic events are in the waiting, "the sun will be darkened and the moon will not give its light, and the stars will fall from heaven, and the powers of the heavens will be shaken." **Revelation 9:18** foresees that, "a third of mankind was killed, by fire and smoke and sulphur."

". . . burning like an oven . . . faces scorched . . . blood and fire and columns of smoke . . . a third of mankind killed in smoke and sulphur" scream out that there is an imminent worldwide catastrophic nuclear holocaust in the making.

"The word of the God of the Universe through **Joel 3:2-3**, reads 'I will gather all the nations to the Valley of Jehoshaphat and I will enter into judgment with them because . . . they have divided up My land.' Division of the land of Israel will trigger the fulfillment of **Joel 3:2-3** and the invasion of Israel," Archangel Gabriel trembles as he quotes the prophecy from Joel.

Unprecedented traumas of this age of man are looming on the horizon. By virulent pestilence, by flesh-eating disease, or by proximate nuclear radiation, the cosmic warning in **Zechariah 14:12** will shake the Valley of Jehoshaphat and all around the world, "And this shall be the plague with which the Lord will smite all the peoples that wage war against Jerusalem: their flesh shall *rot* while they are still on their feet, their eyes shall *rot* in their sockets, and their tongues shall *rot* in their mouths."

 WORLD AHEAD *press*

Self-publishing means that you have the freedom to blaze your own trail as an author. But that doesn't mean you should go it alone. By choosing to publish with WORLD AHEAD PRESS, you partner with WND—one of the most powerful and influential brands on the Internet.

If you liked this book and want to publish your own, WORLD AHEAD PRESS, co-publishing division of WND Books, is right for you. WORLD AHEAD PRESS will turn your manuscript into a high-quality book and then promote it through its broad reach into conservative and Christian markets worldwide.

IMAGINE YOUR BOOK ALONGSIDE THESE AUTHORS!

We transform your manuscript into a marketable book. Here's what you get:

BEAUTIFUL CUSTOM BOOK COVER
PROFESSIONAL COPYEDIT
INTERIOR FORMATTING
EBOOK CONVERSION
KINDLE EBOOK EDITION
WORLDWIDE BOOKSTORE DISTRIBUTION
MARKETING ON AMAZON.COM

It's time to publish your book with WORLD AHEAD PRESS.

Go to **www.worldaheadpress.com** for a Free Consultation